THE TRIALS OF IMPERIUM

LYNDSEY GARBEE

ISBN: 978-1-957723-45-7 (hard cover)
        978-1-957723-46-4 (soft cover)

Edited by: Karli Jackson

Published by WARREN Publishing
Charlotte, NC
www.warrenpublishing.net
Printed in the United States

This book is dedicated to ambition—mine, theirs, and yours. Whatever form it takes, may it be powerful.

DRAMATIS PERSONAE

- **Aoran Jaxis** (*Ay-or-ahn Jax-is*). Liliana's longtime friend, an officer in the Electarian military and member of its Four, and a follower of *Viribus*.
- **Cae** (*Kay*). A magister of the House who follows *Caecus*.
- **Caecus** (*kay-shus*). The God of wisdom. His mark takes the form of a Stone Tree on his followers' right hands.
- **The Captain.** The head of the Electarian military and a follower of *Viribus*.
- **Chauron** (*Kar-uhn*). A guide of *Caecus*.
- **Councilor Ahn** (*Ahn*). A member of the diplomacy council.
- **Councilor Pen** (*Pen*). A dignitary of Nuwei.
- **Dayanara Romano** (*Die-ah-nar-ah Roh-mahn-oh*). An officer in the Electarian military and member of its Four and a follower of *Viribus*.
- **Easternalia Storidian** (*Ee-ster-nayl-ee-ah Stor-ih-dee-uhn*). An ambassador of Aurjnegh. The aunt of Leo Storidian and a follower of *Superbia*.
- **Eliana Storidian** (*El-ee-ahn-ah Stor-ih-dee-uhn*). The first daughter of Juliana and Leo Storidian, second in line to the throne of Electaria, and a follower of *Menda*.
- **Ellegance Fournier** (*El-eh-gans For-nee-ay*). The oldest daughter of the Fournier family and a follower of *Imperium*.
- **Estienne Fournier** (*Es-tee-ehn For-nee-ay*). Co-owner of *Pandemonium*. The mother of Ellegance, Nic, Fitz, Fren, and Penelope and a follower of *Menda*.

- **Fitz Fournier** (*Fitz For-nee-ay*). The youngest son of the Fournier family by two minutes and a follower of *Menda*.
- **Fren Fournier** (*Fren For-nee-ay*). The second oldest son of the Fournier family by two minutes and a follower of *Menda*.
- **Imperium** (*Imp-eer-ee-uhm*). Liliana's wolf.
- **Imperium** (*Imp-eer-ee-uhm*). The God of power. Her mark takes the form of a dragon on her followers' backs.
- **Je Aziz** (*Jay Ah-zeez*). An officer in the Electarian military and member of its Four and a follower of *Viribus*.
- **Juliana Storidian** (*Jool-ee-ahn-ah Stor-ih-dee-uhn*). The former queen of Electaria. Mother to Teo, Eliana, and Liliana and a follower of *Imperium*.
- **Kai Probiat** (*K-eye Proh-bee-aht*). The consort of the empress of Vitria and a follower of *Menda*.
- **Leo Storidian** *(Lee-oh Stor-ih-dee-uhn)*. A former Vitrian merchant who married Juliana Storidian, assuming the throne after her death. Father to Teo, Eliana, and Liliana and a follower of *Menda*.
- **Liliana Storidian** (*Lil-ee-ahn-ah Stor-ih-dee-uhn*). The second daughter of Juliana and Leo Storidian, third in line to the throne of Electaria, and a follower of *Imperium*.
- **Madame Dragonia** (*Drag-oh-nee-ah*). A storekeeper and follower of *Superbia*.
- **Malum** (*mal-uhm*). The antithesis to the pantheon of Gods. Her followers mark takes the same form as the mark for a person's previous patron God but is scarlet red. As a sign of rebuke, her name is not considered a proper noun in any language on *Terrabis*.
- **Marianne** (*Mare-ee-an*). A follower of *Caecus*.
- **Menda** (*Men-dah*). The God of honesty, no discernable gender. Their followers mark takes the form of a series of waves on the left forearm.
- **Nic Fournier** (*Nik For-nee-ay*). The oldest son of the Fournier family and a follower of *Menda*.
- **Penelope Fournier** (*Pen-el-oh-pee For-nee-ay*). The youngest daughter of the Fournier family and a follower of *Menda*.
- **Phil Dahn** (*Fill Dahn*). A servant of the Electarian castle.

- **Renee Probiat** (*Rehn-eh Proh-bee-aht*). The empress of the nation of Vitria and a follower of *Menda*.
- **Ro** (*Roh*). An officer in the Electarian military and member of its Four and a follower of *Viribus*.
- **Seran** (*Seh-rahn*). A guide of *Imperium*.
- **Superbia** (*Soo-per-bee-ah*). The God of pride. Her followers mark takes the form of a Timore hawk on the skin above the heart.
- **Teo Storidian** (*Teh-oh Stor-ih-dee-uhn*). The first and only son of Juliana and Leo Storidian, first in line to the throne of Electaria, and a follower of *Imperium*.
- **Tyn** (*Tin*). A magister of the House and a follower of *Superbia*.
- **Viribus** (*Vir-ree-bus*). The God of strength. His followers mark takes the form of a wolf on the right shoulder.
- **King Wi** (*Wee*). A deceased king of Electaria and follower of *Imperium*.
- **Wren Fournier** (*Ren For-nee-ay*). Co-owner of *Pandemonium*. The father of Ellegance, Nic, Fitz, Fren, and Penelope and a follower of *Menda*.
- **King Zan** (*Zahn*). A deceased king of Electaria and follower of *Imperium*.

PROLOGUE
7014.5.70

Marianne still managed to look beautiful, despite the sallow, yellow skin and gaunt cheekbones that threatened to rip through it.

She sat on the floor of her library, scribbling with such intent that Chauron felt it disrespectful to simply label it "fervid." She wrote like a sinner seeking salvation in the House, desperate and unthinking. She wrote like a sailor lost at sea, thrashing to keep her head afloat. A stack of filled journals rested behind her, and a larger stack of blank journals rose imposingly before her. From dawn until dusk, her hand flew across the page, unwilling or unable to pause for any distractions. Black dye stained her hands and forearms, dark blotches blooming against a backdrop of bulging veins and tight skin. If she were cut open, Chauron wouldn't be surprised if he saw ink spill in the place of blood.

Chauron stood by, carefully watching her as she and her pen dove further and further into the empty pages. Every so often, he pushed a glass of water into her periphery. He nudged a bowl of stew and some bread under her nose. He was beyond the point of attempting to stop the concentrated effort to drain out her soul and put it on a page. He simply tried to ease the process.

They had posed like this for weeks, frozen statues carved of stress and smoothed out with pressure. The small room was never meant to hold occupants for so long. The pungent smell of people who had gone far too long without a wash clung to the wool carpet. Shelves hung on the walls, books placed haphazardly there and clinging to them through sheer willpower and a touch of something even less tangible. Some books were broken, missing entire pages and sections from Mari's searching hands. A year ago, Mari would have been aghast at the idea of mutilating a book in that manner. Necessity had begged a change in outlook. From the disarray of the objects to the miserable state of the occupants, the room had its own miasma that would send any sane person running. The only things in remotely good condition were the walls, recently covered with a bold, golden wallpaper that shined.

Chauron found himself just as entranced as she, albeit for different reasons. His eyes oscillated between drinking in her visage, haggard and stunning, and glaring at the wretched mark on her right hand. Even now, he could feel its faint pulse, its beating inextricably tied to his own heart. Never had such a minute drumming proved to be so maddening.

Time was a vague, squishy concept in Chauron's mind. He struggled to break down the years, differentiate between the days. Sometimes, he imagined himself a fish, swimming in place. The river of time washed over him, and he continued to flutter his pathetic little tail, unable to feel the water brushing over his scales. Unlike humans, his very existence wasn't defined by the ticking of a clock. He did not look at his life as a series of moments that all aggregated to one long descent into death.

No, his existence was tied to the cracking deity in front of him and the damned black tree on her hand.

He had asked her a handful of months ago. They lounged in the long grasses then, back when her smile stretched as wide as the plains themselves. Her hair glinted in the fading light, gray and brown embers beneath a sinking sunset. He asked her how long he had been with her, bewitched by her presence. His lips twitched at the memory, unsure whether to smile or crease into a frown.

She had laughed in that sad, silent way of hers. Her dark eyes creased at the corners, falling into familiar crevices crafted from years of beholding the world with a warm smile. She shook her head, letting it drop into the crook of his neck. Her shoulders trembled, maybe from laughter, though he could never be entirely sure with the clever woman.

"Forty-three years." Her answer washed over his skin like a spring breeze.

He had chewed on the numbers in his mind, mouthing them to himself above her head. They had a heftiness to them. Had he truly been by her side for so long? He still remembered meeting her for the first time like it had happened but an hour earlier. He had beheld her, preciously small and deliciously plump in her black scribes' robes. What a foolish way to describe encounters. There could never truly be a *first* meeting, as two people, once introduced, never formally met again. By the next time those same people spoke once more, each had invariably changed, at least slightly. Chauron felt as though he met Mari for the first time every time the pair talked. That was the beauty of his human's growth. He never spoke with the same Marianne twice.

Chauron had chosen to voice only his initial thoughts. He had pressed his lips against her forehead, murmuring, "That's quite a while for you humans, no?"

She hadn't responded. Chauron watched her now, her black mark emitting a taunting light that only Chauron could see. At first, he took those forty-three years as a blessing. So many years spent together, learning, reading, *existing*. Now, as he watched her suffer and slave over these pages, he remembered that within those forty-three years, he had bestowed upon her a curse.

Mari was sixty-one years old and still had not completed her Walk. The light of his life was a source of near darkness to her peers. They called her "godless." They spat at her feet. Worst of all, they mistrusted her work. The academies of Nuwei and Electaria stopped accepting her research years ago, claiming they wanted no submissions from a *Caecus* follower who lacked his golden seal of approval. They wanted nothing from a woman who could not prove she knew what it meant to be wise.

Chauron had loved her. For forty-three years, he held her close and watched her grow. He witnessed her make discoveries, delighting in that spark that practically burst in her smile when she cracked any puzzle. As she grew older and her mark failed to turn gold, she gave up on the academies. She read books for another purpose, though he had been unable to put a finger on it. The genres lacked any continuity, any common thread. Chauron, instead of pushing her back to the academies, encouraged the independent studies. He hadn't gotten that tug, that indication that told him she was on the right path. But he encouraged her nonetheless, if only to see that brilliant spark.

Now, here she sat. A shell emptied of its dazzling mind to conserve energy, if only to write a little faster. A little longer. She bit her lip so hard as she wrote, it drew blood, dripping steadily against the page. She paid the blood no mind. Against what clock she raced, he could only guess. But he sensed it was fast running out. He watched her, acting the part of the same useless Guide he had been for the past forty-three years.

Yes, Chauron loved her. And in loving her, Chauron had failed her entirely.

CHAPTER I
7055.1.10

The clang of metal against metal rang in Liliana's ears as her warm brown skin glistened with sweat. Bellowing grunts from exhausted soldiers and roared orders from impervious commanders made up the discordant symphony that served as the landscape for the training room. The soldiers moved like a black sea in the peripheral, an ebb and flow of warriors in pressed coal uniforms. The most inexperienced stood out amid the throngs—each one held a wooden rod, their eyes alight with a naive excitement.

Only a few pairs actually sparred, spread across the room. Their blunted swords hit one another with dull clanging sounds. Small groups of rowdy soldiers, jeering and hollering for their favorite, surrounded each fight. To accommodate all the constant activity, the room was one of the largest in the palace. With lofty ceilings, torches blazing all over, floors made up of soft sand, and training dummies everywhere the eye could see, it served as an appropriate testing ground for Electaria's military.

When she allowed herself the luxury of glancing around, Liliana saw those fighting pairs diving in on one another, quick as lightning. There would be a flash of movement, the muted crash of blades, and then they would go back to circling each other. It was a room of warriors, every move she witnessed precise and deadly. Her eyebrow twitched, and the corners of her mouth turned down. She wanted to look just as graceful and, more importantly, predatory when she moved.

Instead, Liliana suffered with the knowledge that she looked like a mangled hunting dog, desperately trying to prove it could hunt with the pack.

The Captain, calm beneath her mask and purple officer's coat, came at her again, and Liliana lifted her wooden rod just in time to catch the strike. She struggled to maintain the defensive block but finally pushed back hard enough to gain some ground. She breathed heavily, shifting her feet and settling down into a sorry representation of Corticus, the Electarian defensive stance.

The Captain jumped back, dropping her rod to the sand below with a thud. She took off her helmet, allowing her bun that had been so carefully tucked within to fall at her shoulders, looking exquisite. Liliana wanted to groan. The Captain's tawny skin was dry—she hadn't even broken a sweat—and her hair was perfect and in order. Liliana stood, admiring, until the Captain began to stalk over to her, her stomps hitting the ground with disapproval.

"Wait, what did I do?" Liliana exclaimed, hands falling to her side and sword hitting the ground.

"Your arms are like twigs," the Captain hissed, grabbing Liliana's arm, wobbling it around like a gelatin cake. "Do you truly believe you could fend anybody off with this kind of kitten strength? This is a waste of my time."

"It was enough to get you away," Liliana replied, eyebrows narrowed, arms crossed.

"Because I am not *trying*. If I wanted to, I could have incapacitated you while sipping tea with my other hand," The Captain growled, taking Liliana's rod and throwing it across the room, an arm's length away from one of the rowdy groups. Liliana flinched; the rod landed and stuck perfectly in the sand.

"And what a party trick that would be!" Aoran called from across the room, picking the rod up and dusting it off. "Tea hour and a coup d'état all at once—quite the show, wouldn't you say, Your Highness?"

Liliana's face flushed a hot red as if *Superbia* herself had poured boiling tea over Liliana's cheeks. She bit her tongue so hard the taste of blood sifted through her mouth.

She could probably count on one hand the number of times somebody had told her she *wasn't* good at something. It wasn't the fact that she was royalty—she was just generally good at most things. How could she have anticipated being so atrocious at something as simple as sword fighting? For centuries, idiots had been able to hold a stick and effectively beat one another with it. She cursed herself for not requesting solo lessons, away from the prying eyes of the other soldiers. More specifically, those of the Captain and resident child in a man's body, Aoran.

Liliana took a breath, willing away her embarrassment. She focused on the Captain, steadfastly ignoring the pest in the background.

"Then how do I fix it? It can't be that difficult."

The Captain stared back at Liliana, her gaze hard. "This is not something to simply fix. I had foolishly assumed you would be in sufficient shape to start basic sparring, but this is obviously not the case. Before ever picking up the rod again, much less a sword, you will need intensive training and conditioning."

"But how long will that take?" Liliana demanded, cheeks hot. She wished she had the power to command obedience. Though, she begrudgingly admitted to herself, she doubted the stony woman would acquiesce even if Liliana *could* give orders.

Liliana found herself looking at the rod, feeling betrayed. She had hoped to learn how to use the damn thing, upgrade to a sword, and walk away a more fearsome, powerful woman. Wielding a sword was an unofficial requirement to serve on Electaria's military council. In order to make her way to its table, she had to be able to stab *something*. Not to mention it made bad sense to be the only person in a room who didn't know how to kill a man. The thought only served to increase her frustration at her present situation. Sword lessons were supposed to be a weekend of her time at the most, not some drawn-out, arduous trial.

"As long as it does take," the Captain said and turned, holding her helmet under her arm, waving Liliana away with a dismissive hand. "Come back to me when I can actually use my sword."

The Captain strode over to a group of practicing soldiers. Her presence inspired immediate reactions. Every soldier straightened their back, sharpening each of their movements into something cleaner, crisper. The Captain snapped at each one of them, finding flaws in every motion. Already, Liliana was consigned to the ash heaps of her to-do list. Liliana's heart burned at being cast aside so immediately. Of course, Liliana was weak! Why in *Imperium*'s name would she have come to the damn dirt room if not to become stronger?

Her head snapped up as she heard Aoran's metal boots approaching. He grinned at her, his teeth white and brilliant, his smile smug and infuriating. His white hair, so wild when they were younger, was tied back in a tight, low ponytail. His warm, beige skin was unblemished, per usual. The years had narrowed his face, defining every contour and angle of his high cheekbones and sharp jaw. Liliana scowled.

In so many ways, Aoran was as conventional a beauty as they came. He had a soldier's perfect frame, sturdy with muscle but slender enough for lethal speed. He had a visage unblemished by nose breaks or scars, sloping eyebrows framing playful jade eyes, and a strong nose that slanted no more or less downward than any nose should. He also had a twelve-year-old's mind and was intent on driving all those around him slowly, but surely, insane.

His curved swords shone on his back, a deadly reminder of what lay behind his smirk. The aureate mark on his taut shoulder seemed to gleam brighter as he approached her. Liliana swore his sign only did that when she was nearby, as if he actively tried to rub the completion of his Walk in her face. The profile of a golden wolf howling upward glowed on his skin, strong and unyielding. The sign of *Viribus,* God of strength.

Aoran completed his Walk nearly four years ago at the ripe age of eighteen. To do so before one turned thirty was impressive. To do so while still a teenager? The insufferable idiot was legendary. Of course, the most annoying person in Electaria would also be one of the most accomplished.

Liliana crossed her arms and tapped her foot, her eyebrows raised. She was ready for whatever clever retort he'd come to torture her with.

"Don't be so hard on yourself, Your Highness! I'm sure you simply thought the sword was a big embroidery needle—now you know! You can take this lesson, tuck it in your little mental princess pouch, and remember it for the next time you want to play with the wolves." He grinned at her again, his canines sharp underneath the harsh lighting of the gymnasium.

Liliana pursed her lips, collected herself, and then gave Aoran the most saccharine smile she could muster. "While everybody in the castle has been debating over the past twenty-two years whether your mother or father was the beast that made you half man, it is comforting to know at the very least that you, yourself, realize you are less than human."

"Less than human means more than nothing, which implies at minimum I am something to you." He winked one green eye at her, smoothing his snowy hair over with one hand. Liliana could have sworn she heard two or three soldiers swoon in the background.

"The same way a good master takes care of any runts in the litter—out of pity for the weak." She stuck her nose in the air, digging her foot into the sand beneath her.

"If I am weak, it could only be from staring at your face for so long, Your Highness! Such dazzling features could drive any self-respecting man to his knees."

"You know what also drives men to their knees?" She tapped her chin for a second before leveling a shriveling glower at him. "The guillotine."

He blinked and then howled in laughter, clutching his stomach as he bent over. Liliana could feel the eyes of the other soldiers on them, gleefully waiting for a continuation of the show the two had put on thus far. She refused to oblige them. Liliana threw one last withering look at the chortling soldiers and turned on her heel. She was through amusing people today at her own expense. She immediately searched for the one thing that could make her feel better after total public humiliation.

The odd man out in the arena met her eyes and immediately started thumping his tail against the ground in excitement. Well, less of an odd "man" as opposed to an odd "wolf." Instead of looking brighter, his black fur somehow seemed darker underneath the innumerable torches. His coat gleamed, though, glossy and healthy no matter the setting. She approached the large wolf sitting patiently at the edge of the gym, some of the mortification from earlier easing away as she stroked the fur on his nose.

"Did you miss me, Imperium?" She scratched behind his ear, and he huffed in response. She laughed and rubbed his chin. "Well, at least somebody doesn't think I'm the worst thing to happen on *Terrabis*."

Imperium had been the largest wolf pup in the litter. Eight-year-old Liliana had zeroed in on him, confident he would be the best and the brightest. Her world then was simple—bigger was better. Every year, the doctors declared the wolf done growing. Every year, Imperium defied reality and continued his unprecedented development. At this point in their lives, his snout bumped Liliana's shoulder when sitting. Liliana still managed to get a kick out of court reactions when those unacquainted to Imperium's legendary size met him. Memories filled with cries of surprise and fear made Liliana snicker as she stroked his fur.

He dipped his head and shook his butt with enthusiasm, the loud smack of his tail against the floor dampened by the sand. Several soldiers looked up, startled. The large wolf enthusiastically wagging his tail did little to assuage their concern.

Aoran, who had moved on to his next source of entertainment, held up a hand and paused his match. He waved his sword threateningly at Liliana.

"Get that *malum* out of here before we see if he's as bad at facing swords as you!"

Liliana snorted and wrapped her fingers in Imperium's fur, giving it a gentle tug. She leaned down to his floppy ear and said, "My room."

He yipped enthusiastically. Liliana smiled and gave him a good scratch behind the ear. Imperium was a better listener than most people in the castle. She swore he could understand her. Imperium followed her loyally out the doors of the training room, bounding alongside her through the hallways. Every so often, he would gallop ahead, stop, look back at Liliana, and excitedly gallop back.

The torches that lined the walls flickered at his passing, threatening to wisp into nothingness. In one particularly precarious area, he slipped on a rug atop wooden floors, his nails scraping against the floor as he yipped and tried to regain his bearings. Able to hear the wolf's footsteps from across the building, servants pressed their backs against the stones. His huge paws pounded against the stairs leading up to Liliana's room, and he outpaced her by a couple of minutes. By the time she reached the top floor, he circled her door in a happy trot.

Liliana laughed and patted him approvingly on the head. He leaned his head to the side, exposing his canines, and allowed his tongue to loll out in a smile. He proceeded to turn around and collapse in front of her door, taking up more than half the hallway. She grinned and patted him firmly on the side of his snout, squeezing around him to get into her room.

If any of the maids saw Liliana's room right now, she imagined they might pass out from horror. She had ordered them to stop coming by a week ago, simply to save them from the ordeal of cleaning and to save herself from having to make everything messy again. Ink jars lay empty on the floor, stacks of books hid in every corner, and sheaths of parchment spilled out from under her bed after years of shoving memos and reports beneath its frame. Traveling to the archives to retrieve records was far too taxing on her time—her room made as good a library as any.

There was a hint of beauty beneath the monstrous mess. Her bed frame, dark wood delicately carved with flowers weaving their way up to the ceiling, held a luxurious mattress with enough lavender pillows to build a small fort. A resplendent chandelier hung from the ceiling, dazzling the room with its icy, white candles. The white marble floors cooled her feet. A negative floral design, finished in a more severe white, spun throughout the floor, courtesy of the kingdom's most famous artist, Seraphinus. To the dismay of her father and the kingdom's coffers, Liliana could barely admire the artistry due to the textbooks haphazardly strewn across the floor.

She hopped around the snares in her room like a seasoned veteran, her feet lightly skipping over *Political History of Electaria*, *Siege and Seas: The Greatest Battles of Our Time*, *Aloan: Banking When Left Unchecked*, and *Plagues, Plaques, Parasites: Cautions of the Modern Era*. Just as she was about to reach her desk, she tripped over a hidden astrolabe and went sprawling across her floor. She yelped as the edges of books and rulers bit into her sides. Cursing, she stood up and stared at the things on her floor with open malice.

"I created you. I can end you," she threatened with a scowl. A death trap of her own creation was still a death trap, no matter how much time and energy she invested in erecting it.

She reached her desk mostly unscathed and quickly found a quill. She produced a fresh piece of parchment and glared at the empty page for a second. Sometimes she wished the words had the courtesy to just appear on their own. Thus far, no such luck. She pressed her quill to the notebook and began scribbling:

Esteemed Councilmen of the Treasury Council,

I beg an answer to the following question: Are you all simply imbeciles, in which I might have you declared legally insane under statute 700.4.2, or do you simply harbor such a desire to see our nation destroyed that I should have you tried for treason under criminal statute 100.1.1?

I would not have you hope for even one second that your clandestine vote, held in the dead of night, away from prying eyes, would escape my attention. I can only imagine you did so in some vain attempt to keep me from speaking on the matter. While you may have stifled my castigations of your stupidity on the open debate floor, the pen will serve as a sufficient vesicle for my rage.

Last night you passed a new law concerning domestic economic issues. You and your equally simple-minded colleagues proposed a massive public service project for the construction of a fleet of fishing vessels, the size and scope of which have never been seen on our side of Terrabis.

Never mind the fact that current interest rates are astronomically high, meaning these newly ordained fishermen will never be able to pay off their debts to their Electarian overlords. Never mind that this project demands a level of human capital that Electaria will be unable to supply unless we import cheaper labor from Vitria (which, considering the nature of the project, I have low hopes for). Never mind the fact that you have failed to create new laws within our international statutes (thus failing to deactivate current trade deals that are contradictory to your plans)—you have passed this statute in bad faith of the Electarian people. What business do you believe the Electarian government has in subsidizing our nascent fishing industry?

The Vitrians have dominated all aquatic realms for the last thousand years. In no reality will your government-funded fishermen pull in flounder and trout at prices lower than where the Vitrians have them set. The Aujrnegh and Nuwei will continue to buy their catch from the familiar economy of yesterday instead of the quixotic markets of tomorrow, brought by Electarian hopefuls. Even Electarians will find themselves hard-pressed to conjure up enough nationalism that they might give five more of their hard-earned iron bits for Electarian fish.

The Vitrians are operating with superior experience, superior systems, and superior economies of scale. You are setting up these misguided pioneers for failure and throwing away precious governmental funds in the process. I demand this vote be taken up once more in a public setting with all councils present.

I doubt your fishy plan will fare as well under such circumstances.

Cordially,

Liliana Storidian, Princess of Electaria and Councilwoman of the Education Council

Liliana paused, checking and rechecking her language. She closed the book, satisfied. When the historians wrote biographies on her and her various accomplishments, she hoped they would use these testimonials to add some color to the pages.

A knock drifted through her room, the voice accompanying it hoarse and jolly: "May I enter? Imperium seems hungry, and I would hate to have my death come about from his afternoon snack."

Liliana put the quill away, hiding the paper in a mountain of various policy writings. She stood on the balls of her feet, skipping over her scattered stuff to get to the door. As she leaped through her room she yelled, "Come in!"

The king of Electaria entered her room with a gentle smile. The wrinkles next to King Leo's eyes crinkled together whenever he smiled, deepening the crevices there as the years went on. As those same years passed, so went his hair. His face, though, maintained a lively glow. The warmth of his sepia skin never seemed to fade, a warm undertone that Liliana had inherited. His cheeks always held a ruddy tint in them, as if he had just finished drinking or belly-laughing at a particularly funny joke.

Unlike Liliana's sister, he never tried for ostentation in his dress. He wore a cream tunic tucked into black pants, a deep purple vest draping over the whole ensemble. If Liliana blinked, he could just as easily be a banker or merchant from the kingdom. One could have missed the fact that he was king at all, if not for the small, silver crown on his head.

Liliana's eyes caught on the crown. They always did. A few years back, she remembered asking him why he chose such a small, pitiful thing when all the other leaders that attended their balls and meetings wore opulent crowns and headdresses. They wore pieces so big and bright they nearly hurt to behold. Her mother had certainly worn something grander.

He had laughed and leaned in conspiratorially. "Sometimes it serves a leader well to remember what gives him strength in times of trouble. A leader must never forget that he leads with this," he tapped his brain, "and not this." He took off the crown and put it on her head, walking around the rest of the night without his one sign of authority. Somehow, he looked more regal than usual without it as he floated between groups and laughed with the dignitaries.

Liliana had walked around that gilded ballroom with the silver crown on her head, going up to all the leaders and launching into conversations like she had every right to stand there. She pretended, just for the night, that the crown belonged to her, and she belonged there. It was stupid—she knew that. But still, wearing the crown and pretending had felt nice, even if the feeling was as ephemeral as a melting snowflake.

She knew her place, now more so than ever. Still, the sight of him brought out a small smile on her lips.

"How is my favorite, youngest child?" Her father approached with his chubby arms open and his brown eyes sparkling.

Yes. With the exception of that night, Liliana had never forgotten that unless Monarchic Trials were declared, the crown went to the next in line. The person destined to sit upon the throne would be the eldest child, her brother, Teo. And in the unfortunate case of his death, the monarchy would go to her older sister, Eliana. The death of someone with the *Imperium* mark was the only way someone with a different mark could sit on the throne.

Loathe her siblings as she might, Liliana lacked the constitution to climb her way to the throne. She would have to commit too much fratricide before the world ever entertained her as queen, and that was assuming she wouldn't be sent straight to the guillotine after she was inevitably found out.

"Recovering from my exchange with the Captain." She let herself be embraced, sinking into the warmth of his torso.

"Really?" She could almost hear his signature eyebrow raise.

"Because from what I heard, you did more verbal sparring with Aoran of the Four than anything else."

Liliana groaned. She detested the castle's affinity for gossip. She had no doubt in her mind that somebody spread the story of what transpired in that arena before the dust from Imperium's paws had even settled. *Conniving serpents, the lot of them.*

She leaned back and batted her eyelashes. "Is there any chance you won't tell Teo about this? I'm simply a little inexperienced, and in a month or so's time, I'll be as good as the Four themselves."

Her father snorted, an obnoxious sound that she grumpily realized resembled her own. "Teo is hardly as good as the Four themselves. I have a suspicion that Aoran would be offended if we tried to compare the two." He chuckled, a belly laugh that resounded throughout the room, and patted her arm. "I'm sure with some practice he'll be more than happy to let you into his war council."

"I don't think Teo knows what the word 'happy' means," Liliana muttered, rolling her eyes as her father swatted her on the arm. She offered a sheepish, but unapologetic, shrug in return. "And what about your diplomatic council?" She followed up hopefully, leaning back to catch his eye.

Her father rotated as head of one of the five councils every four years while serving on the other's committees. With two years left in his diplomacy tenure, Liliana still had a chance to find herself a seat.

He released her and slid down her wall with what sounded suspiciously like a "harrumph." His body hit the floor with a loud *thump.* "I don't even know what to do with them. We're either constantly on the verge of war from taking too hard a stance, or our merchants pound down our doors from being too soft. I truly think we have a need for some fresh blood in there."

"I couldn't agree with you more!" Liliana burst out, a burning feeling spreading throughout her body starting from the mark on her back. "We should also, of course, think about putting some new people on the spiritual council as well, but we can get to that later. If we are thinking about fresh blood as in *truly* fresh blood—we should consider an overhaul of the entire diplomatic council. I can name several outstanding candidates—"

"Not now, Liliana." He cut her off as he stood. He got up slowly, as if every movement was a burden almost too difficult to bear. Liliana watched her father and blinked away the image of a clock ticking down over his heart. Liliana worried he practically worsened by the second. He clasped a firm hand on her shoulder, looking weary, but strong. "We'll discuss this another day. I did actually come to your room with a purpose."

Liliana paused, surprised. For some reason she just assumed he had come to ask of her sword lessons.

"Our extended family is coming to visit us in a few days' time—"

"Who?" Liliana had the courtesy to look slightly embarrassed at interrupting him.

He crossed his arms, giving her a knowing look. "Your great-aunt and some others in tow." He held his hand up before she could interrupt again, and she bit back her words, annoyed. "We might have other guests, but it's unclear. In the meantime, we are to welcome them in particular with open arms. Family is family." He raised his eyebrows at her disgruntled look. "Now I want you to spend these next few days practicing being charming. I don't want you walking around ready to bite anybody's head off as you did Aoran's. He thought it amusing. They will not."

Damn Aoran. Of course he would end up inserting himself into her present and future misery. Her expression sour, she nodded.

Seeing her reluctance, her father added, "It would do you well to be able to be charismatic when you wish. It's certainly the harbinger of a good diplomat."

Before she could ask more questions or demand an explanation of the implication, he pushed the door against Imperium's body and wriggled out, sucking in his large gut to fit through. Liliana dropped to her floor, the mark on her back throbbing with a dull burn. She currently sat on the education council and had accomplished a decent bit in the past three years. If everything went her way, Liliana would sit on three of the five advisory councils: education, military, diplomacy. She could coerce her way into the spiritual and treasury councils later. For now, this would be enough.

Because that was how the youngest child could make waves. Liliana knew she would never be queen. Teo could keep the title as far as Liliana cared—she would be his right hand, advising him all throughout his reign.

That was how you could lead without wearing the damn crown.

CHAPTER 2
7055.1.12

"Ahh, wreck!" Elle's da cursed, yanking back his thumb from the furnace and running to one of the water basins.

"Language!" Penelope reprimanded their father, extending an open palm with the sternest slant to her eyebrows. "That's two irons to the swear jar."

"Call them *bits*, Pen," Nic said. "Everyone calls them bits. You sound so wrecking stiff when you talk like that."

"Four!"

"Son of a *malum*—"

"Six!" Penelope's voice was shrill.

While Da searched his apron pockets begrudgingly, Nic's ire only grew, and he proceeded to grab Penelope's hand, twisting it behind her back until she cried out. Da immediately tried to wrench him away, but the sixteen-year-old's strength was beginning its slow transcendence of their father's.

In some families, siblings took different traits from different parents, each becoming a unique concoction of genetic inheritance. In Elle's family, she and her siblings simply inherited varying shades of their da's taupe skin and purple eyes and different lengths of their ma's raven hair. The three quickly turned into a mishmash of brown limbs, Da's shock of dirty blonde hair the only distinguishing feature among the flurry.

Elle ignored the chaos unfolding behind her to the best of her ability as she grinned broadly at the nervous woman in front of her. Elle handed the poor woman the Sword Bread, affectionately titled for the way it resembled the blade of the weapon, and threw in a couple of copper candies with a wink.

"They're just playing. This happens all the time! Don't worry about it." Elle put as much assurance into the phrase as possible. She clapped the woman on the shoulder and led her out of the bakery. Though clearly not convinced, the woman relaxed slightly beneath Elle's grip and gave a weak nod.

Elle closed the door quickly behind the woman and locked it briefly, turning on her fighting siblings and struggling father. "Now, wait just a minute! How dare you all act so irresponsibly!" Elle shouted, causing the three to freeze for a moment. A grin crept across Elle's face. "Without including me!"

Elle launched herself over the front display counter, leaping up the two stairs that led to the landing where they baked their goods. She jumped into the fray, scrapping at Da to allow Nic's continued torture of Penelope. When the twins, Fitz and Fren, descended from the second floor moments later, they wasted little time before delightedly joining the tussle themselves. The tussle soon turned into a lively brawl, rolling pins and elbows flying in every direction.

The bakery, named Pandemonia, was a place of comfort, and home, both to its operating family and its patrons. The name stemmed from the Vitrian word for bread, "pande," shoved together with the Vitrian word for "demon." The name served both as an advertisement for their goods and a simultaneous warning of Elle and her siblings.

The sweet aromatics of rising dough and their signature rosemary bread never failed to leave Elle a little bit warmer. The bakery was a generally well-run ship, with Elle's ma overseeing daily operations and her da handling the most skill-intensive baked goods. The division of labor almost always worked out into an orderly, efficient working environment. That was, until any one of her six family members got riled up, at which point all order was shoved out the window in favor of its much more entertaining brother, chaos.

Laughter and shrieks coiled in the air like springs, bouncing off one another and amplifying the sound. It was likely because of this manic joviality that everyone failed to hear Ma walk in through the back door until she bellowed, "What in *Imperium*'s name is going on here?"

The family screeched to a halt, a tangle of limbs and horrified faces, creating an altogether incriminating sculpture.

Elle's ma stomped over, rolling up her sleeves to expose a pair of thick forearms, strengthened from years of pounding bread and wrangling children, the golden mark on her forearm practically seething. The family scrambled—but failed—to unravel themselves before she reached the group.

With a snarl on her face, Elle's ma grabbed and yanked her children one by one and tore them apart with the practiced hand of a woodworker removing old paint on a cabinet. Her da had the sense to clamber backward on his large hands as Elle's ma pinched Nic's ear particularly hard.

"I swear," Ma growled, prowling around the upper level of the bakery with a predatory danger, "I thought I could leave for the bank for one hour—but no! And of *course,* you're involved, Wren. I was so foolish to think you could handle the kids and the bakery. I can't leave you all alone for one *second.* Look at this place! *Imperium*, help me—this is a total disaster! And no, young lady—" Elle's ma cut off Penelope's protests. "I do not care who started it. I expect this all to be cleaned up by the time I come back downstairs."

Elle's heart shriveled beneath the weight of her ma's disapproval. Above any proclivity for levity and fun came Elle's love for her family, and above *that* came the respect for Ma. Elle felt a lot like a weathered sailor in that way. After nineteen years of easy sailing and stormy thrashings following the same captain, some level of admiration was not only necessary, but natural. Elle's mark gave a gentle thump, and she resolved to try and make amends, even if in a small way.

Ma turned to stomp up to the second level of the bakery. Da scrambled to his feet and mouthed "sorry" with a quick wink. Elle grinned at her da and waved him forward, giving him a thumbs-up. He flashed a quick grin in return and hurried after Ma to do some damage control.

"All right, cretins." Elle jumped to her feet and surveyed the damage with a wince. While immersed in the fight, she had somehow missed the many pans and ingredients they had managed to fling about the room. "Nic and Fren, you're in charge of putting the baking things back in their place. Fitz and Pen, you two throw out the ingredients that are no good now, but save anything you think we can still use. But wait!" Elle stopped them before they set about their tasks, holding her hand up sagely. "Before any of that—Nic and Pen, I command you to make up."

Nic rolled his eyes, and Penelope poked her lower lip out unhappily, but both turned to each other, clasping their hands on one another's right shoulder. Penelope, at the tender age of twelve, had to stretch her arm, so Nic bent slightly at the knees in accommodation. The concession, small as it was, appeared to wipe away any lingering sourness. Nic's mouth twisted into a wry smile, and Penelope responded with a toothy grin of her own. The Fournier family had never been particularly good at holding grudges. Elle clapped her hands happily.

"*Etiam*! Now get to work, runts."

The mark on Elle's back grew warm as her siblings spread out to complete their tasks with gusto. Once Elle gave instructions, they almost always followed through without further complaint. Perk of being the oldest, she supposed.

Elle unlocked the front door, and one of their regulars immediately swept in, grumbling underneath his breath.

"Ridiculous that I should wait—I'm a councilor after all. And of the diplomacy council no less. *Imperium* help the children these days."

Despite his grievances, Elle couldn't remember a day in her lifetime when she hadn't seen his stern face pop into the shop, perpetually on the hunt for a temporary cure to his interminable sweet tooth.

Fren popped up behind the gleaming counter of goods, black hair sticking in many directions and face bright. "Councilor Ahn! A pleasure, truly." Fren slipped beneath the counter to stand by the older man, holding him tight on the shoulder and guiding him around counters the councilor had likely viewed a million times.

Despite this, Councilor Ahn still viewed the selection with the same scrupulous squint as he did yesterday, last week, and five years before.

"Would you like some copper candies today? Maybe some donuts?" At Councilor Ahn's predictably negative reaction to both offers, Fren lowered his voice conspiratorially. "Ahh, clearly a man of finer tastes. Might I then interest you in a new, secret recipe Da's been working on? It's loosely based on the Nuwei 100-Day Pastry but has a Vitrian twist." Fren winked at the end over the older man's head at Elle.

She snickered as she brushed by her younger brother, giving his head a firm ruffle without remorse. It wasn't like his hair could get any messier. Elle brushed her hand against her other siblings similarly, giving them encouraging nods before taking the steps two at a time to the upper level of the building. The two-story building, though, couldn't be confused with luxury. The bakery itself was hardly wide enough to fit five people standing shoulder to shoulder and was barely long enough to accommodate both their baking and selling operations. This same format, repeated one floor above, made for cramped living spaces for the seven members of Elle's family. Though Elle knew the word "privacy," it took her many years before finding a practical application for it.

Elle's parents stood leaning against the side wall, their foreheads inches apart from one another and voices low. Though it lacked the vigor with which many of their arguments occurred, the general theme always stayed the same. Ma wanted increased responsibility on behalf of Da. Da wanted more levity from Ma. It was like the tune they used in every nursery rhyme, only changing up the words—it was still the same song at its core.

Still, something Elle had long taken comfort in was the way they argued: they always faced one another. Their feet never turned outward, as if they wanted to run away. They never turned their backs to one another, as if they had nothing more to say. They maintained the decency of facing each other head on, never hiding from their feelings or the words of the other. Elle figured that stemmed from Da's Vitrian upbringing and Ma's time there with him. They fought—quite often, in Elle's opinion—but they always did so on clear, communicative terms. Elle lingered in the doorway for a moment longer. *There was something sort of beautiful in that*, she thought.

In such a small area, though, it was hard to go unnoticed for too long. Especially given her family's general height; the Fourniers simply took up a lot more space than others. Ma glanced up, analytical brown eyes registering Elle and immediately flickering to Elle's left forearm. The tense furrow of her eyebrows relaxed the tiniest bit, seeing that Elle's arms were covered, as usual, with long sleeves. Elle avoided rolling her eyes. Nineteen years later and she figured she and her ma would have gained a little trust in that department.

"Shouldn't you be helping your siblings right now?" Ma placed one hand on Da's chest and cast him a long look, a clear sign that their paused conversation was far from over.

"They're taking care of it." Elle swore, offering her forefinger and middle finger up in a cheap imitation of the Deal. She knew Ma wouldn't take it, but the promising sentiment remained.

Ma sighed, a tiny, tired sound nearly indiscernible to the layman, but a familiar noise to children and other mothers. It was a small, resigned creature, a sorry attempt at an outlet for feelings left unexpressed and things left unsaid. Her brown skin, a shade or two darker than Elle's own, was dull, the way it often looked on days she went to the bank. Like she hadn't gotten enough sleep the night before and didn't expect to for a good long while. Elle chewed on the inside of her cheek, a feeling caught in the cross wires of guilt and sympathy gnawing at her.

"What can I do for you, then?" Ma finally asked with a small smile.

"I just wanted to ask if I could sell some of our stuff by the Landing." Elle returned the small smile, knowing the upward pull of the left side of her mouth came directly from Ma's lineage. "You know, to make up for any lost sales 'cause of our shenanigans."

Ma's smile pulled higher. "That would be wonderful, Ellegance. Just make sure to be back in time to help with closing."

"Ma," Elle threw down the word with aplomb, expression wounded, "since when do I not come home on time?"

Ma pinched the bridge of her nose. "Since you were old enough to toddle on two feet. So hurry back, *etiam*?"

"*Etiam*!" Elle laughed, holding her hands up. She turned to leave, catching Da's glittering, violet eyes and approving nod before she bounded back down the stairs.

Penelope waited at the bottom of the stairs with her gapped smile, a result of two front teeth without enough mutual appreciation to saddle up next to each other. She held out a worn and gray wool sack that had been with the family longer than Penelope herself. The sack had one strap whose gray coloring had long since faded to an ashy white, bleached by years under the sun.

Elle grabbed the strap of the sack and slung it over her torso so that the heft of it lay against her back, and the strap nestled atop her chest. She blinked in surprise, registering the weight, and looked at her sister. "Did you already put stuff in this?"

Penelope looked down bashfully, displaying the careful plaits of her black braids. "I wanted to make it up to them too. You are going to the Landing, right? I made sure to put in extra rosemary bread 'cause the people there love it so much."

Elle gaped at her sister before settling for shaking her head in disbelief. "You're far too clever to be working in a bakery."

"Well, I won't be working in the bakery forever." Penelope looked up to inform Elle in the matter-of-fact way children always managed to convey their dreams. As if the path to fulfillment was straightforward, and to indicate otherwise was to lack sufficient imagination and conviction.

In the eight-day week, kids from the ages of six to sixteen attended Electaria's primary schools. They learned basic mathematics, writing, and science as well as a passing knowledge of Electarian history. At the age of eleven, students took classes that drifted away from the abstract and focused on more specific skills and professions. Penelope had found herself enamored with all things economics over the past year of her schooling.

Ma and Da hadn't bothered to have the conversation with Penelope yet. The conversation they had with Elle, Nic, and the twins. The conversation that pursuit of those professions after school required enrollment in a trade school. And trade schools were a kind of expense that the Fourniers couldn't afford. After school, Elle and Nic had both simply transitioned to doing more tasks for the bakery. So for now, Penelope held this dream tight in blissful ignorance. Elle knew she would pity her sister one day, but for the time being, she relished her sister's fierce optimism.

"*Etiam*," Elle finally said her with a grin. "But before you go work for the Kingdom's Treasury and make us all very rich, you need to stay here and keep helping us. Did you put copper candies in here too?"

Penelope looked affronted. "Obviously! To both things! Now leave—before everything goes cold!"

Elle laughed and ducked out of the building, strolling over to the Landing. Spring was by far the kingdom's greatest season. Winter was far too cold for Elle's liking. The way it froze her hands made scaling buildings and running around the city all but impossible. But summer was torture in and of itself. Unlike the Vitrians who lived close to the ocean and the Nuwei with their many mountains,

Electarians rarely had a consistent breeze to keep them cool. This meant summers simply consisted of a melting sun whose heat had no relief except in the shade and at night. That left spring, the perfect average between two intolerable extremes, a rare offering of environmental peace to the people of Electaria.

As Elle offered waves at the various people she passed, a pleasant warmth spread throughout her body. She looked upward and smiled at the gentle sun, shielding her eyes and mouthing a quick prayer of thanks to *Imperium*, queen of the Gods and namesake of the month of spring, Impe.

The path from the bakery to the Landing was a straight shot to the west, but Elle eventually found her feet straying. She took a couple of turns down smaller alleyways, the vague connection she had always felt with the city guiding her course. Finally, she reached a throng of teenagers—a small group of ten or so—throwing out dice and laughing. One of the boys looked up at her arrival, his expression caught between curiosity and wariness. Elle offered her forefinger and middle finger. Unlike her ma's earlier dismissal of the gesture, the boy immediately relaxed and approached her, linking their fingers.

Elle loved the community of the streets. Its simplicity and durability were a testament to its accessibility. To Ma's constant exasperation, Elle had begun wandering the city's streets before she had even started school. At age five, Elle followed the older kids around with a scampering trot, tolerated by them, if not genuinely liked. She learned there were few rules to being accepted: be young and be trustworthy. That was pretty much it.

The low barrier costs to entry brought together children of all kinds of backgrounds. While orphans were definitely the most common character lurking and playing—or oftentimes, scavenging—Elle had found children of councilors, military members, and sailors all playing together. Elle was slowly aging out of the group of accepted members, but the pimples that never went away along her jaw and forehead always made her look younger. A blessing, in street-specific scenarios, but mostly a curse.

"Want to join?" the boy asked, jerking his head backward.

Elle bit her lip, wanting very badly to join, but ultimately shook her head. "Can't. I just wanted to see if you all wanted any copper candy. I got loads extra."

His blue eyes lit up, and Elle laughed, needing no further confirmation. She reached into the bag and dropped the candy into his hand. Named for their shiny resemblance to copper coins, copper candy was a knuckle-sized treat that practically dissolved upon contact with somebody's mouth. Apparently only Electaria made them—*What a pity for the other countries*, Elle thought. The boy immediately turned to share the confection to the delight of his companions, who forgot all about their dice and descended upon the boy with reverence.

Elle smiled and walked toward the Landing with renewed gusto. The streets and its people had taken care of her for years and still did. Whenever she recognized an opportunity to pay them back, she made sure to take it.

Per usual, Elle smelled the Landing before she saw it. Because the small port was built next to Electaria's largest river, The Wi (named after some king who Elle could never be bothered to remember anything about except for his decision to rename the river after himself), there were rarely winds strong enough to clear the odors of everything coming in and out of its docks. Though many of these scents weren't terrible on their own, together they formed a wicked combination of fish, spices, lumber, metals, and animal dung. Elle wrinkled her nose and steeled herself.

The Landing bustled with activity. Da constantly boasted that the Vitrian ports were far more impressive than anyone else's, but Elle had no frame of reference for comparison, so she was sufficiently impressed by the Landing.

Boats that traveled around the world—as big as buildings and full of shouting sailors and red-faced captains—docked in Vitrian and Aurjnegh ports. Smaller boats that traveled up the river to Electaria's smaller towns loaded themselves with finished goods from the city's artisans and unloaded the raw materials sourced from the Riphs. *The rural areas*—Elle mentally corrected herself. She'd been trying to break herself of the street slur for years with little success.

Elle made a beeline for the first cluster of sailors, who lounged on crates a short distance from the port's action. Despite the temperate nature of the day, their peeling, copper-colored faces were coated in sweat and turned up toward the sun. Their sleeveless tunics revealed the many marks of *Viribus* on their shoulders and *Menda* on their forearms. Their skin tones indicated they could easily have hailed from Vitria or Electaria. Elle muttered a prayer under her breath that they were Electarian because her Vitrian was utter garbage.

"Hard day of work?" Elle approached the group with a grin, gesturing to the sweat dripping down their faces.

One of the women smiled wearily at Elle, her head drooping backward. Thankfully, she responded in Electarian, but with a slow, dripping accent. "You have no idea. Impe and Supe are the busiest," she waved her hand, "with the weather being so nice. The next two months are going to be bad."

"But anything to get away from the Riphs, right?" The man to her right elbowed her in the side.

She scowled and gave him a firm shove, right over the side of the box he sat on. Elle's grin grew—she liked this woman.

"The *other parts*," she stressed the words slowly, as if daring the man to use the derogative again, "of this country are wrecked, but it's not our fault. It's the kingdom that's the problem—any resource worth a damn always ends up here."

Elle's head cocked to the side curiously as she mulled over the statement. She didn't hear much about the other parts of Electaria. Relegated to the back both in public policy and public mind, she supposed. Elle shook her head. *Not the time to get distracted.* It was time to sell, and to do that, she needed to sell herself first.

"It is a shame." Elle shook her head solemnly. "You'd think the king could do more, right?"

"The king"—a man opposite of the woman spit to the side—"can barely put on a pair of trousers by himself. It's the classic bar joke: How many kings does it take to light a torch? Just the one—and his hundred servants who will end up doin' it for him."

"My ma and da always said that a king without his servants is just a normal guy in a very big house with a very silly hat on his head." Elle shrugged.

The group burst into laughter, the man splaying out his hands. "Exactly! What's with the crown, anyway? Damn thing looks ridiculous." He looked at Elle, eyes crinkled in a smile. "You got some smart parents, kid."

"And talented too." Elle brought the sack around, undoing the top latch so that the bread was on clear display for the sailors. The mouthwatering scent of rosemary cut through the overwhelming stench of the Landing just for a second, but it seemed like that second was enough. Elle smiled at the hungry look in all the sailors' eyes. "They save the best in the store for the hardest workers in the kingdom."

The woman scratched the back of her head. "I don't know about you guys, but I don't really have the money to pay for these things on a whim."

Elle's mark warmed. She spent so long living with its pulses and its reactions, she rarely spent time thinking about their significance. Her mark was a secret anyway—no reason to dig deeper and threaten to expose it. But even if she didn't analyze it, she tended to keep an ear open to its suggestions.

Reaching into the satchel, Elle grabbed one of the smaller loaves and tossed it in the lap of the woman. "For just being a hard worker, then. You all deserve these kinds of things more than anyone." Elle looked at the bemused eyes of the rest of the group, telling them sternly, "But the rest of you need to pay if you want some."

Their expressions were quickly replaced with laughter and calls for Elle to come over and exchange bread for coins. The woman looked back and forth between Elle and the bread with a surprised, but pleased, face. As more sailors called Elle to them, the group into which Elle had entered grew larger, the good-natured ambiance growing. Elle's mark continued its warm pulses.

In about an hour, all Elle's goods were gone, and her bag was heavy with coins. A skip in her step, she waved goodbye to the group, who cheered her away. Elle walked to the edge of the dock and sat down, throwing her legs over the side and turning one of the iron coins through her fingers. She gazed at the gently flowing water, far enough from her feet that whenever it lapped against the dock, it failed to come even close to spraying her.

Though satisfied with the outcome, Elle was still surprised by the effectiveness of a little goodwill. People were simple like that, in a way. Just be good to them, and they'd do so much in return. Perhaps the easy formula could help Elle get a life that was a little more interesting than simply selling bread.

It wasn't that Elle didn't enjoy doing these things for her parents. There were always little joys to be found in easing the financial burden of Ma and Da, and she enjoyed the people she met when she went on runs for ingredients and embarked on adventures toward the Landing. But Elle had done these things since leaving school three years ago. In between the love she had for her family and devotion she had to making their lives better, there was a thread of tedium that tied it all together.

Gripping the coin tighter, Elle imagined for a second tossing it to one of the captains, asking for passage on one of their ships. Before the talk with her parents, Elle had wanted to be a ship captain. Leading a crew across tumultuous oceans and traveling all across the world was a dream she had so many nights she lost count. She had wanted to visit Vitria, Da's homeland and where he and Ma had met. She wanted to sail to Aurjnegh and see the gaudy country herself. There were places to explore that had yet to be discovered, creatures that had yet to be seen. There was so much to *do*, and Elle had wanted to do it all.

But it was the same song her sister would one day hear. Trading schools, even for sailing, were a cost her family couldn't afford to pay—especially not for each of their five children. The money went into keeping up the bakery and keeping everyone alive. *And shouldn't that be enough?* Elle put her head on her knees and watched the sailors laugh and shout to one another. Her mark burned, a low, painful thing. She wished it were enough.

Her parents needed her help, though. The bakery had teetered back and forth on the brink of ruin before Elle and Nic had started pitching in more. Now that all the children helped in some way, the bakery was slowly but surely becoming less of a financial burden and more of a financial investment. If Elle left, the careful equilibrium of their division of responsibilities would shatter.

Elle groaned to herself. "There should be a way to make *money.*" She glared at the iron coin, adding quietly, "Not just survive."

Despite knowing she would get in trouble, Elle stayed on the dock until the sun was practically gone from the sky. The drunks would soon be joined by their more sober companions hoping to achieve a similar state. The nightwalkers, scantily clad and on the hunt for any gentlemen or women willing to pay for their services, would start prowling. Ma would soon start yelling at all Elle's siblings, wondering where in *Imperium*'s name Elle was. Heaving herself up, Elle began a slow walk back toward her house.

CHAPTER 3
7055.1.15

"Aoran, would his ladyship care to join us for drills?"

Sometimes, when Aoran bothered to think about his dead parents, he cursed them for his name.

On those exceedingly rare occasions, he pictured them as contrarian philosophers or disgruntled artists, the kind of people who drank cheap liquor with obscure names and lived on a cloud of intellectual elitism. The kind of people who really thought they were sticking it to society by subverting its norms and intentionally bestowing their son with a long, effeminate name. Shorter names were easier to shout, whether in jeering or warning. For hundreds of years, men had tended to serve in occupations like military service, sailing, or just hard labor. Concurrently, shorter names developed.

And yet, he was stuck with Aoran. Those three syllables haunted him wherever he went. While surrounded by hard and fast names of male his age like Je and Ro, his sumptuous name stood out as embarrassingly soft.

"His ladyship doth decline the invitation." Aoran put the pipe back between his lips and took a long drag, the smoke expanding his lungs with a familiar caress. With his other hand, he flipped Je off by pressing his forefinger and middle finger together. "Thanks, though, *malum*."

Je raised one well-manicured eyebrow, a dark strip on his gold skin. He crossed his arms and shook his head. "Do you kiss your mother with that mouth?"

"Only when she begs." Aoran flashed a grin—a signature, wicked kind of smile that could send a delighted shiver down the spine of any poor soul caught in its snare.

Je choked, his face caught between total surprise and laughter. Aoran could always count on the famed archer for an easy audience. Five years had passed since they met, and the Electarian merchant's son still had enough good humor to laugh at Aoran's jokes. Whether it be the field of war or the field of witticisms, Aoran repeatedly concluded that the two worked marvelously well together.

Aoran snorted and put his pipe on the ground, pressing sand into the smoldering chamber. At this point in his life, he could barely feel the fading embers against his fingers; what had once been many small calluses had morphed into one massive, rough patch of skin. He rose with the grace of an old war veteran, his joints creaking like corroded armor.

The Captain came over and eyed the discarded pipe with a disgusted expression. She glared at it with her icy blue eyes as if she could make it disappear through sheer force of will. While sunweed wasn't technically illegal, its reputation accompanied that of crime lords, mercenaries, and *malums* of most varieties. Its ten-minute highs provided a temporary bliss, and the effects usually faded shortly thereafter. Sunweed had its more insidious brothers, whose effects lasted far longer, but Aoran had yet to be so inclined.

The Captain herself, of course, was far above the sweet release that sunweed provided. She stood so high on her pedestal of principles, it was a wonder she got enough air to breathe.

"The next time I see the king, I'll be sure to let His Majesty know that the kingdom's tax money is being squandered on manipulative grifters like yourself," the Captain said coolly. Aoran winced. "Get your wasteful ass up and go do Rotations with the rest of the Four.

I will be assigning you all a security task with the royal family shortly thereafter."

Aoran's penchant for doing nothing crumpled beneath the steel of her voice. People called her "Captain" for a reason. Her eyes sent men to their knees. Her commands drew legions to battle. And if some poor *malum* ever found himself at the business end of her sword, people whispered that terror would kill them before the blade did. The legends on the streets claimed she never received a real name and had simply been chosen by *Imperium* to be the one, true Captain.

That was, of course, all wolfshit, but dammit if she still wasn't more intimidating than an Aurjnegh soldier cut off from his beer. Aoran shuddered.

King Leo certainly liked her. She was effective and beloved by the people. From her establishment of the Four to her command in the War of Hawks back in 7051, she had done plenty to earn her reputation. Her very presence in the military lent legitimacy to the throne. Even though monarchies meant politics, and politics meant messiness, it was hard to oppose a regime protected by a woman so revered throughout the land.

Aoran lined up with his three cohorts. They stayed in the back corner of the training room, far separated from the novices that held wooden rods in their unsteady hands. The Captain walked away with a brusque gait, on to yell at a poor group of unsuspecting soldiers.

They were the fearsome fighters who had completed their Walks early on in their lives. Brought together through the cleverness of the Captain, they made their heroic debut in the War of Hawks. Aoran remembered being excited by the prospect of taking his place on the world stage. He had been brimming with electricity the day the Captain summoned the four of them five years ago and commanded they begin training together. By the time Wren, a border noble on the edge of Electaria and Aurjnegh, attacked an Electarian town a year later in the Riphs, the Four had turned into a lethal machine.

Aoran never understood why the Captain didn't fall into the group, making it the notorious Five. The title was, in his opinion, a clear misnomer, like missing the head of the snake—the most dangerous part of its body.

Aoran slowly pushed his body through the motions of Scissura Rotations, his movements a beat behind everybody else's like a heart with a stammer. His muscles ached from training the day before, and his legs felt like two sticks of softened butter, mushy and useless. He gradually scraped away the rust coating his thoughts and his actions. His first few movements were akin to pushing through an ocean of molasses. Gradually, the viscosity of the air lessened, and he moved smoothly. He bent down a little lower, the tension and thoughts melting through his body and onto the floor. His muscles relaxed, his body loosening up and gliding through the air more fluidly.

Rotations centered Aoran. Kings changed, people grew wiser, and battle tactics evolved, but Rotations always remained the same. He had started his training with these same sets of steps and lunges and had continued for as long as he could remember. Soldiers had jabbed and thrusted with these motions for hundreds of years. He was nothing more than another tick on a line that stretched far behind and would go far beyond him. There was comfort in that.

He crouched and lashed his fist out in a quick punch, straightening back up and feigning to the left. He leaped with a swift, rounded kick and landed close to the ground, ducking underneath an imaginary attack. Aoran swept between Rotation forms so fluidly he didn't spare the switch a thought. From the more defensive Corticus Rotations into the offensive Mordercus forms, Aoran adjusted and continued seamlessly.

His senses turned on and off, compensating for one another. His sense of smell disappeared entirely, while his vision sharpened to the most infinitesimal detail. His hearing faded, making Je's heavy breathing and grunts to his left sound miles away. They registered as watery and muffled, as if Aoran had dunked his head underwater. But in exchange for that hearing deficit, he could feel every nerve in his body with an intense electricity that left him almost twitching if he paused for even a second.

Vitrian fighting styles taught explosive maneuvers that caused harrowing damage if one landed. Aoran learned that the hard way when a hulking Vitrian left him broken and bloodied on the cobblestone after too many drinks and a few ill-timed quips. Aoran took away something from the beating if nothing else—he had no desire to return to the city and roam its streets like a half-starved, small-time thug. To this day, very little compelled Aoran to do anything in his life. He had few aspirations and fewer inclinations to find some. But the one thing he knew is that he wanted more from his life than that.

Electarians took a different approach. Precision, speed, patience. Fighting with Electarians was the equivalent to courting a woman. They took their time, approaching cautiously and dancing around the opponent. Then, after a healthy (borderline exorbitant) amount of time, somebody would finally make the first move. Boring? Maybe. But the approach provided the sturdy foundations of a top-notch military. It made for bad entertainment but good soldiers.

Aoran finished his Rotations by pounding his fist against his chest. The sound of all four hitting their hearts at the same time reverberated with a dull echo. He waited, right fist pressed to his heart in an Electarian salute, for the Captain to walk by and signal the end of the drill. The mark on his shoulder buzzed against his skin, almost painful with each electric jolt. He wondered if the others' marks were equally active beneath their skin.

"Everybody, up!" the Captain barked from a short distance away. "Four minutes for water and rest. Then we get to work."

Everybody relaxed at once. Aoran fell backward, his muscles both exhausted and exhilarated from the workout. Sunweed slowed him down to the point of a walking coma, energy expended only for basic living functions and talking. Rotations electrocuted him back to life, charging his mind and body in an incomparable way. They were both drugs in their own right, just with very different types of highs.

"Who do you guys want to work with for this thing?" Je rolled over and shouted at a younger soldier across the room. The soldier turned white and immediately ran to grab him water. Je frowned and pushed at a few obsidian curls that had managed to escape from his fortress of gel during Rotations.

"I hope I get to be with Eliana." Dayanara sighed, her eyes cast with a dreamy look.

Dayanara's black hair was cropped to her skull, a contrast to the alabaster skin beneath. When she flexed, her skin stretched against the size of her biceps. Her sturdy frame mimicked the form of a tree trunk, differentiated only by the slight feminine curve at the waist and hip. While Aoran wielded his dual blades and Je mastered the bow, Dayanara decimated enemies with a battle-ax half the size of her body. While women were allowed in the military, they were few and far between, causing most adversaries to underestimate their prowess in a fight. Dayanara and the Captain were Electaria's best kept secrets—women, yet deadlier than ten men a piece.

"You know being a bodyguard has less to do with the body and more to do with the guard part, right?" Aoran grinned, canines flashing.

"Of course! I would patrol her perimeter and secure all her entrances..." She fluttered her thick eyelashes and fell back on to the floor with a dreamy sigh.

Aoran and Je burst into heavy laughter, the kind that had its own infectious delight. Ro, the fourth of their lot, made no comment, but Aoran would have sworn to anybody who asked that he saw the hint of a smile on the stoic man's face.

Another thing people frequently got wrong: they assumed that just because the Four were warriors, it meant they were all serious stick-in-the-muds. They lauded the Four as a group of stars, meant to swoop in and lead the troops when enemies came knocking on Electaria's doors. Aoran learned a long time ago that people just perceived what they wanted to perceive. Those interested in knowing the truth would figure out in an instant that the most elite soldiers of the kingdom happened to also be some of the most mischievous *malums* the kingdom had to offer.

Except for Ro. Steadfast Ro. Simple and deadly, like the spear he always kept at his side. When Aoran sat at a bar with a potential companion for the night on either side, he made up stories for the soldier of mystery. Aoran wove tales of a rogue pirate turned dutiful civil servant. He painted stories of an assassin who fell in love with somebody in the royal family; rumor had it that Prince Teo still fled from his bedchambers at night to meet in secret with the soldier.

One day, Aoran knew these outlandish stories would catch up to him. But *Menda* knew that for now, they were great bait for the women of the kingdom, and it was hard to give up that kind of allure.

"What in *Imperium*'s name are you all still doing on the floor? Stand up!" the Captain snapped.

Aoran scrambled to his feet. He might be a miscreant, but even foxes had a sense of self-preservation.

The Captain stalked back and forth in front of the Four, displeasure radiating from her narrowed eyebrows and glowing in her eyes. Nobody said a word for about a minute, the feeling of the Captain's disapproval acting as its own physical force that seemed to push the air out of Aoran's lungs. Apparently, he, Je, and Dayanara managed to look appropriately chagrined—Ro would have never misbehaved in the first place—and the Captain's shoulders relaxed the slightest bit.

"I shouldn't need to say this in the first place, but I will because I have as much faith in you four as I do in a small child."

Out of the corner of his eye, Aoran saw Dayanara wince. Je stared straight ahead, but his perfectly trimmed nails nervously scratched at the gray pants of his training uniform. Ro stayed still, his cool, brown face neutral. Aoran felt his fingers twitch, wishing he had his pipe in his hands.

"Royals from all around will be visiting for an indeterminate amount of time. This means outsiders, and a lot of them." The Captain's face resembled the ominous and murky skies before a storm. "Let me make this clear: They are not your concern. They are not your charges. If I see you pull a sword or stand at the ready in their defense, I will dismiss you from this retinue. I will personally see to arrangements of their safety. You imbeciles," she jabbed her finger at them, "are in charge of *our* royalty."

When he had first enlisted in the army, he had been scared nearly shitless from the Captain's sharp tongue. Now Aoran saw her words less as criticism and more as an incredibly useful tool to keep an army together. It instilled humility and respect. Coddling was for artists and magisters—not for soldiers.

"Ro, you will oversee King Leo. *Imperium* knows you are the only one with enough brains in your head to keep him alive. Je, you will be with Prince Teo. Dayanara is guarding Princess Eliana, and Aoran will look after Princess Liliana."

Dayanara squeaked in excitement, and the Captain's frosty eyes narrowed into slits. The Captain refused to even try and conceal her anger as one word—"What?"—passed between her lips.

"N-Nothing, Captain," Dayanara stammered, bowing her head and staring at the ground. "Thank you for entrusting us with these positions."

The Captain glowered at her for a second longer before waving off the comment. "Yes, well, it's not as though I had a choice. You all are my least incompetent guards. Now go change into your uniforms and meet your charges before they enter the main hall to greet everyone."

When they didn't immediately move, the Captain barked, "Now!"

Aoran pounded his right fist against his heart in synchronization with the other three before sprinting away from the scene of the crime. His legs yelled at the sudden jolt in movement. Aoran ignored them. No need to stay around longer than necessary and get yelled at again. He gave a brief wave to his friends and some of the training soldiers as he ducked out of one of the exits and then disappeared entirely.

Aoran emerged on the bottom floor of the castle, lungs embracing the sweet, musty air of the corridors. A horrendous ancient smell—to the unacquainted of sunweed's delights—seemed to radiate from the center of the castle. The farther somebody walked down from the throne room, the stronger it clung to the carpet and walls. The servants complained, and rightfully so. Most people preferred the impervious scent of wet towels and old people to the burning sensation of sunweed.

The Equator, a small fissure just beyond the stairs, appeared in the floor that separated the stone floors of the official palace and the meager wood of the servants' quarters. While staff frequently polished the stone floors so that they shone with regal authority, the wood looked like the best it had received was a half-hearted scrub back in King Ri's reign nearly a century ago. The man's rule had been reflected in the state of the castle: half-assed and left to fall into total disarray. The brown had faded into a sickly gray, the same kind of aged ash color found in a mausoleum. Nails stuck out of the floor, and nicks marred the wood; anybody caught walking barefoot found themselves picking splinters out of their feet for weeks.

Still, the Equator marked home. In the castle's subbasement, that wooden death trap meant peace, quiet, and alone time. Beyond that fissure lay the servants' working area and the door to Aoran's room. He was the only one who lived down here, either a courtesy or a curse from the former queen. The rest of Electaria's military had normal homes in the city where they retired each night.

When he was first placed in the quarters by Queen Juliana, he could only find his way back to his room using the Equator. In a castle that always seemed to change, filled with twists and turns, the Equator was a constant. He would search for that marker, for the line that delineated his world and theirs.

That sounded bitter. Aoran shook his head and crept toward his room, careful to avoid any particularly dangerous protrusions. He opened the old planks of wood haphazardly slapped together that dared to call itself a door. His heart practically heaved in a sigh at the familiar sight.

One bed, one trunk, one sink. Aoran's feet usually dipped over the edge of the bed, its small frame unable to accommodate even his average figure. Its sides dented and scuffed, the trunk looked like a gang member had given it a lesson it wouldn't soon forget. More rust covered the bottom of the sink than the original material of the bowl, but clean water flowed out of the spigot, and that was the only important thing, really. It was about all Aoran had to his name, and it was perfect.

He shucked off his sweaty practice garb and gingerly pulled on the official Electarian uniform. The black pants, sharp and professional, clung tightly to his legs and pressed into every wound he had accumulated over the past week during training. He slipped his arms into the long sleeves of the purple officer's coat, his fingers fumbling over the tiny golden buttons that held the two sides together.

"*Imperium*...Gotta be wrecking kidding me...Son of a *malum*!" He grunted and swore, finally clipping together the last two pieces.

In the back of his mind, he thought maybe he shouldn't complain so much. Once he managed to get the bastards together, the clips weren't that bad. At least he could move in this uniform. The black shit they made the cadets wear was barely better than a straitjacket. The scratchy, stiff fabric left every soldier with rashes and an aching desire to be promoted to a position with more comfortable clothing.

Screw the golden mark, the respect, the status. The only reminder he needed of his accomplishments was the smooth, breathable fabric he had the pleasure of wearing to all the official events.

Aoran tied his hair back into a fresh bun, pulling his platinum strands taut against his head. Liliana used to tease him about it when they were younger. "It looks like somebody sucked out all the color and left behind the dead corpse of your hair."

Even at the age of eleven, she used her tongue as her fiercest weapon. Sharper than any whip, more dangerous than any sword— it took years before Aoran was anything more than a dummy she could practice her lashings on.

Once his scalp started to scream in protest, he knew the bun would be tight enough to receive only minimal criticism from the Captain. She would nag, but she wouldn't pull out her sword to sheer it off where he stood. It was only with strict care and careful presentation that she permitted him to keep his hair this long.

He lingered in the room for a moment longer, his fingers twitching with an absent desire to take a drag. He shook off the feeling. He couldn't tell whether his lungs expanded with relief or distress when he put his hand on the doorknob instead of his pipe. He opened the door and immediately barreled into Liliana, knocking her to the ground.

"Wrecking *malum*," he cursed under his breath, reaching out his hand to help her back to her feet. He desperately hoped that she hadn't fallen onto any of the stray nails. It was his first day as her bodyguard, so he didn't know all the facets of the job. And yet, he felt confident that bashing the body he should have been guarding was not in the description.

"Are you sure we went to the same propriety classes?" she griped at him, dusting off the layer of dirt and dust that always seemed to coat the hallways. "I swear, you have the worst mouth this side of the river has ever seen. If I didn't know you better, I would think you were one of Imperium's brothers that just got separated from the litter." She paused, her face turning thoughtful. "As a matter of fact, I do know you better, and I do think that."

"As much as I would love to uphold our traditional parley of barbs and cruelty, I really have to be on my way. I seem to recall a minor tea party of some sort happening relatively soon." He put his burning hands against the silken fabric of her waist and turned her around so she faced the staircase.

"And by 'minor tea party' you mean the first gathering of the entire royal family in about seven years?" Her mouth puckered, as if unsure whether to drop in surprise or pinch further in displeasure.

"That," he gave her a light push toward the Equator, "is exactly what I mean, Your Highness. And what luck that I should find you!

Now people will think that I'm being proactive about this whole bodyguard arrangement."

"I dare say that the thought of you being proactive has not and will never slip across anyone's mind for as long as we both shall live," she said hotly.

Aoran's mouth quirked up into a smile. A follower of *Imperium*, the girl had more dragon in her blood than anyone he had ever met. "Then I suppose we will just have to wait until we both perish tragically in a lover's quarrel gone wrong—then they will sing songs of my name, and you will see. They will call me Aoran the Proactive. And it will all be thanks to you, my dear."

He batted his eyelashes and barked out in laughter at the faint red that dusted across her cheeks. One of the drawbacks of the dragon blood was that it was impossible to control the fire that spread across her face.

It took a moment for the pink to fade from her warm, brown skin. On the inside, Liliana manifested as a fire-breathing monstrosity that sent all who saw her running in terror. Unfortunately, her exterior proved to be much more pleasant, which made it hard to find her utterly annoying all the time—not for lack of trying either. Her skin just looked too silky, as if somebody had taken glazed terracotta and buffed it to a transcendental smoothness. Her eyelashes flipped up dramatically, brushing the top of her eyelids and framing two clear, determined eyes. Their color reminded him of stained glass, like they would be translucent if they weren't tinted by that bit of brown.

It went beyond just her appearance, though. It came from the way she walked, the way she carried herself. It came from that upward tilt of her chin and the defiant straightness of her spine. It came from the way that her very *being* wouldn't allow anyone to mistake her for anything but royalty. Fortunately for Aoran's sanity, all this perfection was marred by one thing: her stick-and-bones frame.

In the Nuwei empire, her figure would be prized above all else. They enjoyed women slender and slight, more angles than curves off of which their eccentric robes could elegantly drape. However, most Electarians and Vitrians considered her body type distinctly unattractive. The dresses tailored to accentuate the curves of Electarian women ended up making Liliana look withered as they clung to the hard lines of her body.

Most potential suitors stopped their pursuits once they met her in real life, switching their attentions instead to the fuller frame of her older sister. Aoran personally had no problem with her thin figure. Her bony frame made Liliana's presence slightly less distracting.

Speaking of presence.... "But I digress: What brings you here, princess?"

The pink returned to her face and she huffed, clasping her hands behind her back and staunchly refusing to meet his eyes. She stared at the ceiling, the door behind him, a particularly interesting splinter in the floor. Those clear hazel eyes trailed around the room like a wolf on the prowl, hunting for a reason to avoid his gaze.

He smiled, folding his arms, waiting. He could deal with silence. To him, it was another companion he spent pleasant time with on any given day. To people like Liliana, though, silence had a weight and texture, neither of which was bearable.

She cracked. "Fine! I came because I need you to teach me how to fight. Preferably to fight well, but I'll start with the basics."

Aoran couldn't help the wolfish grin that spread across his face. "Well, this family reunion should be fun, huh?"

CHAPTER 4
7055.1.15

"Can't say I'm surprised you came asking for help from the most skilled fighter in the kingdom." Aoran grinned, shrugging. "But how could I possibly find the time for you amid all my other charity cases? I am but one man, Your Highness."

Liliana tried not to snap at the barely concealed glee dancing across his face. She recited the Nuweinian alphabet backward to herself. She repeated the hymns of the magisters. Dreadfully long things, but perfect for distractions. She reminded herself that Aoran and his smug, irritating face were just stepping-stones. A grim pleasure rose in her at the thought of stepping on Aoran's face.

Finally, she took a deep breath and stared, defiant, at Aoran, her brown eyes meeting his playful and curious green ones. "Fine. I will offer you a position as second in command to the Captain once I am on the military council."

Aoran stared at her for a beat before clucking his tongue and shaking his head in despair. *What she must think of me, to try and offer such a thing!* He appraised her before giving another disappointed shake. "Either you have forgotten what we both learned in civi, or you are trying to play me the fool. No matter which it is, I must decline. We *both* know," he popped the word both out of his mouth with sickening satisfaction, "that only the monarch and the Captain herself have the power of appointment in the military—and as far as I last checked, you are neither."

Liliana bit back a curse, trying not to stoop to Aoran's crass level for once. Deep, deep down with a resigned bitterness, she almost admired his craft. Just as an expert clockmaker could navigate the inner workings of any clock with ease after repetition and practice, Aoran had cultivated his ability to the point where he could send her into an angry spiral with just a few words. From the damned civics class he had thrown in her face to virtually every other word he uttered, he wound, tweaked, and tinkered until she was thoroughly vexed.

"Fine. When the time comes, I will talk with Teo and negotiate into having you appointed."

"Even if you had the grounds to negotiate with the royal heir, which," he gave her a pointed look, "I doubt you do, you're barking up the wrong tree, princess. Titles don't appeal to me—I'm happy where I am."

The words came out and all but slapped Liliana on the face. She examined his expression, trying to find some sign that he was lying. He met her probing gaze, and she couldn't find an ounce of doubt hidden there. The mark on her back throbbed with a faint burn.

She couldn't grasp the idea of being content with one's station. The only way anyone could get anything done was by moving up in the ranks of the world. So much of her life had been centered on bettering herself, improving her mind, improving her ideas, improving her spirit (though, she had yet to complete her Walk, so she supposed the last bit was still a work in progress). If everybody decided they were happy where they were, nothing would ever move forward. Their world of *Terrabis* would slow to a halt, stalled by complacency.

It was especially appalling to hear from someone who originally had nothing. Given Aoran's meteoric rise from his humble—and that was a polite designation—beginnings, Liliana expected more from him. Where would she be if she shared that attitude? She stopped herself from laughing out loud. Attending to the poor and devoting her life to somebody else's charity case, probably, as is the norm for every third child with no hope to ascend the throne. Bile churned up her throat at the mere thought.

Steel in her gaze, Liliana looked back at Aoran. The look stood somewhere between a glare and a stare, an expression so intense and forceful that Aoran almost seemed to flinch. The life of a third child was no life at all. Liliana refused to accept such a fate when so much more waited at her fingertips, so long as she was strong enough to simply reach out and grab what she wanted.

"How about this, then? You will teach me to fight. You will get nothing in return, other than a promise that I will not make your job a living nightmare over these next few days." Her voice was hard, chiseled from stone and made into a bludgeon.

"And I had really hoped our vast history together would have absolved us of the whole 'I threaten you, you threaten me, we end up enemies' thing," Aoran said with a smile spread across his face. Despite the playful grin, his tone held a sharp edge that Liliana rarely heard.

She did not respond. That edge in his voice would never be hard enough to sway her. Liliana simply cocked her head to the side as she stared at Aoran. Not now and not ever would she be cowed, *especially* by the likes of him. They held each other's gaze in the silence of the undergrounds of the castle, Liliana's heartbeat pounding loudly in her ears.

He stayed silent before finally breaking with a heavy, dramatic sigh. "Fine! I'll teach you how to fight. You're only marginally less attractive than Je, so it shouldn't be too torturous."

She couldn't even find it in herself to quip back. The mark on her back flared in time with her heartbeat, thumping against her chest. A triumphant breath of air filled her lungs, making her want to yell in excitement or just run around the castle. Only years of training in proper behavior kept her legs still and her mouth closed. To Aoran, it must have seemed such a small concession. To Liliana, it was her entrance into the next phase of her legacy.

Struggling to keep her mouth in a straight line, Liliana turned to the hallway and began marching. For that second, while facing the opposite direction, a clear beam stretched across her face. It was the kind of beam that spoke of good things to come.

Aoran complained as he jogged to catch up. Liliana composed herself and managed her expression into just a small smile. The bottom of her dress scraped against the floor as she all but danced her way to the throne room. Even the pale purple monstrosity and suffocating corset that her maids had forced her into could not spoil her good mood.

Some of Liliana's first memories were of her grumbling as attendants pushed her arms through the leather confinements of corsets and silken cages of court dresses. Her mother directed from the background, demanding a tighter stitch here, higher heels there. Unlike Vitrian women in their robes, Electarians were ensnared from birth in their tight clothing and heeled shoes. Even the maids weren't spared; they suffocated in their own cotton traps as they shoved Liliana's head through high-necked collars.

Once she and Aoran started their fighting lessons, she would have a plausible reason to wear pants. *Thank* Imperium, she thought gratefully. She would be able to ditch the fitted, Electarian dresses that made her sticky frame look "sickly, but in a cute way!" as Eliana so sweetly put it.

Obviously, Liliana would have to keep wearing her small, golden earrings. The pentagon studs had been present on her person since she turned five, a cherished age in Electaria. Those who hadn't completed their Walk tended to wear some kind of gold on their person. Liliana had worn hers since then, well, religiously. She doubted the jewelry would be the difference between spiritual enlightenment or not, but still. She raised her hand to brush against the earring. *It couldn't hurt.*

"So what should I be expecting in there?" Aoran broke the silence, fingers twitching as if looking for something to hold. "Royals and elites stroking one another's ego until everybody is sufficiently erect? A political orgy where everyone takes turns thoroughly wrecking each other? Because I could be amenable."

Liliana threw him a withering look, and he responded with a grin that might have been considered sheepish if she didn't know him better.

He eventually broke into laughter and held his hands up apologetically. "I kid, I kid. Seriously, though. It's got to be something pretty important for the Captain to assign the Four to guard the family."

The Captain. Liliana avoided scowling at the name. A rancid feeling flashed through Liliana's chest as she remembered the Captain's dismissive attitude. Her back throbbed. She stopped the fire inside herself, taking a deep breath at the memory of Aoran's promise. "I don't know, honestly." The tight sleeves of her dress made it hard to shrug properly, but she managed. "Father's been pretty evasive about the whole thing. He just said to be ready and be on my best behavior."

Aoran sucked his teeth. "I never thought him the type to make such impossible requests of the people beneath him."

"He hasn't asked you to not be an unmanageable prick yet, so I would say he's still acting within the realm of reason."

"Touché," Aoran cackled, his green eyes sparkling.

A smile crept across Liliana's face. As annoying as Aoran could be, she viewed their repartee as its own form of art. There was something sort of beautiful about a dangerously sharpened barb and a forceful retaliation. The ease and grace of their back-and-forth reminded Liliana of ballroom dancing.

She winced, the memories flashing across her mind. Taking courtroom dancing at age thirteen with Aoran had been a nightmare. He loved messing up the steps, making her trip up, and just generally being a pain in the ass. Liliana couldn't count the number of times she had gotten in trouble for Aoran's shenanigans. *Still*...Liliana had to admit to herself that they'd had fun. They snickered and trounced their way through that class, testing the teacher to see how far they could go.

The second Aoran thought he would get in real trouble, he grabbed Liliana by the waist and spun her around the room. Though her dance moves had always been passable, she looked slow and clumsy in comparison to his effortless gliding. It frustrated her to no end. So long as it suited him, he could put professional dancers to shame, his moves uniquely elegant and playful. His seamless but dynamic fluidity always reminded Liliana of a wolf.

Liliana saw that same wolf in Aoran when she watched him fight. He moved as a controlled tempest. At any moment he could unleash a storm. Every step was reserved, every lunge teasing. It was as if he were a master puppeteer: He wanted to see how far his opponents could go if he gave them a little more string. But at the end of the day, he still held the controls.

Aoran the wolf. She glanced at him out of the corner of her eye, catching his pensive stare at the ceiling. If she had learned one thing from Imperium, it was that all wolves held a deeper side. The side that gazed at the moon and howled for all the mysteries they would never know.

Aoran caught her eye and winked at her. She ignored the heat that immediately spread across her cheeks to the best of her ability and resumed staring straight ahead. Liliana took it all back—how could she have ever mistaken him for anything but a fox?

**

Other than a few tender spots from some particularly candid insults, they made their way up two flights of stairs to the throne room relatively unscathed. Liliana almost sighed when they came to the entrance. The cream doors were thrown open, partially hiding the golden marks that decorated its face: A hawk on the bottom left for *Superbia*, waves on the right for *Menda*, a wolf on the top left for *Viribus*, a tree on the top right for *Caecus*, and a grand dragon whose wings touched the ends of both doors when closed. All for her majesty, *Imperium*.

Four guards stood in front of the large columns that framed the doors. Two obvious recruits were dressed in the tailored black uniform of the Electarian military, while the more seasoned pair mimicked Aoran's purple coat and black pants. Liliana studied the four, deciding it was probably an arrangement of mentorship. Simple swords hung at their waists, more than enough to handle any misbehaved nobles. Their broad statures barely covered half the width of the gargantuan pillars. They offered small nods to Aoran and short bows to Liliana as the pair passed.

Imperium sat dutifully on his hind legs beside one of the pillars, always attuned to where the action was in the castle. Liliana gave her panting wolf a scratch beneath his large chin and a murmur to stay before entering the throne room.

The vaulted ceilings opened the white room, its floor-to-ceiling, golden-stained windows allowing light to shine in no matter the time of day. The openness of the room and the large windows were subtle nods to *Menda* and the Electarian monarchy's honesty. Liliana never knew if the symbolism was aspirational or just ironic. After all, the throne room was ultimately a place of politics, and honesty tended to be pushed aside for other interests. The room was devoid of color except for the golden patterns that swirled across the walls. Each flower and curl contained real gold, carefully designed by Seraphinus and molded by elite craftsmen from the kingdom.

Decorations were sparse, save for a few fixtures that truly enthralled Liliana. She imagined sinking her heels into the deep, purple rug that led to the two gorgeous thrones. In an ideal world, *her* two thrones. The two chairs stood taller than two men put together, courtesy of the golden dragon that made up their backs. Their heads craned toward the ceiling, ferocious mouths opened in a partial roar. Their wings stretched out into two sinuous armrests, talons outstretched as if reaching for the audience.

She closed her eyes and pictured herself sitting down on the plush, purple velvet of the seat, cradled by the dragon. Leaning her head back against the textured scales of the chair. A shiver went through her body as Aoran gestured for Liliana to walk through the doorway. She didn't think the thrill of entering the throne room would ever fade. It was truly a hallmark of Electarian excellence.

More people filled the room than Liliana had seen in years. She frowned after a cursory scan. The people far outnumbered the extended royal family. She squinted her eyes, looking more closely at the faces. Certainly not just family.... She spotted the proud posture of the Aurjnegh court. The critical stances of the Nuwei council. Even the Soj were present, and the Soj hardly got invited to *anything*. A natural political byproduct of being Nuwei's protectorate territory and all their people being born without marks; the whole of *Terrabis* wrote the Soj off as a generally subjugated group of heretics. The mark on her back began to pound, humming throughout her body.

What in Imperium's *name was going on?*

Aoran's eyes darted around the room, his back tense. It was the most alert Liliana had ever seen him (though, to be fair, about half the time she saw him he walked around in a sunweed-induced stupor). He leaned over, ever so slightly, angling his body away from the rest of the room. He muttered under his breath, the words somehow still totally clear: "Who are all of these *malums*?"

"These '*malums*,'" Liliana said, resisting doing actual air quotes, "are the governing bodies of the two biggest nations in the world." She paused and frowned. "But if they're present, why wouldn't the Vitrians be here, too?"

"Liliana!"

An older woman waved furiously at her, her gargantuan bosom shaking in time with the force of an earthquake.

Liliana remembered her promise to her father and offered a weak smile in return, certain the force of it made her look sickly. Easternalia beckoned her over, and Liliana feared for one moment that the woman's breasts might pop out of her dress entirely.

"And *that malum*," Liliana closed her eyes and sent up a prayer to *Superbia* for the humility to stay patient, "is my great-aunt. Wish me luck."

Aoran played the part of a dutiful guard for once and bowed, bending slightly at the waist and no lower. It appeared as though he did remember a thing or two from their propriety class. Anything more than that was reserved for the kings and queens and would come off as a political slight. *He was a frustrating man, but a smart one,* she thought begrudgingly. Though she hadn't expected such a who's who of politics, she geared herself and adapted too.

She pressed a kiss to her forefinger and middle finger and then brushed them against the area of his sleeve where his mark of *Viribus* lay underneath. It was a relatively formal way of showing appreciation to someone. It typically meant well wishes on one's Walk. Considering Aoran had completed his and she hadn't even finished hers—a source of serious consternation—it was more symbolic than anything else. Aoran and the other soldiers constantly misappropriated the sign, transforming it from a "good luck" into more of a "wreck you."

Liliana wasn't sure, but she thought she saw Aoran's green eyes burn through her as her fingers brushed his shoulder. She did her best to ignore the look and walked to meet Easternalia with as much grace as she could muster.

Now to be clear, Liliana didn't have anything specific against Easternalia. The woman was attention seeking, but she was passive. The most dangerous thing about her was the low-cut, extravagant dresses she wore that always threatened to expose her…lady parts. She would not murder, wrongfully convict, or do anything exceptionally malicious to further her own social agenda. However, she *would* buy her way into power at the Aurjnegh Court. She *would* monopolize three and a half hours of a diplomatic meeting talking about her children and their minute accomplishments. She *would* spread false fidelity rumors about Liliana's mother around the court. She *would* change her birth name from Easter to Easternalia, giving it three more syllables and so much more "feminine charm!"

So no. Liliana did not have anything against Easternalia, other than the fact that she found her great-aunt to be utterly insufferable.

Easternalia squealed as Liliana got closer, grabbing her with more force than Liliana thought lived in the woman's sagging, ivory arms. As Easternalia crushed her to her generous chest,

Liliana looked longingly toward the throne, where her father sat in quiet conversation with her two siblings. She pulled back, looking at Liliana fondly with her sharp eyes. Having lived in so many countries and worked in diplomacy for so long, Easternalia started chattering in Electarian with ease.

"Liliana! Why, look at you, dear. It's been so dreadfully long!"

"It really has, Auntie," Liliana said, struggling to focus on anything other than her aunt's horrific outfit. The dress was a garish red, making her aunt look like a rotten cherry that had been squished and stitched into clothing. The dress itself dipped down and hiked up in the most perilous areas, leaving the room in constant danger of seeing more than anyone wanted.

Easternalia was born in Nuwei and moved to Vitria to marry Liliana's father's uncle when her father was young. After Liliana's great-uncle died of sea sickness, Easternalia whisked her way out of Vitria and into Aurjnegh. Upon arrival, she assimilated immediately. The breezy robes went out the window, replaced with overly embellished fabrics that masqueraded as real clothing. Between the gems and feathers that swallowed every outfit, Liliana found herself dizzy just looking at her aunt.

"Oh! And I'm sure you remember your relatives," she gestured proudly to the small armada of people behind her, "Ie, Tatiana, Ren..."

Looking at the pack of people, Liliana tuned her out. Carbon copies of one another, they shifted awkwardly as their mother (grandmother, in some cases) introduced them. Liliana absently wondered if they even knew how to speak. She would be impressed if they managed to get a single word in with Easternalia beating the conversation into submission. An aching pity flashed through her for just a moment. She understood how it felt to live underneath somebody else's shadow.

"But enough about me." Easternalia fanned herself, as if holding up the conversation left her drained. "Look at you! Now look at you. What a lovely lady! How long has it been since I've last seen you? It feels like an absolute *eternity*, dear."

"Three years ago, at the Nuwei Education conference." Liliana tried to infuse some pep into her voice but found it extraordinarily difficult.

Some of the most powerful people in the world stood around her, and yet she had to talk to her great-aunt. If this moment wasn't a perfect encapsulation of Liliana's life, she would eat Imperium.

"Of course! The Nuwei Education conference!" Easternalia exclaimed, seemingly horrified at the idea of forgetting what had been a relatively unimportant meeting. "If I remember correctly, the idea you proposed caused *quite* the stir." Her aunt patted Liliana's arm sympathetically. "But it's all right. Not all of us are cut out to be changemakers."

Liliana's eye twitched. "I suppose you're right, Auntie. But if you remember even further," Liliana stressed the word "even," a smile on her face, "you'll recall that my proposal for educational cultural exchanges ended up passing almost unanimously. Only two votes against."

The image of Easternalia's plump hand in the air when the head ambassador asked for "those who stood against" burned in Liliana's mind. Easternalia's head tilted to the side, her eyes narrowing by a fraction.

"I'm sure if I thought back hard enough, I would remember that. It truly was so trivial, though." Easternalia waved off the subject breezily. "But really, look at you, dear. Three years and you've barely changed a bit!" Easternalia's eyes flickered down to Liliana's flat chest, her smile curling up at the edges.

Diplomacy be damned. Liliana laughed, a high, piercing noise. "I wish I could say the same for you!" Liliana dropped her voice to a stage whisper, making sure she still spoke loud enough for others to hear. "My mother used to have this great salve for wrinkles, and I'd be more than happy to find the recipe for you."

Easternalia's smile froze in place, her words quiet and for Liliana's ears only. "And how's that working out for her?"

A dull noise roared in the back of Liliana's head, touching every one of her thoughts and smothering them in anger. Her breath caught in her throat, somewhere between wanting to run and wanting to cut the tongue out of the woman in front of her. The mark on her back pounded, begging for release.

"Liliana, come stand with your siblings!" her father called, walking his way down the plush carpet to his seat.

Liliana took the excuse and hurried away, unable to quite look her aunt in the eyes as she gave a small curtsy. She took her place to the right of Eliana, some part of her still in shock from what happened. Eliana appraised Liliana out of the corner of her eye, still facing the front of the room. Teo barely seemed to have noticed Liliana's presence, his eyes focused on Leo's ascent to the throne. Liliana resisted the urge to goad him. He could ignore her for now. She would be valuable to him soon enough.

"What in *Imperium*'s name just happened?" Eliana smiled gently at the crowd, her words still managing to be accusatory. Though Liliana easily stood a head taller than her sister, Eliana had a knack for making her feel small.

"Aunt Easternalia was being a total *malum*," Liliana said, unable to force the composure her sister displayed.

Eliana made a disgusted noise in the back of her throat, her eyes flickering over to Easternalia fussing over her children and grandchildren. "Stop being offended by truths of the universe. The sun will shine. The rain will fall. Easternalia will be deplorable. Move forward."

"She made a joke about Mom."

Eliana turned her head to look Liliana in the eye. Liliana resisted flinching underneath the piercing gaze of Eliana's black eyes. "So what? Mom is dead. Another truth. Work through your emotional turmoil and act like you're ready for the most important meeting of the century."

Liliana could find no retort in her body, only a deep pain, like an old wound before it rained. She looked away from her sister before Eliana could say anything else. Her mother was a topic untouched in Liliana's mind, an ancient artifact better left alone than played with and potentially broken.

Their mother, Queen Juliana, had died seven years ago. During a meeting with her advisors, she collapsed, never to rise again. Liliana could still hear the screams of the staff from her bedroom. Before she could focus on the noise, hordes of military personnel pounded on her door, demanding entry. They whisked her to a secure location, isolated from her family in the event that her mother's death was deliberate.

Liliana had spent hours in a guarded room, alone and weeping for a tragedy of which she had no knowledge. Her mark had ached like an open sore, oozing and raw. To bear the mark of *Imperium* was rare. To lose a monarch with that mark was devastating. Thinking back, nobody even told Liliana about her mother's death until the next day. Liliana cried that night simply because every fiber of her body told her that devastation had struck.

It all happened in the cyclical way most tragic things do. Their mother died, they mourned, they moved on. Wash, rinse, repeat. Or at the very least, most of them moved on. Liliana had the sinking suspicion that she was the only one left clinging to the memory of somebody long gone. If Liliana's father had been a warm star when Liliana was a child, then her mother was the universe itself. Incomprehensible, unending, magnificent. Her father made a good king, but her mother had made an unmatchable queen.

She couldn't blame her father for that, though. The mark of *Menda* lay on his arm. The Gods themselves had decided him a man of honesty, not one meant for power. Eliana glanced over, looking as though she wanted to add something to her last comment, but Teo turned to both of them and put a finger to his lips, his face stern. Eliana stood, effectively silenced, and Liliana focused on her father.

"Thank you all for coming here today. It has been quite a while since a group of this magnitude has been assembled." He chuckled in that hearty, pleasant way of his. Despite the eclectic group of visitors, he spoke in Electarian, the general language of diplomacy on *Terrabis*. His voice was bold, his words warm and genuine. "For that, I thank you. For the seas you fought to get here, the mountains you braved to arrive, and the family squabbles you endured to take your place in this room. Thank you."

Liliana could have sworn he glanced her way for a split second and raised an eyebrow at her. It took all of her will to keep her eyes in place instead of rolling them. Her father had as much subtlety as a dragon in a porcelain market.

"A special thank you to our friends from Aurjnegh and Nuwei for joining us," he added.

Like the subject of any sufficient scorn, the Soj were left out of the king's open remarks. Liliana glanced at the silent delegation, wondering what ran through their minds at the moment.

"I hope our Vitrian allies will be able to join us soon." Her father cast a look at the door, his expression unreadable. He looked back toward the room, spreading his hands out in front of him. "Shall we begin?"

Eager eyes glittered around the room. The same question flashed across everybody's face: Why had Electaria called such a meeting? Liliana almost saw the speculations fill the room like cobwebs. What would it be? A new wife? A bastard child? Embezzlement and corruption? Each held its own allure. She wondered in which one the truth would become entangled.

Her father opened his mouth to speak, but the doors of the room slammed open, cutting off his words. Two large figures burst into the room, their arms open and their faces bright. Their loose, sky-blue robes flowed behind them, leaving even their hulking forms looking graceful. A girl waited back at the door behind the pair, her violet eyes wide. Liliana resisted the urge to wrinkle her nose; the girl's clothes were in the same state she would expect if she had just gone grave digging.

"Leo! You'll never believe the time we had coming here!" The woman laughed, the sound echoing throughout the room.

"It's like you wanted to keep us out, making this city so confusing!" The man waggled his finger disapprovingly at the king.

"How cruel! And from our old friend Leo! Isn't that just terrible, Kai?" the woman exclaimed, leaning on the man.

The picture reminded Liliana strangely of two trees struck by a storm, only staying upright through the other's sheer mass. Their size only made the pair more striking, which was pretty hard to do. Between their sharp jawlines, tanned, tawny skin, and wide smiles, they shared a distinctive look that Liliana couldn't quite place as beautiful or overwhelming. Maybe a little bit of both.

"Dreadful." Kai shook his head, a smile playing on his lips.

Her father smiled and raised a hand, acknowledging the Vitrian empress and her consort. "Kai, Renee, would you like to join the rest of the kingdoms so I can finish my speech?"

Kai and Renee looked at each other, looked at the rest of the room watching the theatrics, looked back at each other, and burst out laughing. They sounded like two sonorous church bells, clanging in harmony. Even Teo looked like he wanted to smile. Though, being Teo, he didn't.

"Sorry, sorry. We'll talk later." Renee winked at Leo and grabbed Kai's arm, marching down the stage to stand next to the Nuwei council. The groups greeted each other formally but with warmth. The Vitrians nodded to the Aurjnegh Court but made no move to interact with the delegation otherwise.

Her father cleared his throat, redirecting the attention of the room. "Now that everyone is here," he shook his head with a small chuckle as the Vitrians waved excitedly at him, "I will make an announcement that should be of interest, in one form or another, to everybody here."

Everybody became quiet. The air in the room buzzed with electricity. If somebody reached out, they would surely shock themselves on the tension. It was terrifying. It was empowering.

This particular kind of anticipation was more than a simple feeling. It was an ocean wave that filled a room, rising and swelling until it reached its peak, threatening to crash over the shore. That wave could drag Liliana down beneath its roaring currents for all she cared. She would drown in the torrents, so long as she was there to watch it fall.

"In two months' time, I will be stepping down from the throne."

The wave crashed, and a volcano erupted. A clamoring, the likes of which was normally reserved for Vitrian festivities and meetings, exploded, raining down on the room. King Leo stood, calm, watching the lava pour and burn through any semblance of decorum. Diplomats turned to each other with shock and excitement in their faces. Easternalia's expression morphed from surprised to hungry in an instant. The Vitrians, uncharacteristically silent, studied King Leo, curiosity playing on their faces.

Within every conversation, unease underlined the mood. Politics, as a rule, did not like change. It adored frivolous squabbles and mistakes, like cheating spouses and unclaimed babies. But an abdication was not frivolous, and succession was not so stable. No, it was the kind of maneuver that could destabilize geopolitical relationships across *Terrabis*.

Teo froze in place, his terror reminding Liliana of a spy caught behind enemy lines, someone captured far from where they should be. Eliana, on the other hand, looked like a cat salivating over a particularly fat bird. The magmatic reactions washed over Liliana, but they didn't burn her. In fact, she couldn't feel anything. She existed outside her body, confident that somebody could have run a sword through her stomach, and she wouldn't have flinched. Her mind began to turn.

What would this mean? It meant the throne belonged to Teo. Liliana was astonished at her own surprise. Her father's reign had always been an ephemeral thing, after all. He had been given an interim power, gifting Teo a little bit more time to learn and grow before taking on the soul of the nation. Why should she be shocked that he finally relinquished the throne to the next in line? Liliana glanced at her brother again. In fairness, he looked as ill prepared for the news as Liliana felt.

She shook her head. More importantly, what would that mean for Liliana? She struggled to decide whether this would fast-forward her plan for the councils or stop it in its path. She needed to regroup, rethink. She needed to talk with Teo and lay out her ideas for the other councils, especially before anybody else could access him. To her perpetual annoyance, Liliana had often found that people took on the mantle of the first idea rather than the best idea.

Her father raised his hand. The room quieted so fast, he might as well have kicked an ambassador in the crotch and screamed, "Listen, everyone!" He smiled, almost apologetic. "To finish what I was saying, I will be stepping away from the throne. Following that, the person who assumes the throne will be a bearer of the mark of *Imperium*." Teo stood up straighter, and a sour taste filled Liliana's mouth. "They will lead our kingdom with the traits decreed most important by our Gods. Honesty, wisdom, strength, humility, and power.

"And they will…" He took a deep breath, almost as if steeling himself. He staunchly looked at the crowd, not making eye contact with Teo, his heir incumbent. "They will be determined through the Monarchic Trials, an old Electarian practice of determining leadership. They will be administered by the leaders of the nations assembled here, which is why you all have been invited."

Her father gave the different delegations a stern look. "It is for diplomatic goodwill that I grant you this opportunity. In return of this goodwill, I expect you all to remain objective and diligent in your assigned tasks for carrying out the Trials.

"The public will not be notified of the passing of the Trials until a winner is declared. There is no need to plant confusion in the country's mind. Per tradition, anybody with the mark of *Imperium* is free to compete," her father added, pointedly looking at Teo and Liliana. "Though I will remain in the castle after the Trials to guide and advise, ultimately, the victor will totally and completely assume the crown."

The room and the mark on Liliana's back erupted into an inferno so intense she swore she could have burned the very kingdom to the ground.

CHAPTER 5
7055.1.15

"Nobody's ever stealen from Madame Dragonia's stall," the young boys whispered, hands covering their mouths but their words clear as day. "What I wouldn't give to see someone walk outta there with one of her trinkets."

Elle stopped in her tracks, looking back and forth between the basket of ingredients hanging from her arm and these boys. A wild naman scuttled by, startling Elle as its puffball form bounded to a nearby trash receptacle. It rubbed its upturned button nose against the metal, a green acid slowly releasing from its purple gums. Slowly but surely, the naman's saliva ate through the metal of the wall, leaving behind a smoking hole the size of a dragon egg. Namans usually hid out during Mend and Cae, the cold forcing them into hibernation. Once Impe rolled around, though, the creatures reemerged in full force, in search of any food to be found.

And when they reemerged, new potential hiding spots cropped up all around the city. Taking note of the new hole, Elle chewed the inside of her cheek before turning back to stare at the pair of boys, longing clear on her face. Her ma was waiting for these ingredients. Penelope and the twins were at school, and her da and Nic were busy filling orders. Due to a large order for a feast at the castle, a small army of bakers in the city had been recruited to deliver additional goods. Elle was officially Pandemonia's last line of defense and had been sent on an urgent mission for "more eggs, butter, and please, *Imperium*, more flour!"

But Elle went to fetch ingredients all the time, and this seemed like an opportunity for a delightful break in an otherwise prosaic day.

Madame Dragonia's did look intimidating, relative to Electaria's typical stores. The cheapest shops operated on the feeble skeleton of planks haphazardly nailed together. The shameless vendors of those places yelled at passersby on the street—usually unsuspecting tourists—squawking at whichever poor soul had the misfortune of entering that vendor's realm. The vendors badgered the person until they capitulated to the aggression, reluctantly walking forward to purchase something. Elle's family learned to circumvent the nonsense. Eggs came from Ianara by the city statue of *Viribus*. Spare cloth came from Yae; his children had all left the house, so he all but gave the stuff away. The list went on.

The stores a step up from the hawkish stalls, like Pandemonia, were their own buildings. Nothing fanciful to gawk at, but sufficient to both conduct a business and house a family. The combination helped avoid superfluous rent.

The *truly* wealthy ones, though, existed as their own kind of artwork. Madame Dragonia's fell into that last category. Stone walls with an alluring archway hung with crimson velvet curtains that protected the mysteries inside. Outside, torches blazed—the most expensive kind, the kind that burned even when it rained. Elle blinked, mesmerized. The fires burned brightly against the gray sky, defiantly existing even now as the clouds began to weep.

Two younger women dressed in Electarian cotton dresses lingered at the entrance of the store. They craned their necks to look inside until they both uttered sighs and linked their arms in solemn solidarity as they walked away from riches they could never afford. Unlike other stores of similar status, no guards protected the entryway. Elle's heart skipped a beat. That probably meant they would look to catch thieves on the inside. She would have to be exceptionally sly, especially considering she had no clue what the inside looked like.

Elle never had a reason to enter a store like this. *Until now.* She grinned, eyeing the entrance. She would get a royal beating with her ma's spatula if she knew Elle stopped for something as stupid as this.

Yet somehow, the ingredients still ended up hidden inside the hole the naman created as Elle crept over to the boys.

"Out of curiosity, what *would* you give to see somebody walk out with one of her trinkets?" Elle asked, violet eyes glittering.

The two boys jumped up, swearing their surprise with mouths only true street rats could manage. She raised her hand and wiped her mouth, doing a poor job at covering up a laugh. Judging from their only slightly wrinkled but mostly clean clothes, Elle guessed they were some of the kids who had homes but had chosen to ditch school for the day. One of the boys scowled at her reaction, but the other tentatively smiled in return.

The first boy regarded her warily. He kicked his feet against the wet cobblestone beneath them, muttering, "Doesn't matter. Nobody can do it."

"But what if they *could*?" she pressed, pushing back the black bangs that fell into her face. She huffed at the unruly pieces. All it had taken was one stray pair of scissors and Fritz's determination— now her choppy locks bore a tragic monument to his "artistic craft."

"I'd give 'em five irons." The other boy shuffled around in his pocket, procuring the five bits.

Elle's eyes widened slightly. If she wasn't sure before, now she was convinced: the kids without parents never ran around betting five bits for something as small as clout.

Even on a gray and rainy day, those five coins sparkled in that happy way all new money did. Elle eyed the irons, chewing her lip. Her ma surely wouldn't be as mad if Elle returned home with the ingredients *and* five extra bits. She glanced back at the basket of ingredients, assuring herself that it hadn't moved. A little detour wouldn't hurt anyone, she justified, rocking back and forth on her heels, pleasantly imagining curling her ma's fingers around the five coins.

She squeezed her forefinger and middle finger together, extending them toward the friendly boy. "Try to fool me and go blind."

"Try to fool me, lose your mind." He extended his own two fingers, and they clasped them together.

Elle leaned back, satisfied. Even as she grew older, she carried a great deal of faith in the Deal. Adults always wanted somebody with the mark of *Menda* before making any deal. When her ma and da came to Electaria together, their only form of work was witnessing painfully boring contracts and making sure everybody told the truth. When she was thirteen, Elle had informed her ma that the extra step seemed like too much a hassle. Her ma had shaken her head, warning that street oaths meant nothing. Elle still rolled her eyes at the conversation.

Well, of course street oaths meant nothing to older people. Adults could rarely be trusted. They lied as often as they washed the laundry or cooked. Younger people like Elle, though—they could be trusted. Elle was aging out of the "young" category but still maintained the same spirit of honesty and trust. Younger people knew the weight of the Deal. If they swore under it, that agreement was as good as gold. Or, her eyes flickered back to the coins, iron, in this case.

The other boy—Grumpy, Elle dubbed him in her head—shook his head in pity. "If you lose your hand, it ain't our fault."

"Of course not!" She grinned at the two before ducking underneath the curtains of the shop. "We blame that on the sword."

The interior of the store looked just as beautiful as Elle pictured. While her home constantly smelled of baking bread, raw flour, and rosemary, this place smelled of royalty. Well, what Elle imagined royalty smelled like, anyway. Cinnamon incense burned heavily in the air, the kind of smell that stabbed at the backs of her nostrils each time she took a breath. The sharp, heady scent hurt her nose at first, but became more pleasant after a few, deep intakes.

Dim lanterns kept the room lit in a way that forced Elle to squint to read any labels, but it wasn't so dark that she stumbled through the aisles. The few other patrons that haunted the store didn't seem to have any trouble with navigating. Red curtains, like the ones at the entrance, hung horizontally from the ceiling, draping so low that even with her shoulders hunched, her head still nearly brushed them. Elle's half-Vitrian blood that stretched out her torso during puberty followed her wherever she went, whether she liked it or not.

All the decorations, though, paled in comparison to the aisles themselves. Rows and rows of jewels. They seemed to stretch on endlessly, each gem more precious than the last. Reds, blues, greens twinkled at her, vying to be pocketed and given a home. The jewels glittering beneath the low light reminded Elle of stars. She wandered through the rows and felt like she was taking a stroll through the galaxy itself.

While Elle desperately wanted to grab the most beautiful piece of jewelry in the store and run, it felt too dishonest. She came in here to prove her sleight of hand, not use brute force. She found a woman behind the counter. The lady's sharp eyes followed Elle's every move like a bird. Elle got the distinct impression that nineteen-year-olds in bakers' garb did not frequent her store.

The woman wore an outrageous hat, feathers dripping over the broad edge in a way fit only for the Aurjnegh. Unlike the Vitrian migrants to Electaria, the Aurjnegh tended to bring the style of their motherland with them. Her dress, though, looked distinctly more Electarian. It draped down to the floor, its material silken and luxurious. It was conservative and close necked except for an opening over the heart that showed a golden bird against her cool, white skin, its talons sharp and its chest pressed forward with pride. The mark of *Superbia*.

Elle, in her simple long-sleeved shirt, apron, and trousers that she had stolen from her brothers, looked kind of like a school textbook in comparison. Plain, unassuming, and, most importantly, boring. Based on the almost aggressively elegant way this woman presented herself, Elle took an educated guess.

"Madame Dragonia?"

"Speaking. And what can I do for you" —her lips curled on the next word—"*madame?*"

Elle couldn't lie; she got the tiniest bit of pleasure from that moment. Elle straightened her spine and smiled in what she hoped was a demure way. She bowed her head and twisted her foot on the ground, looking up shyly at the older woman. Madame Dragonia softened by a fraction.

"I came looking for a present for my ma—my mother." Elle caught her slang, glossing over the stumble. "It's her birthday, see. I don't have much money, so I was wondering if you could show me some of your more inexpensive things."

Madame Dragonia narrowed her eyes, trying to pin Elle as somebody either too poor for her time or a thief. Elle ducked her head lower, shrinking herself into the least suspicious pose she could imagine. Elle wondered if the woman's mark tingled with *Superbia*'s pleasant warmth at Elle's modesty. In fairness, Elle did legitimately feel humbled by the sophisticated woman before her.

Madame Dragonia gave an exasperated sigh, emerging from behind the counter, and Elle held back a grin. Her dress swished as she crossed in front of Elle and curled her finger impatiently. "Come on, then."

Elle followed, obedient and attentive. Madame Dragonia swept through the store, a lithe and flowing stream through the bends and turns of her aisles. She walked with the confidence of somebody who knew where she stood in the order of things— and with that, knew she belonged at the top. As expected from someone who completed her Walk following *Superbia*. She knew who she was, with no inflated or depressed sense of self-worth. Madame Dragonia, much like the gems of her store, radiated beauty and confidence.

Elle cocked her head to the side, curiosity kindling in her heart. What was the source of the woman's confidence, and why was Elle so unfamiliar with the way it looked? The woman's mark could feed off pride, but Elle didn't think it created the feeling itself. Madame

Dragonia moved with a sense of purpose that people like Ma seemed to lack. A lot of people like Ma scurried with their heads down, looking to please and serve. A burn spread throughout Elle's body, starting at the center of her back. Why was that the case? What about this woman allowed her to hold her head up higher than the woman who kept Elle's family afloat every single day?

"Here is our selection of...lesser jewelry." Madame Dragonia sniffed, waving her hand dismissively at a cabinet in the back of the store.

Elle hid a frown. She hardly had the answers to her own questions but knew that something about the entire situation was amiss. The cabinet was distinctly more run-down than everything else. Instead of beholding the same mysterious beauty as the rest of the store, it looked like it had suffered from several unfortunate moves, a handful of careless owners, and maybe even a few namans in its time. The small, puffy creatures made for cute house pets until they started excreting their acidic mucus on somebody's furniture.

Elle decided the cabinet was well loved, but it was an eyesore for a store like this. "Could I possibly have a few moments to look through them? I'll be brief," Elle said to the woman.

Madame Dragonia paused, obviously ready to deny the request, but *Imperium* smiled down upon Elle. Another customer, dressed far nicer and obviously ready to pay far more, called Madame Dragonia over. This settled the woman's mind. She pointed at the cabinet and at the counter, her finger rigid.

"Fine. Come to the counter the *second* you're finished."

"Of course," Elle promised, already trying to decide which gem to steal.

Madame Dragonia swished away, leaving Elle to survey the inventory. She peered closer, pressing her nose against the glass. Almost immediately, she had to close her eyes, the dazzling reflection of light too strong. She slowly reopened each eye, hungrily taking in the sight before her. Each piece of jewelry twinkled happily at Elle, begging for her to appreciate their beauty. This kind of jewelry would die without sufficient adoration, much as a flower would wilt without water or sun. The colors collided and complemented one another, their gems an iridescent garden that only blossomed under the gaze of others.

Elle struggled to reconcile how these pieces could be considered lesser. If anything, she stood in front of the most stunning jewelry she had seen yet. Unlike the rest of the store, these necklaces and bracelets transcended simplicity and modesty. Nothing about them spoke of Electaria, and that foreign splendor in and of itself was beautiful.

One necklace in particular vied for her attention. The thick, silver chain held a charm at the bottom. Carved out of beautiful silver, *Imperium*'s mark stared back at her with amethyst eyes. The rare mark showing *Imperium*'s dragon roaring flames to the sky gleamed, making the other gems look dull in comparison.

She breathed out, unknowingly fogging up the glass. Elle pictured the necklace bouncing up and down on the chest of a queen storming the battlefield, her trusted pendant giving her power in the direst of times. What must that feel like?

Her hand reached forward before she even registered her own actions. She slipped open the cabinet window and pocketed the necklace with barely a second thought. Before starting her discreet exit, she frowned and rubbed her breath off the cabinet with the sleeve of her shirt. She leaned back, satisfied. Now she could go.

Elle crept along the side of the wall, staying as low to the ground and as far from Madame Dragonia's vision as the store would allow. Her long limbs made it difficult, sticking up conspicuously like weeds in a well-managed garden. Luckily, Elle knew how to hide. She spent her younger years as a shadow on the cobblestone and was experienced in disappearing in plain sight.

The chain cooled her hand, and even though she felt guilty, she couldn't stop the jitters making her almost tremble from excitement. Or maybe fear. Success and failure were two suitors taking her by the hand, whispering promises to whisk her away and whip her heart into a clamor. She took a deep breath, the incense filling her nose, and decided her nerves resulted from a delicious combination of both.

She glanced over. Madame Dragonia appeared to be utterly distracted by her customer in the front. Still, it felt like each of Elle's cautious steps landed on the floor with the rumble of an earthquake, each tiny inhale coming with the howl of a hurricane. The gems danced around her, their glow more menacing than dazzling. Elle swallowed hard. Their soft sheen had turned into a spotlight, ready to catch her red-handed.

Elle slithered and dodged her way to the entrance, pretending that she played the part of a young heroine in those operas her da liked. The drums played a slow, ominous beat in her head as she approached the door. They sped up as she reached toward the curtain to open—

"And what do you think you're doing?"

Shit, shit, shit.

She turned around with the grace of a rusted statue to see one of the customers standing behind her, his arms crossed. She had barely noticed him when she first entered, though she struggled to look away now. At first glance, he looked like any other rich person. The kind of person Elle's da would curse at the dinner table and her ma would throw dirty looks at after passing in the street. His smooth cloak and leather boots told the typical story of wealth.

Except…this man hunched over a little bit more. His nail beds, ridden with sores and hangnails, lacked the delicate skin of the nobility. And, most notably, he had a sword hanging from his belt.

Elle was proud that she guessed there would be a guard on the inside. As usual, her deductive instincts were spot on. However, this pride immediately gave way to fear as the man reached for his weapon. She made a weak attempt at a smile.

"I was headed back to ask Ma which jewelry she'd like best. I'll be back soon, I promise."

The man raised one eyebrow at her, taking a step closer. Elle saw Madame Dragonia watching carefully in the background, her arms on her hips with a haughty jut.

"Ma?"

Elle stopped herself from groaning out loud. Her lies, like water, began to dissipate the second somebody administered any kind of heat.

She took a step back, her mouth moving faster than her mind. "Yup. Ma. That's the name of my...fiancé! Yes, Ma, my fiancé. Ma fiancé Ma, if you will. Good man, that one. Comes from a long line of...fishers. Fish people. It brings in money at the end of the day, but at what cost, am I right?" She laughed, more uncomfortable than a jester at a funeral, holding her nose to prove a point.

The guard did not laugh. He did look confused. Elle had a feeling her kind of humor might be lost on a guard assigned to catch thieves. To his credit, though he was slow with wit, he was quick to draw his sword. He brandished the blade for a second before swinging it over his head, aiming for Elle's right hand.

She squeaked and whipped her hand away, her feet slipping against the carpet as she scrambled for the door.

She heard Madame Dragonia screech as Elle burst outside. "Bring me back the necklace *and* her hand!"

Elle was going to be so very late with these ingredients.

The man chased after her, sword resheathed but arms out and ready to grab her if given the opportunity. She used the one edge she had: she owned the cobblestone. The streets she ran on now were the same ones she traced back and forth as a child, making the city her own in small ways. A nook here, a hideaway there. If somebody were to chase her in any capacity, she could at least thank *Imperium* it was on her home field.

Elle flew around a corner and grabbed the wheelbarrow that the local Aurjnegh dyers *always* forgot to bring in and flung it behind her. A noisy clatter and booming curse gave Elle a little more time as she ran into a city plaza. The open space that held warm people and vibrant life in the afternoon looked practically dead in the early light of the rainy day. A handful of people sat scattered about, focusing on their meals and keeping to themselves.

She took a turn at the only bar in the city that opened in the morning. The drunken fools yelling songs from the inside before noon were always a dead giveaway. She twisted its corner and leaped, her rough hands finding purchase on the deck of the nearby Vitrian laundress. The business of hanging wet clothes made the wood just soft enough to prevent tears of pain as Elle swung and muscled herself up to stand on the edge of the balcony.

Digging her fingers into the balcony above the laundress's—the wood hard and cruel on her poor hands—Elle repeated the same move twice more until she stood, panting, on the ceiling of the building. If she put her ear to the ground, she was sure she would hear the Nuwei musicians who lived on the top floor and played most nights at a different bar across town. Elle took a second to survey her city, grinning. The adventure of the day wasn't yet over, but that didn't mean she couldn't enjoy herself a little.

The guard scrambled around below the building, his chest heaving and mustache trembling. He stalked around the open clearing where each tavern had outdoor seating and demanded answers from all the patrons. Elle took particular delight in watching him interrogate the drunks, who all seemed insistent that the guard join in their festivities.

Elle nodded, satisfied. Assured they would keep the man busy, she turned to shimmy down the side of the building and claim her prize.

Gently easing herself off the ledge, Elle took hold of an iron pole that ran the length of the building on the backside. She slid down slowly, protecting her hands from further agony. Despite years of jumping on these same buildings, nothing could fully prepare her body for what she put it through. She sent a silent prayer of thanks to *Superbia*; Elle would not forget to take pride in what her body did for her.

As Elle neared the bottom, she let go and dropped to the ground. The one thing she didn't account for? The drunken man sleeping below the pole. Both Elle and the man shrieked as she hit his soft stomach with her feet, stumbling off him and nearly running into the neighboring wall. Elle didn't know if it was her scream or dumb luck, but the guard poked his ruddy cheeks around the corner. His eyes lit up as they caught her form, and she yelped, springing away once more.

She took a few successive turns, the soles of her shoes burning with each scrape against the ground. A shout echoed behind her, and her heart jumped into her ears. *How did he find me? Doesn't matter. Keep running,* she reprimanded herself. Rights and lefts, she took twists and turns to make a circle back to her starting point near Madame Dragonia's. She grabbed onto the side of a building, flinging her way into a different alley, her fingers burning from the change of direction. Finally, she spotted her prize.

She sprinted up to the boys, gasping for breath. They gaped at her, shocked. Elle reached into her pocket and brought out the necklace, holding it up with no words, only desperate swallows of air. Grumpy looked terrified, but the other boy simply grinned and handed her the five irons.

The sweet, clinking sound they made and the warm glow in Elle's chest almost made up for the fact that somebody wanted to chop her right hand off. *Now to make it home alive...*

Elle slipped the necklace and irons back in her pocket and found the basket of ingredients. She picked it up and gave one final curtsy, an end to her show, before flying off again, the footsteps of the man growing louder as he approached. Her legs groaned in protest, unused to the extended abuse. She sent up a silent prayer to all the Gods individually. *Caecus* for a touch of wisdom, *Superbia* for faith in her body, *Menda* for an honest path forward, *Viribus* for some strength, *Imperium....* One by one she beseeched some kind of help or divine intervention. Her lungs ached, and she added a prayer on the side: *Gods willing, if I keep my hand, don't let Ma take it herself just to beat me with it.*

At the next turn, she caught a glimpse of the man's cloak fluttering behind her. She cursed to herself, wind stinging her eyes, her chest tight. Stupid Elle. Stupid pride. Her craving for adventure had landed her in trouble before, but never like this. She barked out a bitter laugh as she ran. Well, rest assured if she lost her hand, she would consider the lesson learned.

All these thoughts were interrupted when Elle ran into a behemoth of a woman, slamming her down to the ground. The sound of blades being drawn filled the alley as a group of men moved to surround Elle. She watched, almost in slow motion, as the ingredients poured over the street. Her vision blurred, and for a few seconds, she lay motionless on the ground.

"Dammit, what if I killed her?" a deep voice groaned. "We'll never make it to the meeting then. Also, not thrilled that my personal guard, feared throughout the land, couldn't stop this infant from assaulting me."

Elle rubbed her head, the streets spinning as she stumbled back to her feet. The woman stopped her faltering about, tilting Elle's chin up with rough fingers and staring at her with intense, dark blue eyes. "Are you okay?"

"Man...chasing..." Elle mumbled with exhaustion and adrenaline swirling in her head, twisting all her thoughts.

The woman's eyebrows rose into her hairline. She stepped back from Elle, sharing a knowing look with her partner. A group of nearby armored men watched the woman's movements warily.

The guard from the store arrived on the scene a few beats later. Elle took some satisfaction from the fact that he looked about as worn out as she felt. He took out his sword once more, stalking toward her. Fear started to encroach back into her mind, washing away her deliriousness. Elle crawled back slowly, her raw, shaking hands barely supporting her.

"Oh, cut the shit," the woman snapped, stepping in front of the man. Though he seemed hulking before, this woman stood over him like an oak tree next to an acorn. She plucked the sword out of his hands and tossed it to the side, letting it clatter against the ground. The guards moved in to extract the weapon immediately. Elle mustered enough energy to wheeze out a laugh.

The man looked appalled. "Ma'am, you don't understand. She's a *thief*—"

"I don't think *you* understand." She pointed her finger in his face, waving it around with the ferocity one might wield a dagger. "I said cut the shit. Do you want me to say it again?"

"Best if you run now," her companion added, smiling and rubbing his closely cropped beard. "I barely escape her wrath, and she claims to love me."

The man's nostrils flared, and he took another step forward, standing toe-to-toe with the woman. The guards nearby obviously stiffened, taking quick steps forward. The woman held up a hand, communicating for them to stand down. The woman looked down at the lone guard with disdain, the way an ocean wave might view a pebble. He met her piercing eyes, and his face turned white. Elle recognized that expression. Penelope looked just as horrified when years ago, their parents had caught her eating bread baked for a customer.

The woman turned from him. "Collect your sword and leave. I have no interest in discussing this any further."

Whatever the man saw in her eyes stopped his arguments. He grabbed his sword from the outstretched arm of a guard, all his anger from earlier draining from his body and flowing away into the grates of the street.

Elle studied the pair and their armed entourage. The giant frames spoke only of Vitria. The woman was about a head taller than Elle herself. Their accents, dipping back and forth like the sea, sang the same song. Even their tawny skin was tanned in a way only possible from living life by the sea.

The only thing Elle had trouble pinning was their clothing. They wore traditional, loose, blue robes, the silk rippling over their skin. It was the silk that puzzled her in particular. The material was far nicer than anything normal Vitrians owned.

The woman refocused her attention on Elle. "Considering I may have just saved your life, I believe a few questions are in order. Yes?"

Elle nodded, her head bobbing up and down with ferocity.

"Wonderful. Name?"

"Ellegance Fournier. But everyone calls me Elle."

"Fascinating. Why are you here?"

"I bet a pair of boys I could steal a necklace." The woman's eyebrows rose once more, either surprised or impressed by Elle's honesty.

"Interesting. Parents?"

"They run a bakery a few streets down."

"Delicious." The woman seemed to finally take in Elle's stature. "You got some Vitrian blood in you?"

"My da's from Vitria, and Ma's from Electaria. They moved here after getting married." Elle switched to broken Vitrian, the grammar rough but the swaying accent strong. "*Vineis kuan investum.*"

Elle tried to say that her parents came to Electaria when they were young but obviously failed because the woman burst into laughter, her companion chuckling behind her. They moved together with their own ebb and flow, acting and reacting to each other's motions with ease.

The woman clasped her hand on Elle's shoulder, and Elle's limbs almost turned into goo with relief. The Vitrian greeting reminded her of home. Even her ma, who lived her most formative years in Electaria, greeted everyone like that after living with her da for so long.

"*Iuvenistium,*" the woman said slowly, punctuating each syllable. She tapped Elle's shoulder, and Elle repeated it back, tongue tripping over the word. "The words for seed and young are very similar. It is easy to get them confused."

"Thank you." Elle offered a tentative smile back.

She eyed the golden laurels resting on the woman's head and the golden band around the man's arm. From the entire interaction, Elle knew they were important, but she had no idea to what degree. She figured she'd just have to ask—direct and honest were the only way with the Vitrians, after all. "What are your names?"

"I am the empress of Vitria, Ruler of Truth, Protector of—you know what? We'll save the titles for court. I am known to friends as Renee Probiat," she declared. She winked back at the man. "That is my manservant, Kai."

Elle's limbs grew weak, her heart tumbling into the pit of her stomach. It was just Elle's luck: to go from fleeing a small-time jewelry guard to crashing into one of the most important people on *Terrabis.*

The man rolled his eyes and stepped up for the first time, clasping Elle on the shoulder himself. "I am Kai, right hand to the throne and life partner of Her Majesty."

"He basically does the paperwork while I get to do all the fun things. Like starting wars." She laughed, deep and pleasant. The sound washed over her like a salve.

Elle laughed weakly herself, trying to quell her panic.

Kai groaned, wiping his hands down his sharp features. "Please leave those jokes in the alley. The Aurjnegh diplomats will not find them nearly as funny."

"No, but they will laugh all the same because that is their way," Renee grumbled, her eyes holding a dangerous glint.

A broad smile stretched across Elle's face, the distinct feeling that somebody was playing a massive prank creeping over her. It was something Elle would do if she had the resources, so she wouldn't put it past anybody she knew. The world faded around her as she imagined the lengths through which somebody would have gone. At any moment, she expected one of her siblings to jump out with an "aha!" Nic would absolutely put in the effort for such a complex prank. She would bow down to the elaborate nature of the joke. Hiring two people to look like Vitrian royalty really showed dedication—she gave them that. A clever and elaborate joke, indeed.

Otherwise, the whole situation made no sense. Things like Vitrian royalty showing up out of nowhere to save a random girl from doom made some of the fairy tales Elle grew up on seem realistic. Part of her wanted to suspend her disbelief and simply enjoy the fantastical story she found herself in. The other part of her just wanted to wake up so she could deliver the ingredients—

Elle's face fell. The proof that this was real life lay right in front of her, in the form of flour and eggs splattered on the ground. She stood in some random alleyway, the Vitrian royalty beside her. She knew because even in her worst nightmares the ingredients would have made it home. *Imperium*, she was *so* dead.

"She's not listening. What the hell just happened with her?" Renee asked Kai, looking concerned. She snapped her fingers in front of Elle's face, and Elle shook her head, snapping out of her reverie.

"I'm sorry. What did you ask?"

"We wanted to know if you had enough free time to escort us to the palace." Renee scratched her head sheepishly, the laurel almost cemented to the thick, black braid piled on top of her head. "I'm all but useless with directions on land, and my legendary guard over there"—she rolled her eyes on the word "guard," and the armored individuals shrank appropriately—"somehow have less navigational sense than I do."

"Why not?" Elle shrugged, staring at the ingredients with lifeless eyes. "I just realized that without those ingredients, Ma is going to chop me up and feed me to the royal family instead. Might as well help out while I still can."

Kai and Renee shared a look before turning back toward Elle. Kai approached her, kneeling down; even doing this, he still stood almost at Elle's gargantuan height. "How about this. If you take us to the castle, we will accompany you to your house thereafter. I'm sure your ma couldn't be too mad if you brought us home for dinner, *etiam*?"

The word fell over her ears with honey-like sweetness. Her da used it to mean compromise. The Vitrians stumbling home from the bar used it to signal agreement. An agreement, an exclamation, a promise, a sympathy—*etiam* was a word that knew no limits. It took a different shape in each mouth, the core remaining the same. *Etiam* meant promise and safety in a way that the Electarian tongue didn't know.

Elle breathed out slowly. "*Etiam*."

"Wonderful!" Renee clapped her hands and shooed Elle forward. "Now let's get started. I fear the window for arriving fashionably late is rapidly closing."

A small, budding sense of excitement planted in Elle's stomach and began to spread, the kind she could feel from the tips of her fingers to the bottom of her stomach. It felt like somebody had poured one of those pink, fizzy drinks Penelope loved into her head and allowed it to race through her system. Elle supposed that escaping death and finding royalty all within a couple of hours would have that effect.

She began a swift walk through the streets. To Elle's pleasure, the monstrous Vitrians kept pace with her long legs. The retinue of guards shadowed the group from behind, occasionally shoving nosy pedestrians to the side. Despite the cloudy day, the streets gleamed more than usual. Even the grime-covered walls, green from mold and neglect, glimmered just a little bit. The streets and buildings had a funny way of doing that. The city existed as a reflection of Elle and she a reflection of it, in a bizarre form of kinship. The kingdom and Elle lived as one heart, just separated in two vessels.

Renee and Kai did not seem as fascinated by the city as Elle might have hoped. They appeared content to talk to one another. Elle paused, reconsidering. Maybe a more accurate description would be a conversational battle of shouts. Though the content of their conversation was innocuous enough, their voices scaled the rafters, and they nearly yelled to outmatch the other's noise. A spike of pity flashed through Elle for the buildings of her city. They did not have the luxury to cover their ears from the din.

They entered the Aisle, a long stretch of vendors one had to pass to access the castle. It essentially served the same purpose as the moat in the Vitrian capitol, except the lizards of the Aisle had fangs of sweet words and fake deals. The vendors identified the two foreigners immediately, yelling out to Renee and Kai with promises of foreign wonders they "wouldn't find anywhere else on the globe."

"A charm blessed by a living Guide! Sure to help you complete your Walk!" A man with a squirrelly face and rodent smile followed the trio as they pushed through the crowd. "My lady, my lord, if you or anyone in your service wants help in achieving the blessing of the Gods, this is the way to go!"

Elle glanced back, impressed by the man's persistence. Typically, vendors gave up and found different prey after Elle walked a few feet away. Unfortunately, the Vitrians must have looked like very attractive targets. He dodged in between the crowd, attempting to keep pace. His gnarled hands grabbed at the slips of their robes, trying to find something to which he could anchor himself.

"You are losing the chance to offer yourself or someone you love eternal happiness, living with the Gods! Otherwise, they may fall prey to *malum's* grasp! If you don't do it for yourself, do it for a loved one's soul!"

Renee whipped around, getting so close she could have leaned forward and chomped off a piece of his nose. Her mouth curled into an unpleasant scowl, flexing the knuckles on her hands. Her nostrils flared; her chest puffed out. The man faltered in his sales pitch.

"Do you honestly think that any of this wolfshit could help my soul?" Renee jabbed her finger in his chest, causing him to stumble back a few feet.

The crowd parted around the confrontation, otherwise oblivious. Renee and the vendor were simply rocks that the stream had to flow around.

"O-Of course! It—"

"It does *nothing*," she said, venom coating her words. "This is what I hate about you Electarian merchants. You lie, and you lie, and you lie, and there are no lines your deceit will not cross. If the Gods are not sacred to you, what do you hold dear, little vendor man? Or do you simply exist as a vase? Empty and without conviction?"

The beginning of an argument bubbled up and died on the man's lips. He turned around and ran, his shoulders shaking. Elle frowned. It felt like a bit of an overreaction. The poor man had tried to do his job; Elle could see no fault in that. Vendors sold fake religious relics all the time. They could help their embellishment so much as a rose could help its thorns.

"Right, then," Renee said with finality that left no room for any word otherwise.

Elle cast thoughts of the man aside, though she did search for the back of his head in the crowd. She sent a quick prayer up to the Gods that he would find one gullible person to buy from him today, especially after that ordeal.

A subtle smile danced across Kai's face as Renee stormed ahead. Elle cocked her head, curious. Renee did not even meet Kai's eyes, and yet Elle still felt like she intruded on the moment. The gentle intimacy they shared warmed Elle's heart with the same familiar heat of her da's bread. Elle's parents told Elle and her siblings that love existed in many different forms. For family, for friends, for lovers, for enemies even—love involved itself in almost every interaction, whether for better or worse. In this case, Elle was convinced she could practically see a thin webbing of trust and affection between the two.

They arrived at the front gates of the castle. Its clean, vast structure stretched into the sky, the white turrets cutting into the clouds above. The sheer power it held in its walls felt effortless. No unnecessary pomp or grandeur—the castle and the people within it knew their own might. The city might have been Elle's other half, but this castle called out to her in a different way. Not to who she was, but to who she could be.

Elle's back began to burn with a painful ache. She gasped, the feeling surging through her body like a flame licking down her back.

Renee furrowed her eyebrows. "What in *Imperium*'s name is wrong with you?"

"Back!" She tried to reach her arms around herself to touch her mark where the pain centralized.

Renee crooked a finger, and Kai stepped around Elle, his fingers pausing above her shirt. "May I?"

An image of her ma appeared in her head, warning her to keep her arms hidden. Let them think it was *Menda*'s mark beneath Elle's clothing. Her ma always said there was no need to stir up trouble where there was none. A childhood of sleeves covering her forearm and lying about her Walk, her strides toward honesty. A follower of *Menda*, just like her ma and da because there was no reason a street rat should bear the mark of power.

Hunched over, she looked up briefly at the castle and the mark pounded, her back on the verge of exploding. "Yes, yes, yes!"

Kai, his strong hands surprisingly gentle, lifted her shirt. He froze, letting out a harsh breath and laugh at the same time. "You're going to want to see this."

Renee frowned and walked over, her eyes widening at what she saw. A black dragon, its wings outstretched across the expanse of Elle's back, seemed ready to breathe fire up her neck. The claws on the dragon wings skimmed against the ends of her rib cage, its wing a web of shimmering charcoal. Its five black horns dipped backward, its ferocious jaw tilted toward the sky. The mark covered the entirety of her spine, its tail curling around the tip of her sacrum. The mark twisted just so that it was possible to see the lighter contrast of the dragon's belly. Instead of the distinct scales of traditional dragons, the mark's scales were so small they seemed to form a snakelike casing around the dragon's trunk. The mark was majestic, intricate and detailed in a way the trees, waves, hawks, and wolves simply weren't.

Renee began to laugh, disbelieving and quiet at first, but growing in sound and strength. After a few seconds, she was doubled over, tears in her eyes. Elle might have found this amusing in any other scenario, but the inferno still blazed throughout her body with no intention of subsiding. Renee seemed to remember Elle was in pain and coughed, covering up the laugh.

"Well, I'll be a daughter of *malum*. I think we're going to have to take you inside to meet old Leo. I don't think I've ever heard of a nonroyal brat with the mark of *Imperium*."

CHAPTER 6
7055.1.16

Liliana paced back and forth outside her father's chambers. Imperium lay on the floor with his head on his paws, uncharacteristically quiet as his eyes tracked Liliana's movements. Aoran was within earshot should she shout, but he was also far enough away that she could speak in privacy. Every so often, she paused, tapping her foot furiously against the floor before resuming her pacing again. If she thought diplomatic council meetings ran long before, apparently, they ran much, much longer when royal transition was at the top of the agenda.

Liliana's mother first started sneaking Liliana into council meetings when she was eight. This was Liliana's first real introduction to the castle in which she was raised. These precious moments came when Teo was otherwise occupied, which, as he grew older, became more frequent. It was in these spare moments that their mother stepped away from helping to groom the monarch and watered Liliana's blooming mind instead. She laced her fingers with Liliana's tiny hand and led her into the meeting rooms, each of which always shared the stale smell of age and paper.

Utterly rapt in the conversations from an early age, Liliana would sit in the corner and try to imprint every detail into her mind. Every councilor's name, every bill introduced—she wanted to remember every single thing. Afterward, her mother would quiz her on the assorted topics discussed. When Liliana was eleven, her mother broadened the scope of the quizzes to ask about the repercussions of the subjects discussed, forcing Liliana away from regurgitation of facts into taking her own stances on the issues.

Without her mother around, Liliana had no one left to ask her what she thought of this or that. With her mother gone, few people cared about the opinion of the third born. Her brother was the golden child, her sister the famed beauty. Of course, her father loved Liliana and supported her, but he saw her as a daughter—not a future, intellectual equal. Her mother's death didn't rid Liliana of her ideas. It just reduced her outlet for them.

That was one of the things Liliana had loved most about her mother. Everyone else regarded her like a speaking dog, a thing of novelty and intelligence but of little significance. Her mother had been one of the few people to believe in Liliana's mind.

Her father had only asked for Liliana's appointment to the Education Council after Liliana's tenacious insistence that he do so. Therefore, Liliana had approximately a million questions as to why her father had finally chosen to give the forgotten daughter a chance.

In truthfulness, Liliana still didn't believe the situation was real. There was something so fantastically convenient about the path to her dreams opening up that Liliana nearly threw up her hands and declared the whole thing a ruse. The Monarchic Trials were a custom so antiquated that any writing on the matter was buried deep in the annals of the castle library. Following her father's announcement, Liliana hunted the literature down, only to find it checked out to the very man himself. That meant Liliana knew very little about what was to ensue, and it made the entire thing feel even more like a fevered hallucination from Liliana's wildest dreams.

But enough of her wanted so badly to prove it all was real that now, Liliana paced outside her father's door to force him to spread his plans out before her; she needed proof so she could know that the remorseless prick of hope growing in her heart wasn't just the remnants of a quixotism bred from childhood.

Liliana's gaze whipped to the other end of the hallway, hearing the steady thump of many footsteps ascending the stairs. Her father turned the corner moments later, surrounded by a small retinue of guards that were led by Ro. Beneath the torches of the hallway, the silver crown matched his thinning hairline almost perfectly. For a second, Liliana could hardly tell that the crown was there at all.

Leo halted at seeing Liliana's expression, his surprise quickly melting into a smile. He turned to the guards and said something quietly that caused them to disperse, leaving only herself, her father, and Ro in the hallway.

"Here to discuss the latest legislation from the Spiritual Council, are we?" her father asked with a chuckle.

Liliana laughed slightly in spite of herself, responding, "Yes, I hear they're doing some interesting things in there."

Silence fell, its presence all at once foreboding and rousing. Even though the reticence bothered Liliana, she breathed quietly, not yet daring to break the peaceful stillness of the air. These were the last moments she would have between her and her father before everything changed. What that *everything* would entail, Liliana could hardly say. And yet, she held onto the silence for a moment longer.

Her father allowed the lull without question, watching her quietly. For all her mother's pushing, which Liliana cherished to this day, her father had always been far better at the exact opposite: knowing when to step back and allow his children the space they needed.

Liliana finally found the words she needed to process what had the potential to be the best or most devastating day of her life. "Is it true?"

"Yes."

Liliana's blood rushed to her face, and she nearly forgot how to breathe. Her mark pulsed, a hot, demanding beat. Her mother had nurtured Liliana's mind, but she had done so while reminding

Liliana of her place. Third child, third to the throne. Liliana spent years cultivating her love of Electaria and its systems, devising ways to make it better, all the while knowing she would never have all the power to make it so. It was like waking to the same nightmare every day, where Liliana was thrown off a cliff, and her fingers were always too weak to find purchase. Inevitably, she tumbled to her demise. And yet, after years of living in last place, the power to make change, have agency was closer to her fingertips than she could have ever hoped.

She grasped for a semblance of sanity amid the torrent of her emotions and was only able to find one word. "How?"

"You know, you and Teo are not the first siblings to both bear the mark of *Imperium*," her father began, voice wry. While he spoke, he fidgeted with the crown on his head in an absentminded manner. "Obviously, it's a rare occurrence, but not unheard of. Which, in a way, reflects the Trials themselves.

"The Trials were created thousands of years ago. It's first referenced in a book so old that the story is mostly written in symbols, lacking names—or punctuation, for that matter." Her father shook his head with a wince, as if even the memory brought him a headache. "I had heard historians in the castle mention it in passing, but I only recently had them bring and translate the original account. A pair of twins were born—"

Liliana snorted. "How very vaticinal."

"Quite," her father said, and Liliana shrank at his raised eyebrows, which conveyed a clear, "Are you finished?" expression.

He tended not to raise his voice, knowing what he could accomplish simply with a look. Seeing Liliana somewhat chagrined, he continued, "A pair of twins were born with the mark of *Imperium*. Questions of succession erupted immediately, and the solution born was a series of trials to determine suitability for the throne, the philosophy being that the trials would expose growth or flaws in the candidates' characters.

"Then, around six hundred years ago, during the reign of King Zan, a younger sibling with the mark of *Imperium* used this event as precedent to challenge his older brother, also bearing the mark, for the throne. This account was far more specific in its recount, especially with regard to the Trials themselves. Building upon this history, there was one more instance, around three hundred years ago, when the king in power demanded the Trials be held, believing his oldest daughter unfit for the throne. In doing so, he allowed his younger son an opportunity at the throne—and his younger son succeeded. That was King Wi's father," Leo said, chuckling nervously. "A fascinating bit of Electarian history, as you might imagine."

Liliana shook her head. She would not allow her father such an easy escape from the conversation. "But *why*? Why did you do this?"

"Would you prefer I undo the whole thing?" He smiled gently at her, teasing.

"Of course not," Liliana snapped before trying to take a breath to calm herself. She was a jumble of thoughts and emotions, a collection of brush being tossed about in the wind of her mind. "I-I just need to know why you did this. To Teo. For me."

Leo stared at her before giving a heavy sigh, as if the very act of breathing was a laborious task. "Because I am tired, Liliana. I'm tired of second-guessing everything I do because I follow *Menda* and not *Imperium*. Electaria is a country ruled by *Imperium*'s followers; the only time it has had other followers have been ad hoc and incredibly temporary. I think I have reigned longer than any other in this regard, and yet I have felt such the fraud while treading water in this crown."

"But then why the Trials? Why not simply give the country to Teo?"

"I could have. I still wonder if that would've been the better option," her father replied. He shook his head at the ground before looking back up, a weary smile on his face. "But you try simply handing over the crown to the oldest when the youngest has put her entire mind, body, and soul to the task of improving this country. Tell me you wouldn't have given her the chance to have everything she's worked for and make all the smart, innovative changes she's dreamed of."

He raised his hands up defensively. "In a way, I had no choice. Now, the burden is off my shoulders. It is up to you and Teo to prove yourselves."

Liliana did not consider herself an emotional person in the slightest, but her throat grew tight at those words. She walked toward her father and wrapped him in a hug, squeezing for all she was worth. Squeezing with every ounce of joy she felt in that moment, knowing that from now on, her fingers were close enough to the ledge to hang on and fight. She leaned back, barely conjuring enough air to speak. "Thank you."

"Do not thank me." He waved a finger at her. "I have merely shown you the door. It's up to you to walk through. Now, if you would like to accompany me downstairs, I believe I have some Trials to announce."

Liliana nodded, unable to speak. While she had felt a rush of thrill when her father first announced the Trials, she had quickly quelled the feeling at the fear that the prospect was simply too good to be true. It was like someone had erected a protective glass wall between Liliana and all that threatened to overwhelm her. Now that she knew she truly had a chance at being Electaria's queen, there was no emotion sufficient enough to describe her staggering joy.

They walked down the stairs to the throne room, Aoran silently joining the group as Liliana's heel hit the first step. For all his ability to butt in and annoy Liliana, he also excelled at knowing when to pull back. From his insults to his indulgences, there was a certain amount of thoughtfulness that Liliana could swear was there, even if he claimed otherwise. *Quite the dance partner, indeed*, Liliana thought absentmindedly to herself, mulling over the idea.

He fell in step beside her, raising an eyebrow at her in question. Though he had less cause to be suspicious of the announcement than she, he still had the decency to act like he had empathized with her doubt. All she could manage was the smallest smile and nod. Aoran grinned back, jade eyes glittering, and Liliana's heart skipped a beat. There was far too much going on in her mind today.

The throne room, located two flights of stairs down from the royal quarters, was zipping with activity by the time they arrived. Inside and overflowing into the hallway, envoys of various nations gossiped with one another, alight with excitement. The Trials were a novelty the likes of which hadn't been seen in centuries. The prospect of witnessing them firsthand would lend bragging rights of fantastic proportions in the future.

The Captain stepped up to the group as they approached the grand doors, giving curt nods to Aoran and Ro, who responded with an Electarian salute, right fist to heart. She turned and barked at the guards at the doors, parting the gathered gaggles to open a path for their entourage. Liliana's heart thumped, and she took slow steps forward, trying to both process and savor every second of what followed.

Liliana struggled to take in the room around her. Excitement and tension shoved against one another, each scrapping to dominate the room's atmosphere, creating a collision of energy. Easternalia sat in the corner, her back turned to the room as she whispered furiously to her children. As if sensing the presence of social clout, Easternalia's head twitched and immediately zeroed in on the king. Liliana and her father skipped by her aunt, focusing on the dais and pretending not to hear her call or see her emphatic wave. Liliana was actually shocked: her father's body achieved speeds she previously thought impossible for his swelling knees. The miracles Easternalia inspired deserved more acclaim; the woman could galvanize a mountain to flee from its place.

The Vitrian empress and her partner offered a jolly wave to her father from the side of the room, and a young girl watched curiously beside them. The girl's head was cocked slightly to the side, her eyebrows furrowed together, and bottom lip tucked firmly beneath her teeth. The Nuwei council nodded respectfully but otherwise ignored the entourage to talk among themselves. The Aurjnegh court bowed, a few bosoms becoming completely exposed with the movement. Liliana blinked rapidly at the cavalier way in which the women's breasts just *fell* out of their clothing. The scandalous clothing and the ample chest were both unfathomable to her. She shook her head, hurrying forward with her father.

The Soj leader all but hid behind the Nuwei council, his white gaze tracking their every movement. Liliana had never formally been introduced to one of the Soj. Though they had been invited to a handful of dignitary events, their presence was more of a formality than anything. Liliana found the group and their infamy fascinating, even if the characteristic Soj eyes unnerved her. With irises so silver they were almost nonexistent, their crimson pupils stood out like fire in a winter storm. For better or for worse, though, the Soj and their unsettling irises were the Nuwei's problem. Liliana watched her father smile at the man briefly with what seemed to be some level of sincerity before she hurried to her siblings.

Liliana took her place beside Eliana, and her father moved to the front throne. She used to loathe the arrangement, being forced to stand next to the sister with whom she shared little love. It made every royal meeting both an embarrassment and a torture. However, for the first time in her life, Liliana didn't feel so invalidated by the positioning. A heat grew from the dragon on her back, its claws slowly stretching over her body.

In fact, being so close to the throne had never felt so gratifying. Liliana's mark pounded, and she vaguely wondered what Teo's mark might be whispering to him. Though Eliana stood with a placid smile, Teo clenched and unclenched his knuckles, turning his brown fingers pale.

Her father adjusted the crown on his head, looking more relaxed than Liliana had seen him in many years. Such comparisons were hard to recognize when she believed his natural state to be that of stressed monarch. In some ways, she understood his desire to give up the crown. She followed the logic of his uncertainty, his lack of preparation or desire for the role in which her mother's death had placed him. And yet, in other ways, his decision had Liliana utterly confounded. He had everything she had ever wanted and was simply going to *give it up.*

Liliana traced her father's face, shining with a thin layer of sweat, marveling at how someone so different from her could look so similar. For all the shared blood that ran through their veins, they lacked so much common ground in their minds. Though far from towering, Liliana's height was entirely attributed to her father's Vitrian heritage on *his* father's side. Liliana inherited the red undertones of her father's brown skin, the lighter brown of his eyes. While Eliana and Teo had always been deemed the spitting image of their mother, Liliana had always taken after her father. But in between everything physical they shared, there was so little emotional depth that could thread the two together and provide mutuality.

It was a strange thing, to look at someone and see a reflection with which she had nothing in common.

Eliana's dark eyes slid over to Liliana, the movement breaking Liliana out of her reverie. "I suppose you're quite pleased about this whole affair."

"How could I not be?" Liliana shook her head, incredulous, gripping the edges of her silky, lavender dress. "This is my chance."

Eliana rolled her eyes with such subtlety Liliana only caught the movement from years of watching for her sister's snubs. Her sister focused back on the front of room, her voice soft and words sharp. "Teo should have been king."

The words hit Liliana's skin with a corrosive sizzle, and her heart flared with an infectious heat. And her sister still wore her wrecking, calm smile. Liliana's hands shook, unable to contain her anger. She lacked her sister's composure but did not desire the facade. Even when they were children, Liliana's sister had always been a viper. Her words were equal parts alluring and dangerous. A treacherous bite hid behind soft laughter, a suffocating strength hidden behind sweet curtsies. Liliana balled her hands into fists. She was sick of avoiding stepping on her sister's tail.

Her father faced the audience, and the room fell into a hush, as if somebody had thrown a wet blanket over the inferno of their gossip. The collective pressure of their gaze was opaque, its own wall that separated their family and the audience. He was not father or Leo to the aristocrats and dignitaries, no more than they would care to know the name of a flea. Only titles existed on their side of the wall. Representative of this, councilor of that. He was the king, and solely from this title did he warrant their attention, though only for a few weeks more. Once somebody else assumed the throne, his name would be little more than a few ink prints on scrolls collecting dust.

"Thank you all for coming today." His voice echoed across the expansive room.

The people, packed together to the point where some had to stand on other's shoulders, tittered.

"As you know, this is an important moment in our kingdom's history. For years, Electaria has been supported by its strong leaders," he continued, his voice strong.

Liliana wondered how he felt facing the merciless crowd and whether he stood strong or his heart raced with anxiety.

"My late wife, Juliana, was evidence to that. She commanded armies, won battles, supported an expansive economy, and was, of course, a devout member of the faith. She completed her Walk before she was twenty-five."

The room hummed in approval. Religious fervor varied wildly between kingdoms and even then, between people. But whether a fanatic or apathetic, everybody put on a show of faith whenever an opportunity arose. Liliana's mark thumped at the remark, as if reminding her all that she still had yet to be.

"Juliana also bore the mark of *Imperium*. She, like all of Electaria's monarchs, had the dragon on her back, symbolizing a powerful and just ruler." Out of the corner of her eye, Liliana saw Renee fold her arms over her chest, her eyebrows and mouth pinched together. Liliana watched her father purposefully ignore this.

"I served as monarch with the mark of *Menda*. I did this to maintain stability after Juliana's death, as a handful of others have done before me in times of necessity. But after years of being the bridge between the old and new, it is time we welcome the new. It is time somebody with the mark of *Imperium*, a true ruler, takes my place."

The room pounded its feet in agreement. Every person leaned forward, excitement rocketing through their bodies with a tangible electricity. It was the kind of electricity that came with dramatic endings and spectacular beginnings. It was the kind of electricity that came with the terrifying delight of the unknown.

"Those with the mark of *Imperium*, please step forward and prove your right of inheritance. Step forward and declare yourself as a candidate for the crown of Electaria."

Liliana brushed forward before Teo blinked. She strode over, every step with a dragon's strength. The room froze, its patrons looking back and forth between her and Teo. Some people looked horrified. Others looked positively gleeful. The courts of the world did not like change in their own fragile ecosystems, but ferocious upstarts in other kingdoms? Well, those were perfect fodder for that night's dinner.

Liliana wore a fitted, lavender dress, the neckline tied together at the base of her neck. She turned around, her blazing and clear brown eyes staring challengingly at Teo, her back toward the crowd. Two servants hurried forward and untied the strings of her dress, holding the front up while she exposed her back for the room to see. Everybody gasped, though there was no shock in the sound. That was to Liliana's design. The drama of the display would prove to be far more memorable than the mark. The black dragon on her back craned its neck toward the sky, breathing flames into her hairline. She rounded the top of her back, allowing the crowd to see every detail of her mark's majesty.

Teo shook himself out of his stupor, marching up to stand next to Liliana. He cast away his purple cape, then ripped the buttons from his shirt and yanked it off to show the identical mark on his back, with the exception of one detail: the golden shine of Teo's mark. A small din began to grow in the crowd as they looked back and forth between the golden and black marks. They murmured fervently over the one who had proved his understanding of power and the one who still sought its virtues. Teo stared down, but the strain of his muscles and shoulders shone with clear pride.

"I will not go easy into the night," Liliana muttered to Teo under her breath. "I will be this country's queen."

Teo's face remained stoic, focused on the ground. "We both have the mark, Liliana. Gods' will be done from there."

If there was one commonality among Liliana and her siblings, it was that the children of Juliana did not sit idly by and wait for the world to bestow them with its gifts. She and Teo pointed their own spears at *Terrabis*—one of determination, one of steadiness—and demanded it bow to their will.

Leo waited a few seconds before approaching Teo and Liliana. He gave them both small nods, looking back up at the crowd. "We have two candidates—"

Somebody stepped on to the stage, interrupting Leo's speech. The room froze so immediately Liliana was surprised snow did not fall from the ceiling. A young, tall girl with gangly arms and legs like those of a spider slowly walked to stand next to Teo and Liliana. Though the girl said nothing, her face lit up with thrill. Liliana watched the entire thing happen in slow motion, her mouth partially agape. She was glad to have no mirror in front of her because she was sure her expression would be deadly.

Teo's expression could only be described as absolute and total befuddlement. Eliana hid any reaction brewing beneath the surface, simply leaning in closer to see what the girl had to offer.

The young girl, wearing a buttery dress that hugged the base of her neck, turned around to display the backless detail of the garb. The lack of fabric on her back made one large, very important detail apparent to everybody in the room. A black dragon spread across her shoulder blades, trailing down to the base of her spine.

It was at *that* moment that the room dissolved into apocalyptic mayhem.

The Captain leapt into action, barking out orders and ordering her guard to contain the frenzy. Aoran and Je crept closer to the group, their eyes narrowed into slits as they prepared to defend Liliana and Teo. The aristocracy lit up with a child's excitement, passing around speculations like copper candy at the market.

Liliana and Teo should have been the only ones on that stage. And yet, one more stood beside them. The young girl appeared to be no more than twenty. Aoran whistled lowly, and Liliana heard him remark to himself, clearly delighted, "What a day, what a day."

The young girl was certainly a complication with profound implications. Either everything they were taught as children was wrong, or members of the royal family had consorted outside their marital beds. Liliana wondered if her mother could have hidden an illegitimate birth from the prying eyes of the court. She knew her parents had married more out of convenience than love, but she thought their loyalty true. The idea made her furious. Or sick. Or both.

There was no way of knowing yet. Liliana's face was white, and she could only stand in shock. The one thing she did know was that her father had given a commoner a chance at the throne.

CHAPTER 7
7055.1.17

"So...," Ma said slowly, her voice blanched with disbelief, "you're saying my daughter can't come home. Until these Mystical Trials are over, you're taking my oldest daughter away from me. Am I understanding this correctly?"

The composure with which King Leo received the question was remarkable. Though Elle was sure he had no idea what came after that kind of question. She'd been on the other side of that voice many times and knew it was a petrifying path that only led to scathing admonishments.

Ma stood in front of the king in the castle's throne room, firm arms crossed in front of her chest so tightly they looked like a set of armor. Da stood close by, violet eyes narrowed with the left side of his lip sloping down into an almost frown. Her siblings lingered with Elle, removed enough from the scene to whisper among themselves but close enough to follow the exchange.

"I'm afraid so, Estienne." Leo's pudgy face was downcast as he managed to make even Ma's name sound apologetic. "We simply can't risk having one of the Trials' contestants living in the city where anything could happen to her. She could be the future queen of Electaria—we can't afford to treat such a prospect lightly."

Ma looked ready to tell the country's king exactly where he could shove that prospect. Elle prayed to *Imperium* Ma wouldn't get herself jailed; Elle didn't know if sass was a jail-worthy crime, but there was enough insanity going on in her life that she didn't want to tempt the Gods.

Nic fidgeted at Elle's right, pulling at the tight neck of his shirt. It was the nicest one he owned, a whiter dye and more refined fabric than all his other tunics. It also hadn't seen the light of day in about three years and was that many years too small. While her parents continued to argue with the king, Nic raised his elbow, as if preparing for a cough, and whispered to Elle, "This is wrecking wolfshit. You know that, right?"

"Of course, I do!" Elle huffed back under her breath, keeping her eyes trained on her parents.

"Can you imagine Elle being queen?" Fren asked, his long, round face gleeful.

"A literal Stone Tree being queen seems more likely." Fritz shook his head.

"I think Elle would be a *great* queen," Penelope said hotly in as quiet a voice as possible while still sounding annoyed.

"Thanks, Pen."

Ma turned around and flashed a deadly glare at her children. They gave a collective gulp and quieted down as she returned her focus to the king.

"As I was saying, the Vitrian empress gave my daughter little idea what the repercussions of revealing her mark would be. She practically tricked her into entering this little contest of yours. And now my daughter will be stripped from her family for some unknown amount of time, and by the end she might be *queen*? You have no right to put that kind of burden on her shoulders. This never should have happened in the first place! For all the world knows, she has the mark of *Menda*, like the rest of us."

"You're correct—I have no right." Leo nodded, face weary and wrinkled hands clasped before him. "But neither I nor the empress placed that burden on your daughter's shoulders. That was the work of the Gods themselves. Mrs. Fournier, as much as I would love to tell you your daughter can return home and return to her life, that simply isn't the case.

"She is the first common child to be born with the mark of *Imperium* in history—even if she didn't need to compete in the Trials, which the law requires her to do based upon precedent, she is a remarkable case. Through her mark, she has become one of the rarest people on *Terrabis*, and she needs to be protected."

Leo sighed, rubbing a hand down his face. "Besides, even if she did return home, rumor is eventually going to spread. There are hundreds of people in this castle. Keeping this a secret from here on out would be, frankly, impossible. The people would demand to know why this child, this miracle, was not given a chance at the throne. There would be mutiny, chaos. I cannot throw this country into such instability with a good conscience."

Elle wrinkled her nose. It was a strange thing to be referred to as rare, as if she were some newly discovered animal from a faraway place. She never pondered on her mark very much—a consequence of her ma's perpetual insistence that Elle didn't look at, touch, or think about it—but for the first time, Elle felt uncomfortable about the dragon on her back.

Penelope reached out to Elle's left hand, giving it a firm squeeze. Elle looked down and was met with her sister's toothy smile, violet eyes glittering. "You hear that? The king thinks you're rare. That's so cool!"

And just like that, the disquiet in Elle's mind settled, replaced with warmth and a kernel of pride. When the king referred to Elle's mark, she felt wrong. When Penelope talked about Elle's mark in the exact same way, she felt remarkable. Elle grinned back, squeezing her sister's hand before a thought popped into her mind.

"Excuse me, Your Majesty," Elle interrupted, biting her lip. Ma glowered at Elle, but the king looked at Elle with expectant patience. "You said that keeping my mark a secret is going to be impossible, so I have to stay in the castle. I get that." Elle did her best not to notice the crestfallen look that flashed over her ma's face. "But does my family get to return to the bakery? What happens to them?"

"Of course, Elle." Da gave a chuckle at the ludicrous notion. "We're going to—"

"Not quite." Leo grimaced.

Penelope's hand tensed in Elle's. Nic leaned in with narrowed eyes, his expression copied straight from their ma's own critical glare. Fritz and Fren froze, mirrored images of disbelief.

Da opened his mouth, closed it, stayed silent for a few seconds before finally asking, "What does that mean?"

"Your family could be at risk during the Trials. Any Electarian in the castle with hopes of influencing the outcome could threaten Ellegance through you all. As a result, you'll need to be kept at an off-site location until the termination of the Trials." Leo faltered, face sagging. "I-I'm sorry."

"You're sorry?" Ma stomped toward Leo and the soldier lingering behind the king stepped forward, one hand tight along the shaft of a lethal-looking spear. The other hand reached out and held Ma at arm's distance, stopping her from advancing. Ma, true to herself, did not seem deterred.

"You don't get to displace my family from our lives and offer an *apology* as compensation. What about our business? Our customers will disappear if we stop operating for too long. And what about our children? How are they going to attend classes if we're forced to live in *Imperium*-knows-where Electaria? This, *this* is why the people of this city have so little faith in their leaders," Ma thundered, throwing her hands back and practically gnashing her teeth. "We are your pawns, shuffled around and toyed with as you all please, with no regard to the lives that we lead. We are not your toys, the byproducts of your *whims*." She hurled the word with such virulence it sounded like an insult. "But still, you treat us as such and have the audacity to say you're sorry. Don't make me wrecking laugh."

Penelope, eyes wide, said softly in her shock, "Language."

"The details of your living arrangements will be discussed with you by our Spymaster upon your return to your house. They are one of the most capable people I have ever met, and they will make sure you're duly cared for," Leo responded, voice hoarse, eyes concentrated on some point beyond Elle's shoulder. Instead of meeting her ma's furious gaze, he glanced at Elle, eyes pained. "And if you have no faith in your leaders, then now is your chance to put your faith in a new one. One of the guards will now see you out."

Ma ripped away from Ro. "We'll see ourselves out, Your Majesty."

Never in Elle's life had an honorific sounded so venomous that it sent chills down her arms. Ma stormed out of the throne room, the family following close behind. Despite walking through halls more opulent than any of them had ever seen in their lives, everybody stayed focused on their ma's stomps, leading the way.

Elle found she didn't have the same reservoir of anger as Ma. Instead, a resigned, sad feeling settled over her. In spite of Ma's searing criticisms, Elle had confidence that the government would take care of her family during these Trials, whatever they were. She was also sure that after the mysterious Trials were over, regardless of the outcome, she would be able to see her family again. *Maybe even as queen.* She snorted to herself. *Yeah, right.* Still, the idea of being separated from her siblings and parents for the first time in her life made her feet heavier and her lips curl downward. Elle always figured when she eventually left the house for her life of adventures, it would be on her own terms and very likely include at least one of her siblings. She trundled after her ma, her thoughts getting tangled.

As they zipped through the castle halls, Ma's rage seemed to lose its source of fuel. Like a fire whose kindling had been burned through, her shoulders slumped down, and her gait slowed with every step. By the time they reached the gates, Ma had fizzled out.

The spring weather was offensively beautiful, an intense juxtaposition to an otherwise painful day. Instead of rain and gloom, like would be appropriate for such an occasion, the sun gleamed, and the birds chirped in a way so ridiculously pleasant

Elle wanted to tell off *Imperium* herself. The guards had already opened the gates, standing on either side and gesturing outward. Elle kind of wanted to tell them off too.

Ma turned to look at Elle, her light brown eyes shining. She reached up and stroked a hand over Elle's choppy, black hair, her hand pausing on the side of Elle's cheek. A shock of fear flew through Elle; in her nineteen years, she had never seen her ma cry. Elle bit her lip, unsure of what to say to fix things.

"Everything's going to be okay?" Elle had meant it as a statement, but her uncertainty slipped through, turning it into a question.

Her siblings watched warily in the background, as disoriented as Elle in the new emotional territory they had entered.

Elle's accidental inquiry seemed to clear something in Ma. She shook her head, her eyes losing any teary gleam, and gripped Elle's cheek with callused fingers. "Everything's going to be okay," Ma repeated back to her with the same firmness she used to order them into doing chores. It offered no room for compromise—it was a way of saying, "This is the way things are going to happen, whether you like it or not."

Da came up behind Ma, reaching over to clasp Elle on her shoulder. "*Etiam.*"

And with that simple word, Elle's anxiety rescinded. It felt like when a naman was backed into a corner and began expelling its mucus, only to relax, the mucus returning slowly back into its pores. In both cases it didn't disappear entirely. Elle's anxiety and sadness over seeing her family go lingered, but it quieted enough that Elle took a breath and didn't feel like her chest had turned into a cage that her heart was trying to bust out of. "Maybe they'll let us exchange letters," Elle finally said, forcing cheer into her voice. "I might be queen after all—that's got to mean something around here."

"Yes! And when you're finally queen, can you get me in with the treasury?" Penelope pushed past their parents and clung to Elle's sleeve, pleading. "I promise I'll never give Fritz scissors to cut your hair ever again!"

"Wait, that was you?"

Fritz flashed a grin, and Penelope gave a sheepish nod. Elle grabbed her sister's waist and swung her around, ignoring her mix of squeals and cries. "You better hope our time apart is enough for me to forgive you little *malums*."

"Language!" Penelope forced out between gasps as she tried to wriggle out of Elle's vicelike grip.

"Okay, *okay*." Ma forced Elle and Penelope apart, looking at Elle with exasperation, though affection peeked through. "I think that's quite enough. We'll go and leave you to...to...," Ma huffed, "well whatever this is going to be. Just...be safe. Be smart. I—we *all* love you."

An affection so intense crushed Elle's heart into a tiny ball. She ran forward and wrapped her ma in her long arms, burying her face in the crook of her neck. Breathing in, Elle was hit with the perfect smell of rosemary and flour, feeling an ache as she did so. She was already homesick for the scent.

Her da and siblings came in around her, piling on top into a giant group hug. Elle laughed, wiggling to accommodate everyone into the tiny area. Like a pyramid, their foreheads formed a kind of apex, meeting in the middle and pressing against one another. Well, except for Ma and Penelope. Without the Vitrian blood giving her a little height boost, Ma was about Penelope's height, though Elle's own height was an indicator that Penelope would soon surpass that point. The two were squished in the middle of the hug, underneath the dome of everyone else's heads.

"Be good. Be powerful," Ma whispered fiercely to Elle, reaching through the embrace to wrap Elle's forefinger and middle finger with her own two.

Elle almost recoiled in shock; she never thought she'd see the day Ma used part of the Deal. Elle closed her eyes and smiled to herself. She never thought she'd see the day she'd compete to be queen either.

"*Etiam.*"

Her family broke off the hug, slowly and begrudgingly, like trying to yank a child away from his favorite toy. Eventually, though, they managed to separate. Elle's skin seared where their hands had touched, a burning memory she tried to savor for as long as possible. They turned and, as a collective, made their way out the gates, shouting and laughing as they walked back to the bakery. Penelope turned around to give Elle one last grin and thumbs-up, which Elle returned half-heartedly. Elle's legs twitched, as if trying to follow suit. She pinched her thigh and shook her head, turning to walk back into the castle. Her home for the next...however long.

The guards pulled the iron gates shut, the harsh clang of metal making Elle flinch with the jarring finality of it all. She exhaled a huff of air upward, blowing her bangs off her forehead. The spring wind sighed, curling over her shoulders in gentle commiseration. Elle glanced up at the sky and managed a lopsided smile. "You don't make things easy, do you?"

Though her patron God offered no response, Elle's mark gave a tiny pulse. Elle smiled, reaching back to idly rub the tip of her mark that stretched to the top of her spine. If there was one good thing to come from all the dramatics, it would be that Elle no longer had to worry about hiding her mark.

Ma had first talked to Elle about her mark when she was barely four years old. She had firmly explained that Elle had to pretend to have the mark of *Menda*, like her parents. Elle never got much else by way of an explanation from her parents. In school, she learned that the mark of *Imperium* was reserved for royalty, a sign only meant for those who could one day rule the nation. Elle got the message and stopped asking Ma questions; Elle was an anomaly at best and a threat to the monarchy at worst. From that point, she saw no need to stir up any trouble for her family concerning her mark.

Still, Elle had to refrain from guffawing during that particular lesson. Elle had no idea where *Imperium* got her sense of humor, but the God surely must have gotten a kick out of the nobody-baker's daughter bearing her sign. Otherwise, why would Elle have her mark?

As Elle strolled back into the castle, this thought lingered. She wandered slowly into the entrance hall, unable to notice any detail in particular as she delved deeper into her own ideas. Elle still struggled to see herself as anything more than the daughter of her parents. She used to dream of being a captain, but the lack of actualization left her with only the one identity. And yet, here Elle was, embarking upon the Trials, potentially being *queen*—perhaps *Imperium* had more foresight than Elle ever could have considered.

"Your family is very…affectionate."

The voice interrupted Elle's musings, and she halted, whipping her head up to meet the clear brown eyes of the youngest princess. Elle still remembered how Liliana had stormed to the front of the room, showing her mark to the world without a hint of trepidation. Elle had watched the young woman with admiration, having kept her own mark hidden her entire life. There was something beautiful about the princess's confidence.

Liliana stood in the middle of the entrance of the castle, eyebrows furrowed, arms crossed. Much like Elle, Liliana erred on the taller side due to her half-Vitrian blood. Unlike Elle's ever-present hunch, though, Liliana's posture was the picture of perfection, her shoulders drawn backward and chin tilted up, literally holding herself up higher than most.

"We're Vitrian—it's kind of the only way to be," Elle joked.

Liliana didn't laugh, but one of her thick eyebrows raised skeptically. "In that case, my family could use a lesson in Vitrian customs," Liliana remarked, her lips twisting into a small, wry smile.

"Does your da not do anything like that?" Elle asked, surprised. Based on her experiences with Da, no matter how far removed a Vitrian was from his country, it was hard to remove the country from the Vitrian.

"My father is as watered down a Vitrian as they come." Liliana rolled her eyes. "After he married my mother, the Vitrian customs were replaced with Electarian ones." As if defending the choice,

Liliana added shortly, "Of course, an Electarian monarch with a Vitrian identity is hardly an easy sell to the country. The change was necessary."

"Of course" Elle nodded her head. "Ma told me that changing for someone you love is necessary sometimes. That's why Da moved with her to Electaria when she asked."

"My parents' marriage was hardly based on love." Liliana laughed, the sound short but not bitter. "From what I've learned, most royal marriages aren't. You marry for connections, utility. Marriage when you're royal is more like...being executed." At Elle's drop of the jaw, Liliana held up her hand, explaining, "In the sense that at some point, the outcome is inevitable. So the best you can do is pick the least painful route. Save yourself some suffering, at the very least."

"That sounds awful!" In contrast to her words, Elle found herself snorting with laughter.

Liliana's lip curled upward in a small smile. The analogy the princess drew stuck in Elle's mind, the tragedy of the picture making it all the funnier.

"Let no one in this castle sell you a love story," Liliana warned with the same, small smile. "They are either a liar or a fool or quite possibly both."

"In fairness, Your Highness, most people fit into one of those three categories anyway," Elle snickered. "We can't save those titles just for people who believe in love."

"Truer words were never spoken." Liliana's smile grew slightly, her arms loosening against her chest.

With her high cheekbones and jutted chin, Elle doubted Liliana could ever look warm. Even her way of speaking was aloof, her sharp diction and impressive vocabulary far removed from the realm of casual conversation. But with the slight smile, her eyebrows not so narrow and lips not so tightly pressed, Elle figured it was as close as the princess was going to get to friendly.

The princess tilted her head to the side, looking Elle up and down. "You know, you're much cleverer than I thought you'd be," Liliana remarked.

Elle gave a weak grin, unsure how else to respond to the pseudocompliment.

"Though, in truth, my expectations were remarkably low—the empress quite literally found you on the streets. Which, I suppose, brings me to the question burning through the entire court at the moment: How did you end up with the mark of *Imperium*?"

"*Imperium*, I have no idea." Elle laughed, scratching the back of her neck. "The same way anybody ends up with any mark, I guess. Before being taken to the castle, I never thought about it much."

Liliana's eyebrows slid back into intimidating slants, as if dissatisfied with Elle's answer. "I see. And what are you planning on doing should you win the Trials?"

Elle blinked, taken aback by the serious turn of the conversation. "Well...I don't really know yet. I'd have to have more time to think about it." Elle paused, continuing with slow thoughtfulness: "But I imagine I'd want to do something to help people like my parents. They talk a lot about how people outside the castle have a hard time getting in—I'd probably try and make the government more accessible to the people. And maybe do something to help families financially. We only survived because Ma's smart as anything and Da bakes a mean bread." Elle laughed.

"What about foreign policy, like dealing with the Soj? What about trade deals and Electaria's growing machination industries?" Liliana ticked off her fingers before giving a sad shake of her head. "It's a nice idea, but you're thinking too narrowly."

Liliana took a step forward, brown eyes gleaming, and Elle felt her mark pound. Though Elle couldn't feel Liliana's mark, she knew the two were pounding in sync, a kind of challenging rhythm to one another. Even though Liliana and Elle were about the same height, Elle sensed Liliana looked down at her.

"You're fine, Ellegance. Witty, approachable, likeable, even. You would make a perfectly adequate queen. But Electaria needs more than adequacy." Liliana's eyes flashed, like a bonfire momentarily crackling skyward. "If you want what's best for our country, keep that in mind as we move through the Trials."

And with that, the youngest princess of Electaria turned on her heel and walked away. Elle stood there, a little dazed, a lot overwhelmed, and wondering what in *Imperium*'s name she had gotten herself caught in.

CHAPTER 8
7055.1.18

All the air rushed out of Liliana's chest as Aoran knocked her to her ass. Again.

He dug his wooden spear into the sand next to her head, leering over her with a grin that made her want to tear his trachea from his throat.

"You know, they have that phrase about being down to earth. Based on how much you've been on the ground today, I would say you've nearly achieved the quality."

Liliana thought her mind had acclimated to Aoran's taunts, had developed a sort of mental shell to shield her from the constant irritation he provoked. She dealt with his quips now on an almost constant basis between his bodyguarding and their training. And yet, every time she thought she transcended to a spiritual peace beyond the reach of his gleeful grin, he managed to find the chink in her armor again.

Releasing something between a shriek and a growl, Liliana pushed herself to her feet, grabbing Aoran's spear in the process. She tucked the weapon under her arm, lunging forward to pound Aoran in the chest with its wooden point. He danced out of the way, stalking her as she whipped around, desperately scanning for an opening to attack.

She felt like a stone giant compared to his nymph-like elegance. Her feet plodded along the floor, weighed down with bricks of inexperience. Aoran skipped around her, his stance prowling and perfect. He watched her with a delighted, predatory grin, the same way Timore hawks watched baby rabbits fumbling out of the den for the first time.

He feigned forward, and she spun the spear around, successfully managing to bat him back into his slow circles around her. Liliana's scratchy tunic clung to her chest with sweat, her legs wobbling in the sand from more than an hour of back-and-forth. No other soldiers fought as she and Aoran sized up one another. Nothing occupied the space of the training room except for the fighting pair, Imperium, and Liliana's labored breathing.

Aoran's eyes drooped, his green eyes slumping with what could only be called boredom. Liliana's breathing picked up, her muscles tight with the tension of a tightrope. Had she managed to lull the wolf to sleep? *Only one way to find out.*

She jumped at Aoran, bringing the spear above her head for a blow to leave him reeling. She slammed it down, preparing for the impact of a body and the sound of wood hitting bone.

Neither of these things happened. Aoran ducked out of her way, jumping and rolling to stand behind her. He grabbed the end of the spear, ripping it out of her hands from behind. He spun it around so the blunt end faced her. With a swift, calculated jab, he knocked the weapon into her back, her body smacking against the floor. Her head hurt magnificently. She could barely raise her arms, so covered in nicks and bruises that Eliana would only shake her head at Liliana's lack of regard for her own appearance.

Amid the utter exhaustion and the resounding pain that threatened to send her hand up in a plead for mercy, her back began to burn. Her blood roared, and she crouched on the ground, every part of her body trembling. She dug her fingers into the dirt, the rough particles digging into her hands. Unlike having her other hurts, her mark was a grounding, humanizing pain that brought her mind back into reality. It cut through the aches and soreness, and she focused on that feeling as she gritted her teeth. Imperium yipped from the sideline, and Liliana planted her foot into the sand, attempting to find some kind of solid stance amid the soft ground beneath her.

Aoran looked over her, his fanged grin replaced with subdued curiosity. "What's the plan here, princess?"

Liliana offered him a weak, wicked grin in return, wiping away the sweaty hair plastered to her forehead. She heaved her way over to him, each foot slamming down after the other. Her fingers, covered in dirt, crooked forward, beckoning him toward her.

"What the plan always is—to win."

Aoran's face, caught between confusion and delight, turned into immediate annoyance as Liliana threw the sand she clutched in her other hand at his face. Aoran, wiping his face, pulled back the spear to keep it from her grasp. She laughed, the sound sharp. Liliana didn't give a shit about the stupid spear.

She feigned lunging for the spear before coming up on Aoran's other side, elbowing his ribs. He wheezed, grabbing his side. The one perk of Liliana's thin frame? Bony elbows.

He growled, but before he could move forward, Liliana kneed him in the crotch and dropped him. Aoran collapsed to the ground, an unintelligible gasp squeaking from his chest. He grabbed her arm and yanked her down as he collided with the floor, throwing her to the ground with him. Liliana fell next to him, her wrists screaming as they broke her fall.

They sat there in total silence for about thirty seconds before the feeling of the empty air pressed down on Liliana. "Does that mean I win?"

He glared at her with a kind of hatred Liliana was glad she earned. He rolled on to his back, covering his eyes with his dusty arm. "It means you cheated."

"There's no cheating in fighting!" Liliana argued, her voice hoarse but insistent. "You either win with the weapons you have, or you don't win at all. Your...male weakness is a weapon I have. Are you to tell me that I shouldn't use every advantage available in a battle?"

He rubbed his head, covering his platinum hair in dirt and sand. If his hair wasn't so fair, Liliana might have never known he fought in the training room that day. The dreadful, military-issued pants and shirt he wore looked totally unchanged by their brief spat. Where normal recruits had spots that wore thin or stains from nights of drinking, Aoran was pristine. As much as Liliana wanted to believe it was a sense of pride, she had a feeling it was simple superiority. It wasn't that Aoran didn't want to get dirty—it was simply that so few were able to actually bring him down in the first place.

Liliana stared at him for a heartbeat, her eyes moving up from his clothing to trail along his sharp jaw and his pained expression. When they started using real spears, both she and he would upgrade into metallic helmets to protect from lethal blows. *Until then*, Liliana thought as she watched the sweat and sand streaking down the side of his face. She turned her head away and gave a half-hearted attempt at brushing the sand off her own stained tunic. Aoran usually looked handsome, but dirty and defeated, he almost looked beautiful.

"Yeah, well, most male weaknesses are covered in armor during a battle." He slowly stood up, wincing. He put his hands against his knees and groaned, face contorted. "This is the first and last time you'll be able to pull a dirty trick like that."

Liliana watched Aoran struggle to stand, his hands fluttering down to his injured spot in obvious distress. No irony, no witty retort. Just a thoroughly beaten Aoran, and at *her* hands, no less. A smile ghosted across her face. "I believe I can live with that."

Aoran walked over to his discarded spear, his feet moving gingerly along the floor. Liliana, with victorious shanties soaring through her head, all but floated over to Imperium on the high of her narrow win. She scratched the large wolf behind his floppy ears, a sweet warmth spreading through her body. She closed her eyes, cherishing the moment the same way she treasured the first juicy bite of a cherry on a summer day. Pleasant and perfect.

The pungent smell of sunweed wafted into her nose, decimating her transient happiness. Liliana put her hand up to her nose, trying to block out the putrid stench. Sunweed was more than a relaxing drug; it was a selfish one. It only provided comfort to the user—everybody else suffered in the wake of its noxious smoke.

Aoran sucked on his pipe as he meandered his way to Liliana, considerably more relaxed. He held his breath, his fanged grin turning into a lazy smile as he stepped no more than half-an-arm's length from her. Liliana gave Imperium a firm push, urging him out of the room. No need for her poor wolf to suffer too.

"Doesn't relishing in your own depravity ever get boring?" Liliana scowled at him, pressing the sleeve of her tunic to her nose. The rough fabric against her skin was a small price to pay to minimize the smell.

Aoran finally hissed out the breath he held, wisps of yellow smoke curling against Liliana's clothing and hair. "Thus far, no. But perhaps you can successfully shame me where so many have failed before you."

Liliana's eyes narrowed. "Don't tempt me."

"Ah, but Your Highness," Aoran smirked with such wickedness Liliana saw *malum*'s hand reach up to draw Aoran's smile herself, "temptations are my specialty."

A snarky remark burned on the tip of her tongue at the same time that a foreign feeling, as sinister as Aoran's expression, burned through her body to the tips of her fingers. She closed her mouth, a familiar red rushing through her cheeks. A wave of relief swept through her at the sound of boots crunching against the sand. She prayed that *Imperium* bless whoever walked in and spared her from the rest of the conversation.

Except that the intruder was Teo. *I take back my blessing*, Liliana thought and glanced with warning up at her patron God.

Teo marched in, full of his typical, self-righteous pride. His purple cape fluttered behind him, gold lines framing the edge. His black boots practically shined under the lights of the arena, his white uniform underneath crisp and clean. Liliana glanced down at her own training uniform, her formerly cream tunic dirty and her charcoal pants blotched with sweat. She closed her eyes, breathing sharply through her nose. *Superbia* had a funny way of bringing her down a peg at any given time.

Je followed obediently, crossbow resting against his shoulder, amused, hazel eyes at contrast with his stiff posture. He only broke his dutiful guard persona to look at Aoran with wide eyes and miming a pipe. Aoran, as if just remembering the sunweed clutched between his fingers, threw it on to the ground, pushing sand over it before Teo noticed a thing. The two shared a wink before resuming their masquerade of professionalism.

The jovial camaraderie of Je and Aoran escaped Liliana. All embarrassment and nonchalance disappeared, incinerated by her stormy wariness. Even before the tension brought on by the Trials, Liliana had little interest in speaking with her brother.

For all her mother's attention to Liliana and her intellectual betterment, the vast majority of the late queen's time was spent grooming Teo. Liliana had been snuck into council meetings, but Teo was the only child their mother ever took on diplomatic missions for the country. Liliana had been given gifts from faraway places, but Teo was the only one who had a sword requisitioned to his exacting desires. No matter how much Liliana craned her neck and how much acclaim Eliana gathered, Teo, at the end of the day, was the only one of the three who would be king.

Liliana cherished each moment with her mother. She savored their debates, the challenges, the praise. And yet, Liliana simultaneously felt that each conversation was her chance to pitch why her mother should spend more time with Liliana, as if each conversation was a contract to be renewed based on Liliana's worthiness of her mother's time.

Until this point, Liliana repeated to herself firmly. She spent her whole life believing that she would need to lick his boots to even get a glimpse of the power he could never appreciate. While Teo dined on the decadent cake of being the eldest born, she sat at the bottom, scavenging for any crumbs of his power that fell through the cracks. The moment Liliana realized she might be able to take the throne herself, he transformed into just another obstacle she needed to overcome.

And after busting her ass for twenty-one years, Liliana had no intention of failing now.

Liliana wasn't worried about Elle. Her lack of training and inability to rule would show themselves through the trials. She would take care of herself through sheer ineptitude and inferiority. Teo, on the other hand, represented a serious threat. They were competing wolf packs—taking him down and killing him was the only way to win the hunt.

"Liliana." Teo nodded, stiff. Liliana rolled her eyes. Her brother had the personality of damp wood. He looked past her to Aoran, nodding a little more fervently. She avoided grinding her teeth too loudly. "Aoran of the Four."

"Prince Teo." Aoran stood and bowed at the waist. His mouth quirked, but he kept all comments to himself, his respect appearing to be mostly genuine. Aoran ran his fingers through his hair, nodding his head to himself. He loped over to Je with his easy grace, bowing slightly toward Teo. "May I steal your bodyguard to run through Rotations?"

The way Aoran addressed Teo made Liliana's blood heat up. Her back began to warm with a slow, simmering rhythm. He was *her* bodyguard. Why did Aoran, the respectful soldier, only appear when her brother entered the room? She glared at Teo, her pale, brown eyes baleful.

"You may." Teo raised his right hand, dismissing the pair with a miniscule brush to the air. He controlled every movement. Every instant of his existence was defined by restraint. Restraint and timidity. Liliana's eyes narrowed. Power would never find its home on the head of such a man.

As Aoran and Je jostled around with one another in the periphery, Liliana found herself locked in a staring contest. Statues could have taken a lesson from the enduring stillness with which the siblings faced each other. They both waited, fire clashing against ice in a silent battle of wills.

Finally, Liliana huffed and crossed her arms, standoffish. "I don't know why I thought I could beat the human equivalent to a haystack in a silence contest."

"In fairness, silence was never your strong suit," Teo pointed out, his hands clasped behind his back.

Liliana's mouth dropped open, her conviction waning from surprise. Unlike Liliana and Eliana, who took open jabs at one another with whatever words came to mind, Teo usually refrained from doing the same, out of inability or indifference. "Did you just try to insult me?"

Teo's stern face flashed with something unnamable. "We have lived with one another for twenty-one years. It would be impossible to not learn a thing or two from you about insults."

"The magisters always say time proves to be the greatest teacher of all. I suppose two decades is nearly enough to teach even you," Liliana retorted, her eyebrow twitching slightly.

Liliana tried to find a semblance of a center while watching her brother. She couldn't remember a time in her life when he had sought her out, or vice versa. After their mother passed, the three siblings had avoided one another with admirable effort, and even more admirable success. But here her brother was: stoicism, cape, and all. For all his equanimity, something about him looked...off. *Why is he here?* Liliana tried to place it, ideas running back and forth across her mind.

While her thoughts raced, she looked expectantly at Teo. "Well? To what do I owe the pleasure?"

Teo opened his mouth to speak and immediately paused. His lips squeezed together in a tighter line than usual. His nostrils flared by the slightest amount, and he closed his eyes for one second before saying, "You will drop out of running for the throne."

In true form, the sentence came not as a question or request, but a command from a man who had expected everything delivered to him his entire life. Now, Liliana typically thought that she knew what was funny and what was not. It wasn't so much that Liliana considered herself a grand comedian, but she could recognize a joke when she saw one. However, as Liliana now almost dropped to the floor laughing, she reconsidered everything she thought she knew about comedy.

Teo watched her, his face stony and pinched. "Why are you laughing?"

"Ah, beloved brother." Liliana wiped an imaginary tear from her face, standing up and walking over to him until a sword would barely be able to fit between them. The grin dropped from her face, replaced with slow words and a dangerous glint in her voice. "Because you, dear, golden child of the family, might have just said the most ridiculous series of words in the existence of humanity."

He frowned, his chest puffing forward more—if that was even possible—and his tone deepening. Liliana felt her back pound a little bit harder in response. She wondered how fast his stupid, golden mark beat while hers screamed.

"Is it really so ridiculous to want the best person on the throne?"

Liliana blinked. "Oh no. Not at all. So long as we both agree as to whom that person is, which, I have the tiniest suspicion that we do not."

He glared at her, his arms still folded behind his back, but they seemed to be straining with effort to stay put. With his control fighting against his anger, his eyebrows furrowing but arms staying in place, Teo reminded Liliana so much of their mother she almost paused. Liliana found herself caught between admiring and detesting her brother's restraint.

"And do you really think you're the best person for the job? You, who can barely walk through the hallway without picking a fight with one of the torches?"

"At least the torches have some passion and fire," Liliana hissed. "Who will follow the king with no spirit?"

"And who in their right mind would bow before a reckless queen?"

They glowered at each other, hearts pounding. Their accusations dangled in the room, their bloody words dripping down the swords they attempted to drive through one another's hearts. Unfortunately, they were both raised to have armor much too strong to be penetrated by simple words. The lights shone down on them with a painful, blinding glare. Liliana breathed in the scent of the training room, searching for that familiar scent of dust and sweat. All she smelled was blood.

"I am the rightful heir," he growled, his voice booming throughout the room.

Aoran and Je stopped their Rotations, curiously watching the scene unfold.

"If you're the rightful heir, then why would father have declared the Trials?" Liliana challenged.

"I don't know!" Teo bellowed, his hands twitching as if he wanted to hit something. Maybe even hit her.

A dark part of Liliana's heart prayed he would. She wanted to see him lose it. She wanted to see him lose that carefully controlled facade. As it was, this was the loudest Liliana had ever heard her brother.

"All I know is I have studied and trained my entire life for this role, and yet I am forced to compete against my own sister and a *commoner* over a title for which I have waited *years*."

"If you've studied and trained for so many years for the damn job, then show it," she shot back at him, launching her arms forward to shove him in the chest.

He stumbled, looking back and forth between where she hit him and her contorted face, flushed with anger.

"If you were really the perfect person for the job, you wouldn't find yourself so ragingly insecure that you feel the need to step on your opponent before the competition has even started!"

Teo took after their mother. With sharp features and stoic expressions, they walked through life with countenances that spoke of strength and steadiness. That was probably why Liliana relished so heavily in the fact that the red undertones in Teo's dark skin grew into a crimson rash. It was the kind of red normally reserved for the cheeks of Liliana and their father. The flush smattered across his cheeks, blotching away his normal equanimity. *Red really was his color*, Liliana thought gleefully.

Liliana took a step toward Teo, her chin stuck defiantly in the air. She felt strong. She felt powerful, her mark burning against her back. Poisonous words burned on her tongue, venom poised to kill.

"Personally, I don't consider you a threat. You are an apathetic incarnation of mediocrity, and the only importance you'll ever experience is that which has been given to you through your birth date and your mark. I, on the other hand, have been training my entire life for an opportunity like this," she hissed at him, her expression a tempest of rage.

"*Imperium* herself could not stop me from winning this crown. This is my one chance—my *one* opportunity to do something for this country. I have the chance to make Electaria *legendary*, and I refuse to let you or the girl stand in my way. So if you think I will yield to you, you who *reeks* of the fear of losing," her back pulsed, drumming with the beat of her racing heart, "you are even simpler than I could have ever possibly imagined."

The words fell through the room like acid rain, singeing everybody in their vicinity. Aoran and Je winced. Liliana's ferocity dripped down the wall, thicker and darker than any blood the training room had ever seen. She hoped its stain would be stronger than blood too. Frustration and bitterness made the words sharp; years of grasping for Teo's coattails made them strong. She wanted Teo to remember this moment every time they passed one another in the castle. Every time they saw one another in the Trials. She wanted the memory burned on the inside of his eyelids, unable to escape from the truth no matter how far into his own mind he might try and run.

Teo's hand twitched, rising ever so slightly, but he didn't strike. His eyes frosted over with a cold determination. He gave her a stiff nod and turned on his heel. He marched out of the training room, his shoulders pushed back, his chin tilted slightly. A tiny pang of something thumped in Liliana's chest. Guilt? Regret? The sensation soured a fleeting feeling of victory.

Je patted Aoran on the shoulder, scrambling after Teo and resuming his serious, guarded face. Aoran approached Liliana, moving without his usual, nonchalant lope. He observed her with watchful eyes, all playfulness subsided. Words unspoken kept him at a distance, a tangible pressure separating them. Liliana felt that if she reached forward, a magnetic repulsion would force her hand backward.

She prodded the bubble of their silence, attempting to pop it. "What?"

A weak attempt at conversation but an attempt nonetheless. It was more than he offered her in return. He simply stared at her, the new expression unfamiliar beyond his traditional, fanged grin. Liliana put her hands on her hips, staring at him expectantly. "Are you going to talk? Or are you going to continue this act into a career as a court mime?"

"Do you not feel like a total *malum* after talking to your brother like that?" His question dropped through the room with the force of the guillotine, cutting into her confidence.

"Finally, it speaks." Liliana grinned, but the expression was fake. The feeling in her chest wriggled around, a reminder of her regret. But his accusation made her feel defensive and want to stand her ground—it wasn't like she could change the past anyway. "Since I don't make a habit of feeling guilty over telling the truth, no. I don't."

"Wrecking *Imperium*, Liliana." Aoran shook his head, laughing incredulously.

Liliana's eyebrows shot in the air. She was under the impression her name didn't even exist in his dictionary anymore.

"The fact that you don't see what's wrong with what you just said worries me. I know we mess around, but that was something else. That was something—" his mouth moved soundlessly. He looked up at her, deciding on the word. "That was cruel."

"He told me to drop out of the contest!"

"Just decline, like wrecking anybody else would!"

Liliana bit back a comment on how their specific situation was hardly anything like anybody else would encounter.

"Did that option not even cross your mind?"

Her heart squeezed, a foreign loneliness icing the edges. Aoran was a frustration, but a frustration that usually stayed by her side. Why did he defend Teo, her only real competition? The icy feeling turned sour, her lips screwing together. Liliana threw up her hands, annoyance and defensiveness creeping through her body. "What would you have me do? I said the words. Unless you care to try your hand at time travel, what has passed has passed."

"You should apologize, Your Highness." His green eyes flashed. "If that's the way you talk to all the people with whom you disagree, you'll be needing the practice for the future."

Liliana opened her mouth, seething. Her response was cut short by a rich, bored voice. "Before you two continue with your lover's quarrel, might I ask where someone might find some wrecking sunweed in this *Imperium*-forsaken kingdom?"

He was a few years younger than her father, his black beard speckled with gray. Much like her father, his head, empty of hair, shined as he meandered by the torches. Lines creased the sides of his deep, umber chin, imprints from years of practice in frowning. His coat was covered in a marginally less garish pattern than normal Nuwei clothing. The muted gray and black lines and dots that arbitrarily danced on his clothes matched his stormy mood. He watched Liliana and Aoran with arms crossed and a snarl planted on his face.

The argument on Liliana's tongue disappeared, her mind distracted by the newcomer. Aoran recovered quickly, shaking off the conversation. He plucked his pipe off the ground and presented it to the stranger, a friendly ease returning to his posture. The man eyed the offering suspiciously, slowing reaching out to grab it.

Liliana attempted to collect the fragmented pieces of her anger and force them together into a semblance of decorum. "To what do we owe the pleasure of a Nuwei council member's presence?"

The man scowled at her, walking over to a torch to light the pipe. He sucked in, swirling the air around his mouth while pinning Liliana with a deadpan stare. He coughed out the yellow smoke, his voice harsh. "Had no idea a brat with a mouth like that could also be acquainted with the word 'pleasure.'"

Aoran guffawed, instantly doubling over from laughter. Liliana gaped at the newcomer before quickly closing her mouth, spinning around to escape the training room. Teo, this stranger, Aoran—they were all distracting her when she needed to focus more than ever. She needed to redraw her bow, her arrow straight and true, aiming for what truly mattered.

She didn't need to entertain Aoran's arbitrary calls for justice. She didn't need to argue with strangers. They were tiny things beneath the weight of what was at stake. The first trial was to be announced soon. She needed to be—no, she *would* be—ready. She would prove them all wrong when she led the kingdom into a kind of success and prosperity it had never known before.

She paused, sparing a glance back at Aoran, who was laughing with the stranger. A part of her wished he would look up, erasing the past ten minutes. Of course, he didn't. Liliana continued her march out the door, chin high. She would sooner apologize to Teo than Aoran would stop being an immature imbecile.

The odds of either didn't look so good.

CHAPTER 9
7055.1.18

Elle peeked around the corner of the hallway. More ridiculous statues and pictures but luckily, no people. She spent the past few days being cornered by Aurjnegh diplomats attempting to curry favor, Nuwei councilors trying to gauge her future foreign policy (which, after Liliana's scathing remarks, Elle decided to talk to Renee about to form a more concrete opinion), and Electarians turning their noses up at her. Apparently, their court didn't look too kindly on an upstart challenging the throne right of their prince and princess.

She tried at one point to escape to the kitchen in the subbasement of the castle. Elle thought she might find some kinship among the kitchen staff. Instead, she found droves of busy commoners sweating over fires and stoves, too busy to entertain conversation with the newcomer. She frowned the entire way back to her room. They obviously worked in conditions that didn't tolerate levity.

Elle would attempt to interact with them again at some point. She could hardly fault them for being so engrossed—or enslaved—by their work that they didn't have time for her. Everyone deserved a second chance at connection. Sometimes even a third, or fourth, if circumstances and forgiveness permitted.

There was no point in trying to prepare for the upcoming Trials, whatever they were. Not that Elle didn't care, but there was nothing she could do to prepare for what she knew so little about. There was supposed to be a big announcement to all the candidates the following day, but the amount of time before that wasn't substantial enough to do anything of importance. So instead, Elle explored.

She pranced down the corridor of the tortuous first floor, her shoulders relaxing as she pursed her lips at the passing "art." Try as she might, Elle would never understand these royals.

The busts all looked the same: cracked, marble faces with dead eyes that tracked her as she snuck around the hallway. Elle tried to differentiate between the king of this and councilwoman of that, to no avail. Some sculptor must have made a ton of money making one statue, so they decided to make the same statue for every subsequent commission. Elle almost felt bad for this one, unable to help her giggle as she waltzed past. *Poor Juliana.* The queen's bust was nearly indistinguishable from that of King Wi. It was almost cruel.

The paintings were worse. Elle lingered over each one, admiring them the same way one might a battlefield, with wretched fascination at the scene. The opulent colors that coated each canvas seemed to jump off the wall, intent on wrenching their way down her throat and suffocating her in their vibrant dyes. She shuddered. And this was the *Electarian* court. She could only imagine how horrifyingly ornate the Aurjnegh castle must be. Her heart and back fluttered in unison. She wished she could see the monstrosity herself.

Criticisms aside, Elle loved the grandeur in its own way. It was so interesting, so *new*. She rejoiced in everything unique, loved the strange and obscure. Though her heart ached for places and things much grander than the kingdom, she reveled in trying to unearth the secrets of the castle.

She stopped in front of one particularly heinous piece. Elle coughed her surprise. It showed three naked people wrapped up in one another, their faces thrown back in rabid ecstasy. Elle could almost hear her ma's reprimanding voice. The phantom growl echoed: *Ellegance, look away! Do you think the Gods would approve of such things? I said look away!* Elle snuck one more look, sheer curiosity getting the better of her, before scurrying past.

A faint ache hit her chest as she moved onward. It was the same kind of ache that came with running an old bruise into the side of a table. Elle had been separated from her family for far too long, missing an extension of herself she never realized had become so embedded in her identity. She chewed the inside of her cheek. Without the background of her parents and siblings, who was Elle? In the lonely corridors of the castle, with nobody else around to shape her experiences and behaviors, who was left?

Elle missed them all so much; she would have even settled for her ma coming simply to yell at her. Elle felt that desperate for her family's affections.

The Vitrians were kind, no doubt of that. Renee's exuberance and Kai's warmth provided great company when around Elle. But they typically weren't. The two practically drowned in bureaucratic responsibility. Much as Elle enjoyed the castle and its new sights, she wanted to go home. She wanted to wrestle her siblings on the scratchy carpet of their living room and scare them into doing her chores, like running errands or keeping the oven fire stoked. She wanted to slip through the alleyways of the kingdom and feel the hum of the city race through her bones.

But no. The castle lacked two quintessential things: her family and her freedom. The Electarians allowed her free reign of the castle, yes. But *only* the castle. Its many doors and strange people only offered so many adventures. At the end of the day, her heart cried out to wander. Though Elle had felt stifled within the confines of the city, never in her life had she felt so trapped.

Instead of roaming, she stayed inside the castle walls, throwing hungry looks outside every window that she passed. Each one offered a tantalizing morsel of the outdoors. As far as Elle could tell, guards patrolled the castle at nearly every hour. She passed by a window, her neck craning back longingly before shaking her head. Even her quick feet wouldn't be enough to bound by the three guards stationed immediately beyond the glass.

The necklace from Madame Dragonia's stall bounced against her chest as she slipped through the corridors. She brushed the silver dragon with the side of her finger, clutching the pendant in her warm hand. It began as something beautiful, but now it was something indispensable. The necklace was about the only thing she had control over in her wardrobe.

Elle wore the silken dresses of Electarian royalty, the long skirts constantly getting in her way. Ma wore dresses of a similar style but with fabric that had much more stretch. Though Elle had never felt anything so smooth against her skin, the tightness disallowed much mobility. She mourned the loss of her brother's pants and shirts, scratchy as they were. The maids had peeled Elle's original clothing off her, stiff with sweat and dust, barely concealing their disgust. While one maid forced Elle into the creamy yellow dress, the other held Elle's old clothes an arm's length away to throw it into the fireplace of Elle's room.

She envied the Vitrians and Nuwei, with their flowing and functional clothing. Robes and pants made navigating the world a breeze. The dresses made tripping through the day a newfound torture method.

Every day a different maid entered Elle's chambers, pinning up her choppy, black hair and shoving her arms through the rigid sleeves. She grimaced and waved off hands near her face when she could. Elle wasn't really beautiful by anyone's standards. Her eyes were a bit wide set, her skin spotted in areas where acne scars had left their marks. The maids were convinced that with some rouge and creams, Elle's long face could be rounded, and her thin eyebrows could be thickened. Elle didn't care for the treatments; she wasn't beautiful, and she had no interest in pretending to be.

The maids certainly weren't a talkative bunch—though not for lack of trying on Elle's part. She broached every topic from loaves of bread to the most infamous merchants of the Aisle to even the Gods themselves. It was like Elle was trying to communicate through a glass wall, impenetrable by sound. An intangible *something* separated Elle and these women. Elle couldn't quite place her finger on it, but it gave her a bitter taste.

She laughed to herself, the sound bouncing around in the empty hallway. Or maybe they simply tied their own dresses so tight that they no longer had the air to speak.

Since the day she exposed her back to the world, the royals of the court had stolen her entire life. Overcoming any initial caution surrounding Elle's newcomer status, the royals turned her into a brand-new toy. Elle was novel, shiny, her newfound political importance making her stand out in any room no matter how small she tried to be. Or maybe that was just her height. It didn't matter. Either way, she quickly grew weary of serving as everyone's dinner entertainment.

They laughed at everything she said. Everything! They chuckled at her words, chortled at her stories. They put their hands to their chests, their cheeks pink as they admired how "absolutely charming" she was. After years of Ma and Da yelling at her for her lack of manners, she knew with certainty that "charming" was one of the few things that fell outside the scope of her glittering personality.

Elle stopped in front of a small painting, brushing her hand against the dragon printed on the canvas. It flew on the horizon of the ocean, its scales rolling beneath the sun. The waves reflected the light, glowing against the dragon's ashy stomach. Its wings paused in a downward stroke, rippling with muscle to drive the dragon onward. She wondered to what horizon it flew. That dragon explored edges of the world of which Elle could only dream. Her back gave one warm pulse. Elle yearned to roam wild and free, swooping and diving into the unknown. The Trials, and queenhood, as unlikely as it seemed, offered a tantalizing possibility to turn that fantasy into reality.

More than her own desires, if Elle was queen, she could change everything. The bakery, the house, her siblings' and parents' futures—the world would become malleable in her grip, and she could make everything better for the people she loved. If she were queen, her family would likely move into the castle. No more sharing a crowded space to sleep and no more worrying about rent payments. They would be treated like royalty, a luxury her ma and da deserved after so many years. With that image in her mind, the idea of winning felt so *real*.

Elle shook her head, dismissing the notion. Just because a thing was possible didn't make it plausible. She tried to tie a rope around her heart, keep it from running away unchecked with grand visions. In all likelihood, Elle would lose in the Trials and return to her old life. Back to the bakery and back to the city streets.

She paused, a crown in a case catching her eye as she passed. Its glittering threads spoke of delicate hands and a determined mind. Elle pictured the careful concentration it took to connect each string of material. Unlike the gaudy nature of much of the castle, this complex crown looked simple, and in its simplicity, it was breathtaking. It caught the beam of the torches, pinning fractals of light up against the wall. Her back throbbed, a rush of desire flooding through her body and severing the rope of her rationality.

That was the problem, she thought, running her finger along the casing of the crown. She loved her old life. But a very small, very *loud* part of her wanted nothing more than to win. The dragon on her back burned her, pulsing every time she even thought about wearing the crown. Think of the adventures *then*—every day filled with new people, new countries, new ideas. And she could live at the center of it all, her hand brushing every corner of the world.

Her blood surged. Elle bit her lip, her fingers bent toward the crown. Beat Princess Liliana and Prince Teo. *Elle*, a smooth voice whispered in her mind, *someone must lead this kingdom into the future, must take charge of moving everyone into the unknown. Why not you?*

She squeezed her eyes shut, pulling her fingers away from the display. It was so very difficult to ignore the dragon's roar.

Elle walked farther down the hallway, turning to the right, and immediately yelped. A couple stood in front of her, knotted together in such a way that would have made the earlier painting envious. The man practically swallowed the woman, his height dwarfing hers. *That didn't appear to be stopping them*, Elle thought to herself wildly. They split, breath heavy, cheeks hot. Even though they technically parted, they still clung to one another with a ferocious tenacity. The man's hands seared into the woman's curvy hips, stroking his hands over the hills of her body while he watched her with heavy lids.

The woman slowly turned to eye Elle, her arms draped around the man's neck. She gave Elle a lazy smile as she licked her lips. Centuries of volcanoes and fires filled Elle's cheeks, transforming her face into a color that made blood seem dull. The woman's beauty surpassed her mussed state, her perfect lips and watery, black eyes making Elle's heart skip a beat.

"Well, if it isn't Lady Ellegance, contender for the throne," Eliana drawled, her words slow and sensual, dripping off her tongue like warm honey.

"P-Princess Eliana! That's me. Or, they call me Elle. I don't think we've officially met before. Which, of course, is probably why you called me Ellegance. O-Of course, you can call me Ellegance, if you want!" Eliana's eyes never left Elle as Elle stumbled her way through a battlefield of words, tripping over every trap set forth.

Eliana smirked, one dark eyebrow quirking up as she put her lips close to the man's throat. He breathed heavily, melted copper candy in her hands. "Ellegance suits me just fine. Why do you wander the castle, dear Ellegance? One would think with all the excitement, better things exist with which to pass the time."

Eliana's dark eyes tracked every one of Elle's fidgets with a predatory gaze while she moved the man's hands to her waist, allowing him to pull her even closer. Taller than her by about a hand, he leaned in, desperate just to be closer to the princess. Elle, gradually thawing from her shock, recognized the man's loose robes and pastel colors. Wasn't he one of the Vitrian dignitaries?

If Elle stood close enough, would she tower over the princess in the same way? *Stop, stop, stop.* Not the path of thoughts to follow at the moment.

Elle needed to extract herself from the interaction as soon as possible. Caught between terror, embarrassment, and intrigue, escape seemed more desirable than any woman or crown. She laughed, the sound awkward and forced, and she closed her eyes, desperately wishing to be anywhere but the corridor. Taking a shaky breath, she attempted to conjure some semblance of normalcy within herself.

"The meetings and dinners aren't really for me. The people in the castle talk like they're playing a Dragon and Wolves game." Elle shook her head, eyes still closed. "I was raised by a Vitrian da, so it's not really my style, I suppose." She huffed out a half laugh at herself.

In spite of their inability to be straightforward, Elle still admired the poise and confidence everyone carried. They were a bit like some of the paintings—beautiful and illustrious, their mystery both alluring and a little overwhelming. "In all honesty, I find them intimidating." Elle finally strung the sentence together, like a haphazard pearl necklace. She opened her eyes and met Eliana's amused gaze. The princess's eyes twinkled with mischief and mystery.

"That is the way they tend to be," Eliana murmured, releasing her clawed grasp of the man.

When her hands came off his shoulders, he gasped, appearing to burst forth from a nightmare. He breathed heavily, looking wildly around the room. He said nothing, just clutched his chest and searched in the hallway for something Elle could only guess at.

Eliana stepped quietly toward Elle, her voluptuous figure swaying with every step. Elle considered herself mentally strong. But in that moment, she had a feeling she might pass out.

"Well, if you ever find yourself in need of escape from the drudgery, you may always come and find me." Eliana leaned forward, standing on tiptoe, whispering the last part in Elle's ear.

Her breath blew hot against Elle's neck, the syrupy, caramel scent of her perfume overwhelming. Elle's head grew light, each one of her senses focused on the woman in front of her. The room, the paintings, the statues—everything disappeared behind Eliana's wicked smile and silken words. Forget Elle's plan to leave. Elle was pretty sure she would die right then and there.

The sweet pain of Eliana biting her ear and the sound of her whisking away only registered with Elle long after the princess had gone. Elle eyed the man leaning against the wall, still stirring from his stupor. They both looked like drunks waking up after a long night out. A shiver rushed down Elle's spine. If Teo and Liliana were anything like their sister, she wouldn't need to worry about losing—she wouldn't stand a chance in the first place.

She stumbled out of the hallway, deeper into the castle, her brain sloshing around her head like molasses, sticky, sweet, and slow. Nobody from the royal court acted like that. *Imperium*, nobody from the city acted like that. Though Elle had seen very little of the world, she felt confident that Eliana was one of a kind on all of *Terrabis*.

The boys on the street ran around with the energy of namans, only slightly more house-trained than the beasts themselves. Their waves of energy carried with them hopes of going into the army, a tide of desire to fight for their country. The best of them joined Electaria's finest. The mediocre fell into ranks with the merchants, marching instead to the cacophony of raspy wheedling. The worst landed in fighting houses. Girls typically stayed in the house, learning whatever skill might make them useful. Teach her to bake, to write, to fish—something to support the merchant when he came home as empty-handed as the rest.

The people of Elle's life were snowflakes, drifting from the sky. Perhaps one was different from another, but at the end of the day, they were all still snow. No matter how interesting or unique, their paths followed the same torturous spiral downward before disappearing on the ground. Elle fought against the blizzard, seeking out adventure to keep her afloat. Anything to keep her from falling into the snowdrifts that littered the kingdom. Anything to keep her from being just one of many people who failed at being individuals.

But Eliana was not a snowflake. She was the storm itself.

Passion draped languidly from Eliana's shoulders, clinging tightly to her like the dress that latched onto her curves. Her energy screamed control and somehow purred with rawness. Eliana wore her personality with confidence. Despite seeing the passion, the energy, the confidence, Elle couldn't put a single word to Eliana's personality. The Princess Eliana who waved at dignitaries with a sweet smile on her face was not the same succubus that just melted Elle's brain. A shiver again ran through her body. Elle sent a quick prayer up to *Viribus*. Should she ever run into the princess again, she would need as much strength as she could get.

Elle gulped in a deep breath of air; today was officially too much for her heart to handle. She looked up, and the emotional exhaustion creeping through her brain was immediately dispelled. She yelped at the picture in front of her, her shoulders jerking up and her knees buckling, making her smaller within seconds. Eliana stared right back at her with dismissive black eyes from the canvas.

Except it wasn't Eliana. Elle caught her breath, mentally chiding herself for being so shaken. Eliana warranted caution, not fear. Elle studied the picture, feeling as though the clouds that had wrapped her head had lifted, dissipating into the stale air of the room. No, not Eliana—the nameplate read Queen Juliana.

She took a step back, her heels sinking into the plush of the carpet. Elle bit back a curse; bakers didn't bother with such inconvenient footwear. Beautiful carpets covered the entire palace, but the maroon beneath her feet looked like wool just shaved from the sheep. Silence smothered the room like a lid on a pot, squelching any boiling activity that happened therein. Thorny black torches allowed Elle to see but only by squinting. Instead of another room in the castle, it felt more like a shrine.

Though the walls were simple, the gigantic pictures that lined them more than made up for that fact. Rows of faces glared down at her, giving Elle the distinct impression that she wasn't welcome. She pictured spirits standing beside each of their respective portraits, stewing with ideas on how to get rid of Elle, the intruder. Elle decided the risk of staying was still less than that of leaving the room and running into Eliana again.

"Hello?" Elle asked into the darkness, unsure whether she wanted anyone to answer her. Like pesky dust mites, the shadows of the room swept away Elle's bright voice. A bud of interest planted in her heart. Though the room crawled with ominousness, it didn't scare Elle so much as it intrigued her.

"I hope I'm not breaking any rules. If I am, tell me now." She paused, waiting for any kind of sign. Her heart leaped, squeezing out a staccato beat. She took the lack of response as a tacit agreement from any spirits and turned back to the painting of Queen Juliana.

Elle wracked her brain, folding her lips together as she held her arms, trying to locate the piece of her mind that remembered the significance of the name. Her memory looked a lot like its own city. She walked through its streets, a familiar stroll, searching for thoughts and images she hid in its buildings. A translucent version of herself pushed open a door, idly meandering around a room before a statue at the side of the room of a man—or woman, all the *Imperium* forsaken statues looked the same—caught her eye. Her city of memories melted away.

The image of the bust from earlier appeared in her mind, and Elle laughed incredulously, the sound filling the room in the same way that a single drop of water filled a bathtub. The walls absorbed her amusement, giving her back nothing but the impervious silence of monarchs past. Elle put her hand against the painting, the waxy oils rubbing against her hand, leaving a faint residue.

Queen Juliana's likeness to Eliana was uncanny. Elle's brain itched, settling on a memory. Elle vaguely remembered learning in class about the woman and was pretty sure Juliana was Eliana and Liliana's grandmother. "Turn Eliana's soft arms into willowy branches and have the painter draw deep frown lines down the princess's chin, and *etiam*, you would have a perfect replica," Elle whispered to herself, eyes wide.

Though the woman fascinated Elle, the background grew to be much more interesting. Instead of being embossed against a dark background like the other portraits, the queen appeared to have had her portrait sketched in the middle of one of the city's markets. People posed in the background, skeletons of the real world. They sold goods, hurried past, cleaned streets, their positioning stiff and awkward. Elle's mouth quirked into a smile. Somebody must have paid Electarian nobility to pose for those; real people would never look so unnatural living their lives.

Except, the people couldn't have represented Electarians. Each one wore their clothing to expose their marks, neglecting the modest, sleek fashion of the kingdom. Her eyes trailed around the painting, counting quietly to herself. *Superbia, Vitria, Caecus, Menda*…each God represented in black on the common people in this market. Why show off the marks if they hadn't completed their Walk yet?

One more figure watched from the street, no expression on his face and no mark on his body. Elle peered closer, wrinkling her nose. In fact, he appeared to be completely naked. Despite this, he was the only one in the painting, the queen included, that did not look totally out of place. It was as if a painter had accidentally dropped them in the wrong masterpiece. He had the silver irises of the Soj.

The queen's shoulder blocked the lower half of his torso, but Eliana saw no *Menda* mark on his forearm, no mark of *Caecus* on his hand, no *Superbia* mark on his heart, and no mark of *Viribus* on his shoulder. She pressed her lips together again, an uncomfortable feeling tugging at her. Everyone was born with a mark. Everyone had a patron God. Elle's eyebrows furrowed, and she tore her eyes away from the man, feeling deeply unsettled.

"But why this background?" Elle thought aloud, trying to divert her thoughts while taking a step back from the painting.

"She wanted to show the juxtaposition," a voice echoed from behind her. Elle whipped around, the bud of excitement blossoming into a flower of thrill and fear. Spirits! The thought fluttered away as her eyes traced the corpulent frame of something distinctly human. She tried hard not to look as disappointed as she felt.

King Leo walked toward her, regarding the painting with an unreadable expression. "She wouldn't let anyone be painted with a golden mark. She wanted people to be able to make the direct comparison—the superior versus the inferior."

"Your Majesty!" Elle bowed down, her back crying out from the quick drop. Her da lectured her in her head, his rocking Vitrian accent stern: *Elle, when you meet the important ones, you bow. When you meet the real important ones, you bow until your nose hits the floor,* etiam? Her face hovered a few inches from the floor, the clean smell of castle carpet tickling her nose. She figured that was low enough.

"Rise, child. Who knows? I may need to bow to you in the coming weeks." King Leo chuckled, the lines beside his eyes wrinkling together. Elle slowly rose, her smile growing easily in return, the way a flower responds to the sun. He nodded toward the painting. "Do you know who this woman is?"

"Queen Juliana," Elle responded, confident. Teachers had paintings of monarchs hung up and down classrooms and hallways, but they all blurred together into one vaguely royal face. She drooped a little bit after speaking. "Though, honestly, Your Majesty, I can't remember the specifics about her. I usually slept in civi classes. More than that, the class was at least eight years ago."

The king erupted in uproarious laughter. His stomach jiggled, and his hands squeezed his sides. He took to the pose like a dying fish took to the sea—familiar, natural, and most importantly, necessary. King Leo was a temple, purposeless without the praise of laughter. The dim lights brightened, the shadows curling in on themselves in the corners. Even the paintings looked less stern. Elle watched King Leo, admiration shining in her violet eyes.

"Your honesty is refreshing. Very Vitrian of you, *etiam*?" King Leo winked at her, obviously having noticed her slightly taller frame. Her chest warmed; even if Liliana decreed her family had no Vitrian customs, her father apparently retained more of his heritage than he let on. It made Elle feel as if she was only out of place for her upbringing, not her heritage to boot.

"If I may, what did she do?" The question dropped out of Elle's mouth before she remembered to add any formalities. She tacked on sloppily at the end: "Your Majesty."

The king waved her off, his beard rustling against his clothing with each shake of his head. "Queen Juliana, ruler of Electaria. She bolstered the military, created economic prosperity in new ways with other nations, and made Electaria into a kingdom to behold. The dragon of foreign policy, snake of the trade deal. Made of steel, resolute and firm. My late wife."

Elle nodded along politely—hopefully politely—up until that point. A profound horror dawned on Elle then. Not only had she mistaken the late queen's bust for that of a man, but she told the widower to his face she knew so little about the woman. Elle moaned to herself, sending silent, voracious prayers up to the Gods. She pictured *malum* watching her from her cracked throne, licking her lips as Elle inched closer to her damning grasp.

Her mortification must have been evident because King Leo hastily followed with, "It has been many years since she passed. I am sure you were much younger when the ordeal happened. There is no reason you should have knowledge of her."

Somewhere in Elle's city of memories, she remembered the funeral. Elle had been around twelve at the time. The kingdom had dressed in its mourning reds, *malum's* favorite color, in an attempt to drive the evil God's attention away from the spirit as it traveled to live with the Gods. But Elle and her parents had been slaving over an open fire the entire week, having been commissioned to bake for the many royal gatherings that followed such an event. The smell of copper candy lingered in her mind much stronger than the death.

Elle attempted to circumvent the historical piece, asking tentatively, "Do you miss her much?"

King Leo's face turned thoughtful, his mouth scrunching up as he squinted at the ceiling. Liliana's description of her parent's marriage sat in Elle's memory, a reminder that the princess grew up confident in the belief that marriage was, at its core, a transaction. Eventually, King Leo shrugged his shoulders, reminding Elle of the way her mother looked when her da accidentally burned a loaf of bread. *These things happen.* She never thought the phrase applied to wives.

"I miss her leadership terribly. Making decisions for an entire kingdom can be quite difficult, as you have probably imagined." He stared at the queen's stern face, searching for answers the strict portrait refused to give.

Probably, Elle thought absentmindedly. Memories of her ma and da arguing over the queen and king drifted across her mind, vague dandelions from times when Elle was more focused on wrangling the twins or taking Penelope to school. Though Elle couldn't remember the specifics, she could remember the tone, like a skeleton left without any muscle or skin. Her parents rarely approved of the decisions made by Electaria's monarchs. She wondered if the difficulty in leading lay in accommodating to people like her parents or simply dealing with their repudiation when things went awry.

For the first time since entering the room, the king looked less like a puppy in an old body and more like an ancient Stone Tree, its roots sinking into the earth. Weariness dragged his shoulders down with leaden claws, leaving its cavernous mark as he beheld the room. Elle cocked her head. In front of the towering portraits, King Leo looked much shorter. She didn't recognize the expression on his wrinkled face.

"Power is a lot like lenses, I'm afraid." He sighed, averting his gaze to the floor. "The effect is not immediate because as you age and your eyesight worsens, the magister makes the lens stronger. With councils and the like, you can take corrective measures as a monarch for a long while. But that only works to a point.

Because even the magister, servant to the Gods, cannot fix your eyes themselves. I am afraid many kings and queens leave the crown blind."

Queen Juliana frowned at the pair, overshadowing every person behind her. The men and women worked in the background, their very lives made insignificant by her crown and the mark on her back. Did she see the people in the background? Or was she blind, her eyes so focused on the horizon and the future that she failed to see what lay right next to her? One of the men in the painting wore baker's garb. A hollow feeling settled over Elle's chest, as if somebody reached in with a spoon and ladled out her mood, one scoop at a time.

"And how do you feel?" she whispered, unable to tear her eyes from the baker. Her back ached, tearing and pleading with her. "How weak will your eyes be when you leave the throne?"

He glanced back up at Elle, smiling the smallest smile. The golden mark, exposed on his forearm, glowed a little bit brighter. "Queen Juliana's actions taught me many things. Her inaction taught me many more, not the least of which, to carry a stick in front of me everywhere I go. Then it matters less how blind I may be. I may be helpless to change what I feel before me, but I will know it's there." He lost himself in his wife's picture, his countenance hard with a strange grief. "At the very least, I will know something is there."

CHAPTER 10
7055.1.19

"The naman rifling around in Prince Teo's ass is more active than usual," Je complained, fussing with his hair. The perfect coif of curls remained in place, its strength surpassing that of Je's fidgeting fingers.

Aoran internally rolled his eyes. The hair's stubbornness still failed to exceed that of a particular princess.

"Impossible," Dayanara declared, leaning back on her forearms. "The Gods could never create one of those animals that could make him even more uptight."

The Four were technically on a noon break. Such breaks were supposed to be reserved for food and not much else. Aoran, Dayanara, and Je took a more liberal approach to the concept.

Aoran sucked in the lingering smoke from his pipe, breathing it out slowly through his nostrils. The yellow wisps danced along his sleeves, a familiar friend. The Captain's harangues and Liliana's disapproving snipes were nothing compared to the feeling. Habit, addiction—whatever word they chose to use didn't matter. Different songs with the same refrain still sounded like music to his ears.

The sickeningly sweet smoke razed his throat, caressing every nerve ending in his body and soothing them, one by one.

He hummed absentmindedly to himself, letting the gentle touch of the sunweed pluck out his negative thoughts, replacing them with its own distinct brand of comfort. For the first time in the month of Impe, he relaxed. "Princess Liliana hasn't been nearly as nightmarish as usual." Aoran offered the pipe to the group.

Dayanara plucked it from his hands, taking a drag. "You sound disappointed," she coughed out, voice raspy as she passed the pipe to Je.

Je, defeated, dropped his hands to his sides and sucked in the smoke with the sulky features of a reprimanded toddler. He presented it to Ro, who responded with a blank stare. Je sighed, somehow managing to look even more pitiful, and passed the pipe back to Aoran.

"The same way a mother is disappointed when her colicky child finally falls asleep. I'm *not*." Aoran laughed. "For the first time in a while, I am finally at peace." He closed his eyes and let out a sigh. The statement held a pinch of the truth anyway.

He ignored the way his heart hissed at him. Aoran hushed the tiny rattlesnake, locking it back in its cage, content to let it shake the bars. Pitiful thing, really. Like all small serpents, his heart believed itself to be bigger than it was. Caught up in its own venomous selfishness, it tended to forget who was truly in charge. It forgot how easy it was to let his mind do the talking instead. What need did he have for such a creature in his life?

Je and Dayanara chuckled with him, elbowing him in the ribs. Aoran smiled and jostled the others around, the playful wrestling of wolf pups who just grew in their teeth. Aoran rolled around, his hands grappling Je's shoulders as Dayanara jumped on top of them, knocking everybody to the ground. Her face glowed, breathless and alight. Je took advantage of the opportunity, rolling away and pouncing on her once more with a hearty cackle. Aoran backed off, feeling the sunweed's brief presence melt away.

Ro watched the ground with empty eyes, motionless with the intensity of the sea before a storm. Despite having fought side by side in battles and assassination attempts, he never joined the roughhousing.

Aoran sometimes found himself longing for that kind of silence. Better that than the sound of insincere words. Some part of him *was* disappointed. Since their argument, Liliana appeared with a tumultuous fervor, sparring with Aoran and taking all his instructions with tight lips. He couldn't tell who she was most angry with—Teo, Aoran, or herself. Every time he attempted to instigate an argument, she settled back into the Mordercus offensive stance, attacking him before he could provoke her. He never realized how much the conversations between them meant to him until they were slashed to bits by wooden swords and spears.

It wasn't even that she ignored him. Liliana registered everything he said, her eyes flashing and shifting, every withheld emotion channeled into those clear, hazel windows. She simply focused all the anger and the energy she had into training. She grew stronger, more confident in her strikes. Their friendship grew brittle, a fragile chrysalis of its former cocoon.

He envied the followers of *Menda*, the lucky *malums* that said whatever they thought simply because of their God. *Caecus*'s people sought wisdom above all else, allowing for clarity. Those who followed *Superbia* knew their strengths and weaknesses, understood the people around them, gracing them with total confidence and clarity of social orders. Aoran groaned to himself. He'd kill for any of those things right now.

Instead, he followed *Viribus*. The wolf on his shoulder, electrifying and golden, served as a constant reminder that above all else, he had to be strong. Being strong meant keeping uncertainties to himself. Being strong meant freezing feelings and leaving them for dead. Being strong sometimes meant being somebody that Aoran had no desire to be.

Aoran turned abruptly to Je, grabbing him by the shoulder and hauling him off Dayanara. "I need you to hit me."

Je paused, laughing for a second before registering Aoran's face. Apparently whatever gaze he leveled with his green eyes was enough to make the man pause. "Wait, really?"

Aoran nodded. He opened his mouth to say something, perhaps a better explanation, but Je's fist crashing into his cheek stopped him. A fierce pain erupted from his face, his mouth and teeth throbbing. He stuck his finger into his mouth, pulling it out to find it covered in blood. He presented the finger to Je, waiting for an explanation for his friend's immediate and destructive reaction.

Je shrugged. "You looked serious. Figured it would require a serious punch to wipe that dumb wrecking expression off your face. You're better off when you just mess around."

Ah, the sweet words of wisdom. Life was much simpler when he contained his thoughts within the borders of serving the kingdom and wreaking havoc in whatever time was left to spare. He grinned at Je, his fangs flashing. "Je, your consistent ineptitude had me fooled for most of our friendship. Is it possible that you are...smart?"

"Let's not get crazy ideas, now." Dayanara snorted, rolling on her stomach and giving the pair pointed looks. "Since day one you two have been some of the dumbest *malums* I've ever met."

"Shit, remember that?" Je exclaimed, shaking his head. His hair and head moved together, not even one follicle straying from the gelatinous mass.

"That was back when we were wrecking fifteen. Before we were even the Four. And back when Daya still sort of looked like a woman. I miss those days." He sighed, casting Daya a wistful glance.

Dayanara cocked her head, nonplussed. She raised her eyebrows, her sharp chin jutting out. It was the sly type of look only privateers and smugglers could give, full of mystery and adventure. "And yet, even with all my mannish charm, I still get more ass than you and Lady Aoran over here," she said, and she ignored their feeble protests of "not enough time" and "Aurjnegh women are better anyway."

She ran a hand through her tuft of hair, her features wicked and taunting. "Plus, unlike you two *malums*, I actually know how to please a woman."

"I always find it interesting how exactly you all choose to waste your time instead of training to live up to your woefully overblown reputations," a voice said.

Dayanara's face slipped into horror, the inevitability of her demise written on her face in stark ink. Aoran knew that face. He used to see it on the people of the streets when they saw a storm rumbling toward the kingdom. He used to see it on maids' faces when Queen Juliana was in a particularly foul mood. Aoran couldn't remember the last time he felt that unique brand of anxiety and terror churning venomously in his stomach. He could never forget the feeling itself, though. She turned around, throwing her forehead to the ground at the Captain's feet.

The Captain slammed her foot down next to one of Dayanara's hands, leering over the woman, her features drawn in utter disgust. "Get off the floor. You are a soldier of the Four. Act like it."

Dayanara flushed, scrambling to her feet. Aoran snickered, making a poor attempt at disguising it with a cough. There was about as much sincerity in the effort as a young follower of *Menda*—someone who manipulated the truth instead of living by it.

The Captain's eyes flashed. She marched over to Aoran, raised her back hand, and snapped it forward. His face crumpled beneath her blow, strengthened by an arm experienced in disciplining soldiers.

Aoran held his throbbing cheek, the mark on his shoulder buzzing alongside. *Fight,* it hissed. The same voice that used to purr to him when he prowled shoeless in the streets of Electaria. The same voice that growled the second they threw him in the military's fight rink to claw for his battalion placement. He gritted his teeth, keeping his eyes trained on the ground. Years of being screamed at by the woman in front of him held his tongue. Years of yelling with Liliana nearly let it loose.

The Captain put her face into his, a snarl on her lips. "Is there something funny about this imbecile shaming the station you all so precariously hold? Or is her embarrassment somehow the reason behind the wrecking smirk on your face?" She punctuated the word with such ferocity that she spit in his face.

The acidic smell of armor cleaner burned his nose, making his eyes water. *Fight*, it roared. Aoran closed his eyes and breathed a slow, quiet stream of air through his nose. He opened them, meeting her eyes, his green gaze the cool patience of a full moon. "No, Captain."

That voice whispering the word "fight" had taught him many things. It taught him how to command fear, his name a wary whisper on the lips of those who roamed the streets. It taught him how to capture respect, his sickle swords a symbol of power in the ranks of the soldiers.

More than anything else, though, it taught him that fighting and winning required as much strength as standing and doing nothing at all.

Her flared nostrils retracted, her cold fury tampered by his acquiescence. The Captain studied him, as if waiting for his composure to shatter like glass, jagged and terrible.

He kept his fists at his side, his eyes focused on the wall at the end of the room. He squashed any pride, any anger, any feeling that wasn't obedience, leaving himself a void waiting to be filled with a command. Aoran was a lot of things. Handsome, charismatic, gifted beyond reasonable imagination—but before all that, he was a soldier. He had enough pride in that title to stay silent.

Queen Juliana was the first one to teach him that lesson. She originally found his roguish nature charming; who wouldn't? She scooped him up from the riffraff of Electaria, putting a sword in one hand and a pen in the other. She cultivated him, firing the kiln, smoothing her hands over the unsavory and roughest parts of his personality. He could never tell what exactly she saw in him that she didn't in the others, but he was never stupid enough to inquire and make her question the decision that saved his life.

And, of course, the second he started to think he was special, she cut his confidence to ribbons, wielding knives of serrated truth.

She reminded him at age fourteen, the first and only day he snarked back at her, and each time he saw her thereafter until her death that his purpose was to put the country's existence above his own. If he started to believe he was worth a damn, he would no longer be worth shit to her.

With such a mother, it was a wonder Liliana turned out to be the delightful sugar puff she was, he thought to himself as the Captain redirected her attention. He let out the tiniest breath of air, his shoulders relaxing. He rolled his neck slightly, his fingers twitching for his pipe, his arms aching for a fight. Something to help his mind fade into goo, even if temporarily—he had used entirely too much brainpower for one afternoon.

She turned on her heel, striding over to behold Je and Ro. "Do you two have anything to say about all this nonsense?"

They adopted Aoran's strategy of hush. Well, Ro's strategy, he supposed. Aoran had to give credit where credit was due. His need for one of his habits nudged harder at him, making him curl his fingers into fists. The Captain, satisfied by that day's psychological torture session, faced all of them, her face pinched and severe. They braced themselves for a tirade, sure to include a dash of duty, a splash of nationalism, and a generous helping of fear.

Instead, she raised one eyebrow, her tone clipped. "I find it absolutely fascinating that you four idiots are still standing here like a group of useless Stone Trees instead of guarding your charges."

Aoran escaped from the room before anybody else had moved. He whisked his way through the palace, a shadow against the walls. The only sound he left in his wake was the faint whipping sound of his swords swinging back and forth. Despite having to sprint up three flights of stairs to make it to the royal chamber floor, Aoran made it in record time, spurred by his adrenaline. As he crept his way over to Liliana's room, the itch scraping beneath his skin slowly subsided. He brought up his fist to knock on her door. Had he not had years of near-death experiences under his belt, the voice that interrupted him might have made him jump.

"You're late. Let's go," his sugar-filled princess snapped at him from behind.

Imperium towered next to her, an obsidian wall of fur and fangs. Aoran passed the princess, giving the wolf a scratch under the chin. It tilted its head up, a content rumble shuddering through its body. At least *somebody* was happy to see him.

"As a great philosopher once said, 'Time is relative,'" he said. But as Liliana started her march down to the throne room, his excuse caught in his throat as he jogged to catch her. "So as much as I may have been late, you may have very well been too early. I suppose we'll never know either way."

She shot him a dark glower but otherwise said nothing. A maid had pinned Liliana's walnut hair against her head, all strands pulled away from her face. Her cheekbones seemed to stretch higher when none of her locks bounced around her face. Liliana had discarded her typical dress, swapping it instead for a long black tunic with a sweeping, golden cloak. She sported black pants and black boots with golden inlay. She even wore a sword at her side, its hilt intertwined with white and gold vines.

Aoran made a noise in his throat. She looked like the female version of Teo. He had a feeling she would not appreciate it very much if he chose to voice this thought. A ghost of his fanged smile flashed across his face. That being said, he never much cared whether or not she appreciated his commentary.

"Princess, you have to tell me who you have doing your wardrobe," he enthused, grabbing the bottom of her cape and giving it a playful tug. "What you're wearing seems to be all the rage nowadays—why, I believe I saw Prince Teo wearing the same thing just the other day."

Her eye twitched. Princess Liliana paused, turning to Aoran, fire burning in her hazel eyes. "Aoran, as cute as your whole routine is, I really need you to shut the wreck up today." Her voice was low and intense, leaping like the main hearth that burgeoned to warm the entire castle. "*Imperium* help me, I'm going to win this whole damn thing, and I do not need your shit."

The grin on Aoran's face was full-fledged and undeniable now. He loved when people tripped into traps he never meant to lay. "You think it's cute?"

She opened her mouth, seemed to think better of it, and continued stomping down the hall, considerably less poised than moments before. It comforted him, in an odd way. He walked behind her, a pleasant skip in his step. If he could no longer torture Liliana, the easiest person to set off in Electaria, he would have had to seriously sharpen his skills.

* * *

Aoran and Liliana arrived at the grand doors of the throne room without incident. Aoran's eyes strayed to the golden wolf on the top left of the white door, his own mark buzzing faintly in response. Despite having visited the throne room a million times, he always caught himself staring at his mark. Strength. Depending on the day, that wolf could feel like a reminder of his duty or a warning should he fail. Imperium plopped down on his belly in the hallway, his snout peeking through the door.

Whispers burst through the room as the pair entered. Like the skin of a cooking turkey, the aroma of gossip popped through the room: the princess's wolf—the one she named after *Imperium*, for *Imperium*'s sake. The disrespect. She was a prodigious education councilor and had passed plenty of reforms in her fledgling tenure. However, small councils like that were where smart people born last were always thrown in order to prove their worth. But she wanted to be *queen*? Aoran caught the dubious looks they threw each other. Liliana held her tongue and ignored the heady scent of idle prattle.

Aoran bowed, his low ponytail skimming against the back of his uniform. He stopped at the waist, holding the pose for two seconds before rising again. Electarian royals and their ridiculous customs. He would never understand why the angle at which one bent their back and stuck out their ass could spark such offense.

Liliana kissed her fingers, pressing them to the fabric that covered his mark, her features impervious. His shoulder buzzed with electricity. Liliana was fire and flame but never so much as when she turned his blood into lava itself.

She took her place with Teo, who already stood at the dais, his hands clasped in front of him. The silence between them was awkward, uncomfortable. It sank iron hooks into the mood of the room, dragging the excitement into a murky and tense abyss. Aoran snorted, walking over to a wall of the room to observe the day's proceedings. The miry air between the two could have given *malum* new torture ideas for her unlucky victims.

Aoran posted himself in front of one of the many torches that dominated the walls of the palace. Just outside the gentle touch of the torch, he glided into the shadows, melting against the wall until he was nothing more than another piece of the backdrop.

The throne room that awed him as a child brought dread to his heart now. It meant long meetings and standing around, waiting for calamities that never came to fruition. The guards were drawn bows with no arrows—taut and ready, but utterly pointless. The opulence that awed foreign guests and brought petitioning citizens to their knees failed to impress him, so instead he focused on the people.

Je walked into the room, a pond of calmness. Pond in the sense that on the surface he appeared professional and ready, but Aoran knew, life and chaos teemed beneath the steady shores. Aoran saw the heavy rise and fall of his chest, the undone button on the top of his uniform. Clearly the meeting with the Captain earlier had rattled the poor man. Aoran sniggered to himself as Je found his way to an opposite corner of the room, his eyes on Teo.

"Captain won't be happy," Aoran mouthed to Je when his friend finally looked across the room.

Je drew a slow thumb across his throat, gesticulating very obviously to the crossbow at his hip. In smaller settings, the archer traded his war bow for a more close-ranged weapon. Aoran couldn't exactly read his lips, but the premise of "I will murder you" felt pretty obvious. Aoran caressed his own swords tenderly in response.

Before Je responded, the room slowly fell quiet, the same way the maids of the castle peacefully passed out after a night of drinking wine and giggling with one another. The king strolled in, his features jovial and his cheeks rubicund. Aoran liked to think *Menda* swiped his thumb over Leo's cheeks as a blessing, leaving the man a perennial rogue from simply knowing everyone's truths.

The large empress of Vitria flowed in behind him like a tsunami, graceful and terrible all at once. Her mouth quirked upward on the verge of a smile as she sank into a chair staged for her on the dais.

Aoran raised his eyebrows, watching the young female contestant hop behind her. She had a long face, her arms and legs thin and on the lanky side. Compared to someone like Eliana, the girl was basically a scarecrow without the stuffing. She stood up a little bit straighter than she had that first day and had violet eyes that gleamed beneath the lights of the throne room. She took her place at the front, a faint smile on her face and her features bright.

Je caught Aoran's eyes, pointing to the girl and slicing his thumb across his throat once more. This time, though, his features were drawn in pity. Aoran's heart twanged but he had to agree. Her effervescence next to the palpable intensity of Teo and Liliana made her look like a snow beetle in front of a blizzard.

The king stood to the side, and a young magister rose to her feet. She strode to the front before speaking, her voice filling the space to the rafters, the projection effortless. "Thank you, King Leo, for letting me speak today." The magister's Vitrian accent rocked over the words, rising and falling on the different enunciations.

Aoran closed his eyes. Listening to Vitrians made him nauseous.

"As a representative of the House, it is my honor to be here with you all today. To the Nuwei, the Vitrians, the Aurjnegh, the Electarians, and the Soj"—there was an intake of breath from the audience at her address of the Soj; *Imperium's* sake, Aoran wrecking hated politics "—it is an honor to play a role in these ancient traditions as the Gods pick our new ruler."

"New Leader—try to give Vitria a better trade deal this time, *etiam*?" Empress Renee shouted from the dais.

The younger girl's tinkling laugh rippled in response. Liliana looked annoyed. Aoran grinned. *Ah, universal order restored,* he thought.

"King Leo has graciously allowed me to introduce the format of the Trials. There will be five in total, each one honoring one of our Gods. You will have two days between Trials to prepare, allowing for a brief time of prayer to each God, if you so choose. In the second Trials ever recorded, both participants prayed every single day of the competition." The young magister eyed the three contestants meaningfully, and Aoran held in a snicker.

"The rules of each trial are determined based on a collaborative effort between the House and the participating foreign dignitaries. We will base rules on existing precedents and divine guidance from the Gods." She looked upward and murmured a brief prayer, which the audience followed with varying levels of fervor.

Focusing back on the audience, she continued in her dizzying accent: "There will be a scoring system based upon your respective performance in each Trial. The foreign dignitary conducting the Trial alongside a representative from the House will calculate your score after each Trial. A perfect score in a single round will constitute one point, adding up to four points in total, for the first four Trials. However, being that this competition is ultimately a dedication to *Imperium* herself, success in her Trial will be worth two points.

"As a loyal follower of *Menda*, I am honored to announce the rules of the first Trial, dedicated to *Menda's* name."

Liliana closed her eyes, the lines of her body tense. Aoran was sure if he walked over and poked any part of her, the bands holding her together would snap in half.

"In two days' time, the candidates will meet in the House of the Magisters. One by one, the candidates will undergo a series of private questioning. Chosen for their understanding of *Menda's* path and the political environment in which you may enter,

Empress Renee of Vitria and King Leo of Electaria will administer the first Trial.

"The premise of the Trial is simple: tell the truth. Your performance will be gauged entirely on this factor. A country is not a *gambling chip*. Bluffing is not how alliances are won or how peace is maintained. A leader must be honest and forthright. This Trial will determine your ability to do so. And be careful how you answer," she smiled, "for the *Menda*'s chosen pair will know if you lie. I wish every candidate the best of luck for the first Trial."

The magister nodded toward the candidates before walking away from the dais. Liliana opened her eyes, her gaze steely. Nobody left the room, their mutters rising into loud chattering. Aoran turned to the door, uninterested in seeing the bigwigs drool over one another as they attempted to curry favor and incite rumors about what was to come.

Liliana appeared to be in a heated conversation with Eliana, his only indication being the red flush across Liliana's face. Eliana beamed at her sister, her hands folded primly in front of her. Dayanara watched the two with careful eyes, obviously on edge from the Captain's treatment earlier. He nodded to her, slipping through the throngs of people to the door. At least he could pet Imperium while Dayanara prevented assassinations.

Aoran came up to the door, pausing as he heard voices arguing. His blood spiked and his mark pounded. *Fight.* He pressed his back against the door, pretending to observe the room as he listened to the conversation.

"...She can't rule a nation. *Caecus* ripped me from my wrecking bed to tell you that simple fact. Completing her Walk is different. She can get the gold without the silver. If that girl gets the helm, the state will be dead as soon as she puts the ridiculous-looking crown on her head," a coarse voice like frayed yarn said.

A rich voice replied, running like velvet over Aoran's ears. "And how do you propose she finish her Walk without winning the trials?"

"*That* is not my wrecking job. That is for you to figure out, dear friend." The first voice dripped with false sympathy.

"This is why none of the other Guides talk to you anymore, *malum*," the second growled back.

Aoran's brain stopped. Guides? He barked a laugh to himself, attracting the concerned stare of a few people in the back of the room. Guides were myths, legends made up by people seeking divine intervention to help them complete their Walk when their moral ineptitude proved too strong. It was a story made up for the hopeless, the elderly whose bodies were still stained with black marks, the wayward youth with no clear future. They were *stories*.

Aoran stepped into the hallway, closing the doors behind him, his mouth open and ready to question the conversationalists. The words caught in his throat, staying there with a suffocating pressure as he looked at the only two things in the hallway that could have been the source of those voices. The Nuwei representative from the other day in the training arena, his features pinched and grouchy. And Imperium?

The man from Nuwei stopped and looked at Aoran, taking in his pale, shocked features. He looked at Imperium and back at Aoran. Aoran stayed frozen, unsure of what to do. With a loud sigh, the Nuwei representative reached forward and grabbed Aoran's arm, hauling him fully into the hallway. Aoran's mark buzzed, and his senses took over. He whipped out one of his swords, its hilt catching the knife aimed for his throat.

The Nuwei representative sneered at him over the blade. "So, *malum*, what did you hear?"

INTERLUDE
SEVEN YEARS AGO

The scratch of lead on wood ground against his eardrums, a tenacious *scritch, scritch, scritch* buzzing through his skull. It was worse than the shrieking sound of a rusted saw slicing into stone. One after another, the din of writing congregated around his head. Every time he attempted to block out the sound of one pencil, three more sounds happily replaced it with their own distinct drone.

He squeezed the edge of his desk, grimacing to the floor. Having a ferocious naman taking up residence in his brain and destroying each cell might have been preferable to the unending and insufferable sound of note-taking. He took a deep breath, the pressure in his head clearing momentarily as the feeling of fresh air fought against the injustice of noise.

The sweet smell of flowers wafting in from outside nearly offset the gnats of discordance. The classrooms were separated from the rest of the House, liberated from the suffocating chains of its incense. Their open windows allowed for the garden's perfumes to be enjoyed without involuntarily gagging from the perennial smoke in which the House drowned itself. These classrooms saved the students from olfactory torment. The average worshipper was not so lucky. If anything, the self-inflicted torture required to pray proved the city's unyielding devotion to its Gods time and time again.

"And what did the Gods spend the first hundred years doing?" the Head Magister droned on, his voice so unimaginably dull it could have put a Stone Tree to sleep.

"Building civilization!"

"Teaching their followers!"

The exceptionally enthusiastic sycophants continued to offer suggestions, the same words packaged in different ways. The Gods spent the first hundred years creating the world as everybody knew it. The next hundred years fighting *malum*. The last hundred years they devoted to creating marks for their people and placing Guides on *Terrabis*, leaving residuals of their heavenly presence so humanity might still follow their ways. A lesson taught to every child in the Electarian school system and a story hammered into the brains of magisters in training. He put his head down on his desk. It hurt his head to discuss the same story they practically bathed children in as babes. He was too old for this.

"Very good!"

The genuine sound of pride made him hurt even more. The brightest minds were said to be fostered within these walls. Was this really the best they had to offer?

"And what about the next hundred years?"

And so on and so forth. They stumbled through the timeline of the religion that served as the foundation of their universe, as if its history were some new, recently discovered gem. The disappearance of the Guides, the division of the nations based on differences in culture and belief systems, the emergence of the House—basically a how-to guide for their faith, should anybody truly want to try the whole thing over again. His lower lip stuck out in a near pout. He would not be sad to see his classroom days over.

"Cae, have you finished copying down what I said?" The Head Magister's voice cut through his musings with a whip's force.

Cae arranged his face into what he assumed was something sincere. "O'course, *vici*."

A gentle wind licked past his skin as the Head Magister approached Cae, the man's footsteps heavy and uneven against the floor. Cae imagined an uneven gait and a crotchety man, older even than Cae, equal parts frustrated with his students and his own life. Cae felt that distinctly human pressure and heat against his forehead as the man leaned over.

"Then why is your paper blank?" he rumbled.

Cae smiled in the man's general direction, his blue eyes staring ahead. "Aye, so it is! Seems as though ya spent the hour talking without sayin' a thing, *vici*. Very nice!" Cae lowered his voice conspiratorially, still talking loud enough for everyone in the class to hear. "Ya know, the great *Caecus* once said: 'A man who talks with nothin' to add is the same man that spits inta the flour to bake his bread.'"

A pause, and then the man hissed, spit flecking against Cae's face like the spray of the ocean. "I believe you are done in this class for the day. Tyn will escort you back to your room."

"I see I'm not wanted." Cae paused for a heartbeat before bursting out into laughter. "Aw, come on! Get it? See? *Vici*, even *you* gotta be wise enough to think that was funny!"

A firm arm grabbed his shoulder and navigated him out of the room, warding against any further comments from Cae. His feet hit the wooden planks of the hallway before he had the time to protest. Tyn's hand was warm against him, his vice of a grip nearly stopping the blood flow in Cae's arm. Cae waited, still grinning, silent and expectant.

Eventually, Tyn broke. He sighed, disappointed, in that way only he could be. He had a drizzling kind of frustration, a gentle shower that rained distress with hopes for sunnier skies. Cae didn't believe Tyn capable of anything more volatile. Most of the other magisters in training grew used to Cae's behavior, much in the same way weary mothers grew accustomed to their toddlers' rampages.

Tyn still found room in his heart to believe in Cae and still found the capacity to be upset when Cae, once again, failed to meet his lofty expectations. Tyn's breath hitched, that hiccup that always materialized before he spoke, as if he needed the extra second before he was sure what he wanted to say. "Why do you insist on scrapping with the magisters? They're trying to enlighten us to the ways and minds of the Gods."

Cae's fingers itched, wanting to trace the frown that likely found itself on Tyn's face. Cae never spent time wishing for his sight. He laughed away the question each time, finding the notion funny even after all these years. Humans dreamed of wings and flight because they saw the birds up above, the seed of envy planting in their heart. Cae pitied them in their yearning. He was a Stone Tree, his rocky roots planted firmly in the earth for as long as the Gods willed him to stand. He knew no other life, and thus had no longing for what he couldn't know.

"Aye. And do ya think the Gods spent those hundred years fightin' *malum* inside or outside a classroom?" Cae felt around for Tyn's hand, grabbing it with squeeze, but Tyn shook off his hand. "Aye, they mean well, *vici*. But the evils out there ain't gonna be afraid of pretty stories. We need ta do the work ourselves."

"And we can do that once we're assigned House or Garden," Tyn said, walking Cae forward.

"I hope ya do that when ya assigned Garden." Cae grinned into the air. "The Ol' Head Magister will have ta finally leave me alone when I'm given House."

They stopped walking. Tyn grabbed Cae's arms and shuffled him off to the side. Tyn gently pushed Cae's head down below an unseen barrier, and Tyn squeezed in next to him. Cae got the distinct impression that Tyn chose the tiniest place imaginable to hide. Thanks, *Superbia*. Nothing like his lover hiding him in some kinda closet to wound his pride.

Tyn leaned in close, his breath hot against Cae's cheek. His voice filled with hurt, he whispered, "Don't think like that, Cae.

You might still be able to get out of the House and work with the people."

"Maybe," Cae said, smiling to the man in front of him.

Cae had never seen the sun. It existed through a warm pressure on his skin and promises handed to him saying it was so. As far as he knew, the ball of light everybody talked about was really some kind of volcanic ash in the sky, keeping *Terrabis* warm. So much of his world was built on those promises—assurances that this texture really was brick and that this sound really was a fiddle. So much of his world came purely from external validations.

Cae found that he didn't really care whether the world he fabricated was realistic or not. He paid no mind to whether it matched the stories people saw and told. As far as Cae was concerned, Tyn was the sun. Regardless of what the world really was, it was *his*, Tyn right along with it. Running fingertips over the man's thin arms, marinating in his soft tones, breathing in that earthy scent of the flowers and *Caecus*'s temple, feeling Tyn's warmth? That was the world Cae knew.

Tyn put his hand against Cae's cheek, stroking his thumb over the top of the cheekbone. His thumb pads scratched over Cae's skin, their salty coarseness a consequence of hours spent copying notes and studying. The hands of a perfect little magister in training. Cae's hands, to Tyn's constant chagrin, boasted no calluses. If somebody shook his hand, they might think him a royal, not a man devoting himself and his life to the Gods.

But then after seeing the heavy robes adorning his body and the absent look in his eyes, most people figured that there was no place for Cae in this world outside of the House's marble walls. How could a blind man help create textiles, bake bread, sell his wares? No, as far as every other Electarian was concerned, Cae's only useful role lived with the Gods.

"Let's get you to your room. I need to head back to the classroom." Tyn's soft sigh feathered over Cae's face. That warm pressure edged closer until Tyn dropped a chaste kiss against Cae's cheek.

Cae grinned and fumbled around for Tyn's hand, holding it tight. "Shouldn't ya stay to make sure I behave myself?" Cae raised his eyebrows.

Tyn laughed, the sound a soft flutter of bells through the room. "Cae, I don't believe even *Imperium* could make you behave yourself." Tyn gently pulled Cae from the tiny space, slowly leading him down the hall once more.

"I'm sure the ol' woman could find a way," he cackled, throwing his head back toward the sky. "Ain't that right, *vici*?"

"Cae! You can't talk about the leader of the Gods that way!"

"Ol' *Imperium* won't care. She knows how to laugh at a good joke."

Tyn continued his diligent spluttering up until the point that he ushered Cae through the door and eased him onto his bed. Cae rolled his eyes. The man embodied so many wonderful things, but his prudish devotion to courtesy was not one of them. Cae sometimes felt that he met Tyn specifically to help loosen up the tightly wound strings that controlled the man's every movement.

"I really can't believe you," Tyn said one more time before falling silent. Cae pictured the prayers flying through his partner's head, soaring up to the ether and begging for forgiveness. Only *Superbia*'s own Timore hawks had the strength to support the sheer might of Tyn's faith. Uptight, yes. But undeniably sweet.

"Then go to class and back to believin' in ya Gods," Cae said, flopping back on his bed and closing his eyes.

"*Our* Gods."

"Aye, aye. Our Gods." Cae waved off the correction. The mark on his hand cooled, as if a wind brushed through the room, emphasizing Tyn's reminder. As if Cae could forget the very beings to which he dedicated his life.

Caecus. God of wisdom, most trusted advisor to *Imperium.* His followers sought truth and knowledge throughout the world, the trees on their right hands leading them through every conceivable query and question about existence. That tree symbolized *Caecus* himself: a foundation, a protector, something solid amid the raging pantheon of his brothers and sisters. He served as a neutral ground between the pride of his sister *Superbia*, and the candor of his sibling *Menda*.

He paused, listening for the faint sound of Tyn's light breathing. The lullaby allowed his arms to relax behind his head. The low sound of Tyn's heart and breath, those small confirmations of his existence, were sweeter than any song ever could be. "Have fun. Be good."

"I should be saying that to you," Tyn said, exasperated. His footsteps clipped against the wooden floor as he bent down to Cae, pressing another light kiss to his forehead. A smile spread across Cae's face. "Pray a little while you're here. It'll do you some good."

Tyn left the room, though his flowery scent lingered for a few moments longer. Cae's heart tugged, urging him to follow. He resisted, opening his eyes and staring into nothing. He rested like this for a few seconds, waiting. And waiting. And—

"Are we gonna talk, or are ya just gonna watch me lay here, *vici?*" Cae huffed.

The familiar presence always pressed against his head, always lived with his thoughts like the clouds. It was just another part of his sky, so natural he didn't think about it that much. But much like the clouds could grow stormy, the presence grew more insistent on some days. It filled his mind and heaved against his skull, as if trying to break out from a prison. Like today.

"You seemed...busy." The voice was amused.

The smell of Tyn filled the room once more, a sharp reminder of to what—or to whom—the voice referred. Cae breathed out slowly, reminding himself of Tyn's retreating footsteps. His right hand cooled, his mark's breeze a reminder of reality when reality felt too dreamlike.

The manipulation was subtle, unable to cause storms and raze cities but more than capable of producing a scent to mess with Cae's head. The scent disappeared, leaving a vaguely stale, sterile smell in its place. The voice's point was made—no need to continue with the tricks.

As it turned out, the Gods *also* thought Cae's only useful role was with them.

When *Caecus* first started speaking to him, Cae thought he had gone crazy. Cae had already begun to feel wrinkles form in his skin and figured that with his appearance, so went his sanity. But the golden mark on his hand provided him with the clarity to trust in his own lucidity, and his sightless eyes provided him with perfect hearing—apparently so perfect that his patron God could communicate directly with him. *Caecus* tethered himself to Cae, an indirect connection to the humans for which the Gods sacrificed everything.

"Aye, *vici*, I'm always busy." Cae threw his arm over his eyes. "Trainin' ta be a magister is a full-time job."

"It is," *Caecus* agreed. The voice took a shape, forming into something almost tangible in Cae's mind. It gave off the impression of someone standing in the room, the presence neutral like the earth with a touch of vague curiosity. "Though I imagine it only counts as a full-time job if you're able to actually stay in the classes for their entirety. At this juncture, you barely qualify as a part-time student."

"Ey," Cae griped, the sound heavy and harsh, "call me crazy—"

"The others do."

"—*but* it's a lil' backward ta take a class about the Gods when one of 'em won't leave ya alone." Cae tried to force the magnitude of his exasperation on that pressure in his head. The pressure pushed back, acknowledging but dismissive.

Cae learned long ago that the task of annoying the God of wisdom was close to impossible. In myths, *Caecus* provided council to the Gods and warnings to the humans. His legacy persisted as serious and stern, unyielding and dispassionate. And he could be. Like all the Gods, the duality of his wisdom caught up to him on occasion and bared its teeth. On those days, Cae held his tongue with every ounce of willpower he had, listening silently to the deity's thunders. For the most part, though, *Caecus* retained the goodness of wisdom, in all its gentle, intellectual curiosity.

"When I finally managed to connect with one of my followers, I truly did expect more reverence," *Caecus* mused, ignoring Cae's annoyance and focusing on Cae's words themselves.

Cae resisted rolling his eyes. Talking with the God was like having a conversation with an intelligent toddler—he only discussed what he wanted to, paying no heed to his audience.

"Tell me, do you truly hate me?"

"'Course not," Cae sighed, letting his exasperation melt away. *Caecus* approached the emotion in its place, prodding curiously at Cae's lingering weariness. It was undoubtedly a strange feeling; having an ethereal being pressing against the threads of your emotions was not a sensation most experienced. "What do ya need, *vici*?"

As much as Cae wanted to believe the God communicated with him for the sake of Cae's delightful company, it was never that easy. Cae's charm, though legendary, was not that astounding. No, the God only tuned in when he stood at a crossroads, his logic paralyzing him from choosing one route or another. The God sought Cae when he was able to admit he needed a human.

Caecus paused, chewing over his words. His thinking burned through Cae's mind, a whirring of millions of ideas Cae could never hope to contemplate. Cae grimaced at the feeling, even though he wanted to smile. *Caecus* thinking alongside Cae's own thoughts in his tiny, human head was less than pleasant, but feeling uncertainty from the wisest God always allowed him a sense of comfort—even the most perfect of beings experienced a semblance of doubt.

"There is a meeting of the Gods today." He spoke slowly, laying down his sentences brick by brick. Cae wondered how many of those bricks held the truth and how many were fabrications specially designed for Cae. "*Imperium* wishes for an update on the human world. *Superbia*, *Viribus*, and *Menda* have nothing but praises for your people. In their reports to *Imperium*, they will only see images bathed in light. They so fawn over their creations, unaware of your faults. They exist so consumed with their own images made to live on *Terrabis* that they are blind to your species' many, many flaws."

"Aye, *vici*, ease off," he said, the word coming out like "awf." "We're the only things that make ya dusty lives up in the heavens interestin'."

Caecus's presence twitched as if deciding whether to laugh. He ignored the inclination, his mind uninterested in tangential conversations. "My point being, they will go to *Imperium* this day and tell her all is well on *Terrabis*. But the truth of the matter is it's not. And it will not be so unless corrective action is taken. Unless corrosive action is taken, to boil out the cancer existing among you. And I have, well, less than ideal guidance to provide."

Cae snorted. "When's the wisest option eva' been the ideal one?"

"Well, therein lies the root of my problem." *Caecus*'s voice picked up, a new rhythm to his words that Cae imagined was the God pacing back and forth. "Wisdom from whose perspective? Certainly not mine. She might very well imprison me for a few centuries or so, simply for the notion. Wisdom from her perspective? It very well goes against her interests on *Terrabis*."

"Then who's ya advice really protectin'?" Cae asked softly, the familiar feeling that first led him to the House creeping up inside of him.

Caecus did not bring Cae to this place. He only broke through Cae's head later in Cae's life. Cae first decided to travel to the House more than two decades earlier, one of the longest magister-in-training tenures the House had ever seen.

The idea that a divine hand existed, moving pieces around to help humans achieve their best selves and live harmoniously together, drove his feet to the white steeples. *Terrabis* existed in a constant state of decay, and yet some people fended off their end against all odds. Despite the inevitability of death, they clawed their way through the slough of their lives, crawling from one day to the next. It was a terrible thing. It was beautiful too. Why did they fight? How did they manage to win such tiny successive battles? What forces ultimately felled them in the war?

Cae began at the beginning—he looked to the Gods. He studied their history, had others read aloud their texts, attempting to demystify the minds of immortals and the world they created for their people. It was a lost sense of wonder, knowing how insignificant he was next to their power. *Caecus*'s voice eased some of the awe, but it always persisted in the back of his mind, knowing how much of the world those five deities touched. How much perished beneath their watch. And how much they protected all the while.

Caecus never responded to Cae's question. Either bored with their conversation or having obtained the answers he needed, the pressure in Cae's head evaporated. A twinge of annoyance flashed through Cae, fading as quickly as it came. Cae couldn't blame the God for leaving. His near omniscience made him a strong and sure God to follow, but he was a terrible conversation partner.

Cae shook his head, wrinkling his nose as he searched for peace in the dark and quiet. He prepared himself to go to class tomorrow. Maybe he would actually try and engage for once. *Tyn might faint if he ever heard me say that*, he chuckled to himself. He sank into himself, leaving the world behind for the sounds and smells of his dreams. As he attempted to submerge himself beneath the waters of sleep, screams pierced through his slumbery solace.

Cae shot up out of bed, stumbling around as he searched for the walking stick he used when by himself. The sound of his door flying open whisked by, familiar footsteps clumsily falling toward him. He reached his arms out, almost collapsing as Tyn's figure melted into his embrace. Shaking hands pressed against Cae's face, swept against his arms, brushed across his throat.

Tyn nearly sobbed in relief. He rested his head in the crook of Cae's shoulder, his tears hot against Cae's neck. The screams cut off, leaving a more disturbing reticence in their place. "I'm so happy you're okay." Tyn's voice came out muffled against Cae's collarbone, his breath watery and warm.

Cae's heart swelled and froze all at once, oscillating between a profound kind of love and an acute kind of horror. He found the will to speak, brushing back Tyn's hair with his left hand. "What happened, *vici*?"

Tyn sniffled, wrapping his hands in Cae's robes and yanking on them as if he had to confirm that Cae really stood in front of him. "The House and castle are on lockdown. Everybody is advised to hide in whatever sanctuary they can find while the guard launches an investigation. Queen Juliana is dead."

Cae, shocked, numbly patted Tyn's back. He looked up at the ceiling in muted disbelief. Caecus, *what the wreck did you just do?*

CHAPTER 11
7055.1.21

Liliana balanced on a tightrope, a sensationalistic act that would have made any troupe performer envious. No audience tracked her journey. She wobbled forward, totally and utterly alone. She tilted back and forth, the wind taunting her as it whistled past her ears and danced around her shaking legs. The abyss beneath her reeked of failure, the sour sweetness of its corpses making her lightheaded. Her toes cramped from latching on to the rope beneath her, her legs burning from the effort of maintaining the precise balance necessary to keep her from spiraling down, down, down.

Her heart slammed against her chest, each beat reminding her of the proximity between her and her demise. Liliana and her fate stood close to one another, lovers whose warm breath fanned over each other's face. She prayed to stay far away enough that they never came close enough to kiss. Yes, Liliana balanced on a tightrope, her situation so very precarious.

Years ago, Liliana used to cry every time a thunderstorm cracked across the sky. She pictured *malum* wielding thunderbolts toward *Terrabis*, the electricity laced with the vengefulness she had spent millennia fermenting. Liliana always cradled the fear that *malum* threw these lightning bolts down, seeking Liliana specifically. It was an immature fear, and she knew that even as a child. Logically, the lightning bolts would never hit her. But if a man pointed a sword at her chest with no intention of running her through, she still might tremble. So, she prayed. She prayed to *Viribus* for strength, to *Superbia* for courage, and to *Imperium* for safety for one of the God's few followers on *Terrabis*. The lightning bolts never hit. She continued to pray.

Yet Liliana would always jump at the first boom of thunder, attempting to play it off in front of her family as excitement. She didn't want Teo to know of her powerlessness, for Eliana to know of her weakness. Around one another, they were always the best versions of themselves, cracks disavowed.

Despite the wobbly smile and brave face Liliana attempted to put on, her mother had always seen through the facade. *Imperium* bless her father, but the queen seemed to be the only one with that sixth sense for knowing when her daughter's strength crumbled, even when appearances signified otherwise.

She followed Liliana to her room, holding her until the storm passed. The heat of her mother created a barrier between Liliana and the dangers outside. Liliana found sanctuary in her mother's graceful fingers when she stroked her hair back and her mother's soft words that swirled around in Liliana's head like a warm bath. Queen Juliana was an impregnable force, as a queen and as a mother. Liliana could only burrow deeper into her embrace and dream of one day standing as strong.

Beyond those temporary bubbles of her and her mother, Liliana didn't think she ever knew the blissfully tranquil feeling of safety. Liliana never let her mother stay long, intent on being strong even when she felt the boom of the thunder crackle through her bones. Her mother loved Teo's strength, and Liliana knew she could be just like him in that way. As she grew older, she dismissed her mother from her room sooner and sooner. Eventually, her mother stopped coming. Liliana stopped praying.

Then her mother died. The skies did Liliana a favor the day of the funeral. They wept with her, masking her silent tears amid the raindrops. When she returned to her room that night, she curled into a ball, a corrosive pain in her heart that felt like it might consume her entirely. The idea of dissolving in on herself in the acidity of her own grief seemed appealing. Far more so than living with the grinding and gnawing ache in her chest. She screamed into her comforter, slashing her throat from the inside as she tried to empty out the pain.

Teo came into her room. He sat on her bed, staring at the ceiling, unsure of what to do. He said nothing. He offered no words of comfort. He did not touch her, keeping all comforting embraces to himself. He simply sat there, unflinching, as she cried into her bed, her shrieks unyielding. They coexisted together that night, giving each other nothing more than the simplest gift of human company. Liliana still didn't know why he came at all.

This moment made up one of only a handful of fond memories Liliana had of Teo. Beyond a few companionable miracles, they mostly spent their childhoods avoiding one another. Separated and trained for their respective paths in life, there was no time to form anything more than a cordial bond at best. It was competitive and toxic at its worst.

Liliana fought tirelessly to claw her way to a title that amounted to more than just princess. She spent her days learning skills to dazzle dignitaries—flute lessons for the Aurjnegh, the Dragons and Wolves strategy for the Nuwei. She even studied agriculture and irrigation to interact with the shunned Soj. Instead of making people take her more seriously, she only succeeded in getting them to view her as a palace pet with exceptional traits.

And while Liliana growled at the world, gnashing her teeth and demanding to be recognized, Teo drifted away to his own private lessons. The magisters served information to him on a silver plate, secrets of the castle spoon-fed into his tight-lipped mouth. She craved to know what he could. Liliana begged to be privy to some of his knowledge, given a morsel of the inside world like her mother had given her through the council meetings. He brushed her off. Why did he need her? He had his pick of advisors. After all, he was going to be *king*.

Liliana dug a hole in her mind and buried the memory of her and Teo there, kicking the dirt back over with the fervent hope that her feelings might rot underground. Her prayers now were more than the irrational fears of a child. She prayed to *Viribus* for strength in each contest; *Superbia* for courage in doing what needed done; *Caecus* for wisdom in her every step; *Menda* for honesty when she faced the first trial; *Imperium* for support in all contests ahead. She didn't need to rely on family. She had herself and—hopefully—the blessing of the Gods.

After all, Liliana balanced on a tightrope. And she refused to let senseless sentimentality be the straw that tipped her over into the deadly abyss.

She gathered her hair, twisting the walnut-brown locks around her hand and pinning them to the back of her head in a tight bun. The dexterous movements of holding, clipping, and brushing came easily to Liliana. No harder than plucking the finicky strings of a mandolin or sculpting an ice beetle's thread. Years ago, she made one of her attendants teach her how to do her hair. It allowed her a semblance of independence, even if a small one. The maids offered to help her dress for today—she dismissed them, granting them the morning free. If she couldn't even manage her own self from time to time, how in *Imperium*'s name would she manage a country?

Liliana watched her deft hands in the mirror, her eyebrows furrowing. She paused and brushed the tips of her fingers against her skin. A darker complexion with red undertones, quick to react to anything and anyone. Her mother had cooler skin, steady and unchanging regardless of the circumstances. Liliana found it hard to imagine a queen staring back at her. What made one face regal and another common? Such a thin line society drew in the sand, and yet it marked such a stark difference in fates. It distinguished the high and low, the worthy and unworthy.

She only saw the same smooth complexion steeling itself, as if constantly in preparation for tragedy. Liliana scoffed softly to herself. The Gods had given her reason to be at the ready.

She rose slowly, the back of her golden cloak falling behind her. She commissioned it days before the announcement of the first trial, moments after her spat with Teo. It billowed and swayed from the same silk that Teo's did, the only difference lying in its deep, aureate color. She savored the look on his face after he first saw her wearing it, the sweetness of the memory sharp in her mouth. It was a victory over her brother for which, this time, she needn't feel any guilt.

A *scritch scritch scritch* at her door melted her smirk into a smile. She danced around the mess of hobbies that consecrated her floor, flinging the door open to a fanged grin. Imperium lay outside the door, head near the bottom of the doorframe, steadily shaking the floor with a rhythmic wag of his tail. His tongue lolled out, earning a laugh and a firm rub on the back of his ears. She leaned into his coarse fur, meant to protect the canine in even the fiercest winters, and sighed.

"Couldn't you just eat the other contestants so we might be done with all this pomp?" She waved her hand, and Imperium yipped. She gently curled her fingers into the fur under his face, guiding his head down and plopping a kiss on his forehead. "I'm sure Teo's bitterness would give you indigestion, but it's nothing that a few remedies and roots couldn't fix."

"I prefer to think of Teo more as a dark chocolate," a deep voice said from behind Imperium's enormous rump. "You just need to keep trying him until you begin to understand his sweetness."

Liliana frowned at her father. "If anything, he's like that atrocious coffee-grime the Aurjnegh drink—no matter how they may frame it, the muck is no more than an acrimonious stew," she said, her response flying off her tongue with an arrow's accuracy, swift and stinging.

King Leo sighed, the disappointment muffled by the small mountain of fur in the hallway. Liliana waited, arms crossed and eyebrows raised, as her father said, "I really wish you two would treat each other more like family and not enemy spies found in your encampment. Or is cordiality simply too elusive for two people vying to be monarch?"

A crawling feeling shuddered down Liliana's back, her father's displeasure prompting the first spark of doubt she had felt since stepping up to the dais and exposing her mark. Leo, his thick eyebrows furrowed, finally managed to move Imperium to the side. Spiders slowly inching their way up her spine would have been preferable to his withering gaze. He waited for her answer like a swinging axe, prepared to whistle down and hack at any unsatisfactory reaction.

She squared her shoulders, jutted her chin out, and declared, "That's an overly simplistic way of putting it—you know the situation is far more complicated than that."

Chop. Wrong answer. He shook his head.

Her mark pulsed, flaring up and scalding her with flames of autonomy. Liliana bit her lip and ignored the throb. While there was so much her father could not give her that her mother could, she still loved him. When her mother had been too busy, as was frequently the case, Liliana had practically been raised by her father. Though her mother was her only source of stimulation, her father had been her only source of real companionship. The flame died as quickly as it had burst, leaving her with an empty sense of humiliation.

"I know how complicated it all is," he said. His words were soft, a desperate plea wrapped in a velvet blanket. "But regardless of the outcome, you two will have to figure out a way to coexist with one another. *Caecus* might find it prudent to find some semblance of peace now—before your relationship is beyond repair."

"*Caecus* might find it prudent to use whatever means necessary to beat my competition, even if that means cutting down the heartless skeleton we've dubbed Teo," Liliana muttered.

She meant it as a joke, but a jolt of conviction zipped through her body. The sentence was a weed, seemingly easy to yank from the ground and remove from the garden. Unfortunately, its roots ran much deeper and it was much more complex than a simple yank could assuage.

"No." Her father's voice was hard, absolute.

Liliana looked up, stunned. She nearly forgot her father held the capacity to reprimand her, though, in fairness, even the most well-behaved pets were prone to snap from time to time. Liliana readied herself to argue back, arming herself with weapons of words as she had for years, but his glaring countenance stopped the rebuttal in her mouth.

He stood up straighter, his shoulders thrown back as he stared at Liliana. Though his aging back made him hunch more and more, Liliana had never seen a man stand as tall when he loomed over her in that moment. His deep brown eyes, normally crinkled and soft, ran through her harder than a blade. The traces of her pleasant father melted away into a puddle on the floor, leaving nothing but an icy sternness in their place. No hesitation, just sheer resolution as he made Liliana shrink in on herself with one word.

Frosty fingers laid themselves around her heart, constricting it with a firm squeeze. Her mark pounded, making Liliana unsure of whether to straighten her own spine or stand down. Liliana used to trace her father's mark of *Menda* as a child, chubby fingers running over the golden lines. Despite spending years looking at the proof of his honesty, Liliana still found herself doubting everything she knew. She wondered, if she took off the robe and beheld his back, might there be a dragon there instead?

While Liliana chased her own thoughts like a dog with its tail, her father finally spoke, his voice low and charged, like the air just before a lightning strike. "Those ideas, those thoughts are of *malum*. They lack empathy and clarity." He clasped his own forearm, closing his eyes.

Liliana wondered if he'd felt *Menda's* touch freeze through him at the name, a reminder of his patron God's vigilance against *malum's* influence. Her pulse stayed still, stubbornly resistant to such fears.

He opened his eyes, his gaze softer. "Do you understand?"

His weariness blanketed the room, smothering any light. A pang of pity hit Liliana with the force of a small battering ram. Her poor father. The king grew older every day, the fact not helped by his warring children. No wonder he wanted to abdicate the throne. It was enough to drive any sane man to yield his power. A surge of resolution overwhelmed her, as if she just gulped a lungful of air after days of holding her breath.

It was enough to drive any sane man to yield his power. But her mother had never suffered from that pressing exhaustion. The empress of Vitria marched around, her confidence sewn into every stitch of her robe. *Imperium* ruled heaven and earth, for Gods' sake. Liliana plucked the commonality between these rulers and sifted it into a plaster around her heart, providing a structural support she hadn't realized was missing.

Her father, though a wonderful, honest man and a good ruler at his core, could never serve a kingdom with his life. Teo couldn't either. They lacked the passion of the women who cradled the world in their hands, the ferocity that led them to conquer new lands, the grit that allowed them to pour their whole hearts into a nation in hopes that the rising waters might lift everyone higher.

Liliana gazed at her father, understanding rushing over her body with a faint shudder. The bags under his eyes, the gray running through his beard—damning evidence of what she should have known: that her father was never meant to rule in the first place. The same for Teo. Liliana, on the other hand....

She squared her shoulders, looking him directly in the eyes as the burn of her mark sang through her blood. Liliana was quite possibly the only one left in Electaria with broad enough shoulders and a strong enough mark to bear the weight of the kingdom. "I understand," she replied, smiling ever so slightly.

Her father finally relaxed his stance and returned her smile. She told the truth, even if it was her own version. His gentleness coalesced once more around him, creating a sweet outer layer to hide the ice beneath.

"Good." Her father blew out a hard breath, stepping toward Liliana and clasping his hand on her shoulder.

Liliana was surprised she didn't bear an indent from years of the little motion.

He regarded her, eyes slowly lighting up as his stance went from condemning to proud. "In that case, I think it's about time that I escort you to your first Trial, no?"

Liliana reached forward, interlocking her arm with her father's. She opened her mouth, but nothing came out. Before the Monarchic Trials, she had been a dying woman, drowning in the middle of the ocean. And yet, somehow, someway, *Imperium* saw fit to reach down and pluck her from the voracious throes of the waves. She drew the salt water from Liliana's body, replacing it with sweet air, simply on the condition that Liliana went forth and made something great of her second chance. How could she verbalize the feeling of being brought back to life, her new purpose shining down on her with a blinding light? This step marked the beginning of everything, the universe materializing in front of her—all she had to do was reach her fingertips out and grab it. She settled for a simple smile in return, confident that if she beamed any wider, her cheeks would rip through the middle.

They walked in silence to the House of Magisters. The palpable excitement that swirled around the pair squashed any hope of conversation. The atmosphere pushed Liliana with the intensity of a pride of lions ready for the hunt, the primal force causing her heart to beat faster. As they approached the spires, Liliana pressed her lips into a tight line and steeled herself. The air held the bloody taste of anticipation.

Her father took a step back as they entered the House. Her mark pounded, and Liliana stepped outside herself, taking in the moment. Liliana's eyes tracked the stars painted against the ceiling, relishing in the numinous feeling of insignificance. Like one of the phoenixes from Nuwei at its death, true worth first required awareness of what it meant to feel insignificant. Only when one meant nothing could one understand the leaps and bounds it took to mean something.

The galaxy, deep and mysterious, glowed above her, challenging her to try and rearrange its resplendent constellations.

"Good luck, my dear. Let honesty guide you and not your desire to win." Her father's earnest voice and knowing look shattered the glass windows of her reverie. She had nearly forgotten he still stood behind her. He smiled at her, wrinkled face twinkling. "I hope you and Teo pass this day. May *Menda* watch over you both."

Liliana gave her father a nod, sending a silent prayer up to *Menda*. She squeezed her lips together into a line and prayed so hard she felt an uncomfortable tug in her gut. She prayed for Teo and Elle to fail. Cruel, but she prayed it anyway. She could imagine her father's terrible disappointment if he knew her thoughts. Luckily, the man could sense lies, not read minds. In the back of her mind, Liliana recognized the viciousness of her thoughts and even felt a little nauseous from them. But ugliness for the sake of higher purpose had to mean something. *Right?*

She gave the stars above one final look before striding toward *Menda*'s clear, glass dome. Liliana didn't care if she had to slash the stars down from the heavens itself if it meant she got to rewrite history on this day.

No light crept through *Menda*'s broad windows. The ashen clouds turned the glass into gray walls. Though she saw the turrets of the castle popping up outside, a shiver scurried up her arm as she got the impression she had just walked into a prison cell. Without any other furniture in the room to distract from the bleakness dripping from outside, the grimness had a palpable energy not unlike getting hit in the face by a brick. Her heart twisted. For the God of honesty, their place of worship didn't seem that open.

The empress of Vitria sat in the middle of the room, her light blue robes splayed around her crossed legs. Liliana dropped to the floor with as much grace as she could muster. Shuffling her legs around, she finally managed to mimic the woman's stance. She would never understand Vitrian customs, not the least of which included their annoying need to contort their bodies when praying.

Liliana's blood swelled and pressed against her skin, the pressure of her heartbeat turning her body into a single, throbbing pulse that thrummed through her veins. Each breath jumped in and out of her body, quick and burning. Her face flushed with the fire of the moment, leaving pink embers along her skin. The empress looked perfectly natural. Dammit, she looked perfectly pleasant. Liliana's eyes darted around the room before turning back to the small smile on the woman's face. Could she not feel the confining walls of the room?

"Princess Liliana," the empress said, blessedly breaking the silence.

Liliana waited, but the woman offered no other words. "E-Empress," Liliana replied, her voice a skeleton of her normal confidence. She growled in her head. Timidity was a word for the weak and would not find itself in her vocabulary today of all days.

"How are you?"

Liliana puffed her chest out, lips quirking up into a sure smile. An easy first question and a painfully obvious transition into rapport. Electarians loved a good back-and-forth, and much like any athletic event, the mental marathon of witty repartee couldn't begin without a proper warm-up.

The immediate, cavalier response of "I am well" rested on the tip of her tongue. As she opened her mouth to respond, a fierce, painful burn *tugged* from the center of her back. Her mark roared against her, catching the answer in the middle of her throat.

The empress raised one eyebrow at Liliana, waiting with an anticipatory tilt of her chin.

A simple enough question. But was "well" really the truth? Her mark pulsed, and Liliana swore she heard a velvet voice whispering in her ears, "*No, Little Dragon.*" Liliana's pulse thumped. Was that Liliana's own voice or *Imperium* herself, guiding Liliana toward victory? The idea of the latter steeled Liliana.

Her trial of honesty had started the second her feet crossed over the room's threshold. "Well" didn't describe Liliana's state at all. Her heart still throbbed, her skin still burned, and anxiety continued to gnaw at her heart with an acidic tenacity. She almost burst into laughter. "Terrified," Liliana said, slicing her heart down the middle and opening it up to show the empress its contents. "A little excited, but mostly terrified."

The empress grinned at her, a knowing twinkle in her navy eyes. "Well, it appears as though Ol' Leo taught his kid something after all. A pleasure to finally meet you, Liliana."

Liliana caught her own hardwired answer, throttling the "nice to meet you too" to the ground of her mind. Pleasantries had no place in this room. *Menda* plucked out melodies of terrible truth, not comforting lies. It was part of what made the Vitrians such frustrating—and frankly, terrible—dignitaries. Though not all of them followed *Menda*'s path, the few that didn't rarely found themselves in governmental roles.

She chose her words carefully. "I'm glad to finally meet my father's childhood friend, though I wish it could have been under less pressing circumstances."

"Understandably so," the empress said, her long *a* sound rising and crashing the end of the word in that strange Vitrian accent they all shared.

Her father used to draw out his vowels and shorten the end of his words until the court beat the habit out of him.

"Then we might as well get started with the good stuff, *etiam*? Why do you believe you should rule over Electaria?"

In any other room, Liliana might have tempered her pride and attempted a meeker response. But then, Liliana believed she would have failed. Temperance and meekness were weeds she had strangled out as she continued to grow, and there was no truth to be found in those ideals for Liliana. There was no pause, no hesitation, no force of humility. She met the woman's eyes, her eyebrows furrowed and challenging. "Because I am the best."

The empress of Vitria's eyebrows flew so far up they almost disappeared into her thick, black braids. Liliana's heart pounded, not out of fear of failure but the thrill of facing a thought that lurked in the back of her mind for years. She soared and drowned in the moment, freed, and potentially condemned, by the same truth.

"What if you aren't?" the empress said.

Liliana's lips quirked up into a small smile. If her words were a trickle before, now they flowed with the power of an upended dam. Every thought that hid in every corner of her mind poured out, a pounding waterfall of conviction. "That's the thing, though, isn't it? I know I am. Ellegance simply doesn't have the experience or the policy knowledge to change things effectively. Teo is too content with moderation, so nothing great would happen in his reign. But I've spent years studying this country and this world, and I have ideas that would make Electaria great. I have plans that would change our relationship with the Soj, improve financial living for the average citizen. Out of the three of us, I just *know* I am the best."

The empress studied her. The air in the room halted in the same way oceans took a breath before unleashing their fury. A chill scampered up Liliana's arms.

"Let me ask you: How well do you know the other two candidates?"

Liliana paused. It almost felt like a ridiculous question. Though she had only spoken with Ellegance the one time, Liliana didn't think the plucky city girl was exactly an enigmatic puzzle to be solved. And the other candidate was her *brother. Though*, Liliana thought to herself grudgingly, *blood isn't exactly a direct correlation of emotional proximity in this family.* "I would say I have a good idea of who they are," Liliana finally answered, choosing her words carefully so they would remain genuine.

"And couldn't it be possible that they might prove to be of greater potential and value if you took the chance to get to know them better?"

"Empress, I don't understand your line of questioning. Is it possible? Of course, it is. It is also possible that wolves with three heads exist; I don't believe in an idea simply in the absence of evidence contrary to its existence."

"So you *truly* believe that, even without having really gotten to know the other candidates, you would deem yourself superior?"

"*Yes*, I can say it in as many ways as you want, but it won't change the answer—I am the best candidate for the crown of Electaria, and I will secure the title so I can lead my people," Liliana snapped. "Qualifications be damned—not a single one of the *malums* has half the passion that I hold in my heart for this kingdom. I don't care who's older or potentially smarter—I only care about Electaria and its future, and that is why I have to be its queen."

The outburst froze in the air like deadly icicles. Liliana held her breath, sure that one sharp inhale might impale her on the deadly tip of her own words. Her back pounded, her conviction singing through her blood. Despite the situation, she couldn't help savoring the faintly sweet taste of making somebody hear her roar.

She trained her eyes ahead, drilling her focus into the woman in front of her. An uncomfortable feeling pushed into Liliana's heart, like an unwelcome guest trying to force their way through a closed door. A ball of sweat rolled down Liliana's neck. The empress looked up, staring beyond Liliana's shoulder, and a freezing shudder crawled down Liliana's back. The way the empress's eyes moved, following motions blind to Liliana's eyes gave her the distinct impression that something lurked behind her. Disconcerting, to say the least. Liliana bit her lip but did not move.

The empress shook her head, disbelieving at first. This disbelief morphed into something uglier, as the empress's lips curled upward, in a picture of perfect displeasure. The empress's gaze dropped back down to Liliana. The horrible, creeping feeling disappeared moments later, returning the room back to its earlier stillness.

"*Menda*, she really believes it doesn't she?" the empress whispered to herself, unable to keep the disgust out of her voice.

Liliana leaned in slightly, hoping to catch a word of the woman's mumblings.

The empress shooed her away, glaring into Liliana's eyes with a tone that directly contradicted her next words. "Liliana Storidian, you have completed your first test. Congratulations, you will be moving on to the next round of challenges in assuming the throne."

CHAPTER 12
7055.1.21

"For now, let us set aside our differences and give cheers to the passing of the first Trial!"

Leo's voice boomed across the grand hall, merry and warm as he thrust his mug into the air. The foam of his beer tilted over the side, haphazardly spilling on the velvet cloth laid so carefully hours prior. A servant hurried forth immediately, wiping down the area with nervous haste. Leo beamed at the attendant and raised his cup again—not even the frothy stickiness coating his hands could threaten the king's jolly mood.

The air practically glowed with the warmth of the room, bodies packed against one another like a litter of wolf pups. Silver platters covered the banquet tables from end to end, a scrumptious cavern of minerals waiting to be mined. Frankly, Aoran thought the king struggled to compete for the crowd's attention as they took turns eyeing the table in front of them. The chatter ebbed to a polite roar, allowing him his speech as the attendees waited impatiently for his toast to end and the drinking to begin.

"Our history states that before the second and third Trials, the royal family and its contestants celebrated the first night with a grand feast." Leo raised his bushy eyebrows at the crowd. "Far be it from me to stand in the way of tradition!"

With a wide smile, Leo waited for the laughter to subside before continuing. "In truthfulness, though, this road is an uncertain one. We honor those with the fortitude and power to walk its trail. As of tonight, the three candidates remain closely ranked. Between myself, Empress Renee, and our House representatives, we have scored Liliana at 0.85, Teo at 0.9, and Ellegance at 1. The competition is close, which only means we will end with a truly worthy monarch for this country."

Leo raised his glass once again, the rest of the room following suit.

Aoran watched from the edge of the room, trying to make sure his boredom didn't show. Je, Dayanara, and Ro were doing much better at looking engaged in their jobs. For some reason, Aoran couldn't find the will that night. The conversation between Imperium and the dignitary weighed on his mind. It made concentrating on anything else remarkably difficult. Besides, the ranks remained tight, which, in Aoran's mind, meant nothing had changed. A dull affair, in his opinion.

"We uplift those who may yet prevail. Tomorrow, we prepare for the next Trial. Tonight, we rest. For now, we celebrate!"

Everybody roared in agreement, their cheers drowned out by the immediate *clank* of dish covers thrown around and plates loaded with as much food as people could manage. Aurjnegh dresses, with their miles of fabric, draped over anyone within a two-chair radius. To the woe of their neighbors, this allowed the Aurjnegh to reach over all those pinned down by their extravagance, snatching the choicest food in front of their neighbors' lamenting eyes.

Liliana, Teo, and Eliana sat near one another farther down the table but not together. Never together. Aoran noticed the separation early in his tenure at the castle. Juliana had always insisted the three sit apart, forcing them to mingle and make pleasantries with strangers. Juliana used to play the courtroom like a lyre with graceful and deft fingers, plucking each guest to her desired tune. The queen may not have known her people, but *Imperium* be damned if she didn't monopolize the court. While she primed Teo for the throne and nurtured Liliana's insatiable desire for knowledge and growth, her skill for socialization seemed to be the one attribute she desired all her children to have in common.

Useful, certainly, but Aoran always thought that it drove the strange isolation between the siblings that much deeper.

Eliana laughed, her hand carefully placed on the arm of an Aurjnegh court member. Teo, eyebrows furrowed in thought, nodded at an exasperated member of the Vitrian court. Liliana talked in a low, hot voice with a nearby Nuwei diplomat. Her expression, intense and narrowed, sent Aoran's absurd heart thumping. There was something about her conviction that reeled him in every single time.

Aoran tried to squish the feelings, glancing over to watch the king. Leo ignored all the dishes but one, simply grabbing the silver tray of Cloud Biscuits. Each one boasted a rich, golden color; the biscuits were toasted to the point of flaking on the outside but sinfully soft on the inside. Aoran swallowed, trying his best to not think about the light and buttery taste that was surely now dissolving in Leo's mouth. *Imperium*, Aoran was famished. He tried not to look like a hungry predator as he watched the king enviously. Leo finished the biscuit in two more bites as the empress stared at him.

"Are you planning on massacring the other twenty-three in the same fashion?" the empress said.

Leo smiled, popping the entire second biscuit into his mouth and nodding as he hummed with contentment. Renee grinned and leaned over, plucking a biscuit from beneath him with one deft movement. He growled as she slowly pushed the whole thing into her mouth, her long cheeks bulging outward. Kai looked over from his conversation with an Aurjnegh diplomat, flashes of horror and delight fluttering across his face. Crumbs spilled over the front of Leo's tunic, collecting in a small pile at his lap. He chuckled to himself, spraying crumbs over the front of the table.

Aoran caught himself approaching a grin. While watching his children compete for the throne couldn't be easy, Aoran admired the effortless way in which the king allowed himself the small pleasures of life. A stark contrast to his youngest daughter, who seemed intent on depriving herself joy at every turn for the sake of some higher, greater purpose. Aoran shook his head. On the topic of small pleasures, his throat began to burn with a craving for sunweed. Shifting his eyes around, fingers twitching, Aoran searched for anything else to focus on.

He found himself unable to do so, his attention caught by the larger picture of the room. With laughter, food, and drinks abounding, the aloof royals of Electaria and their many foreign embassies almost looked like normal people. Aoran snorted to himself. *Imagine that.* The chandeliers of the grand hall practically beamed with light, their existence made to illuminate these people at their most human. While the royals hid their betrayals, anathemas, and skeletons in the dark, the chandelier's solemn duty was to simply highlight every inch of joy in the room.

A contented pleasure filled Aoran. Not quite as satisfying as the ringing of swords or the sweetness of sunweed but damn close enough. He hated politics, both as an idea and as a reality. While living on the streets, politicians ignored the broken, forgotten children like him until it was most convenient for them. While living in the castle, Aoran watched the royals wasting so much time on one another's pettiness that they never moved beyond that to accomplish actual change. In spite of her almost aggressive determination, Liliana was the only one who got anything done. This all made it damn near cathartic to exist in an instant where there didn't seem to be some sort of political trap afoot.

Which, of course, soured his mood all the more when the shouting between Liliana and the affronted Nuwei diplomat shattered the tenuous peace of the moment.

"Watch your tongue, child." The diplomat trembled with anger, waving his finger in a pentagonal shape with the Nuwei gesture to ward off evil.

Though Liliana was tall for a woman, the diplomat surpassed her by several inches in height. He puffed out his chest and took a step toward her, attempting to impose this superiority in size and will on the young spitfire. "You passed your education reforms *once* at our conference years ago. This does not grant you the wherewithal to overthrow the very system as we know it."

Aoran came to life, moving with silent footsteps to stand behind Liliana. He lurked behind her, his jade eyes drilling in on the diplomat. Perhaps the diplomat was right to be offended, even right to be aggressive. Unfortunately for the diplomat, at the end of the day, it mattered very little who had said what. Liliana was his charge to protect, and the *malum*'s throat would be sliced before he laid a hand on the princess. Aoran's upper lip curled, exposing one of his fanged teeth.

Eliana watched in distress appropriate for her station, her hand fluttering between clutching her heart and the side of her face. Aoran vaguely saw the king moan to himself, trying to motion to Aoran to keep himself in check. Aoran's body was tense but motionless, a lone wolf ready to strike. Easternalia practically salivated, her eyes glazed over and enthralled. From what he had been told, Aoran had no doubt she already had crafted ten different narratives on how the fight began and ten different endings if the real one proved to be too lackluster.

Teo had already swept to the other end of the table, rounding up other Nuwei council members and beginning reconciliations. The councilors all had red, pinched faces, tight with distress. Nuwei diplomats were not prone to shouting, but they flashed their displeasure readily. Though Aoran's body shadowed Liliana's, a piece of his mind broke off to admire the prince. Teo lacked Aoran's charisma and Liliana's passion, but he spoke from a position of confidence and experience. In a scene of potential chaos, the prince, per usual, proved steady.

"The only thing I will *watch*," Liliana bit off the word, "is the total and utter ruin of this cycle of knowledge consolidation you have created for yourselves. Your people have held a monopoly on education for centuries that feeds on the exploitation of *our* workers who barely know how to read the contracts *your* legal experts draft. How do you in good conscience say the elitist hierarchy of knowledge that you and yours have created is a system worth upholding?"

"You speak beyond your station," the ambassador hissed through gritted teeth. Despite efforts of restraint, his hand twitched at his side. Aoran's eyes flashed, his mark thundering with electricity and heart screaming for blood. His hands crept for the handles of his sickle swords.

"I *speak* as the future ruler of Electaria!" Liliana thundered back, taking a step toward the man and raising her own hand. Her thumb curled in, her hand straight and firm—Aoran's lessons had proved to be worth something. She readied to strike the diplomat with a traditional Electarian commander's blow for wayward troops.

Before she moved, Leo hurried forward, grabbing her hand and swinging it down. "Enough!" Leo must have put every ounce of force he contained in his voice. His hand shook as he pinned Liliana's hand to her side. Leo turned to the diplomat and bowed so low Aoran looked away, embarrassed to see a monarch bend that far. "I'm sorry for any offense we may have caused and apologize for my daughter. Please, continue to enjoy the festivities and speak with one of my more"—Leo cast a sideways glare at Liliana— "agreeable children."

The Nuwei diplomat, far from appeased, gave a stiff nod and turned to join his fellow council members with Teo. Aoran stayed close to the pair, but his eyes trailed the diplomat as he walked away. Aoran was unable to let go of the handles of his swords, his mark and heart lighting up in unison and mouth twisting into a scowl. Leo spun Liliana around to face him. The king was met with blazing hazel eyes.

"Your more *agreeable* children?" Liliana laughed, the sound a dark contrast to the merriment that cautiously reemerged in the background. "Yes, please. Send these diplomats to your children who will smile and nod their heads at whatever policies these...

these *crooks* will throw on the table. No matter how wrong, how immoral these ideas may be—let us be *agreeable*, shall we?"

"The Nuwei are among our closest allies, and we should not be bringing policy into a *celebration* of all places—"

"Where else do we discuss these things? In our conferences and meetings where the Nuwei council bands together and refuses to put on the agenda that which brings them a modicum of discomfort? These issues are swept under rugs of policy and promises of future action, overshadowed by the least controversial, least effective, least *important* change we might take on."

"Then why have you not discussed this further with our education council?" Leo's furry eyebrows scrunched together. "Why go after the poor diplomat? Why incite such rancor from the Nuwei?"

"Because the council doesn't *listen*. Nobody here listens." Liliana threw up her hands, gesturing to the room. "I have been on the education council for two years trying to make whatever changes I could as a member and have barely scratched the surface of what I wanted to accomplish. Everybody wants to give themselves a pat on the back for ruling the country the way it has always been ruled. The people want more from us, and we should want more from ourselves!"

"Then we may ameliorate these issues later—these are systemic issues that cannot be resolved by attacking one Nuwei diplomat. You have placed complex diplomatic matters on the shoulders of one man in an entire voting body. How can that be fair?" Leo shook his head. "You are not yet a queen, and you have no right to speak to our allies in this way. We will discuss this tomorrow in a more"—he looked around and all the eavesdropping eyes suddenly found more interesting pieces of conversation on which to focus—"private setting." The king paused, staring at Liliana as if the words he wanted to say were written in her face.

She met his gaze challengingly, blazing brown eyes indignant, even though her hands trembled at her sides. She squeezed her hands into balls and kept her chin high, body tensed as if bracing for impact.

The king's deep voice cracked, ever slightly. "Liliana, I am disappointed in you."

Aoran winced, and Liliana fell into a glacial silence. The admonition was straightforward and stinging, particularly coming from a man Aoran knew Liliana admired and loved. Juliana had doled out praise and reproach with an equally fastidious hand for both. Leo was just their loving father, choosing to leave all stricter aspects of parenting to his wife. Juliana turned validation into a prize to be earned, while Leo simply supported his children through all the seasons.

Liliana opened her mouth, eyes shining with fury and surrounded by a sadness that hit Aoran straight in the chest. She closed her mouth, lips tightening and eyes blinking furiously. Something cracked and solidified in the princess. When she finally replied, her voice was low, wavering, but absolutely certain. "And I am disappointed in you. What is the use of sitting in your throne if you never learn to leave its comforts and take a stand?"

She nailed the words to her father's hands, crucifying him on the cross of his own insecurities. For a moment, Aoran pictured Juliana's phantom drifting behind Liliana, her hands planted smug and comfortable on her daughter's shoulders. Liliana twisted on her heel, her cape fluttering behind her as she marched from the hall, head high.

Leo's shoulders slumped, a man already defeated with another weight added to the torture of his sentence. He turned to Aoran. "Which do you think worse of me—as a father or as a king?"

"Would you like me to be totally honest, Your Majesty?"

Leo nodded.

Aoran shrugged. "Both could use some work. But she does not make either one an easy task."

"Few things worth doing are." Leo sighed, rubbing under his eyes with the palms of his hands. He nodded his head toward the closed door. "Will you look after her? Try and make her see some reason in light of tonight's events?"

"The princess has a particular type of astigmatism toward seeing reason, Your Majesty." Leo looked particularly exhausted, so Aoran quickly added, "But I'll speak with her. On exceedingly special days, she sees fit to entertain some of my thoughts."

Aoran hurried out the large double doors of the grand hall, soon catching a glimpse of Liliana's lavender dress fluttering as she turned the corner. Fortunately for him, her righteous rage didn't compensate for the preexisting disadvantage of heels. *Still, she moves annoyingly fast.* Aoran gritted his teeth. "Son of a malum— wait up!"

Aoran started jogging, finally catching up to the princess as he burst into the intersection of the castle where Liliana's ice beetle sculpture resided. The intricate piece glittered underneath the hallway's torches, a contrast to the princess's stormy demeanor. His chest rose and fell rapidly, trying to catch his breath. Aoran came up behind Liliana, grabbing her wrist. She whipped around.

He expected an immediate tirade, decrying the idiocy of everyone who couldn't understand her. Aoran stood still, posture tense, ready for her diatribe. Instead, Liliana turned to look at him with...was that *hurt* in her eyes?

"They don't trust me, Aoran. Why don't they trust me? I've spent years, *years*, trying to help this kingdom in whatever way I can. I read all the stupid books I could get my hands on, joined the stupid Education Council—quite literally the least significant council there is, but I joined anyway and tried to make changes. I did all the *Imperium*-forsaken things I could do, and it's still *not enough for them*." The last part came out like a plea.

Even with her back hunched and her shoulders drawn inward, her chin stuck out, held up by her aching pride. Her eyes shone under the light of the chandelier, vulnerable and terrible.

Aoran's heart squeezed for this woman in front of him and the girl at whose side he had spent so many years. He had born witness to her struggle to be something more than what so many people consigned her to, admiring her valiance every time her plans fell apart, and she put back together her pride and tried again. Without Queen Juliana, plans dissolved far more frequently, whether by the nature of Liliana's station or by the design of Liliana's plans, which were always so much loftier than what the rest of the country was ready for.

And in her perpetual cycle of failure and renewal, Aoran thought she was one of the most beautiful things in the world. The princess, his dragon—she wanted so much from life, and the fact that she never gave up the fight for more than what society allowed her was remarkable and sent his heart pulsing.

He looked at Liliana with an indecipherable expression, his green eyes burning. His hand, still on her wrist, drifted up to clasp her elbow. "Do you think so, princess? Is it them? Or are you worried that you might not be enough yourself?"

She blinked at him, and he ventured a dangerous step forward.

"Or maybe you're worried that you won't be able to live up to Queen Juliana the way you want to?"

Liliana stared blankly at him and then began laughing, the empty sound echoing in a broken way in the grand hallways. She shook her head, disbelieving, shoulders shaking with her incredulous and raw amusement. "Of course. I should have known better than to speak to you. I should have known you wouldn't take me seriously—just like everybody else. *Please*, Aoran of the Four, continue on with your dreary half existence of oscillating between punching people and smoking in a futile effort to compensate for your total and utter lack of perceived existential purpose. I shall work to avoid bothering you with such matters in the future."

Aoran recoiled, his mark jolting with a bolt of electricity and his aching for the princess replaced with anger.

"And you continue on, using your sharp tongue and prickly personality to cover your insecurities and personal failings. Forget appreciating those who may actually be on your side—it's so much easier to yell and scare them away, right? Worked really well for you tonight," Aoran snapped back at her. His hand around her elbow tightened.

Liliana growled and swept her hand forward, palm open and ready to slap Aoran across the face. A futile attempt, and they both knew it. Aoran caught her wrist in the air. Her shaking hand hovered a few inches from his face. Liliana's face flushed an intense, blotchy red, her breathing heavy. Aoran let out a tiny sigh, releasing his moment of rage. Liliana didn't need a sparring partner or an adversary of any kind right now. Even if the stubborn princess would sooner eat her own foot than admit it, she needed somebody right now. Aoran could swallow his damn pride.

Aoran adjusted his grip and tugged on her arm, pulling Liliana until she practically tripped into his chest. He wrapped his arms around her, one hand on the top of her head, the other coiling around her waist. Liliana pressed her nose to his uniform, frozen for a moment before relaxing in the embrace. Her hazel eyes fluttered, blinking away silent tears. Aoran held her there in that position, the only movement the occasional brush of his finger against the tip of her ear.

After what felt like an eternity, Liliana spoke, her voice muffled and more repentant than Aoran had heard in a long time. "I'm sorry for trying to slap you."

"No apology necessary. I'm so incredibly talented that even with your best effort you would have never been able to make contact."

Liliana snorted, the sound soft and almost watery. "Of course."

Silence pushed through the hallway for the span of a heartbeat.

"We're going to pretend this never happened tomorrow."

"As Her Highness wishes."

Liliana pushed Aoran away with a small laugh.

He clung to her for a second longer before letting her go. He grinned as he watched her back straightening and shoulders rolling back, unfurling to her full height like a cat after a nap. Her eyes and face were rimmed with rose, as if an artist had taken his brightest red and used Liliana as his canvas. Unconsciously, Aoran reached forward and rubbed his thumb underneath her eye, wiping away the makeup that had smeared against his uniform.

Liliana looked at the dark smudge on Aoran's hand, expression mortified. "I can't go back in there looking like this."

"I can accompany you to your room before returning, if you'd like," Aoran offered with a flourished bow. He looked up at her with a wicked grin, trying to bring Liliana back to a semblance of normalcy. "Besides, it's the gentlemanly thing to do to help a girl in the bedroom."

"It's also the gentlemanly thing to do to abstain from fighting, drugs, and general vulgarity." Liliana ticked off her fingers with a raised eyebrow. "Are you sure you want to tempt the Gods by classifying yourself thusly?"

"Princess, as I've said to you before, temptation is my specialty."

Liliana shoved him with both her hands, her cheeks bright. Aoran snickered and stuck his hands in his pockets, walking toward Liliana's room. The two slowly ambled along, for once in no hurry. Though at least three feet of space separated the two as they walked, Aoran couldn't help the fanciful notion that they leaned toward one another with their own gravitational pull.

CHAPTER 13
7055.1.21

E lle had become somewhat of a master in the art of stealth. Whatever clandestine expertise she thought she had gained traveling the streets of the city paled in comparison to her skills now. A week of being gawked and marveled at by the assorted flavors of the elite flocking to the castle proved to be a spectacular incentive. Now, Elle snuck, skulked, and shirked with a thief's precision. She wondered how she'd do at Madame Dragonia's if she gave it another go.

She moved through the castle seamlessly, just another decoration in the opulence of the palace. It was a skill most easily acquired by those who did not grow up expecting attention. Elle noticed this when she first arrived at the castle and had yet to see an instance to disprove her theory. When someone grew up with the belief that *Terrabis* and the Gods' eyes were upon them, they stood tall and spread their legs in a way that took up more space in a room. Elle, on the other hand, had lived with the same anonymity that most people of the city did—knowable only to those closest in proximity and otherwise ignored by the rest of the world.

Tonight's sneaking was more than aimless wandering through a castle of people she would never understand. No, tonight's sneaking held the boon of escape. Her boots shuffled beneath the thick fabric of her robes, delightfully free from the confines of heels and dresses. Empress Renee insisted Elle be put in more Vitrian clothing. The Electarians complained about Elle competing for an Electarian position, but Elle sided with the empress. In the airy, breathable fabrics of Vitria, Elle finally felt a little more at home. She was able to walk more easily through the castle, stand up a little straighter.

The time spent initially learning the crevices of the castle turned vanishment into a manageable task. Elle simply needed to stick to the background and avoid detection, an easy enough task with the feast in full swing. Even then, the faint sounds of Vitrian and Aurjnegh diplomats traveled, muffled, through the thick walls—a testament to both nations' tenacity in noise. One more right and...

Etiam! Elle grinned to herself. The window she sought was mounted at the end of an intersection of three hallways. If Elle took a left, she would find the throne room. If she took a right, she would find the stairwell leading to the upper and lower floors of the castle. Should she turn around, she would find herself stuck in the grand hall. The ceilings of the intersection, like everywhere else in the castle, were taller than two fully grown men standing atop one another. Creamy and simple, the ceiling served as a refreshing contrast to the golden intricacy of the walls it bordered.

The ground floor window before Elle, a resplendent, stained glass masterpiece, depicted *Imperium*'s defeat of *malum*. The towering, eight-foot woman stood over *malum*'s huddled form, face hidden beneath the layers of cloth and pools of golden blood. The other Gods watched, impervious, behind *Imperium*'s shoulder. They stood as solemn witnesses as she drew back her silver spear, prepared to deliver the final blow. In what Elle considered a morbid addition, the stained glass was framed by two thick, crimson curtains, whose elegant, flowing style reminded Elle of running blood.

Apparently unbeknownst to many in the castle, the stained glass windows within were done in panel styling. Elle grinned and approached the bottom panel, pushing it gently. The window creaked from disuse before giving way, opening to the grounds below.

"Lady Ellegance?"

Elle froze, quickly shutting the window closed. Slowly, she turned around to see one of the castle's staff staring at her. She gave the man a sheepish grin, walking toward him with small steps. The easiest counter to her magic of obscurity was someone who was also obscure. Phil, an errand runner for the castle in his midtwenties, more than fit the bill. His job, and thus his existence, was defined by the needs of others. More so, he shared the pale, grayish skin color of the Soj people, which gave everyone in the castle all the more reason to ignore him.

Which meant, of course, that of all the people Elle could have run into, he was absolutely the most likely to notice her.

"Aren't you supposed to be at the banquet?"

Phil was one of a growing handful of serving people in the castle who had cautiously befriended Elle. Though they still stuck to honorifics and superficial pleasantries, they, at the very least, *talked* to her now. Upon breaking past their bustling, stressed exteriors, which Elle understood they naturally wore as members of the castle workforce, Elle found the real, flesh-and-blood people beneath. And the people beneath were, in fact, delightful company. While people like Phil were far from the comfort of her family, there was still something familiar about the focused tenacity many of them shared.

In his arms he held a silky emerald stole, an amethyst stain slowly dominating the green of the finely woven threads. The fabric was wrinkled, as if children had balled the beautiful piece up and decided to use it in one of their games.

Elle pointed at the stole, ducking beneath Phil's question, and said, "Somebody a bit careless with their wine?"

His sigh crossed with a tired chuckle. "More the Aurjnegh being careless with their clothes. The stole had been on the floor for upward of thirty minutes before its distraught owner finally noticed."

"Ah, such are the trials and tribulations of an Aurjnegh court member, no?" Elle grinned at Phil, who gave her a tentative smile back.

His eyes strayed to the right, clearly ready to return to his task, but something gave him pause. He opened his mouth before stopping, closing it for a few seconds, and then opening it again. "Congratulations on the first Trial, Lady Ellegance. I was thrilled to hear you passed with the highest marks."

Elle scratched the back of her neck, a pleased embarrassment written across her face. "Thank you. It was...interesting, to say the least."

The idea of being tested by *Menda*'s standards had felt strange to Elle. She spent her entire life being raised by two people with the marks of *Menda*—in a way, her upbringing had essentially been built around the ideology of *Menda*. King Leo had served as her judge, and the Trial had simply felt like a chat between acquaintances. They discussed her family, her dreams of seeing the world, her thoughts on ruling a nation. Elle never actively thought about telling the truth; it was just something she had been raised to do.

"They say that you didn't hesitate," Phil murmured, gray eyes locked on Elle's violet ones. "Everyone says that while Teo and Liliana paused before saying anything, careful of their words, you didn't falter. You simply...spoke."

Elle raised her eyebrows in surprise. Though she was far from ingrained in the castle's gossip, she figured that kind of rumor would have gotten to her sooner. The idea of Liliana or Teo pausing for anything baffled Elle. Both seemed so steeped in self-confidence that they would sooner be run through with a sword before deciding to change the path on which they walked. Elle furrowed her eyebrows. In fact, she had expected better of both siblings. Elle had yet to fully process the outcome of the Trial, but what did it say about the state of things that she had emerged victorious?

While Elle had yet to witness any of this personally, she could name countless times kids, merchants, her parents, practically everybody, had complained of the lack of transparency in the government. Perhaps Teo and Liliana, both raised in the castle, were subsequently subject to the same type of pressures that veiled governmental action, clouding their communication. Phil, in his proximity to the various government officials of the kingdom, had probably seen his fair share of lies and deceit. *What a tragic idea*, Elle thought, biting the inside of her cheek, *that honesty in and of itself is a novelty.* Elle shook off the morose tinge of her thoughts, giving Phil a small smile. "As any leader should, *etiam?*"

Phil didn't respond, but a slow smile stretched across his ashen face. He nodded and turned to the right, starting toward the washing rooms once more, clutching the emerald stole tighter. He cast one last curious glance back at Elle before disappearing around the corner entirely.

Elle exhaled a harsh breath she didn't know she'd been holding. She cracked one of the window panels open, a brush of clean air running against her face. Luckily, Phil hadn't continued his line of questioning, and Elle's miniature escape could continue. She opened the window further, preparing to slide out of the—

Stomping echoed down the hallway, and Elle groaned, pulling the window closed once more and making her breath shallow. Liliana slammed her way by the intersection of the hallway perpendicular to Elle, a sight to behold. She paced around the ice beetle sculpture in the intersection, muttering under her breath. Elle discovered the other day that Liliana had created the sculpture. However, Elle struggled to imagine the furious princess before her crafting something so delicate.

Liliana's chin jutted into the air, defiance in the absence of resistance. Without anyone around, it looked like she was putting the paintings and chandeliers in their place. Her bottom lip trembled; the inside of her cheek sucked in like she was clamping down on it with all her might.

Elle was struck by the momentary fragility she caught in the princess's face. Liliana, with the pomp of the palace stripped away, was significantly less intimidating. The upturn of her chin looked less arrogant than it did a facade of force, an action not brought about by confidence but rather by trying to instill it. Her fierce eyes seemed less a weapon and more a shield. The princess, in all her beautiful and ferocious wit, seemed like she was pushing down her uncertainty with a painful amount of will.

It comforted Elle, just a little, to know even the girl who normally glowed with self-assurance also sometimes looked like she was stumbling aimlessly in the dark.

"Son of a malum—wait up!" shouted Aoran.

Elle blinked, eyes wide, and she moved before she was caught in a situation from which she couldn't escape. She released her breath and pushed open the bottom panel of the window—the one displaying *Imperium's* discarded crown—and slid down the wall to land in the soft flower beds below. She winced, mouthing "sorry" to the poor plants crushed beneath the weight of her fall.

Elle visited the garden frequently during the day. When her arms weren't pulled this way and that by various people attempting to curry favor, she escaped to the outdoors, putting her nose to the air and trying to catch a whiff of the smoky and damp scent of her city's streets. All she found was the smell of more flowers. Not that she minded; they were lovely. But they weren't real. The lives these people lived—their politicking, their banquets, their competitions, even their *smells*—lacked depth.

A breeze whispered up her arms, flowing playfully through her robes, a cool relief to the sweat already beginning to accumulate at Elle's brow. Whether from stress or the weather, Elle hardly knew, but she seemed to run hotter these days, and she mentally thanked the empress once more for her new clothes. The Vitrians maintained a general sense of style, but unlike Electarians, they changed the fabric of their clothing based upon the season. While they wore wool in the winter months, lighter, cotton fabrics dominated their styles during Impe and Supe.

Luckily, having visited the garden so often allowed her an intimate knowledge of where to slither to escape the watchful gaze of the guard. She ducked and dived, jumping between bushes of flowers as the guards turned their heads to survey a different section. She had to restrain a laugh. Elle nearly forgot how fun it was to test her limits and play with consequences.

When the guards began to switch shifts, Elle relaxed. The shift took around three minutes, giving her plenty of time to stroll the remaining fifty feet. She passed by two people, vaguely hidden in the shadowy areas that the torches failed to illuminate. The pair appeared so thoroughly immersed in one another that Elle doubted she could distract them even by running them through with a spear. It appeared to be a guard and a dignitary, the armored individual pinning the dignitary against the wall, her dress's skirt and frills spilling over the guard's arms.

They broke apart for an instant, and Elle did a double take, recognizing that heavy breathing and those lidded eyes. Eliana pressed her lips against Dayanara's cheek—*wasn't that her bodyguard?*—and to Elle's surprise, Eliana gave Elle a pointed look with her smoldering, obsidian eyes. The princess flashed Elle a devilish smile and sly wink before moving her mouth down to Dayanara's neck.

The guard appeared not to have noticed a thing. Dayanara's eyes pinched closed, her lips barely parted and totally silent except for the occasional gasp. Elle took the wink as a sign that Eliana would keep her lips shut about Elle's escape. *Well, as shut as Eliana might ever keep her lips.*

With a shudder crawling down her back, Elle prayed to *Superbia* as she hurried through the shadows of the garden. While the Goddess had no official stake in matters of love, the nature of confidence and insecurity—*Superbia*'s domain—often found itself intertwined in the heart's affairs. Elle offered up whatever material possessions she had to the Goddess, just to avoid running into the viper princess like that again. Elle wasn't sure she would be able to take another meeting of that nature without passing out.

Distracted by a wink that replayed obsessively in her mind, Elle nearly ran into the palace wall. She stopped, stunned, and did her best to rid Eliana's parasitic presence from her mind, focusing on the task in front of her. She fluttered her fingers against the cobblestone walls, finding divots weathered in over time. For a normal person, these divots would be visual nuisances, nothing more. Elle, with her experience in climbing anything and everything, quickly turned those nuisances into perfect hand- and footholds.

She gripped the protrusions, digging her toes into the niches, and climbed upward. Elle grimaced as the abrasive rocks rubbed against her hands. Barely any time in the castle, and already she worried her hands had grown softer. Ignoring the discomfort, she put one hand in front of the other and scaled higher and higher until she perched comfortably on top of the wall, castle grounds on one side, city on the other.

Elle liked these places. Forgotten by the world from fear or inconvenience, they existed beyond the greedy fingers of those who would never be able to truly appreciate them. People like Teo, blind to a value that expanded far beyond its currency, would question the utility this wall brought. Liliana would demand the wall be higher and greater than ever before. It was people like Elle who asked the wall for nothing but its existence, explored its mysteries, and discover what more might be lying beneath the surface.

The wind grew stronger, whipping her choppy black hair around with a rough hand. She held on to the wall below her, unafraid of the fall even as the gales grew in intensity. She closed her eyes and took another breath, hints of the city burning through her nose. Over the smell of the castle gardens and beneath the odor of the wind stood a scent of wet cobblestone and fruits left too long in the rain. She held on to this damp, saccharine smell, cherishing every second of it that made her stomach turn. She spared one last glance at the castle before hurling herself over the other side and scaling down as quickly as she could.

Her feet hit the ground with a thud that shocked her knees. She glanced around, waiting for some cry signaling her disappearance. No alarms set off; no shouts greeted her. Instead, the sounds of drunken fools welcomed her back into the city. The taste of smoke and stale liquor in the air coaxed her deeper into its recesses. Elle took a tentative step forward onto the cobblestone her feet spent years tracking. Another step followed. And another. Before she knew it, Elle sprinted through the streets of the city.

The buildings pressed against one another, pushed aggressively together like a group of patrons in line for the first loaf of bread. They crowded out the stars of the night sky, forming their own celestial sea of torches and candlelit windows. Elle leaped over discarded boxes in the street. She danced between the nightwalkers of the kingdom, women and men waiting on corners for an iron bit to be thrown their way in exchange for some company. She spun with the delicacy of an ice beetle's thread, weaving through the people and places with ease. As she dashed through the alleyways she had spent years scoring into her mind, an elated laugh bubbled at the back of her throat. She felt like a floundering fish thrown back into the water.

Elle's canter slowed into a jog, her surroundings changing from simply familiar to home. She could point out which candles would be extinguished, and which would still blaze at this time of night. She could match the muddy footprints littering the sidewalks with every child's shoe in the area. She could draw the constellations of clothespins on laundry lines with perfect accuracy.

The lights in Elle's home were off, the bakery's sign clearly scrawled: Closed. Her lips pressed into a thin line, and she nodded to herself. *As expected.* Elle had yet to receive communication from her family. She wondered if Penelope and the twins had been able to continue their lessons, wherever they landed. Nic was probably driving their parents insane with nothing to do himself in the absence of his bakery responsibilities. Whether the lack of letters stemmed from inability due to restrictions from the castle or some other reason, Elle could only guess.

"You'd better be taking care of them. You'd better be keeping them safe and full and warm." Elle pointed at the sky warningly, forcing conviction into her voice. Her shoulders drooped and her voice dropped to a low whisper, "Please."

The wind whipped by her face, and her mark pulsed as the breeze caressed her skin. Elle sighed and nodded. The only reason she truly wanted to come in the first place was just to give herself the space to reminisce and miss her family. The castle made her feel disconnected from them in a way that nauseated her; she hoped that returning to the bakery would allow her to feel their absence in full, ache for them as they properly deserved.

So she began to climb. She grabbed onto the windowsill of the building next to the bakery, fingers finding worn-in notches and pulling herself up higher and higher. The old couple that followed *Caecus* always had bars on their windows in fear of the young riffraff, providing perfect handholds. The family that followed *Superbia* above decorated their window in splendor, silks spiraling down from the top of their window. Elle grabbed onto the bottom, pulling herself up with burning arms.

Years of climbing this building served as her map to the top. She retraced the footsteps of younger iterations of herself, each one more naive than the one before. Elle laughed to herself, legs straining to push herself up to the next windowsill. She probably was still naive in many ways. But she saw what clarity did to those older than her. Stagnant, jaded, cantankerous—age brought with it a kind of poison that wilted blooming flowers, eroding their petals and turning them into weeds simply trying to survive and multiply.

She wore her nineteen years like a cloak, easy to shuck off, and remembered how it felt to be young and free. Elle recalled with perfect precision the way her heart and mark used to pound as she climbed the building's terrain, pretending she scaled the Constans Mountains that bordered Nuwei. A girl who was thrilled by the notion of the world and its vastness, yet to be discouraged by practicality and its cruel sibling, reality.

After making it to the top of the building, she hopped up to the roof of her house. Shoes scraping against the walls, she lugged herself onto the roof, crawling until she sat on the edge of the building, long legs swinging over the weathered edges of the roof. She admired the city, which she held closer to her heart than nearly anyone. The full moon glowed, illuminating the cracks where all the rooftops fit together like a messy puzzle. Elle liked to think of the streets as one entity of the earth, separated narrowly by miniature earthquakes that created seismic fracturing, just enough room for walking and peddling goods. An indescribable feeling overwhelmed Elle as she watched the world beneath her.

How very vulnerable her city looked from above. The buildings, patchwork entities in varying stages of decay, sat upon cobblestone streets whose stones had cracked years prior. While Elle knew it had been a while since the city's last infrastructure project, never before had its face looked so worn down and tired. From her vantage point, the buildings looked like simple pieces in a Dragons and Wolves board game. Playthings to be moved around but never taken seriously. Was that why everything continued to fall apart, ameliorated only through patchwork bandages on much deeper wounds?

How very small, how *insignificant* it all looked from so many stories removed. Though they looked like pawns from so high above, there was so much more to be understood underneath that first glance. This high up, Elle would never know about little girls like Penelope who desperately wanted more than what their reality would allow them. Elle wouldn't be aware of crippling rent payments that stole away her family's income, leaving them with little left over to save for something more. Elle would never understand the inability of the city's people to move the needle on issues they truly cared about.

In some ways, Elle felt a pang of empathy for the royals. From so high up, it was impossible to understand the rot beneath. Is this what Liliana and King Leo saw when they looked down from the castle? Or did they see microcosms of poverty, case studies to be experimented upon with policy draughts in the search for an eternal elixir? Or were they blind even to those?

How could they ever understand the people who lived in these houses from a forty thousand-foot view? People like her family existed under these roofs, living out each day on a handful of coins and a prayer to their pantheon of Gods. Elle's back burned as she looked below at the streets, picturing the people she used to see every day haunting its crevices. These people's problems could never be understood from a vantage point where the watching party was always looking down.

Elle knew these people. She knew this city. She knew its dangers, its problems, its mystery, its beauty, its worn-in lanes and well-loved bridges. The nuances of hundreds of thousands of lives aggregated into one area were something few could claim to understand, Elle among them. But she knew more and would try harder than somebody raised within the confines of palace walls would ever be able to.

"Uh-oh," Elle said out loud to herself, groaning and laughing at the same time. Elle's mark burned and pounded, slowly at first but growing harder and faster. She looked up to the stars, picturing *Imperium*'s steely eyes painted in its glowing dots. "I think I just found resolve. Does that mean I have to win now?"

The question was rhetorical, but a breeze echoed in response, blowing up through her robes and soothing the burning of her mark. The stars spun, radiating brighter and harder than she had ever seen them. Elle closed her eyes and parted her lips, letting the city wash over her.

"*Etiam, etiam*. I hear you." She laughed, throwing herself back over the edge and beginning her descent down the building as she steeled herself to sneak back into the castle. "I guess the competition really begins now."

CHAPTER 14
7055.1.23

The Crimson Cough struck Liliana when she was fourteen years old. When Electaria was still little more than a wriggling notion in one man's mind, the Landing developed. Its growth turned what would be Electaria's capitol city into a booming metropolis and primary trading hub for Electaria as a whole. While the development of a major trading port had a variety of positive externalities, one of the least suspected, but most appreciated, was disease prevention.

Electarian children had legendary immune systems from the constant influx of goods and people from outside nations. The Sea Sickness (an infamous Vitrian novelty), Scholar's Scum (a Nuwei delight), and Silent Suffering (a Soj specialty) were diseases that haunted the globe. To the chagrin of the rest of *Terrabis*, Electarian children avoided just about every single one with their hardened bodies.

However, the Crimson Cough seemed to be the one disease able to penetrate their seasoned immune systems. It was practically an Electarian rite of passage to go through puberty and contract the disease at some point in the process. The Cough rarely killed anyone. It mostly served as a two-week-long ordeal that bonded the kingdom's children together through their companionable commiseration. Electarians delighted in comparing the amounts of blood they hacked up during the experience. If there was ever a lull in conversation at the castle, it could usually be assuaged by mentioning—in an offhand manner, of course—the exact length of time one had been plagued by the Cough. The longer someone stayed beneath the sheets, stuttering through the blood bubbling in between their breaths, the more impressed the audience.

Liliana went through Corticus Rotations now, utterly disconnected from the movements and completely lost in her thoughts regarding the Cough. Aoran had started her on the defensive stance, dangling the idea of teaching her the more advanced poking and attacking stances later. He had served the knowledge to her like a precious delicacy—with an appetizer quip of how she could benefit from learning to let things go. When he first showed her the Rotations, Aoran's body glided through the motion like a bird riding a particularly strong gust of wind. Eyes focused and yet seeing nothing, he looked utterly natural and at ease. She failed to find the same meditative peace. Her body marched through the military's most honored tradition while her mind explored the terrain of her memories of the Cough.

Liliana had a particularly gruesome time of it. For a disease that lasted around two weeks on average, Liliana lay bedridden for twenty-six awful, bloody days. What she did and who took care of her had all but faded into a blurred, feverish dream.

What she felt, though, echoed in her brain with a tenacious insistence. Her chest had burned as if somebody set fire to coal sizzling in the bottom of each of her lungs. Her body ached, each limb swelling with viscous liquid that was about to burst through her skin. When she coughed, she clenched every muscle in her body, terrified she would lose control of all her faculties with each wracking storm.

A miserable experience, indubitably. And yet the entire time Liliana lay there in agonizing silence, a small, comforting voice told her that everything would be okay. She *had* to be okay, and thus, she would be okay. The torture was temporal, a sapling of suffering meant to bloom, wither, and fade away in its own time. Liliana was miserable, but she never once feared for her future.

The past few days had been a lot like that. Liliana never spoke with her father after the dinner. The king never sent her a request for an audience. She supposed the onus was on her to set up the meeting, make amends both with the Nuwei Council and her own family. Liliana laughed softly to herself. He had to have known she could never do such a thing. *Would* never do such a thing. The distinction hardly mattered.

Liliana had been right in standing up for her country. Politicians so often played nice with one another for the sake of diplomatic relations, never willing to push each other to uncomfortable places that might actually result in change. Her mother would have done the same thing, had she been in Liliana's shoes. In fact, the Nuwei's monopoly on the education system was one of the first issues her mother ever lectured to Liliana about. Even if her father's disappointment stung with a constant, tiny pinch, Liliana maintained her resolve that she wouldn't rewrite the night, even if she could.

Instead of resolving the break in their relationship, Liliana dove into her work on the education council. Even while the castle was in the throes of an imminent political transition, the rest of the country did not cease to function. She spent the entire night of the banquet alone drafting new legislation that would seek funding to establish a new university in Electaria. If Nuwei refused to do its part and bridge the vast gap in higher education, Liliana was determined to drive the two separated ledges together by force.

In her focus on this new initiative, she stopped talking to many people. Liliana struggled to talk to Teo, always inflamed by annoyance when she saw him. Eliana, an equally unappealing conversation partner, was never to be found anyway. In the absence of all her family, a new silence existed between the spaces of Liliana's breaths. She stood, her limbs swollen once more as with the Cough, making her unable to move in any direction to mend the peace. Was it uncomfortable? Of course. But she would survive, and Liliana did not fear for her future.

Liliana heard Aoran's footsteps before she saw him, slowing down in her course through Rotations. She could recognize his soft gait through the tumult of a thunderstorm, attuned from years of listening for his entrance to a room. With his confidence, one would figure he would stomp, each step resonating with his sense of self-importance. In fact, it was the exact opposite: Aoran carried a delicate presence. He walked with steps so light that Liliana was convinced the bones in his feet must be hollow. From his smile to the air beneath his feet, so much about him was free of care and the gravity of life.

Beyond his footsteps, Aoran's presence had a tangible feel that extended past his lean body. His very essence took up space in a room, filling the area with a faint warmth. It was a miracle he had the stealth skills he did; Liliana didn't even need to hear or see a thing to know Aoran had come into a room. Her heart simply burned the moment he entered.

It was because she recognized him so acutely that she also knew to jump forward when he approached from behind and tried to take her out at the legs. Growling, she turned around and pushed a few stray strands of hair back from her face. "Forgive me for doing Rotations on my own like you asked."

Aoran stared at her, unimpressed. He wore casual clothing, a simple, long-sleeved white shirt tucked into a pair of black pants and soft leather boots. Even his hair hung free, framing his face and sharp jawline. The only reminder of his soldier duties were his sickle swords, ever crossed and ready against his back. Her heart thumped, and she cursed the damned thing silently.

"If you were doing Rotations right, you wouldn't have been able to hear me, much less have been able to dodge."

Liliana's eye twitched. "Maybe I'm just better at them than you. Ever considered that?"

"Of course." Aoran nodded his head emphatically. "I've also considered the idea that the silent Ro of the Four runs away and becomes the charismatic leader of an uprising of the Soj people. Equally implausible ideas."

"One day I will use your body as Imperium's chew toy."

Aoran jerked at the threat, his eyes flickering around the room. "Where is the wolf, anyway?"

Liliana stared, confused by the turn in conversation. "I don't know—frolicking around the castle and doing whatever wolves do. Why?"

Aoran shook his head. "Just trying to get a gauge on my imminent demise as his chew toy. Until that much anticipated moment..." Aoran paused, his green eyes softening around the edges. He took a step toward Liliana, hands in the air as if to say, "I come in peace." "How are you feeling? Are you ready for the trial?"

An excellent question. One Liliana had pondered herself for the two long nights that had felt like weeks. Toward the end of the feast, it was announced that the trial of *Superbia* would follow *Menda*. Liliana tortured herself with possibilities of how they might test her. They could have her admit her greatest flaws (an event sure to bring joy to Eliana, at the very least). They could have her admit her greatest points of hubris. After decreeing to the empress of Vitria in the first trial that she was the best one to rule over the kingdom, it seemed a strong possibility. She winced to herself. She wasn't exactly thrilled at any of the options.

"I just want it over with," she finally said. Her fears and anxieties, ultimately, did not matter. She would approach the challenge with fangs bared and claws out and pass with flying colors.

Aoran looked at her curiously, the same way wolves poked their noses around corpses found on the forest floor. The animals were playful and inquisitive, always looking for new toys with which to entertain themselves. Liliana rolled her eyes. She couldn't feed Aoran to Imperium—it would practically be cannibalism.

True to his word, he hadn't spoken of their encounter in the hallway. He did watch her with intense eyes, though, as if he were searching for a sign that she might break. Or searching for more parts that were already broken. The gaze didn't feel concerned, the way one might worry over the state of a delicate vase teetering on the edge of destruction. It was more fascinated, as if someone looked into the same vase and found a vast trove of gold. In spite of his obvious interest, he remained silent, letting the memory keep its peace in both of their minds.

Liliana struggled to relive the moment herself. Her feelings had been so...visceral. A culmination of her worries that she wouldn't live up to the one opportunity in her life to do something magnificent, failing years of effort on both her and her mother's part to sharpen Liliana's mind.

The idea that even her father doubted her capacity left her so empty, as if somebody had set acid in her stomach and let it burn until she was nothing left but toxins. It was so incredibly painful.

Liliana pushed aside the thought. Aoran opened his mouth, eyes hungry for more from his prey, but she cut him off. "Are you going into town today?"

He looked down, seeming almost surprised by the linen against his torso instead of his normal steel. Days off for soldiers, especially the Four, were few and far between. Sometimes Liliana forgot that Aoran had any more to his life beyond the armor and swords. She pursed her lips, appraising his outfit with greater interest. *What could he possibly have to do?*

He leaned against one of the training dummies, fingering the handle of one of his swords with absentminded care. "Yeah. I got some business to take care of down there." His eyes flashed, and his cheeks split into a taunting grin. "Of course, I'll be missing your sunshine smile the entire time I'm there."

Her cheeks immediately exploded with red. Any earlier curiosity dissipated with his flirtatious nonsense. She jabbed her finger at the exit and spluttered, "Shut up and get out!"

Aoran cackled, bowing low—far lower than he should have, given her station. "As Her Greatness commands. And princess?" He raised his head, making searing eye contact with her. His jade eyes glinted and twinkled simultaneously, as many parts playful as they were absolutely lethal. Her cheeks throbbed with the blood pulsing beneath the surface of her skin, and she found herself entirely unable to look away. "Good luck with the Trial."

She sputtered, watching him lope out of the room. The training room expanded with his departure, as if a whole legion of training dummies had just disappeared. Refastening the cape around her shoulder, she stomped out of the facility, grumbling softly to herself. *How annoying.* In an instant, he had sent her composure spiraling.

How was it fair? Aoran was one of those people who simply seemed made for living. He drifted through the motions with practiced ease, as if life was a final performance to a play he wrote. Even with actions as simple as walking, he practically glided—the man was unhindered by the weight of social expectations and universal laws of human existentialism. How could it possibly be so easy for him? If she were Aoran, these royal Trials would be nothing more than a comedy series for the traveling entertainers to use as fireside fodder. The *malum* would already be king, dammit.

Unnamable feelings with shadowy faces crawled through her body, some uglier than others. Some curled around her ear, purring for her to call him back. Others nestled in her heart, hissing to be rid of him entirely. Those feelings, those growling, snapping, biting feelings, nipped at her skin like an armada of microscopic fire ants. One on its own was hardly worth her attention, but the thousands setting blaze to her body made the feeling impossible to ignore. She tried to rip her mind away from thoughts of the soldier to no avail.

He wished her good luck. She snorted softly to herself, casting one last, stern look at the training arena from one of its many exits. Luck was the idyllic preaching of those who never came to know the struggles of clawing one's way to an achievement. Liliana was sure that Aoran, gifted with his physical prowess and mark of strength, believed in luck. Teo, groomed for a throne he was sure to inherit for years, likely also trusted in luck (though Liliana smiled slightly to herself; he was sure to have thought his luck changed in recent days). Eliana with her natural beauty was probably also a devotee of the notion.

The only person in the castle who Liliana believed may be exempt from the false faith was Ellegance. Though Liliana ultimately saw the city girl as competition to be defeated, Liliana couldn't help but admit that the young woman may be the only one, both in the Trials and the castle, who knew the feeling of having to work for something.

The Gods did not believe in luck. They handed out cards of strengths and weaknesses the day somebody was born. They plucked out their champions, those able to best carry their virtues through the world, and sent them on their lonesome way. Luck didn't have a damn thing to do with how they played their cards from there.

She stopped in front of the doors of the throne room, taking a deep, harsh breath through her nose. *Focus, Little Dragon.* Another Trial was nothing to fear—if nothing else, it was another opportunity to show her worth. It was a chance to show the people who had brushed her aside for years that she may have the mettle to run their kingdom better than they might ever have imagined. It was an opportunity to show her father that he was wrong to be disappointed, her brother that he was a fool to force her aside, and her mother that she was worth every second they spent together.

Her right hand shook ever so slightly. She pressed it to her side. Lifting her head up and jutting her chin into the air, she shoved the door open with her left hand.

And immediately halted in the doorway. Stacked in front of the throne like prisoners for execution, was a group of people so socially disconnected from one another they had little more in common than a loaf of bread and a dragon: one of Easternalia's children, the Nuwei ambassador, one of the cooks, a handful of the maids, Dayanara of the Four, and Easternalia herself. Most of them milled aimlessly around the dais, sparing each other barely more than a passing look. The group's meandering had stopped only by her abrupt entrance. Her mind raced. What in *Imperium*'s name was going on?

Easternalia's sharp eyes traced Liliana's lanky frame, and Liliana swore she saw the woman lick her dark red lips. Her aunt bounced forward off the dais, arms spread open, and cried out, "Oh, my *dear* Liliana. How good to see you!"

Training with Aoran still failed to physically prepare her for the crushing momentum of her aunt's embrace. Easternalia's feathered hat pushed into her face, suffocating Liliana slowly from a lack of oxygen and an abundance of familial propriety.

Easternalia leaned back and pursed her lips. "Are you not just positively thrilled for this Trial? You're going to do fabulous, dear, fabulous!"

Her aunt was in top form. Boasting an outfit that was more feathers than fabric, Easternalia wore a sapphire blue dress that had likely cost a few hundred Imperials and the lives of a small family of Timore hawks. Two exceptionally large feathers, likely plucked from the male hawk's expansive wings, made a poor effort in concealing her aunt's bursting bosom. From there, the feathers fanned out over her pale, aging body in strategic places, strung together by dainty, lace crochet and the will of the Gods themselves.

The golden bird on Easternalia's chest glowed, radiant. Prideful. The mark practically purred. *What must it be like*, Liliana wondered absentmindedly, *to always be so self-assured and confident of where you stand in the world?*

Liliana shook off the thought and found the will to be pleasant in the shallow depths of her social grace, a frozen smile plastered on her face. "Auntie, I didn't expect to see you here. Is this the Trial?" she looked around the room.

The people on the dais took turns sneaking looks at her, but Liliana focused on Easternalia's mouth, which had already kidnapped, tortured, and run away with the conversation.

"—and I simply *had* to be the one to facilitate your Trial, dear. I promised to be oh so fair to you three—and while I do love my family, don't be expecting any special treatment." She cackled, suddenly waving a blue-feathered fan at Liliana.

A fan procured from where? She's practically naked. Liliana didn't want to think about it too hard.

"But I truly am so thrilled! To be a part of such history! Truly, an honor."

Liliana cleared her throat, trying to appear as polite as possible. "Of course, Auntie. And what is the Trial?"

Easternalia's eyes narrowed the slightest, and Liliana wanted to kick herself. Those who followed *Superbia* could not read intentions and hearts the same way as those who followed *Menda*, but they picked up on social cues faster than her father picked up cloud biscuits. It was part of the reason the two groups of people tended to hate one another—one sought to be honest and direct in all that they said and did, while the other sought to exploit social dynamics to their benefit. It was a wonder the *Menda*-dominant nation of Vitria and *Superbia*-dominant nation of Aurjnegh weren't always at war.

"Why, of course, dear," Easternalia said this through a marginally less warm smile, a tiny but unfortunate indicator that she had registered Liliana's slip. "If you'll allow me, I will explain the task set before you."

Liliana nodded her head quickly, wary to speak again.

Easternalia looked satisfied, broad hips swaying back up to the dais. She turned dramatically toward Liliana, sweeping her arms out in a wide gesture. Her voice, nasally and clear, bounced off the acoustics of the lofty ceilings. "Welcome to the Trial dedicated to the glory of *Superbia*—she who watches over us and reminds us of our place and our worth. When it comes to ruling a nation, it is imperative that a leader be confident in his decisions."

Liliana's mark burned, and her eyebrows pushed together. While confidence was imperative, Liliana naturally didn't believe that the leader being a man was part of that mandate.

Easternalia continued, oblivious to the slip. "But!" She waved a finger warningly, looking awfully excited while doing so. "It is just as important for a leader to be humble, and to know when this confidence has been stretched past its limits. It is important for a leader to know where she has erred."

Liliana rolled her eyes. Pronouns be damned. Her aunt was doing it on purpose, the slimy *malum*.

"Therefore, in this trial, our contestants have the obligation—nay, the *opportunity!*—to humble themselves before others who believe they have suffered from the contestant's mistakes."

Her aunt's eyes lost their sparkle, and she zeroed in on Liliana with a smug simper. Liliana's heart dropped. Had she truly wronged all those people? *It couldn't be.*

"The ones you see behind me are a sample size of those who believe you have caused them harm. Your Trial, Liliana, should you choose to accept it," her aunt cried to the room, shaking her arms this way and that, "is to humble yourself before those who beseech your acknowledgment. You are to apologize, acknowledge your mistakes, and show you harbor the humility so necessary for a truly effective monarch. If you agree to these conditions, you may start with the visiting ambassador from Nuwei."

In that moment, Liliana concocted about a million other things she would rather do than apologize to the pompous *malum* standing before her. The list included dancing in a room lined with serrated hunting knives on the floor and having her trachea ripped from her throat and used as a traveling entertainer's new instrument, among a plethora of other equally gruesome tasks.

"Anytime now, dear," her aunt sang softly, pleasure caressing each note.

She knew it was petty, but Liliana sent a quick prayer up to *Imperium* to cut just one section of that stupid lace and have it all come tumbling down. It wouldn't be enough to ease the fury simmering in her blood, but it would at least give Liliana one thing about which to smile.

Taking a deep breath, Liliana took a step toward the Nuwei diplomat. He beheld her as she approached, a small smile playing on his pudgy, fawn face. Liliana wanted to puke, knowing her vomit would contain trace amounts of blood and hatred from the churning bile in her stomach.

Acid filled her mouth, leaving a putrid taste behind and burning every nerve in her body. Did Teo have to walk through this Trial? Did Teo even exist enough to provoke any emotion stronger than apathy from those around him? Did they intend on humiliating Liliana personally, or was she just the unlucky victim of her own history? Looking around the room, Liliana was almost surprised by the hatred she felt toward Easternalia. The contempt toward the Nuwei ambassador. The antipathy toward every single individual in the room.

And the small amount of scorn she held for herself. When a prisoner found herself locked in a cage of her own making, she spent her time abhorring the guards who held her there, but equally herself for ever being caught in the first place.

None of it mattered. The physical virulence she could feel like a flame had to be ignored. Her thoughts and musings had to be ignored. If she had to hold her nose and close her eyes to pass this trial, so be it. She *would* prevail. With any luck, the vitriol searing through her body and burning her mark would leave her numb enough to power through each apology with nary an extra thought.

Liliana laughed quietly to herself before stepping up to the diplomat. Perhaps she could have used a little bit of Aoran's foolish luck after all.

The man stood there, arms crossed and expectant. At such a close angle, Liliana could see every wrinkle and crease in his aged and ignorant face. His face split into a smile, his lips cracked and blistered. His robes bore the latest geometric pattern that found its home in the elite of Nuwei fashion. Triangles spliced on top of one another, each a slightly different shade of the same awful green against a black background. It was all the Vitrian's shape and form, none of its grace. She tried to shut off her mind, keep it from criticizing and analyzing. That was not what she was here to do. She was here to say sorry. *Right?* For a moment, Liliana doubted she could find the words in her vocabulary, even if she spent a century searching. Her mark throbbed. It burned. *Focus, Liliana.*

She took a deep breath and looked into his beady, undeserving eyes. "I am truly, deeply sorry for what I said at the earlier celebration. It was a contemptible insult, one for which I can see neither defense nor reason. I shamed myself, my family, and my kingdom. Moving forward, I promise I will carry myself with nothing but decorum and respect for you and the Nuwei kingdom. I hope you accept my apology."

She plucked the words out of her brain, planting them in his mind and watering them into beautiful lies. She presented a bouquet of the deceits to the Nuwei diplomat, hoping their false colors and promises might appease him.

"While it was indeed a terrible thing to say, I think I may find room to forgive you," he paused, dangling the next sentence in front of her like a hunt master would to his dogs, "so long as you agree right here and now to make a public statement that Nuwei is not a corrupt society. It is important for future diplomatic relations that we know you support us, and vice versa."

"Could we not settle this cordially among ourselves?" Liliana said. She kept her voice low, sure that raising it would sear the man before her with her rage. "There is no need to lend credence to rumors of the public on the terms of our nations. The people should be led to believe our allyship is as strong as ever, no?"

"No," he responded, his grin widening into an expression so gruesome Liliana wanted to gouge out her own eyes.

Arrogant. Abhorrent. Repulsive. The slimy *malum* had the gall to look her in the eyes and request she lie through her teeth. Liliana almost laughed out loud. No, he was not requesting—the ambassador was practically *salivating* for her pride to be crushed before him. How could it be that such human waste was permitted not only to crawl about the earth but also to serve one of the most powerful nations on *Terrabis*?

Liliana's eyes were blank, her mind somehow even emptier. She smiled at the man, though she could not stop her shaking hands.

"I-I understand. You are absolutely right. The Nuwei society is an upstanding one, and it was preposterous of me to imply otherwise."

He nodded, smug and satisfied. Liliana offered a slight bow, tying her lips together to keep from screaming. She stood and moved on to one of the cooks, continuing with the same garden of lies.

The palace cook had the face of a brick in a wall: underwhelming, forgettable, and a bit flat. Sweat showed beneath the armpits of the traditional mulberry garb of the palace chefs, red stains smattered on the black smock thrown over top. The corners of her lips wobbled, perspiration coalescing along her forehead. Her hay-colored hair, held together by a rough yarn, hid beneath a white cloth. Liliana decided that the yarn was the most notable thing about her.

But for what do I wrecking apologize? Liliana studied the woman, her fury and helplessness growing by the second. In truthfulness, Liliana never thought about the staff enough to consider any of her actions toward them. Perhaps she was too critical of a particular dish? Liliana avoided growling.

The cook interrupted Liliana's consternation. She spoke, her voice barely above a whisper, and looked about, unable to meet Liliana's gaze. "Y-You had my s-sister removed from service when you w-were a child. Y-you complained of her copper candy to the q-queen, and my sister was gone before the n-next morning." The cook cringed, as if expecting a slap.

Liliana's jaw pulsed. She doubted the cook lied, but Liliana had no recollection of such an event. Which, in her mind, made sense. How was she to hold her younger self accountable for that which she could not even remember? She clenched her teeth together, holding in a sigh. Liliana was to apologize for her misdeeds as a *child*? Is this truly what her Gods ordained to find the best ruler for her country?

Impossible. This was not a Trial meant to teach any lesson or from which to draw any meaning. It was nothing more than a line of people meant to shame Liliana. To make her doubt her candidacy. To make Liliana doubt her worth.

She doubted her mother ever had to suffer such injustices to her honor and name. Queen Juliana took no grief from any person. She walked as if she owned the earth on which she stood, ruled the air that she breathed. Liliana's mother would not have stood by and lied to appease these cowards, fools only brave enough to confront Liliana under the guise of the Gods' blessings.

But Juliana had already been queen. She acted like she owned the earth and ruled the air because for all intents and purposes *she did*. Liliana had no such luxury. *Not yet.*

"I'm terribly sorry. Please forgive me." Liliana cocked her head.

The cook stammered incoherently, nodding fervently. At Liliana's pause, the cook pointed to her own chest. A follower of *Superbia*, then. Liliana kissed her fingers and pressed them to the cook's chest. She drifted away before the cook had time to respond.

Dayanara had none of the quaking, rabbitlike energy of the cook. She stood before Liliana, her spine straight and her dark blue eyes cautious. Like any soldier, Dayanara's emotions did not show in her face. They came in the way her fingers tittered along the golden handle of the axe strapped to her back. They showed in the downward tilt of her chin and the way her muscles looked ready to burst through her skin from how tense they were. No, Dayanara was not scared like the cook. But she was certainly nervous.

Easternalia stood at Liliana's back, so Liliana tilted one eyebrow up. She regarded the soldier with the one raised eyebrow, more than enough to signal, *Well?*

Dayanara cleared her throat, a hacking cough that echoed about in the room. Her voice was husky but did not quake. She met Liliana's eyes, wary with every word. "Back when I was a regular soldier, I accidentally got in your way while patrolling the palace, and you fell to the ground. You were so furious you went to the Captain and demanded any promotion of rank be delayed." Dayanara's mouth twisted halfway, as if she wanted to say more but was stopping herself.

Liliana vaguely remembered the moment. She recalled a bruised knee and broken heel and storming to the Captain, insisting that any soldier who hurt the royal family couldn't be promoted to protect them. She had been thirteen at the time, old enough to know the consequences of such pettiness. It was the only complaint that Liliana heard thus far that actually had some merit.

"I'm sorry," Liliana remarked, voice slightly calmer, pressing her lips to her fingers and then to Dayanara's pale white shoulder and golden *Viribus* mark.

The remaining interactions proved just as outdated and outrageous as the first two. She watched the act play out before her of a young princess putting all her pride on the line for the sake of her dreams. Anytime Liliana looked backward at Easternalia, her aunt's lips spread back, revealing a dark smile and approving nod. The entire thing was just another Crimson Cough. Hack up the blood and shriek internally but survive. *Wreck it all.* Liliana knew there was a way to survive even when her stomach roiled, and her blood screamed.

As she plodded through the motions of the Trial, Liliana grew more and more disgusted with herself. She understood the ideal of pride and humility in a leader. Every person had to walk the fine line between the two, careful never to dip too far either way.

What Liliana struggled with was not the importance of humility but its present application in the Trial. What was the point of testing her honesty and commitment to truth if they shoved her into a corner of disingenuity a second later? A ruler should value all the virtues, not only the one most convenient for any given moment. When she was queen, would she forgo following *Caecus* for the sake of *Viribus* in a battle? Might she forget *Imperium*'s touch if she attempted to be honest with her people, as *Menda* told?

The more she thought about it, the more tangled it all became. There should be a way to balance truth and pride, power and wisdom, strength and humility. If the Committee valued more than just *Superbia*'s touch, the Trial would look very different. For if Liliana was being totally honest in that moment, the word "sorry" would have never left her mouth at the start. No words would have, in fact.

If given the chance to be honest, Liliana would have smiled at the Nuwei ambassador, stepped forward, and sawed off the *malum*'s ear before he could even think to speak.

Chapter 15
7055.1.23

Aoran spent the eighteenth year of his life in a military campaign, securing Electaria's border from the tenacious reach of small-time nobles ascending from small-time towns. The War of Hawks came as little surprise, but the ferocity of Electaria's adversaries was a shock. The border nobles had managed to secure far more men and arms than any, the Captain included, previously thought possible.

Sometimes, those nights looked like stained glass in his mind, red and frozen in garish pictures of comrades losing their limbs. Other times, he could barely recall more than a fuzzy, vague idea of the events that transpired, as if he were fishing for memories from his darkest, youngest years.

Some moments stood separate from the horrific and blurry reservoir of wartime recollections. Completing his Walk, for one. It was damn near impossible to forget the stunning feeling of his mark turning gold, the electricity that ran rampant through his body. The other memory that persisted with him was that of the war camp at night. When the sun began to nestle beneath the silhouette of the mountains, he used to survey the encampment, checking in on soldiers and putting out skirmishes. He moved through throngs of warriors, ducking beneath rough back claps and dodging friendly punches. It was a testament to his unadulterated awesomeness that he always emerged from those rounds relatively unscathed.

He put those same skills to the test as he maneuvered the busy streets of Electaria. Dancing over the broken cobblestone, Aoran attempted to flow through the crowd. However, evading the grabbing hands of merchants and the blatant desperation of beggars proved to be far more challenging than anticipated. Despite his best efforts, the crowd pushed Aoran around like a schoolyard bully, forcing him every which way.

The kingdom's disjointed buildings sloped around him in dizzying rows, their old structures lacking rhyme or reason. His heart squeezed, and as he looked up at the towers around him, he felt like he had shrunk to half his size and lost the swords at his back. He watched the kingdom once more, overwhelmed with the same pricks of anxiety that had plagued him as a child. That anxiety had haunted him from the day his grandmother died, when he was six, to his first inhale of sunweed at age nine. Even the smells— the damp, dirty smells of the streets—brought back nauseating memories of the years spent living no better than the city's rats. *Get yourself together, malum,* he cursed himself internally.

A light buzz tingled at his shoulder as Aoran cleared his mind. Aoran's heartbeat slowed down, and he continued his fight against the enemy troops that were the bustling marketplace of Electaria. Dirty and starving, he used to weave in between this overwhelming bustle, searching for anything to put into his stomach. He lived that way for three years until a nasty spat with another street rat caught the interest of a local street lord. His upper lip curled back in disgust. Yes, Aoran had little fondness lingering for the streets of the city he grew up scavenging.

He finally broke out of the tidal pull by escaping into an alley off the side of the street. Impe's sun, harsher than usual, bore down on him from above, and sweat crawled down his forehead and arms. Watching the crowd continue to surge in every direction reminded Aoran of a nasty whirlpool, out of control and dangerous. This natural disaster, this swirling mass of people, was about as close as the annoyingly proper Electarians came to a lack of decorum. *Of course, now. Of course, here.* He grimaced. *Bothersome.* Getting to his destination would be far more difficult than he had thought.

Aoran needed to find this Nuwei ambassador. The other night, after babbling everything Aoran heard to that man and…Liliana's wolf? The two had nodded. The man had snapped his fingers, and Aoran had closed his eyes at the sound. By the time they were open once more, the pair had disappeared entirely. No time for questions or answers, Aoran was left more dumbfounded and confused than he had felt in years. In some ways, he had almost been impressed. Others rarely managed to stupefy him so thoroughly. He probably had a thing or two to learn from this man in the art of screwing with others.

His attempts to get Imperium to talk with him had been both a fruitless endeavor and one that often left Aoran looking insane. After two castle servants caught him yelling at the wolf, Aoran decided to try a different avenue of approach.

So he sought the location of the Nuwei delegation. The highest-ranked among them stayed at the castle, but lower advisors and servants were relegated to a distant inn. Aoran asked some questions, charming certain answers and forcing others. His shoulder tingled at the memory. Strength often meant knowing when the situation deigned coercion or cajoling. He grinned to himself. It was easy to forget how wildly charismatic he was when he spent most of his time around the black hole of joy that was the merry monarch-to-be, Liliana.

Following the trial of *Superbia*, the scores now rang in with Elle at 1.7, Liliana at 1.75, and Teo at 1.8. Despite performing better than in the previous Trial, Liliana was unassuaged. The tightness of the race did little to relax the fire-breathing princess.

Enough stalling. He gathered up his lingering dread, residuals of a childhood better discarded in the streets where it had ended. Aoran willed himself to forget the grimy skin and pangs of hunger, to lock away the hours spent clawing at other children at The Crank for his Street Lord. He siphoned it all down the grates of his body and locked it in the same cage as his heart. "Out of sight, out of mind" was the fallacy of fools. The only way to control such things was to never allow them the freedom to roam, keeping them under lock and key and strict supervision.

Aoran gritted his teeth and pushed his way back into the crowd. This time, he kept a hand against the hilt of one of his swords. He arranged his face into a scowl, his muscles protesting at forming an expression so foreign to his typical grin. The result was immediate and blissfully effective. People parted around him, eyeing his hand nervously. Instead of being pressed against on all sides, Aoran now maintained a small berth of about six inches all around. The scowl stayed on his face, but he couldn't help the delight in his eyes. These people were influenced remarkably easily. Maybe he would have enjoyed his childhood more if he had realized that sooner.

Caught up in the delight of his own facade, Aoran ran right into another person when he refused to move around him. He took one step back, fists clenching at his sides as he readied to give the stranger a piece of his mind. Opening his mouth, Aoran stumbled over his own words when he realized they were going to be delivered to the prince's face.

Teo blinked, eyebrows furrowed, as he rubbed the middle of his head where the two had collided. The image reminded Aoran of an old merchant who, after having become accustomed to traveling the same roads year after year, ran over a divot in the trail. Teo didn't look pained so much as vaguely surprised at the notion that anything could have been in his way in the first place.

Even the casual clothes Teo adopted failed to make the prince look any less serious. It was as though his deep, mahogany eyes and the firm line of his mouth transcended any of the prince's attempts at normalcy. *A shame, truly.* The man worked the latest style of the kingdom well, with a sturdy frame to fill out the billowed, light blue shirt tucked into cream pants that cinched at the ankles. Aoran refrained from emitting a low whistle. He nearly felt bad for the girls of this city, catching their wistful glances as they bumped their way by. Damn if the prince wouldn't do his kingdom proud at any given bar or brothel.

Aoran immediately relaxed his fists and bent over into a bow, low enough to recognize his station but not so low as to inadvertently imply a future for which Liliana would undoubtedly skin him alive for suggesting.

"Prince Teo! My apologies. Having forgotten my armor in the castle, I seemed to have also forgotten my manners." Aoran scratched the back of his head, laughing at his own joke.

The sound died down when Teo continued to regard Aoran with polite confusion. Refraining from a disrespectful eye roll, Aoran remembered why he restricted his teasing to the princess. Teo was about as good an audience as a pile of corpses.

Aoran moved past the conversational roadblock, his eyes jumping around to look behind Teo. "Right, then...I might imagine Je would normally ward off such unfortunate accidents. Where is your bodyguard?"

"Why would I need a bodyguard in the city?" Teo glanced around the marketplace, one eyebrow quirked upward.

The man always appeared to look at the world as if separated from it by a magnifying glass, a scientist with the pleasure of observing from the outside, never having to enter the danger of the experiment himself. The flow of its citizens surged forward with little heed to the two men stalled in the belly of the kingdom's streets.

"The only dangers I face lurk in the minds and swords of those in our castle."

Aoran barked out a laugh, holding his stomach. He didn't know the Prince of Stone-Cold Demeanor had such a joke lying in the graveyard of his sense of humor! What other jokes might be brought back to life if Aoran pushed hard enough?

"That is no laughing matter, Aoran," Teo said, his stern voice crushing Aoran's laughter like a pile of snow on a budding spring sapling. "The truth of the matter is that only the politicians of this world wish me harm. Outside of its walls, few care enough about my existence to consider ill will toward me."

"I see," Aoran trailed off, his mind spinning around the words. Liliana's angry face flashed in his mind, beautiful and terrible as she raged over her brother.

The pair never spoke again of her words to Teo that day. They swept it under the rug of years of friendship, moving forward with barely a second glance. Her look, though, the venom sizzling from every word she spoke.... The unadulterated desire to crush all that stood in front of her remained imprinted on his mind. And that was just the princess. One of many (presumably) vicious dignitaries. He wasn't sure he could blame Teo for his sense of caution.

Teo either did not notice or did not care about Aoran's lapse into silence. He plowed forward, his manner straightforward and his voice matter-of-fact. "That said, I have no idea where Je is today. He was given a respite from his duties, and what he does with the time is no concern of mine. And what brings you here today?"

The prince's eyes drilled into Aoran's, the topic pivoting so fast that it almost left Aoran dizzy. The way the prince jumped and whipped his way through conversations reminded Aoran of a reckless carriage driver—they cared little for the comfort of the passengers inside so long as they made it to their destination as quickly and efficiently as possible.

Pausing, Aoran sent a quick prayer of gratitude up to *Superbia* and her followers; what a blessing it was for the rest of the world that at least some people were naturally ingrained with a sense of social grace and fluidity.

Aoran recovered his footing in the conversation, acting like the question was a simple missed step in a choreographed routine. Of little importance as long as he could remember to continue dancing. "I have some business to attend to in the city. It's personal. I trust you understand."

Aoran hoped this last bit would be enough to dissuade the prince from asking questions to which Aoran would inevitably not be able to provide an answer. *Oh, you know—going to search for a mythological creature of our religion currently masquerading as a member of the Nuwei delegation and seeing what I can figure out. I mean, what do you do with your days off?*

"Of course." Teo nodded, curt.

Aoran smiled at the prince. "If I might ask," Aoran grabbed the reins of their interaction and attempted to steer back into territory where he may remain in control, "why are you in the city today, Your Highness?"

"The Captain was right. You are bad at reconnaissance," Teo replied and shook his head, ignoring Aoran's pitiful protests. "I've been visiting the city once a week for the past six years. Sometimes I help with building and repairs at the outskirts of the city—with the poorest of the capitol—and sometimes I just try and buy the kids on the street something to eat." Teo frowned. "It's quite concerning that you don't know the travel patterns of a member of the royal family."

"Why bother helping them?" Aoran asked, a question intended as his own jab.

What was the prince's angle? Win the love of the people? Earn their adoration so that even if somebody were to be placed on the throne, he might still be seen as their leader? Aoran studied Teo with more interest. Was the man before him truly one of straightforward honesty, or was he more calculating than Aoran ever imagined?

"Must there be a reason?" Teo's voice sounded exhausted, and though the prince's shoulders were thrown back and his back was straight, Aoran never noticed that weary sound in his voice.

"My mother told me my entire life to do this and that, so it might help me with this council member or that initiative. Perhaps you and she recognize something I do not—does there always have to be a deeper, underlying motivation?"

Aoran's mind catapulted out of his body, suddenly seeing a landscape of Teo's life in a single snapshot. A direct, well-meaning boy navigating his way through a system wrought with complex motives and underhanded tactics. Told he must serve the people, the boy tried everything in his power to become a ruler of which they might be proud. Any actions he took, though, always lacked the political deft required by a ruler and demanded by his mother. Intent on following through and leading his people, yet always outclassed, the boy was left constantly scrambling to keep his head above water in the throes of his political arena. It was the equivalent of taking a fish, throwing it in the sky, and demanding it fly.

Aoran's finger twitched at his side, craving the sweet ache of sunweed. All this empathy was exhausting. His head drooped, his cheeks flushing slightly. Those earlier questions reminded him of Liliana, not himself. Since when did her cynicism infect his very thoughts?

"Of course not, Your Highness. You're a good man," he said with more sincerity than he remembered feeling in a long while. The castle walls made excellent shields against authenticity. He kept talking, unable now to keep his lips shut. "You'd make a good king, Teo."

The words left his mouth before he could stop them. They barreled forward, propelled by an honesty Aoran barely knew existed within himself. Why had he said that? He could see it now: Liliana's face, a picture of exquisite rage framed by hurt. This painting of his betrayal would serve as an eternal damnation of any tenuous connection they once held. He nearly laughed out loud, groaning to himself.

Teo accepted the compliment with the barest acknowledgment, tilting his head up slightly. In a rare moment of idle mindedness, Teo looked up at the gray sky, eyes following the lumps of charcoal clouds. "Pray that *Imperium* favors me similarly." The slightest of sighs left Teo's mouth.

"Seeing as I generally try to avoid self-imposed demise, you must forgive me if such prayers never make it to the House of the Magisters' flames." Aoran laughed to himself, a short sound. He cast a look back toward the castle, picturing his pernicious princess. "Princess Liliana's wrath consistently proves to inspire more fear in this body of mine than any potential retribution from my Gods."

Teo's mahogany eyes snapped back into focus, as if he had momentarily escaped the idea of his sister and had been forced back to reality. Any vague semblance of casual conversation tumbled away, blown by the breeze of Aoran's snark.

"Right. Well, I must be going, Aoran of the Four. I suppose I shall see you back at the castle."

Without fanfare, Teo marched forward into the crowds. Either from recognition or intimidation, the crowds parted around him, making way for his stiff walk back to the castle. Teo's exit reminded Aoran strangely of the donuts that occasionally made appearances at particularly fancy feasts: a hard, crispy exterior covered in powdered sugar that practically sizzled on the heat of the fried dessert. Teo simply lacked the delicate dusting of social grace and was therefore left as a hard shell, with no sugar to sweeten his demeanor and mannerisms.

Aoran shook off the strange encounter, pushing it into the sewers of his mind. Sometimes it was better to approach life like a soldier. Take orders, don't speak back, and for *Imperium*'s sake, don't think. Thinking was what got soldiers in trouble. It got normal people in trouble, too, especially if they had a propensity for the wrong kind of thoughts. He rolled his eyes; no wonder Liliana and Teo were such damn grouches. Thinking that much about anything—much less the fate of an entire kingdom—was prone to ram a naman up anybody's ass.

Fingers convulsing for a quick, numbing bliss, Aoran set forth to find Chauron with renewed determination. His thoughts became a loop of cobblestone, one foot in front of the other as he trekked his way through the city. Images of Liliana and Teo were barred from entering the main stage of his mind. Images of Teo wearing the crown, the smallest smile on his face. Images of the people, cheering for a man so far from the drudgery of traditional politics that they might finally stand a chance in his majesty's courts. Images of Liliana, weeping ugly, odious tears, her shrieking cries muffled by the roar of the kingdom.

But first...Aoran jolted to a stop, his nose twitching. A familiar nauseating odor wafted through the air, drifting right into Aoran's nose and into the part of his brain that controlled desire. It was like when he saw a brownie and the saliva exploded in his mouth, anticipating the onslaught of sweetness; his lungs sighed, his body tensing in preparation to let go. He followed the scent to a pair of young teens, passing a pipe of sunweed back and forth. He snatched the pipe from their hands, sure to drop far more copper coins on the ground than the damn thing was worth. Putting the pipe against his lips, he inhaled and finally relaxed for what felt like the first time in an eternity of tension. For *Imperium*'s sake, it was time to stop thinking.

***

If later asked how he found the Nuwei diplomatic residency, Aoran would be hard pressed to come up with an answer that didn't sound like the ravings of a deranged lunatic. A yellow haze hung over the time between his first drag and the moment he arrived. He shrugged to himself, gazing up at the vibrant yellow lines of script overlaid on the bright green flag that proclaimed Nuwei's residency. Insanity or the Gods. People were prone to blaming inexplicable events on one of the two. People usually painted this idyllic picture of Aoran, using watercolors of *Viribus* and the strength the God had endowed the young soldier. He figured he ought to experience falling on the wrong side of the line occasionally.

Though it appeared the Gods favored him nearly as much as any bouts of madness. He grinned to himself as the Nuwei ambassador plodded out the door. Aoran paused to savor the moment, putting the pipe to his mouth and allowing himself one more victorious inhale. He threw the thing on the ground, stomping out any smoldering embers as he watched the slippery diplomat with wolfish delight. Dammit if he didn't love it when things seemed to just work out.

The Nuwei ambassador stopped to look up at the flag above the front door, gritting his teeth and spitting to the side. His frown lines appeared deeper than ever, canyons of misery engraved in his face like the work of a careless jeweler. Despite this, he carried the chiseled, classically handsome features of a mythological hero. He had the lucky kind of features to which a scowl only added depth.

Aoran whistled, and the ambassador's head shot up. "Diplomacy evades our capture more successfully for some than others. It appears as though it's eluded you as successfully as a sailor fleeing from the local hag who spent the night masquerading as a prized woman. Why the grumpy face, friend?"

"You know," the ambassador trudged closer to Aoran, his eyes glinting with the malice that came from years of hatred made to simmer, "I hate the clever ones the most. Not only do they never leave things as they are, but they try to make a damn comedy out of their downfall."

Aoran faintly wondered if he should pretend to feel threatened as the man jumped at him, a knife flashing in his hands. The man did move relatively fast, Aoran thought. His mind, hazy with the yellow smoke of sunweed, opted for less flourish. Aoran sidestepped the attack and grabbed the man's arm, pulling the straightened limb backward as he pushed the diplomat's shoulder forward. The diplomat groaned as his shoulder threatened to slip out of its socket.

The electric zip of Aoran's mark cut through his mental cloud, cracking him back into reality like a lightning strike. Yes, he supposed the diplomat did move fast. Fast to the average man, but hopelessly slow in the face of Aoran's dominance. Dislocation was unnecessary.

He yanked the diplomat backward, pinching his hand tightly against the man's neck before whipping him around and cracking his face into the wall of the Nuwei embassy. The ambassador let out a gurgled moan as Aoran held him pinned to the stones, squeezing his neck a little bit harder when the ambassador attempted to move.

"Now—" Aoran said cheerfully, his body buzzing with energy. He couldn't have stopped the grin on his face if he tried. He didn't try. *Viribus* knew there was nothing like feeling the boundaries of somebody else's strength and knowing it paled in comparison to that of your own. "I think it's time you answered a few of my questions."

A strangled sound answered him.

Aoran considered the noise. "An interesting point. But if I let you go, you have to promise not to run away."

He released the diplomat, and the man slumped to the ground, looking up at Aoran with a baleful glare. Aoran laughed out loud. *Imperium* have mercy—it took *years* to cultivate that kind of concentrated contempt in one look. He was impressed.

The diplomat spit into his hands, slicking back his long, black hair with a slow motion, his eyes never leaving Aoran. Aoran absentmindedly wondered when the sight of fresh, sticky blood matted in another man's hair stopped making him cringe.

"I would rather stick this shiv into your throat and twist than run away. Seeing as I have the strength to do neither in the face of a wrecking *Viribus* brat, you can assume my compliance."

Aoran shrugged. "Not exactly the warm and sugary response I was looking for, but it'll do for the time being."

"Quit wrecking around. What do you want?"

Aoran's eyebrow twitched up in time with his fingers. His entire body wanted to strike this *malum* with a fierce need. His mark jolted through his body, stopping his hand in its place. The dignitary was crushed and on the ground at the mercy of his attacker. There was no strength in further beating a beaten man. The electric thrum in Aoran's body successfully extinguished the urge, instead letting a broad smile spread across his face. "Let's start with your name."

"Chauron."

A classy spit to the side. Aoran felt a giddy feeling rise in his chest. The *malum* was rude, abrasive, and utterly insufferable. He was a weed with thorns that would inevitably choke out the modicum of diplomatic charm the Nuwei delegation carried with them. But dammit if that wasn't *marvelous*. Chauron was a cool glass of water in the middle of the scorching desert that was the diplomatic scene—utterly refreshing. Far more entertaining than the poised and perfect petals of the court.

"Lovely!" Aoran knelt and looked at Chauron in his bitter, onyx eyes. "Now the questions might be a little bit more difficult from here on out. When I caught you earlier in the hallway, were you really talking to Imperium?" Aoran tried his best not to falter, despite the utter ridiculousness of the question. The exchange he had kept firmly locked in his brain unfortunately sounded even crazier spoken into the damp air of the alleyway. If he ever heard Je or Dayanara spout such nonsense, he would tease them mercilessly until their pride was thoroughly and irreversibly ground to dust.

Chauron did not respond. The diplomat watched Aoran with wary eyes, as if he understood exactly how important this answer was to Aoran. He dangled his silence in front of Aoran like a master waved a flank of steak in front of his dog. Aoran, a man normally content with the quiet of a moment, felt it grate against his ears with its harsh nails, a torture in and of itself. *Wreck*, Imperium, Aoran thought to himself, *please let me not be crazy*. Otherwise, he would have to have an incredibly uncomfortable (and likely terrifying) conversation with the Captain considering his fit for service....

"Yes."

"Wreck." Aoran groaned to himself, running his hands over his face. "Of course you weren't. What kind of *malum* would talk to a wrecking—wait. Did you say yes?"

"Brilliant. He's a smart-ass and yet somehow impossibly dim-witted too. Tell me, what kind of genetic lottery did you fall prey to at birth?" Chauron snorted as he rolled his eyes, resting his head on one knee and watching Aoran process the information.

"I am the product of a whore and her penniless lover, raised by the streets of Electaria, the fields of battle, and a cold, dead, royal bitch." Aoran brushed off the question, his eyes wide and staring at the ground.

So! So, so, so. So. Chauron, the cranky Nuwei diplomat, had talked to Imperium. Liliana's *wolf*. The man in front of him, glaring with absolute steel at Aoran, somehow communicated with an animal. And the animal had responded. And the animal belonged to Liliana. Could Liliana talk with Imperium? Was this one of those creepy, ancient secrets that all royal families were obligated to keep? Aoran had a tough time picturing Liliana speaking with

Imperium. The two wouldn't have nearly as good a relationship if the thing could talk back to her. So then why could Chauron—

"Guides," Aoran stated, his mind drowning in its own tide pool of thoughts. They crashed in, one after another, erasing all the sentences he attempted to assemble in the sand. "Guides. You and Imperium—wreck, did you seriously talk to wrecking Imperium?"

Chauron looked up at Aoran, unimpressed. "I believe we covered that bit of the interrogation."

Aoran ignored him. "So do you talk to all wolves? Or just that wolf? No wait—Guides! You two were talking about Guides." Aoran pointed at him with an accusatory finger, shaking ever so slightly. He hadn't felt this wired or nervous since his first battle. He was reminded of the exhilarating rush of a sword tip pointed at his chest, aimed to kill. "Guides. Let's talk about that. Are Guides real?"

"Yes."

"*Wreck*." Aoran released an exhale of breath, his eyes wide and seeing nothing around him. "Are you a Guide?"

A beat. "Some might call me one."

Aoran's brain whipped to a stop, and he stared at Chauron. Every frown line and gray hair suddenly seemed a little more ethereal. "Shit. Shit, *shit*! Should I bow?"

"Much as I'd enjoy that, you're better off saving that bullshit fanfare for the little royal facades everyone here puts on." Chauron began to push off his knees. "I can quite literally smell the smoke coming from your brain. I fear you might have had enough revelations today to last you a lifetime. Now, why don't we both wreck off and chalk this up to an unfortunate, coincidental encounter."

Aoran took his left hand, planted it against Chauron's chest, and shoved him. The man hit the ground with a groan and a bark.

"What the wreck is wrong with you, insolent *malum*? Is this any way to treat a holy figure?"

"Your mouth makes it easier," Aoran replied. "And I have more questions. Who is your person? The person you're, you know, guiding? Do I have a Guide? Why in the hell are you traveling with the Nuwei delegation? Who were you talking about with," Aoran gulped, the wolf's name tasting impossibly strange in his mouth, "Imperium?"

Chauron rubbed the back of his head where it had hit the wall once more. He spit the next part out, nearly hissing with distaste. "Did you not pay attention in your damn history classes? Guides are brought down by necessity, not just made wholesale for all you damn humans."

"Damn." Aoran swore, vaguely disappointed. He ignored the feeling, focusing back on Chauron. "And Nuwei? Why them?"

"*Caecus*—*malum* that he is—told me to monitor the trials. I'm here to ensure certain...outcomes."

An icy rush flooded Aoran's body. The image of Liliana crying and shrieking while the crowd roared for Teo flashed through his mind once more. "What kind of outcomes?"

"Unfortunately for you, your time with me has officially elapsed," Chauron said.

He reached forward and grabbed Aoran's hand. Aoran moved to evade whatever blow was to come his way, but instead the Guide simply dragged Aoran's hand forward and placed it against the wall. When Chauron released, a golden glow emanated from underneath Aoran's hand, and he found himself totally unable to move away from the wall. He gritted his teeth, pulling as hard as he could, bracing his foot against the wall and pushing. Nothing.

"What the wreck did you do?" Aoran said.

"My *vis* may not be what it once was, but I can still charge up enough to put you arrogant *malums* in your place. Let this be your lesson if you try to tell anyone about our little conversation today—I can muster up enough to make your life a living, breathing hell. You'd rather spend a night in bed with *malum* than get further on my bad side. I'm not always feeling this goddamned nice."

"This is your *nice*?"

For the first time in speaking with the man, Chauron's face broke into a small grin. His cheeks dimpled, and his teeth were straight and white beneath his lips. Aoran had a feeling that at one point in this man's life, based on the way his wrinkles shifted with the change, smiling used to be a common pastime.

"This is me at my most compassionate, *malum*. Have an enjoyable day." And Chauron trudged away from the alley, leaving nothing but more pounding questions and a tugging, growling Aoran in his wake.

After struggling for ten minutes, Aoran collapsed to the ground, waiting for a sign he could move. And soon, a faint tingling started at the tips of his fingers, traveling with lethargic pace through his hand. Eventually, he could lift the tip of his pointer finger off the wall. After even longer, the entire finger. After the hour, Aoran gingerly removed his hand from the wall entirely, flexing and stretching his fingers as if to assure himself they were still there. He clenched his fingers into a fist, unable to ignore the faint tremble of his hand. He whispered to himself, caught between incredulity and awe. "What the wreck just happened?"

CHAPTER 16
7055.1.24

"I say this out of sincere love and care: you look atrocious."

Liliana's head jerked up from her work to see her older sister standing in front of her, aggressively emanating her usual exquisite elegance. In typical fashion, Eliana appeared with little notice or even sound. Liliana's head briefly spun in a dizzying way that only happened when she was low on sleep, food, and human interaction. Tucked away on the third floor of the castle, the royal library had plenty of nooks and crannies in which the body might disappear and even more books in which the mind might vanish entirely. Liliana rubbed her eyes, leaning back in her chair and bringing her sister back into focus.

Already frowning slightly at the work before her, Liliana's expression soured upon fully seeing Eliana. Her sister's black curls coiled in tight rings, spiraling down to her shoulders like perfect acrobats. Eliana's black irises surveyed Liliana critically, scanning up and down and back up again. Though the brilliant whites of Eliana's eyes made the irises almost look like black targets, Liliana was the one who felt pinned down. Eliana's bright red dress clung to her form like a dying man at sea, fitting her so well it could have been deemed a sin of *malum*.

Liliana narrowed her eyes and looked back down on the parchment in front of her. Focusing on her sister too hard always led Liliana down a dangerous path of comparison, one which, as long as they both lived, Liliana would never win. Like ivy lounging on a trellis, Eliana's mysterious beauty occurred without thought or effort. Trying to compete with such natural grace would only end in failure, so Liliana zeroed in on that in which she could excel: more work.

"That's very kind and also very necessary of you to point out," Liliana muttered, shaking her head and tapping her pen against the desk, trying to relocate the track of her thoughts. "To what deity do I owe the misfortune of your presence and, as stated, very helpful commentary?"

"Why, your favorite God of them all!" Eliana fluttered her eyes and placed her hand on her chest before smacking that same hand down on Liliana's desk, sending her papers scattering. "Your own ego."

"Wrecking—Eliana!" Liliana scrambled to collect the papers before they got too out of order or the ink smudged.

The papers were a manifesto on the acknowledgment of the Soj nation as a legitimate partner in diplomacy. The more Liliana hated the Nuwei—and after *Superbia*'s trial, she found herself acutely hating the Nuwei—the more she found herself fascinated with the silent protectorate. While she knew some random facts about their economy to make conversation, she had little to say beyond that.

So, following the last Trial, Liliana holed herself up in the kingdom's library, skimming every book she could find on the subject. Liliana grew up knowing that the Soj was an entire nation of people strongly rumored to be born without marks—essentially an entire people damned by the Gods. The Nuwei took over bureaucratic control of the Soj hundreds of years ago, seen then and now as the benevolent protection of a godlier, more developed country. The Nuwei controlled the Soj's diplomatic relations, economic deals and policies, and virtually anything else a bureaucrat could think of. The Soj retained their title—and only that because the Nuwei would never fully incorporate the tainted people.

Over the past day, Liliana read all this with rapt attention, settling on a decision. With the Soj and the Nuwei, she had the opportunity to feed two birds with one scone. She decided to write a virulent manifesto detailing all the ways in which the Nuwei exploited the Soj through their "benevolent proctorship" and to submit it to the Diplomacy Council during a public meeting so it would be read out loud and available on the public record. In one fell swoop, Liliana would defend a wronged people and (ideally) offend some of the Nuwei in the process.

Liliana finally got her papers back in order and glared at her sister, seething. "What. Do. You. Want?"

"I told you I was here because of your ego," Eliana drawled, crossing her arms. Voice and expression cool, she leaned on the desk and obscured Liliana's papers. "While in the past you've scared all your suitors off, you've gotten considerably lazier recently and have just been ignoring every call and letter for the past month. Father sent me to talk to you, given that you and he are acting like children and avoiding one another with commendable success. You need to start responding to the world of marriage."

Eliana fluttered her fingers on the word, as if describing a magical land.

"Wait—what?" Liliana shook her head. "No. No—that doesn't matter anymore. I mean, I had no desire to be married before, but now I won't have to get married. I'm going to win the Trials and be queen."

Eliana laughed, covering her mouth with her hand. The sound was soft and eerie, like wind chimes outside a cemetery.

Annoyed, Liliana blinked at her sister. "What?"

"Oh, nothing. It's just very funny, you realize, this stubborn notion you have that once you're queen, everything in your life is going to change." Eliana sighed, swiping away an imaginary tear. "Dear sister, as much as I love indulging your little fantasies, let me clear things up for you. If"—she pushed out the word with as much force as possible—"you were to become queen, the only thing that would change is your title. But you, Liliana, you do not change. You will still be a stubborn, spiteful, little thing. You will still be third-born. You will still be a woman. You will require marriage more than ever to solidify your position—ideally, to a mild-mannered, noble-blooded individual to balance out all that you are." Eliana shrugged. "Far be it from me to decree man or woman—though, for legacy, man would be ideal—but you need someone to steady the inherent instability you would bring with your rule."

"Mother ruled alone for a time," Liliana argued.

Eliana's mouth twisted, a war between scorn and a smirk. "Mother dearest was queen for one year before stakeholder pressures forced her into a loveless marriage with our father." Eliana paused, tapping her chin. "Who knows? Perhaps if we look hard enough, we might find a rich, Vitrian merchant for you to marry too. Then you can truly be like our mother in all regards. Though, I doubt anyone you could find would bring as impressive a dowry as our father."

Liliana's heart thundered in her chest. Had their mother truly only gone one year before being shackled to another for the sake of opportunity? It was impossible to tell when Eliana told the truth. Being a follower of *Menda* who hadn't yet completed her Walk, she could just as easily be lying to Liliana's face. *But why would she?* The idea of being forced into a marriage made Liliana's stomach turn with a wretched vengeance. Her dream of being queen and changing the world began and ended there; it was not some joint venture on which she planned to drag another along. It was for her, and her alone.

"And that is assuming you do become queen. If you do not win the Trials and still do not marry, you will be failing your country in a most spectacular manner. Anybody can serve on the Education Council. Only royals can produce more royals. Well, theoretically, anyway. Ellegance and all her stupefaction aside. All this to say," Eliana continued airily, "you must stop avoiding your suitors and begin responding to them. Cordially, the king, your sister, and the rest of Electaria."

Liliana stared at the desk, a dull anger simmering just beyond the reach of her fingertips. Unable to fully access the emotion, she asked in a monotone, "What about you? Why do I never hear of you courting suitors? You're second-born. You need to contribute just as I do. Not to mention that you're obviously the lovelier. So why just me?"

"Oh, dear sister." Eliana clucked her tongue softly, but her tone and eyes were sharp. "I'm not a precious child of *Imperium*. The kingdom cares very little about the future of my womb, at least for a while longer. Not when *you* and your babies hold so much more potential. If it makes you feel any better, Teo is equally sought after on the marriage market." Eliana pushed off the desk with a raised eyebrow. "And being Teo, he has the foresight to start interviewing potential spouses, unlike others."

Liliana gritted her teeth, her mark warming. The injustice of the situation overwhelmed her with its sheer absurdity. Why shove her through these Trials if, ultimately, her future was to produce more royal stock? The notion that her mind, her worth as a ruler, might be devalued into her ability to bear children made her blood boil. If their mother married their father after only one year in power, it must have been her own decision. Their mother had been too powerful to simply succumb to the entreaty of Electarian politics. Eliana's cavalier fatalism about Liliana's future only propelled her fury. As if the purloin of Liliana's autonomy was a thing, long ago determined. Liliana refused to believe that to be true.

Of course, Teo has already begun his quest, Liliana thought with disdain. Ever since childhood, Teo followed instructions without a second thought. Liliana never understood how he had completed his Walk before her. His belief in power was founded on subservience, entrenched by preexisting hierarchies. The world told him he was firstborn, he was the best, and he must do this and that to continue to be so. No wonder he lacked such a nuanced view of the world: from birth, the castle, their parents, and the world had divided life for him into easy-to-understand monotones of choice, turning his existence into a series of severed, binary decisions.

Liliana's mark pounded, heated, sang to Liliana. For the first time in her life, she was annoyed by its presence. What held Liliana back from completing her Walk? A part of her blamed the mark itself. Perhaps it was faulty. Liliana felt that she truly understood power, in a way Teo and Elle couldn't understand.

She saw a shattered picture of that same monochromatic life but with ambiguity leaking through the cracks. Liliana grew up with a mark of power yet was relegated into last place. She dreamed of drafting sweeping reform across the country but had to settle for small-time matters on a small-time council. Liliana's understanding of power was the opposite of subservience: it was fighting and clawing against the systems in place to assert one's will, standing with her head held high while the rest of the world stood on her shoulders and tried to keep her down. She wanted to shake *Imperium* and yell at the Goddess: *I understand it all—so why is the damn mark still black?*

"Show me where the letters are," Liliana finally said, voice hard. Pushing all her papers to the corner of her desk for further review, she shoved herself up from the desk with such force her chair toppled backward behind her.

Eliana's eyebrows shot up, dark eyes looking between the fallen chair and Liliana. "Truly? I thought I'd have to entertain at least another half hour of your pontifications."

"Consider this your lucky day," Liliana said, crossing her arms and narrowing her eyes. "Now show me."

Eliana pursed her lips at Liliana, expression sour. "Well, since you asked so nicely…"

Eliana brushed ahead of Liliana, her feet light on the hardwood floors in spite of her black high heels. Liliana followed, expression stormy and fists clenched at her side. They left the depths of the library and descended quickly down the stairs, entering one of many rooms on the second floor dedicated to bureaucratic affairs. Eliana plucked a torch from the outside hallway and lit the torch on the inside of the room, allowing a dim view of the small space.

The area was the size of a closet, covered wall to wall in hundreds of tiny boxes. In a far-right corner, one of the boxes was so full of letters that its covering couldn't entirely shut, a small pile of mail accumulating on the carpeted floor beneath.

Eliana swept her hand, gesturing grandly to the corner of the tiny room. "Here you are, Your Almightiness. The dozens of poor fools stupid or greedy enough to ask for your hand in holy matrimony. Since I'm already being treated as your serving girl today, would you like me to fetch some fresh parchment so you might begin crafting your responses?"

"No need."

Liliana wasted no time. Marching over to the corner of the room, she pulled all the letters out of the box and spread them on the floor. They collapsed to the ground with a papery *huff*. She gathered them in a small circle, making sure the pile was relatively contained. Liliana then grabbed the torch her sister lit inside the room, pulling it from its sconce and throwing it down on top of the pile of letters. The pile of paper caught fire quickly, the creamy sheets turning black at the edges.

"*I like this side of you, Little Dragon,*" a voice said, lifting upward with the flames and circling around Liliana's head like a satisfied cat preparing for a nap.

Liliana's pulse quickened. If *Imperium* herself approved of Liliana's actions, then she could stand through any criticism her sister might throw.

"Are you crazy?" Eliana yelled, and for possibly the first time in her poised life, she looked flustered. She hurried forward, hands outstretched, searching for a way to fix the growing flames. The second the heat of the fire touched her fingers, she yanked her hand backward. She leveled a look of equal shock and outrage at Liliana. "Are you actually wrecking insane? *Imperium*, Liliana—your childishness truly knows no bounds!"

Liliana didn't respond. Eliana made an exasperated noise and fled the room, cupping her mouth and calling for help. Her sister's syrupy voice carried surprisingly far when Eliana put in the effort, Liliana noted absentmindedly while staring at the growing fire.

Let Teo be the one to pass on *Imperium*'s mark. *Wreck him, wreck Eliana, and wreck the notion that her worth was tied to any other person or future child.* Liliana didn't have the time in her life to dedicate to raising a wrecking child—not when she still had her entire future on which to focus. Liliana had enough ideas on raising Electaria's revenue that the councils would be unable to force her into a marriage. No rich merchants, no noble blood, no political connections. Liliana's prowess as queen would exist above and beyond any marginal advantages that could come from having a king.

The fire swelled to a size about half of Liliana's height. The heat pushed against her face, the smoke filling her nostrils with a dizzying scent. Her cheeks turned a bright pink, and sweat began to drip from her forehead. Still, Liliana remained in her spot. She swore to bear witness to her decision that she would rule alone. She hoped the smoke would drift into the sky, right to *Imperium,* and let the Goddess know that Liliana would not be dismissed. Her back burned, its heat nearly indistinguishable from the fire itself.

"Whoa." Ellegance laughed from the doorway. "I thought I smelled fire, but I figured I was just crazy. What in *Imperium*'s name happened?"

"A proposal that just didn't quite work out," Liliana responded with a wave of her hand. She glanced back at Ellegance. "I've always felt a certain kinship with fire though."

"Good for baking bread, not so good for sharing rooms." Ellegance shrugged with a small smile. She took a step forward, the hand at her side rising slightly, her eyebrows concerned. "D-Do you need help putting it out?"

Liliana shook her head, closing her eyes against the wall of heat that grew hotter with each minute. "Tell me, Ellegance, do you have plans of marrying anytime soon?"

"A kind offer, Your Highness, but I'm afraid it's too early for that," Elle joked with a short laugh. She gave the fire a nervous glance, saying slowly, "No, I don't plan on marrying soon. I can't imagine ever getting married, honestly. I don't think I'll find anything like my parents, and I don't really want to do what your parents did." Ellegance quickly followed this with, "No offense."

"Truly, none taken. My parents barely liked each other, much less loved one another. I understand the hesitancy." Liliana continued pressing the girl: "But what if the entire world desired that you did? What if your friends, your advisors, your family all believed you should marry? Would that be enough to persuade you to chain yourself to another?"

Elle bit the inside of her cheek, the skin dipping in and exaggerating her cheekbones. "I mean, if all those people thought I should do it, I guess I would at least think about it."

"Hm. Another divergence between the two of us. Is not power the quality of standing firm with one's convictions and ideas, even in the face of adversity? If you capitulate every time there is a majority, you stand to become commonplace. Just another person subject to the whims of others."

Elle's casual smile drooped, and she looked at Liliana with a gaze that was almost challenging. The fire flickered in her violet eyes, the purple and reds crashing into a mesmerizing whirlpool of color. "The people in this castle have never been subject to the whims of others. That's part of the problem. If people like you and me actually gave credence to the majority, then Electaria might actually make some progress."

Liliana eyed Ellegance with renewed interest. "Ellegance, you've managed to surprise me once more. Where did this backbone come from all of a sudden?"

"It's always been there, Your Highness. I just stood up." She clasped Liliana on the left shoulder with her right hand.

Liliana flinched, unused to the friendly contact.

Elle's eyes glinted, even though she smiled. "If you want to win this thing, I suggest you do the same."

Chapter 17
7055.1.25

Vitrians tended to arrive in the world in various shades of tall. Elle's long legs and willowy arms earned her nicknames like Spider and Stick as she grew older. The natural hunch in her shoulders tempered the effect, to some extent. She had no qualms about her size or the insults. In fact, her height provided her a sense of delight. Her height gave her an advantage, putting her fingertips closer to windowsills, narrowing her body to squeeze through tight places, and lengthening her legs for escaping any adventures that got out of hand.

She had always liked her height—up until today.

Elle stared at herself in the floor-length mirror—one of many ornaments in the overwhelmingly gaudy room within the Electarian palace—and frowned. She stared at her skinny arms and waved them about. In fairness, she had gained some weight since arriving at the castle. It was impossible not to, with the constant, rich dishes the cooks served. Still, she had yet to fully fill out the bones of her frame. The only aspects of her appearance that indicated strength were the worn calluses on her hands and the fierce gleam in her eyes. Normally, that was enough.

However, on the day of the Trial of *Viribus*, the God of strength, her appearance didn't feel all too promising.

Elle arranged her face into her best impression of a snarl, adding a small growl when her expression fell short. Her reflection in the mirror was unconvinced of the charade—even the furniture of the room looked unimpressed. She could practically hear her family burst into laughter in her head. She could picture their mirthful faces behind her in the mirror and the merciless teasing from Nic and the twins. Elle's head perked up, and the second her broad smile began to creep across her face, their images dissipated like mist, gone into a windowed world she could not follow.

She sighed, a small sound that lost all its gravitas in the large, empty room. "You're here for a reason," she reminded her reflection sternly. Her back gave a light pulse, a gentle sign of agreement. Her shoulders straightened, pushing her chest forward slightly. "Besides, the worst thing that happens is you die. That sets up pretty low expectations, so as long as you do better death, than we're really doing marvelously, *etiam*?"

"Should I do you the favor of pretending that there is somebody else in there with whom you could possibly be conversing, Ellegance?" Eliana's drawl slipped underneath the door. Elle imagined the slight, moonlike curve of Eliana's smile, the way her thick, black curls pressed against the door as the princess entreated through the wall. "Or should I simply ignore your blatant relinquishment of sanity and lead you to the Trial without a question edgewise?"

Elle's reflection exposed her distress: her furrowed eyebrows and wide, violet eyes impossible to hide. Her heart twirled in her chest, a giggling damsel the second it sensed its idol's presence. The blushing rouge dug around her thoughts, exploring her mind's city streets until it found the monument dedicated to the object of its affections. It threw open the door with wild abandon and let every feeling—every delicious, burning, painfully mortifying feeling—flood her body. Elle groaned and flopped backward onto the velvet ottoman in front of her mirror. *Viribus* himself could not come up with a task more daunting than spending time alone with the elder princess. She glared up at the golden, vaulted ceilings; the Gods sure did have a sick sense of humor. Elle gave a small laugh. She supposed she, as much as they, could appreciate the butt of a well-timed joke.

"I'm here out of the kindness of my heart, dear Ellegance, but I find my compassion quite limited. Will you be gracing me with your presence anytime in the next century, or must I pine away the remainder of my days waiting for you?" Her words curled with heat like burnt chocolate, bitter and caustic, poorly concealed with a vague sweetness.

"Coming." Elle huffed out a breath of air, whooshing her ragged black bangs out of her face. She appraised her black, long-sleeved tunic cinched at the waist with a golden belt, draped over a pair of loose, cotton pants. Though she enjoyed the Vitrian robes, this was the outfit that made Elle feel the most comfortable. For once in her time at the castle, Elle didn't feel totally at odds with the clothes she wore, as if her personality and the fabric were at war with one another. Though the material was higher quality than virtually anything Elle owned in her life, it still mimicked the comfort she used to feel wearing her brothers' clothes. Elle spared a smile at herself, her shoulders rolling back. In this outfit, she looked more like herself.

Elle threw open her door, willing her heart to please, *please* stop its tumultuous fanfare the second Eliana's pursed lips and dark, round eyes came into view. Before Elle could even utter a word, Eliana was grabbing her wrist and dragging her through the hallways, much in the way rivers whisked fallen leaves away from their harbors of safety with little care for their protests.

"We are running fabulously late—I can already see the smug, little look on Liliana's face when she finds out I towed you in at quarter past the start of the event. *Imperium,* help us all, it's not as though the girl needs any more stones with which to layer the foundation of her vaulted pedestal." Eliana's face twisted into an exquisite scowl, the thundered expression of a displeased goddess.

Elle, so focused on Eliana's elegant gnashing, entirely missed the path the two had taken until they were thoroughly buried in the recesses of the castle. Elle watched their surroundings with renewed interest. She took note of the dilapidated wood beneath their feet, so worn down it felt a lofty judgment to deem it a floor at all. The torches lit their way like comets, sparse and fleeting, providing only the barest glimpses of light before disappearing once more.

"Where *are* we?" Elle failed to hide the amazement in her voice. She thought she had traveled every inch of this castle, memorizing each detail down to the chips in the floor. How in the world had there been an entire underground system hidden from her exploring eyes?

Eliana glanced back, and a softer smile danced across her face, though Elle couldn't be sure beneath the transitory light of the torches. Her voice warmed into something more self-satisfied, the burnt chocolate from earlier turning into smooth, hot cocoa overflowing with pride. "The tunnels. Most castles have them, but most fools haven't enough wit to stumble upon them. Useful little things, aren't they?"

"They're incredible!" Elle exclaimed, her voice bouncing off the enclosed walls. She marveled at their rough, uncut texture, as if somebody had done the bare minimum in carving out their shape and left them at that. The abrasive surface mimed the material of some of the older, fancier buildings within her city. Elle's body buzzed with excitement. The prospect of something new and unexplored teeming beneath her feet sent her back pounding. "How do you know about them?"

"I never kiss and tell." Eliana winked back at Elle and thrust her sideways into a hidden path.

Elle flailed forward in the dark, her hands grappling for some object or surface onto which she might latch. A firm hand settled over the small of her back, grounding her in the dark void and pushing her forward. Eliana wrapped her other hand over Elle's eyes, needlessly obfuscating Elle's sight in the total obscurity.

She leaned over Elle's neck and whispered, the sound sending bumps over Elle's arms. "Be a good girl and stop"—she popped the word with her lips, and her hand at Elle's back pushed a bit harder—"struggling so much."

Eliana held her in this position for minutes longer as they navigated the twists and turns. She turned with confidence, her breath steady as she pushed Elle gently forward, leading from behind. The same question continued to chip away at Elle's mind. Such a secret being known by Electaria's most mysterious royal could be no coincidence. Elle bit back further demands for explanation to the point that her tongue gave a weary sigh of pain. She held her silence, scared she might break the spell of the moment with an inopportune comment.

They climbed up and down stairs, weaved around unknown objects, and walked until a dull burn developed in the arch of Elle's foot. Elle relished the faint ache. It was the satisfying kind of foot pain that came with playing games barefoot in the street or wandering to the point that the mind had ventured farther than the legs could handle. Her toes wiggled delightfully in her thick, leather boots.

Finally, Eliana removed her warm hand. "Thank *Imperium*, Liliana's not here. And, you, the precious treasure, have been safely delivered."

Elle blinked, her eyes struggling to adjust to the sudden brightness that greeted her. *Wait, brightness?* Elle squinted her eyes and quickly realized Eliana had somehow managed to drag her outdoors. The afternoon sun glared high in the sky, rivaling her ma in its overbearing nature. Impe asserted its dominance with as much light as it could muster, shoved down on *Terrabis* below.

Despite the overwhelming brightness, barely a fraction of the light managed to filter its way through the ceiling of leaves formed by the forest. The protective cloak created by the trees allowed for all life beneath to flourish, undaunted by the heat beyond the barrier. Birds squawked and crooned to one another, harmonizing with the scuttling of naman below. If Elle strained her ear, she could hear the occasional howl of what sounded like a very, very large wolf. A drop of sweat dripped down the back of her neck.

They waited behind a large oak, right on the outskirts of a forest where just beyond lay a small ring of military personnel. Elle found she had no reasonable way to explain how they had made it from her room in the castle to this point in the forest. Frankly? It drove her crazy. Elle gaped back and forth at the group and at Eliana, unsure of who deserved more incredulity.

"What—how—*Imperium* help—"

"Not *Imperium*, I'm afraid—just me. Now go complete your Trial." Eliana grasped Elle's arms and gave her a gentle shove into the clearing but not before pressing her lips against Elle's neck in a light kiss and murmuring, "Best of luck, Ellegance. Be sure to return tonight in such a way that you might crow of all you accomplished here."

Elle stumbled into the clearing, feeling entirely off-kilter. From the disorienting route they had taken to the dizzying guide herself, Elle felt the deep desire to turn around and nap away this strange afternoon. The ring of military personnel turned around, their tight eyes zeroing in on her. Within moments, they surrounded her in one very metallic, very intimidating circle. Elle groaned internally, straightening her back as best she could. Too late now.

A woman stepped forward, her ice-blue eyes freezing Elle in her place. Elle vaguely recognized the pin-straight hair and phlegmatic demeanor as the Captain of the Electarian military—though to be fair, it was difficult to forget a woman whose only natural propensities leaned toward weapons and scaring the living shit out of people. Liliana's guard, Aoran, winced sympathetically as the Captain loomed over Elle. A smile shadowed across Elle's face before she looked up and focused on the incarnate of moral fortitude before her.

"Ellegance Fournier, today you enter the Trial honoring the God who guides his strongest and protects his weakest: *Viribus*. He leads warriors into battle, merchants over rocky seas, infants through their plagues. He is as much the God of standing firm as he is the God of overcoming that which stands against you.

"Today you will enter this forest and venture toward its depths." The Captain pointed her finger north of where the group stood. "There are three golden keys therein, one for each of the Trial contestants. Yours will be uniquely marked by the engraving of the first letter of your name. Once you have retrieved the key, bring it back to this location, where one of my soldiers will await your return. You must return before the moon hits the midpoint of the sky; this should allow you plenty of time to complete your task."

"That's it?" The question slipped out before Elle could stop herself, but she found that she meant it. Aoran and two of the other guards seemed to be in immeasurable pain attempting to hold in their collective guffaw.

She blinked at the Captain. There had to be more to the challenge. She used to walk the streets of the kingdom in the depths of the night, skipping over the rocks without a fear lingering in her heart. With its thieves, fighting rings, and traditional city woes, she faced more danger in those block-long jaunts than in this moment. Elle found her lips creeping up into a tiny grin. There *had* to be more, otherwise Elle feared she would have a rather easy go of it. Maybe a dragon would be waiting to eat all her toes once she got halfway there. Or maybe Liliana's phantom would try to possess Elle and simply make Elle kill herself. Elle chuckled to herself. *There just has to be more.*

The Captain's lip curled up, and Elle got the distinct impression that Elle would never be a favorite should she deign to join the Electarian military. The Captain continued, her words clipped and her eyes a wintry blizzard. "If you return empty-handed—turn back before finding the key, lose it somewhere along the way— you should immediately fail the Trial. You will score zero points automatically and will be relegated to a firm last place in the Trials. *That* is it."

Elle suddenly found a lot less humor in the situation. Her eyebrows squeezed together, and she threw a few prayers up to

Viribus. She prayed for the strength to complete the task without fear or a ghostly Liliana murdering her.

The Captain raised one frosty eyebrow. "Well?"

"Understood." When the Captain continued to glare at her, Elle added a trembling "C-Captain?"

The Captain nodded, satisfied. Well, as satisfied as Elle had seen since she came on the scene. With little more fanfare, the Captain disappeared with the soldiers, each one filing in line behind her.

The only one who stayed behind was Aoran. He cocked his head to the side and smirked. "She's delightful, no?"

Elle, taken aback by the friendly demeanor, laughed quick and easy. "How do you do it?"

"Indomitable charm and—" He turned around, and she heard the hiss of a lit flame. When he straightened out, he held a small blunt in his hand, and the butter-colored smoke of sunweed curled from his mouth. He winked at her. "A little friendly help."

Elle laughed even harder, fueled by anxiety zipping through her blood. As it turned out, it was an excellent stimulant for hysterical laughter. When she finally regained her breath, Elle nodded, both to herself and Aoran, and turned to the forest. She squared her shoulders and took a deep breath, a vague excitement and nervousness buzzing through her body. They worked concomitantly through her system, charging her every nerve until she stood there so tense that her body barely contained its tremble.

"You ready, soldier?" Aoran watched her carefully, his posture casual but his tone sincere.

Elle turned back and met his crinkled, green eyes with a wide grin. She felt the severity of the scene melt away for just the second, and her shoulders stretched back a bit farther. Every trial was a step closer to helping her family and everyone like them. Elle could put people like Penelope on the Treasury Council. She could make bureaucratic processes more transparent. Instead of daunting Elle, the prospect of the momentous change she could enact thrilled her. There was so much to be had and so much to be gained by acing the Trials and moving her family into the castle. "Hardly. But that's the fun part, *etiam?*"

She left the forest clearing with Aoran watching her. She disappeared into the trees while an amused grin danced across his face, and sunweed smoke swirled into a spiral above his head.

Elle walked in the direction pointed out by the Captain, very quickly realizing that maybe, *just maybe* she should have asked for more cartographic guidance. She bit her lip, unsure of whether she should turn back to ask Aoran for assistance. But...if she turned back now, Elle had the sinking feeling that it would be considered an early return and drown her chances at the throne entirely. Pursing her lips, Elle trudged forward. *Boldly and bravely,* she thought, attempting to raise her own confidence at her decision.

The forest stole away the afternoon sunlight and dimmed the sun's rays to a dusky haze surrounding the area. It was as if by entering, Elle had put on a pair of black, translucent glasses. Although she could see a few feet in front of her, every object appeared fuzzy and dim. The trees stretched high into the air, their roots crawling and arching over the ground wherever they found purchase. Elle found she had to keep her eyes trained on the ground, unable to watch her surroundings for fear of tripping on a willfully placed root.

The dewy scent of grass lingered on the insides of her nostrils in the soft way wet things tended to, overlaid with the heavy aroma of moss and bark. The cacophony of nature grew in both its volume and discord, as if every living creature constantly participated in the grand competition of noisiest species alive. Elle snorted to herself, chuckling as she wandered forward. The animals of the forest could give the Vitrian empress a run for her money.

Elle's bangs clung to her forehead, pasted on by a thick layer of sweat as she hopped over roots and ducked under branches. Occasionally a forest naman would scurry out of her way, at which point she had to leap over the characteristic trail of acid the adorable beasts left behind. Unlike the namans that scuttled about the kingdom, the forest namans had spiky, dangerous fur.

Otherwise, she failed to run into any animals. This only heightened Elle's nerves as she delved deeper into the woods.

The absence of people and action created a bubble of compression around Elle, pushing in on her with an uncomfortable pressure. Her gaze darted this way and that and always returned to the ground as she stepped lightly around all that lay beneath her. Elle's breath caught at shadows flashing between the trees, her heart crawling up and into her throat. In the castle, she could always sense the people around her, even when she couldn't see them. She couldn't remember the last time she had felt so alone.

Throughout Elle's life, loneliness was never a possibility. If she wandered the city streets during the day, she passed by merchants, students, tradesmen, all bustling about through the rushing cobblestone streets. When she snuck out at night, drunks, scantily clad nightwalkers, and the equally mischievous children of the kingdom haunted nearby corners and alleys. Even if Elle failed to see a single person during the evening, she could always hear laughter and jeering nearby.

The darkness tightened around her, more suffocating than any court dress. Alone, she trekked through the tangled trees and brush. Her eyes burned, straining to piece together her surroundings. She reached for some excitement at the prospect of the unknown, but she failed to latch onto anything except for a growing sense of dread. Adventure seemed to lose its glamour when Elle lost her company.

Elle stumbled briefly and felt her heart drop from her throat to her stomach. Used to her sure footing, Elle was even more caught off guard by the slip. A bead of sweat trailed down the side of her face. She cursed to herself, shaking off the falter. She only messed up because she was alone, in the dark, and trying to complete the stupid Trial.

Elle's brain stalled on the last point. Would this always be the culmination of being queen? Alone and fumbling for a destination she had no idea how to reach? Elle felt out of her league and far outclassed for this position. Her heart skipped a beat, unsure and nervous.

Loneliness surely wouldn't be a problem—there would always be people around her. The thought gave her no comfort. So often, the people of the court felt less like people and more like dolls, going through the motions somebody else deemed appropriate. For some reason, knowing she would be surrounded by dolls made the journey seem impossibly lonelier. Was this the type of adventure she wanted to embark upon?

Shaking her head, Elle dispelled her thoughts. She tried to pretend that she was taking another stroll through the streets of the city. Elle sang an old street song under her breath, her voice breathy and out of tune as she hiked through the foliage:

Try to fool me and go blind
Try to fool me, lose your mind
Loyal is as loyal serves
Ya always get what ya deserve—

Elle's voice cut off the second she heard a distant, wet snarl. Before she could even attempt to pretend this was a simple trick of the forest, another growl echoed in response. She quickened her pace, moving from a simple walk to a light run, her feet skipping over the forest floor. The growls erupted behind her, louder. Closer. Elle whimpered to herself, her breath coming out in short puffs. Did she even dare turn around?

She dared. Elle snuck a look over her right shoulder and felt bile rise in her throat, her own fear so tangible she could have plucked it out of the air and thrown it into dough as an ingredient. Four sets of yellow eyes met her own and, more importantly, four sets of very sharp teeth.

"Oh *shit*," she whisper-screamed to herself, her eyes wide as she flew through the forest, her feet carrying her faster and farther than ever before.

As she sprinted, she heard paws pounding against the floor that sped up in response. Her blood thickened and expanded underneath her skin. Her heartbeat thundered to the tips of her fingers. This was a far cry from the exhilarated fear she used to feel sprinting through the streets of the city. The weight of the moment hit her with a vicious ferocity, a voice in her mind repeating a mantra: "If you are caught, you *will* die. Run faster. Run farther."

"I'm running as fast as I can, son of a *malum*!" Elle cursed in a gasping cry, though to whom she couldn't say.

She desperately scanned for protection, cover, *something*. Her hopes of escape plummeted with every step as her legs grew more tired, and the pack of wolves gained ground. Elle's eyes watered, the wind whipping in her face as she raced to safety—wherever in *Imperium*'s name that was. Her back pounded, burned, *roared*. This was about more than just staying alive. This was about climbing and scraping her way to the throne. This was about her family. Her city.

Elle would be damned if a handful of wolves stopped her from doing that.

The next few seconds passed with the speed of decades. Her eyes zeroed in on a sturdy branch in front of her, much too high for someone of shorter stature. Elle gritted her teeth and leaped. Her fingers scraped over the abrasive bark, gripping the damn thing with all her might. For a split second, Elle thought the sweat on her hands would cause her to slip. A strangled noise slipped out of her mouth as she regripped her hands, her forearms burning from the struggle. She stuck her legs on the trunk and pushed off, heaving herself upward with the strength of a girl who spent her entire life scaling brick buildings.

Elle didn't stop climbing. She reached for branch after branch, propelling herself upward with shaking legs. Her hands grated against the tree, tearing open with each bloody pull. She didn't stop. The wolves howled at the base of the tree, each taking its turn to bump its side into the trunk. After launching herself to the top, Elle looked down and bared her teeth, growling at them with all the force in her diaphragm. "And now, if you'll excuse me, I'm going to get the damn key!"

Elle cackled to herself, a cross between a frenetic laugh and a heaving sob. The fear clung to her skin like the smoke of fire, putrid and overwhelming. Her limbs shook, sweat dripped from her forehead, and she still had the distinct feeling she might puke from terror, but she moved forward.

With the careful grace of a practiced city acrobat, Elle moved between trees. She traveled through the canopy as if the very thing were made as her own personal transit system. Stretching from tree to tree and straining from branch to branch, Elle promised herself that she would never say another thing about her height for the rest of her life.

Elle had no clue where she was headed, but her mark beat a steady rhythm as she slipped about the forest from an aerial view. When she turned in a certain direction, the beat would slow down. Elle followed its guidance, moving wherever her back pounded the fastest. The trees finally broke apart for a small clearing in what she assumed was the center of the forest. In the middle of the clearing lay a small, brown chest, barely bigger than Elle's own head.

She shimmied down the tree, scanning for any signs of disturbance before kneeling and opening the chest with shaky hands. Inside resided a golden key with an elegant *E* burned into its head and a small note in neat, scripted handwriting. Elle mouthed the words to herself, unable to concentrate otherwise.

> To whichever contestant this finds:
>
> Strength is not the absence of fear, anxiety, and their many, terrible brethren. It is the existence of a spirit that is willing to put all those things to the side and do what needs to be done when it is called. You have the key; now finish answering the call.
>
> Aoran

Elle laughed to herself, a tear sliding down her cheek. She took a second to sit there and put her face in her hands, drawing in a shuddered breath. Taking her head out of her hands, Elle looked forward with red, determined eyes. She folded the note and grabbed the key, tucking both into the belt of her trousers.

"Aw, come on! You already found the key?" a tinkling voice whined behind her.

Elle whipped around and lunged for the voice. After everything that happened earlier, there was no way in *Imperium*'s name she would be taken out now. The small individual squeaked, throwing their arms over their face. She tackled the figure to the ground and pointed the jagged end of the key at the intruder's eye.

Chest heaving, Elle quickly realized the fierce strain in her biceps to keep the stranger pinned was unnecessary. The quivering, thin frame beneath her couldn't fend off a tight sweater, much less the full force of Elle's height and weight.

"Wait-wait-wait-wait-wait!" the figure beneath her shrieked, muffled beneath their arms, their eyes pinched closed. Even though this being was dressed like a normal Electarian, in a simple camel tunic tucked into black pants, Elle swore she had never seen somebody so foreign.

"Who are you?" Elle demanded, her black hair falling in front of her face. Her hand shook, but she held the key firmly above the stranger's face. She dragged in air sharply through her nose, waiting.

The stranger slowly opened one eyelid and then the other, peeking at Elle through their fingers with doe-like, amber eyes. The individual's ecru-colored skin was a sharp contrast to the intense coloring of their eyes and hair. The hair was a faint orange, cropped so close to the head it was practically peach fuzz. Looking at the stranger's sloped, thick eyebrows and full lips, contrasted against their male dress, Elle found herself utterly befuddled in trying to determine the stranger's gender.

"If I tell you, will you please not stab me with that key?" The stranger blinked at her with those mesmerizing, golden eyes.

"Tell me who you are first. Then, we can revisit the question," Elle said. She hoped the threat didn't sound as empty as it felt. If the stranger didn't answer, she wasn't sure what she would do. Elle wasn't really in the business of being menacing to others.

The stranger sighed, a soft sound like a summer breeze brushing through long hair. "My name is Seran."

They pronounced the name like "Seh-rahn," their mouth curling over the second part of the name like a wave crashing against the surf, cutting it off quickly and neatly. Where was that accent from? The name lacked the shortness of traditional male names of Electaria, but it wasn't quite long enough to be considered feminine, furthering Elle's puzzlement. She found the key loosening in her group with her uncertainty.

"And…what are you?" Elle asked, eyes trailing up and down Seran to emphasize her confusion.

Seran clucked their tongue, somehow sounding exasperated through the faint tremors that still ran through their body. "Does it matter? A male, a female, something in between, something far beyond—I haven't decided. You're asking the wrong question."

Elle chewed the inside of her cheek. Seran didn't seem to be a threat. She slowly relaxed, rolling forward on the balls of her feet to stand up. Seran carefully followed suit, brushing the dirt off their clothing and unfurling to a height a hand shorter than Elle herself.

Elle tried the question again. "Okay. So you're Seran. *Who* exactly is Seran?"

Seran's pink lips curled upward into a playful, impish smile. A gentle wind brushed through the trees and down Elle's back. "Unless I'm utterly mistaken, Elle, I'm your Guide."

CHAPTER 18
7055.1.26

Liliana stood in front of a door at the end of a hallway, unable to tear herself from the spot. The exit's wandering path eventually led to the House, but Liliana found her feet firmly planted in place. Eyes narrowed, she stroked Imperium's fur. Liliana had requested Aoran's absence for the afternoon, allowing her the time to visit the House on her own. Of course, he readily agreed, so long as Liliana admitted that it was because she would find Aoran's handsome presence too distracting. Her cheeks warmed at the memory, wishing she had hit him harder in response.

This left Liliana alone with her thoughts and her wolf, at least for a little while longer. Imperium reveled beneath her attention, tongue lolled out and head on paws larger than most children. She tried to find a sense of calm in the softness of his fur, something to ease her growing annoyance at the current Trial scores.

Ellegance Fournier: 2.7

Liliana Storidian: 2.5

Teo Storidian: 2.6

Even though the Trials were being kept a secret from the public, within the castle confines, they were the heart of every conversation. It was impossible to talk diplomacy, finances, or even general gossip without the Trials being inserted in some way. The fact that the House regularly posted score updates around the castle, such as the one before Liliana, only served to increase the Trial's salience in every individual's mind.

Liliana's Trial of *Viribus* had been wholly uneventful, which she now blamed as part of the reason for her inferior performance. Rumors from the handful of castle staff she interrogated indicated that Elle had escaped the snapping jaws of wolves, and Teo had fended off a flock of tumultuous Timore hawks. Liliana's grasp on Imperium's fur grew harder. How was she expected to compete with displays of valor if she never had the opportunity in the first place? It felt like both the Trials and the Gods themselves were conspiring against Liliana's victory.

The door before her swept open, and Teo strode back into the castle. Cape fluttering, sword gleaming, and face characteristically neutral, though his eyebrows furrowed a bit in the center. *Speak of the* malum, Liliana thought bitterly to herself.

He halted at seeing Liliana, and she practically saw the debate of whether or not to speak waging in his head. Finally, years of propriety won over, and he nodded to her stiffly.

"Good afternoon." He paused, his methodical mind systematically rolling through the appropriate way to proceed. He continued slowly, "It has been a while since we last spoke."

"Not too long a while, unfortunately," Liliana muttered. "I assume you are returning from prayers like the good son you are?"

"It's not about being a good son. Mother stopped insisting I go pray years ago. I do this for myself," he said firmly, as if trying to convince himself the words as he said them aloud. "My times in the House are some when I feel closest to *Imperium*."

Liliana tried not to let her jealousy show. While she believed *Imperium* sometimes whispered in her ear, she never felt particularly close with her patron Goddess. It was like how a magister could give Liliana advice or tell her what to do—that didn't signify some deeper connection between them. *Imperium* felt less a spiritual force in Liliana's life than a distant teacher. There was this constant hope that through the Trials, Liliana might feel *Imperium* more acutely. Maybe then, Liliana would finally complete her Walk. If the Trials were testing for a true leader, then shouldn't the Trials also be able to reveal the path to finally complete her Walk?

The idea that Teo had a close bond with the Goddess grinded against Liliana. Biting back some of her crueler comments, Liliana simply said, "I see."

Silence stretched between them, glistening and long like copper candy being stretched to its breaking point. Liliana's hand grasped at the skirts of her lavender dress, and she willed herself not to say anything else just for the sake of filling the space. She had no desire to make their conversation any longer than necessary.

Teo studied her with his mahogany eyes while they stayed silent. Liliana's heart twisted, anger and sadness wrenching it in different directions. When he looked at her so critically with those eyes, he looked exactly like their mother. Liliana hated him, just a little bit, for that.

Breaking her consternation, Teo asked, "Eliana tells me you set the mail room on fire the other night? She also said that you've refused to talk to any suitors, despite her and father's pleas otherwise." He looked at her with what could only be considered utter bewilderment. "You've always been brash, but all this? I simply don't understand. Why, Liliana?"

"Oh no." Liliana shook her head with a laugh, one hand tightening on her dress and the other tightening in Imperium's fur. "You don't get to ignore and scold me for two decades and then suddenly request an open pass into my mind. That isn't how this works."

"Ignore you? You detested me, ever since we were children," Teo countered, raising a finger in protest. "Mother and I agreed it was better not to incite unnecessary family drama, so I tried to avoid you. Too much interaction, and we would eventually bicker. I wanted to keep that promise to her after she died." His stoic expression wilted the slightest bit. "Given recent events, I suppose my failure is pretty evident."

"I only detested you because whenever you actually *dared* to interact with me, you brushed off my ideas or treated me like a child!"

"If I treated you like a child, it only would have been because you were acting like one. A lot like you are now," Teo added with a shake of his head.

"And that," Liliana unclenched her dress and shook her hand at him, "is why I will not be answering your question about the mail room. Since you and Eliana are so keen to discuss my affairs behind my back, go ask her. Enjoy your afternoon."

Liliana brushed past Teo's half-hearted protests, exiting the castle and walking toward the House. She fumed, her heels hitting the ground and sinking into the gravel that lined the walkway. Everything about the conversation provoked her ire. Teo's prying into her life, his decision about what was best for her, his disregard of her as a functional adult. Brashness, Liliana admitted, was a flaw of hers. But to apply the label to every one of her ideas and decisions whittled her down to a childish archetype in which she loathed to be placed. Her mind stayed stuck on the idea that her mother had facilitated the frayed relationship between herself and Teo. *Why?*

Arriving at the door of the House, Liliana scratched behind Imperium's ear harder. Once again, she was stuck before another entryway. The entrance looked more like a barrier. She reached deep within herself for the capacity to spare a quick smile for Imperium, wishing the wolf would soothe her raging feelings more quickly. Humans were irrational. Wolves didn't suffer from the same plagues of conflicting heart and mind. They followed their nose and whatever pleased them at the time, loyal to those who treated them well, enemies to those who didn't. It was a one-dimensional world, one that made infinitely more sense than that in which Liliana lived.

The sun shone brilliantly in the sky, a golden jewel bathing everyone beneath its gentle rays. Still in the first few weeks of Impe, the season was a pleasant mistress, but she would turn into a crueler summer soon enough. The white flowers guarding the House's prized magisters strained their necks toward the sky, drinking in every drop of the day their tiny petals could. People in search of prayer and a little good faith whisked around Liliana, bustling and pleasant. They came for guidance. She came for answers.

The House of Magisters had no door separating its halls and the world. Such a contraption would be entirely counterintuitive to the idea; the magisters channeled the will of the Gods, and the Gods existed to help their followers, guiding each through their own Walk so they might find peace within their respective virtue. The magisters—and the Gods themselves, she supposed—would be of no use if they couldn't be reached.

There was no barrier preventing her entrance. "So why," she asked loudly, Imperium quirking his head curiously, "am I still out here?"

A rhetorical question, of course. Her feet cemented themselves to the ground, and her hands locked in Imperium's fur. Her mother's firm, unyielding voice echoed in Liliana's head: "Cae is Electaria's greatest treasure. When you see him, you must have patience. He is …strange. But he is an artist. He shall paint the future before you as clearly as if the Gods themselves had whispered in your ear. He serves as advisor to the throne but may be persuaded to lend his ear and his mind to another. You must be charming."

The memory of her mother's voice was more warped than usual since Liliana's run-in with Teo muddied the waters of her mind. Liliana squeezed her eyes shut, trying to put the interaction out of her mind.

This might have been one of those times she sought the advice of her father, the only parental figure she had left. She might have stormed into his room, banging down his door in search of his audience. Begging for guidance, she would have huffed and puffed and asked, "What in the world am I supposed to do?" He would have smiled, the old and merry twinkle in his eye as he gave her a piece of ambiguous advice. Advice so lukewarm that she would be left to deciphering and pulling meaning from where there was none.

Liliana might have tried so hard to convince herself that the words of her father were the same as the prophetic advice of her mother. Then, maybe, Liliana might have carved out her own destiny from her father's meaningless words and good intentions.

Of course, times such as those were far gone.

She huffed, turning to Imperium and looking her wolf seriously in the eyes. He stared right back at her, his black head tilted to the side.

"Have any tips?"

Her wolf, unfortunately, stayed silent, offering her only a small yip. He gently nudged her with his nose, pushing her backward from the entrance.

Liliana patted his head as he gave her another firm bop away from the House. She tilted her head to the opposite side and laughed, despite herself. "Excellent advice—but we can go back to the castle later. For now, destiny awaits. Wish me luck."

Liliana brushed past the entrance of the House, its splendor and heavy incense barely registering. She moved briskly to the entrance of *Caecus*'s room, her small, golden heels sinking into the ground as tiles morphed into dirt. She collected the hem of her lavender dress in her hand, eyes scanning for the legend from her mother's stories. Queen Juliana rarely had praise for those outside of herself and her family members—and even the latter was rare. The very existence of a man who warranted the offhand compliment and approval of the deceased monarch was clearly one to be taken seriously.

Or so Liliana thought. There was only one man in the room who matched her mother's descriptions: a man stationed at the far end of the room whose sightless blue eyes roamed aimlessly around a world he could not behold. Liliana quickly found such a man but ...Was the old man talking to himself?

Liliana approached with the same caution that she might a skittish animal. The olive skin sagged around his cheeks and jaw, lines from age and laughing creating deep divots and pockmarks in his face. His brittle hair was collected into a wispy bun on the top of his head, silver, broken strands taking up residence on the shoulders of his earthy robes. The ancient man paid no mind to her approach, chatting away to the air in front of him with lips so dry they threatened to bleed every time his statements turned into exclamations.

"And I *tell* ya, *vici*, Tyn near cried he was so rile'd up. So I tell ya what, *vici*, I took his face and tell 'im: '*Eye* believe in ya!' Get it? Eye!" Cae jabbed a finger at his own blind eyes before laughing uproariously, smacking his right hand against the ground beside him.

Liliana took a step back, startled. Embarrassment on behalf of the stranger flooded her cheeks with red. The other magisters in the room regarded the pair with clear aggravation.

Cae heaved a sigh, blue eyes glittering "Aye, Gods as my witness— ey, *vici*, ya know what I mean—damn near funniest thing I ever seen. Now, ya have to forgive me. Got a visitor, I do, and it'd be mighty rude to ignore her. Aye, aye. I hear ya." And with little more warning, Cae's crystal gaze moved down and settled on Liliana.

His tiny pupils, swimming in a sea of a faded and watery blue, focused on hers. Wasn't he supposed to be blind? She took another tiny step back, her skin crawling. Who in *Imperium*'s name was this man?

"What can I do for ya, *vici?*"

Liliana's eyes narrowed, and she stepped forward, waving one hand tentatively in front of the man's eyes. He didn't blink, and yet his eyes remained firmly trained on hers. A shudder ran down her back.

"Cae, correct? It is a pleasure to meet you. My name is—"

Cae's hands shot forward and grabbed her shoulders, squeezing her biceps with morbid curiosity. Liliana's nostrils flared, and it took everything in her power to not break the man's fingers.

"Aye, there ain't no way, right? But I'd recognize that *Imperium* energy anywhere. But-but there *ain't* no way. As far as I know, Queen Juliana has long passed...right?"

Liliana's spine stiffened. Her mother's death felt like a paper cut that never properly healed. On most days, Liliana felt fine. But occasionally somebody would accidentally bump into the wound, and it would hiss the remnants of a sharp pain. Today, too many people had bumped into the damn wound. She arranged a forced smile on her face, even though she was (relatively) sure he could not see her reaction. "I'm afraid not. I am her daughter, Princess Liliana."

"Princess Liliana, a' course! Well, I'll be a son of a *malum*, if the pleasure ain't all mine!" Cae cried joyously. He released her shoulders only to feel around the floor to grasp her hand, shaking it aggressively. "Tell me, *vici*, what does ol' Leo think about my new hairstyle? Tyn don't give it much thought, but I figure a fine man like ya da would be *sure* to appreciate it. Course, Tyn ain't got much time to..." Cae's face faltered for the briefest second before brightening again. "Well, never mind that. What can I do for ya, *vici*?"

Liliana's head spun. Who was Tyn? Her father knew about Cae? A furious divergence of her thoughts occurred, and she wondered if Teo knew about the man too—was there anything sacred in Liliana's relationship with her mother? If Cae was a war general and information his arsenal of arrows, Liliana's troops would be on the retreat. She rallied her thoughts, forming a coherent thought from their scattered ranks. "Ah, yes, of course. Right. That. I came here for a reason." She shook her head, pressing one frustrated hand to her temple. "I came here seeking guidance."

"Lotsa things can give ya guidance, *vici*. Ya thought of startin' with a map?" He cackled and slapped his knee, nearly rocking back to the point of flipping over.

It was official. Liliana was thoroughly flustered. "No—I mean, I'm not looking for a map—I'm-I'm—" Liliana growled out a frustrated breath and flopped down in front of Cae, her lavender dress becoming intimately acquainted with the dirt. *Wreck charm.* No matter how much someone might coax an arrow into being charismatic, it would only ever be straight and direct because it was a wrecking arrow.

"Look. I'm competing in the Trials, and I need you to investigate the future for me. Like you used to do for my mother." She paused, her eyebrows furrowing. "Like I guess you've been doing for my father. Can you do that or not?"

Cae's countenance flickered, as if Liliana had gently blown on the flame of his gaiety. His hand dropped hers, falling to the ground and aimlessly picking at whatever his fingers could find. "Aye, *vici*, if ya parents said anythin' about me then ya know I only talk to the queen a' king. Not the youngins'." His face dropped in apology.

"Are you sure?" Liliana pressed, feeling her frustration grow. "Is there truly no way I could convince you otherwise?"

"Aye." Cae spread his fingers out helplessly in front of him. "Ain't nothin' I can do. Mighty sorry 'bout it, too, *vici*."

Liliana gritted her teeth. Her inferior rank superseded her ambition once again. But the stakes were infinitely higher now. She was in last place for the Trials. The two remaining Trials would be the determinants of the city's fate.

Which meant that now was not the time to play nice. Now was the time to get what she wanted. If there was a potential advantage, Liliana would snag it. She had to.

Liliana took a quick look around to make sure none of the other magisters could hear her. "No, *I'm* sorry." She laughed in a quiet, harsh way. "I must not have communicated what I wanted clearly enough because instead of the future, you just gave me utter bullshit." She leaned her head on her fist, staring at the man. Though he could not see, she hoped he could feel the sheer hostility radiating off her.

"My mother would have never told me to come to you if you would be of no use to me, and I certainly didn't come here for a pleasant conversation. So please, I implore you in all your wisdom," her voice grew hard, "be of use to me."

"Ey, kid," Cae's smile totally vanished, "that ain't how it works 'round here. I ain't on retainer for ya royals. I work for the Gods. Maybe ya should head—"

Cae abruptly cut off, his eyes losing focus and staring beyond Liliana's shoulder. His wrinkled jaw dropped, his chin wiggling around incredulously. "Are ya serious, *vici*? Ya want me to speak with her?" Cae's voice turned whiny. "Are ya kiddin' me?"

He turned silent, sullen, before his blue eyes shifted back to Liliana, petulance displayed in everything from his sulky tone to the slump of his shoulders. "Fine. What do ya want to know?"

Liliana had no idea what just transpired, but far be it from her to argue with a good turn of events (she didn't even want to imagine how vehemently Aoran would have objected should he have heard such a statement from her mouth). A warm smugness curled itself around Liliana's shoulders like a fine fur scarf. The thrill of having answers at the tip of her tongue sent tingles to the tips of her fingers. She leaned in closer to Cae. "First, I need to know what the format of the next Trial is going to be—"

"Ey, ey, ey." Cae cut her off with a slam of his hand on the dirt floor. "Next question. I ain't allowed to answer somethin' like that."

Liliana's eyebrow twitched. "Okay, then I would like to know what my greatest asset will be going into the—"

"Nope."

"Wrecking—okay, then at the very least, what will be my score going into the final—"

"Uh-uh."

Liliana let out a shriek in frustration, her fingernails digging into the dirt beneath her. It took everything in her power to keep her voice at a loud whisper as she seethed. "*Imperium* damn you, you son of a *malum*—what *can* I ask, then?"

Cae cackled to himself, leaning back on his wrinkled, skinny wrists. "I'll let ya know when ya ask a question he says I can answer."

Liliana flushed a bright red. The blind, stupid "prophet" made a joke out of her, in front of her very eyes. The stories around the man were clearly nothing more than myths propagated to elevate his self-importance. Her mother and father had apparently gotten caught up in the sensationalistic idea. She wasted her time in entertaining his nonsense and would not be made the man's fool any longer. She jerked upward, slapping any dirt that remained on the skirt of her dress.

When she spoke next, she enunciated her words to the point of practically spitting at the man. "Clearly *Caecus* has abandoned you entirely, for you lack any sensibility to cooperate with a future ruler when you see one. I can assure you, the next time I return to this House with a crown on my head, you will be the first thing evicted from it." She whipped around to leave.

His voice caught her before she took a step toward the exit. "Ey, vici, ya really want a piece of advice?"

A modicum of hope reared its head in her mind, salivating at the prospect of getting legitimate information. Liliana stalled in her storming off, refusing to fully turn around and give him the satisfaction of having her full attention. Not that he would know either way.

Cae seemed to sense he had caught her interest. He continued, his voice low and solemn. "Exit from the competition. There's nothin' for ya at the end of that road."

Liliana's world slowed down. Blood rushed into her ears. She ground her teeth together, feeling as though her molars would crack if she clenched any harder. Those words. *Those words, those words, those words.* So much like Teo's when the worthless man walked into the gymnasium, beseeching her forfeit. So much like the attitude of the Nuwei ambassador who told her to mind her place. So much like her father's insistence that she make peace and be more like Teo.

Be a martyr. Accept defeat. Support your brother. Just find a suitor. Learn your place. A low, dark laugh rumbled in the bottom of her chest. She never knew how many ways one could say "Give up."

Cae apparently was another man who wanted to force the white flag of surrender on Liliana. Unfortunately for the millions of people who stood at her gate, anxiously waiting for her surrender to walk through its doors, Liliana was not so fragile. She did not live her life pining away for others' approval. Teo and Ellegance could play the part of the good little brownnosers. Liliana's pride would never allow her to be so malleable to others' whims. Not then and certainly not now.

Her fists clenched at her sides, the mark on her back shrieking. The dragon in her thrashed, begging to be heard. The burning agonized her and centered her at the same time. The searing pain gave her a focus. Damn him, and damn that forsaken flag. Liliana fully intended on shoving that same shameful flag down everybody else's throat.

She turned carefully on her heel, descending to kneel next to the old man. He flinched backward, but she grasped his chin tightly between her fingers. She ignored the gasps and gazes that erupted across the room. He met her gaze with his own sightless eyes, an unnamable expression playing across his face. Liliana squeezed his chin a little bit tighter, her nails digging into the soft folds of his skin.

"When I am in power, I will collect all those who denied me along the way. I will place them in a stack at the center of the palace and light them on fire, until any former disbelief in me and what I am *capable* of"—Liliana's fingers turned white as she gripped him inexplicably harder. He made an uncomfortable noise, but did not look away—"is nothing more than dust in the wind."

She dropped her hand to hold his own, crushing the old bones in her hands and taking a deep satisfaction in the way he winced. Her voice grew sweet and soft as she whispered into his ear, "And I promise, Magister Cae, you will be among the first to go."

Liliana stood up and prowled out of the room, leaving the magister sitting there. Everybody in the room watched with terror. Liliana's back pounded and burned, and she met the eyes of every bewildered person in the room. Her mind receded, as if being gently pushed back to make room for something else. Liliana faintly knew in the recesses of consciousness that the term wasn't exactly right. *Someone* else.

A smooth whisper curled faintly in Liliana's head, soft, but firm. *"The Little Dragon has no need for prying eyes right now."*

Some intangible switch clicked off as she stared them down. Their shoulders relaxed, and they returned to their conversations, looking none the wiser by the entire exchange. One by one, the room regressed to its former mood. Liliana gave the phenomenon no further thought and stalked out of the room for the last time.

Aoran waited for her outside the House, ready to return to his post, leaning lazily against the white walls. Imperium had left, and Liliana recognized a vague disappointment at her companion's disappearance through the window of her rage. It was like she could see all her emotions, but each one was inhibited from reaching her through the glass.

Upon Liliana's storm out of the building, he pushed himself off, approaching her slowly. His green eyes scanned her up and down, seeking the cause for her distress. "Hey, princess, you good?"

She whipped around to face him, her eyes wild and cheeks blotchy. "We're fighting in the training arena. Come. Now."

Aoran apparently thought it prudent not to argue for once, as he easily acquiesced. He trailed her at a safe distance from behind, as if worried she might turn around and swing at him at any moment. She ignored him the entire way to the training arena, her thoughts clamoring so intensely in her brain that she could not fathom speaking through the noise.

Liliana threw open the door of the gymnasium, seeing with a dull satisfaction that they would be alone. The gym's empty space amplified the furious racing of her heart. Her fists clenched and unclenched at her side, and a nauseatingly angry feeling squeezed around her heart. Liliana was sick to death of people putting guard rails on where she could and could not take her life. People fed her so many lies and excuses throughout her life on why she wasn't qualified or why she should not dare to take some action— she practically burst at the seams from the banquet of doubt and misgivings she had feasted upon for twenty-one years.

Aoran lacked any of his normal bravado, his face entirely unsure as Liliana led the way. He opened his mouth to say something but was cut off before he could formulate even his first word. The second their footsteps touched the soft sand of the dueling area, Liliana turned around and lunged for Aoran.

Years of training were the only thing that spared Aoran the slam of Liliana's body running into him with all her force. He leaped to the side, falling into a somersault against the ground. Before he could counter, she was springing at him again. Aoran grabbed her leading arm, attempting to twist it behind her back to pin Liliana to the ground. Liliana reached around with her other arm, elbowing Aoran in the kidney. He coughed, and she whipped around, attempting a punch directly at his face.

Aoran lifted his left forearm, catching the brunt of the blow. She withdrew quickly, feigning a punch with her left hand before coming back with her right hand toward his abdomen. Aoran danced away, his agility allowing him to escape the circle of her grip as he assessed the situation.

Liliana's fighting lacked its normal grace and composure. She grappled and lunged with the undisciplined power of Vitrian fighters. She licked her lips, relishing his surprise and discomfort. Aoran narrowed his eyes at her. He brushed off his initial surprise, his fists rising and his fighting stance stabilizing. Liliana growled to herself. She had to move before he could fully get his bearings.

Liliana moved toward Aoran again, attacking with an unprecedented speed. Time spent training together had turned Liliana's frame into something leaner. Unlike Liliana's well-intentioned but adorably weak smacks at the air from their first lessons, Liliana's hits were backed by experience and intensity. Instead of stumbling around the sand, she sliced through the air. While Aoran likely still had the upper hand in a traditional sparring match, Liliana had come into her own and was a force to be reckoned with.

Though Aoran clipped her several times against the jaw, he couldn't seem to land a direct blow. Liliana feigned a punch with her left hand before raising her right fist for another punch. Aoran steeled his abdomen, ready to allow her the hit so he could pin her down immediately after the move.

What she lost in the sharpness of her movements, she more than made up for in pure ferocity. Instead of aiming for Aoran's kidney again, she dipped beneath his hands, getting low and driving her elbow into his knee socket. He dropped to the ground, and Liliana turned him over before he had time to think, pinning his arms down with her knees and holding his hands to the floor. She leaned over him, her chest rising and falling rapidly and sweat gleaming across her forehead.

Aoran looked up at her, a confused annoyance on his face. "Liliana, what the hell?"

Every time Liliana believed she had reached a new level of maximum fury, some poor, stupid idiot managed to exceed her expectations in pissing her off. There was always another person who seemed to excel at making her tick, infuriating her further than she previously thought possible. And it always started when somebody trapped her within the confines of their definition of impossible.

She breathed heavily, her dark hair falling in pieces in her face, glaring down at Aoran. Liliana felt dangerous. She felt powerful. Her mark and heart pounded in synchronization, a drum reverberating in her body. *Imperium* damn them all—not a single person would ever tell her what to do or not do again.

Liliana threw herself downward at Aoran, crushing her lips against his.

He made a muffled noise of surprise before relaxing, his lips molding against hers with a fierce pressure and painful warmth. They kissed one another like they were still fighting, competing for dominance. There was nothing loving or caring about the moment. Anger surged through the connections, making the kiss less a meeting of lips and more a collision of wills. Liliana kept his arms pinned to the ground, biting his bottom lip in a way that would undoubtedly hurt for the next hour.

After what felt like centuries but must have been no more than ten seconds, Liliana pulled back and stood up, leaving the poor soldier dazed and confused on the ground. She wiped off her mouth and walked out of the gymnasium, head high and ready for the challenges to come.

CHAPTER 19
7055.1.26

"So would you prefer I kick your ass first in Dragons and Wolves or in this trade agreement?"

Renee and Leo eyed each other for a moment before laughter erupted between them. Elle swore that as long as she lived, she would never fully understand the empress's cavalier way of conducting official, diplomatic business. Her brassy laugh bellowed through the room in a way that left Elle's ears ringing.

Renee slapped Leo on the shoulder, leading the group back into his room, still chuckling. "Aw, don't worry your precious mind about it, King Leo. I'll save you the trouble—we'll do them at the same time."

Elle followed from behind, a small smile playing on her lips. Leo fell into conversation with Renee easily, like two lost books placed back in their correct shelves. Renee forced the king to the ground and set out to find his board game. Elle sat adjacent to the table, low to the floor, tucking her legs into her chest. She rested her head on her knees and waited. Ro ghosted the group, taking up his post by the front door should anybody enter uninvited.

"So what could have possibly compelled you to voluntarily join the two of us?" Leo leaned over and clasped Elle on the shoulder with a good-natured grin. "I imagine spending the afternoon with two old, stuffy Vitrians isn't anyone's ideal day."

Elle waited, trying to think of an appropriate answer. The real reason was that Seran recommended getting more acquainted with castle workings. The concept of a Guide still freaked Elle out in ways she couldn't describe, but there was something to be said about the advice of a semideified figure literally meant to guide Elle to complete her Walk. Seran's existence was something Elle still struggled to process, but that didn't mean Elle would ignore a thing her Guide said. Plus, while Elle never considered herself dull, there was an experience gap of years between her and the other contestants that she wanted to close the best she could.

"There's a lot of things I don't know about the castle and politics," Elle finally admitted. "I figured sitting in with the empress and you could help give me a better understanding of," she waved her hands in the air, "all this."

"I see." Leo rubbed the bottom of his chin before winking at Elle. "That's a very wise decision for a future queen."

Elle grinned, though the expression felt forced. She did truly enjoy the king's presence—his Vitrian amiability brought her comfort in a castle that most other times felt foreign. But his warmth reminded Elle so much of her family, from whom she still hadn't heard a word. She bit her lip, deciding. "I also wanted to ask, Your Majesty, have you heard any word of my fam—"

"And she is here to learn the art of *oblitus*!" Renee announced, cutting Elle off as the empress dropped the Dragons and Wolves set on the table in the middle of the room. The king offered Elle an apologetic smile, which she somehow returned, despite everything in her body insisting she not.

"And how will she learn the art of *oblitus*, pray tell?" Leo leaned back, bushy eyebrows raised.

"Ah, well, I've told the youngling all about our little spat at the last feast." Renee's dark blue eyes became unreadable for an instant before the woman grinned broadly once more. "Given that we've hardly had the time to speak since then, I decided now is the best time to show the future queen how Vitrians release the past for the sake of the present."

Elle nodded, keeping her mouth shut. While she was far from a language savant, her da had taught her basic Vitrian phrases and philosophies. *Oblitus* was one of the most valued ideas of the nation.

The idea of *oblitus* ultimately stemmed from the fundamental concept that Vitrians abhorred holding grudges. Grudges usually meant secret bitterness, thoughts left unsaid, or feelings left unprocessed. Vitrians discussed everything they thought and felt with everybody, regardless of potential repercussions. Grudges simply didn't oblige their style of living. *Oblitus*, as Da preached, could never truly translate into the Electarian tongue. He claimed Electarians could never own such a merciful word in their language. Still, Elle knew it roughly equated to "forgiving and forgetting."

"Well, consider this a primary example." Leo chuckled. He creaked up to a standing position, clasping Renee on the shoulder, a gesture she emphatically returned. "We move on, *etiam*?"

"*Etiam*, old friend."

Elle watched the two, head cocked to the side. It was so curious to her, how the king's room seemed exempt from the miasma of gossip and intrigue that dominated the rest of the castle. A nervous energy grew in the court like a slow-moving, toxic fog. As time went by, the fog came to dominate people's minds, governing their every conversation.

Elle tried to avoid people beyond the castle staff, spending her time learning from the empress, exploring the grounds, and speaking with the serving staff. As far as Elle knew, Teo maintained his course, either unaware or uncaring of the tornado of gossip that whisked around him. After her little fire, Liliana, according to the castle staff, split her time equally between attending Education Council meetings, reading in the palace library, training with Aoran, and avoiding human luxuries—like sleep and food. *Imperium* only knew where Eliana had drifted off to, a thought that Elle both tried and was hapless to avoid.

Leo and Renee descended back to the ground. Elle tapped the table with her finger curiously. "Do all diplomatic meetings happen over games?"

"Hardly." Leo snorted. "The empress is unique in how she does her dealings. That said, Renee, let's begin to discuss our kingdoms' trade—"

"Ah, ah, ah!" Renee waved her finger warningly, her eyebrows practically as high as her hairline. She smacked the silver Dragons and Wolves board on the table with her hand. "I said at the same time, Leo. Let's set up the pieces, and then we can talk about your damn trade deal."

Leo opened the board up, and the opal and silver tiles gleamed under the light of his room. The obsidian pieces waited patiently to be placed, their features carved with such detail that Elle could imagine feeling the scales on the dragons' bodies.

"Do you know how to play Dragons and Wolves, Ellegance?" Renee asked Elle without looking up from her setup of the board.

"I know the basics from Nic, though we haven't talked about it in many years. He always had a fondness for all the games that were far too expensive for our family." Elle laughed. "I've always been more of a dice player myself."

"I personally have no great love of the game," Leo said, looking up at Renee from under his eyebrows. "I play it for the sake of Empress Renee's infatuation with the thing."

She shrugged and Leo sighed.

"I find it far too complicated for its own good but fear I'm in the minority with this view," Leo added. "Teo and Eliana share a mutual love for the game's strategy. Even Liliana enjoyed it at one point when she was younger." Leo's voice grew softer. "Though she stopped playing when her mother died."

"Bah, enough of depressing talk." Renee scowled and waved her hand, as if she could disperse the negativity into the air. She turned to Elle, her excitement taking years away from her face. For a moment, Elle could have believed the empress was in her twenties instead of her fifties.

"I'll give you a refresh, just to make sure you follow my brilliance as we play. The Dragon player starts with five dragons, each able to move up to two spaces at a time. The Wolf player has ten wolf figurines, but each is only allowed to move one space at a time." Renee stopped abruptly, waiting for Elle. Startled, Elle nodded, and the empress continued.

"Turns happen sequentially, unless, of course, you disposed of an enemy piece, in which case you are allowed another turn or to appropriate the disposed piece for your own team. A player needs two dragons on either side of a wolf to remove the piece, but a wolf player needs three wolves around a dragon to get rid of the piece. A player wins by eliminating all enemy pieces or moving all their own pieces to the other side."

Elle blinked, her head swimming. True, it had been years since Nic had talked them through the game, but she didn't remember there being so many rules.

"There are, of course, contingency rules for scenarios such as four wolves surrounding a dragon, the special abilities of each individual piece, and don't even get me started on playing with Nuwei rules." Renee grimaced. "I've played games in that country that have lasted more than two days."

"*Imperium*," Elle said under her breath, eyes wide. The explanation served as a forceful reminder as to why Elle had stuck to a pair of dice and a deck of cards during her youth.

"Now! Elle, if you please, take these two pieces and shuffle them around in your hands so that we can assign sides."

Elle grasped the tiny dragon in her hand, her breath hitching at the way her mark warmed at the contact. The scales felt so real in her fingers Elle could almost imagine she was stroking the neck of a real dragon. She let out a small breath of air, her mark thundering. Dragon sightings were a rare thing. There was no concrete conclusion on where they lived or even what they ate—only a few academics had concluded that certain breeds fed off wolves. She wondered where in the world she would have to explore, what kind of expedition she would have to lead to see a dragon for herself and feel its scales beneath her hands.

Renee shoved the wolf in her hand, and Elle felt the connection of the moment sever. A shiver ran down Elle's spine, and she put both pieces behind herself, switching them back and forth before presenting two closed fists to the pair. Renee tapped Elle's right hand, and Elle opened it up to display the small wolf piece.

"Wolves!" Renee exclaimed, delighted.

Elle offered the dragon piece to Leo, who accepted it with a weary smile.

"It's as if you ask me whether I'd prefer the guillotine or the noose—all roads lead to the same abysmal outcome." He held the dragon at a distance before beginning to set up his pieces along the board.

Renee began doing the same on her end of the board, her navy eyes gleaming as she continued to chat away. "Kai really thinks he's something special when it comes to this game. But we all know who the true empress is, *etiam*?" She leaned across the table and pushed Leo's shoulder with a laugh. "Now I think for this new trade deal it's important that tariffs are lowered by the kingdom of Electaria. I know you maintain a small import tax on our agronomical products, but it's high time to be rid of that, don't you agree?"

Elle blinked. The transition in conversation had been totally abrupt.

Renee glanced over at Elle and winked at her. Leaning over to Elle's ear, Renee whispered more softly than Elle imagined the woman capable. "As a follower of *Menda*, I can't lie during negotiations with other kingdoms. This gives me a lot of credibility when making deals, but it reduces my bargaining tools. I oftentimes will use sharp tangents to get what I want."

"Unfortunately for her." Leo cleared his throat with a rueful smile. "I've known the empress for far too long to succumb to her cheap political tricks."

Leo, as the Dragon player, made the first move with his *Imperium* dragon, sliding that piece and his other dragon (whose name Elle honestly couldn't remember) two paces forward. Elle remembered the *Imperium* piece, though. With its name, the memory of Nic's explanations seared in the kingdom of her memories. The *Imperium* piece was marginally bigger than all the others and, when used as the dominant piece in the turn, allowed the player to move another one of his or her pieces.

Leo looked up at Renee with crinkled brown eyes. "Your move. While I understand this request, our domestic agriculture sector is still recovering from the drought that occurred five years back. My advisors prefer to stimulate internal demand as opposed to giving out subsidies and creating reliance. Therefore, the tariff must remain in place, at least for the time being. However, we can discuss opening our ports, even the Landing, during certain hours of the night so that you are able to increase the volume of ship exports to our kingdom. In exchange, of course, you would have to officially open up the Vitrian day markets to Electarian merchants."

Renee grinned, praising the king and explaining to Elle, "Leo, I remember when you used to be a baby king, and we all would shove you around in these trade negotiations. How far you've come, my friend! I'll also be moving my alpha piece an extra two paces forward, nulling my beta piece's ability to move for two turns. Now," her eyes cut back to his from the board, "you know that opening the markets to Electarian merchants would have the shopkeepers coming for my head. The Vitrian marketplace, run by Vitrians for Vitrians, is one of the prides of our nation. Try again."

Leo's eyes never again strayed back to the board.

Elle hid her laugh in the sleeve of her tunic; she believed the king had already given up on the board game. Even while observing the king, the contents of the conversation didn't escape Elle. She had actually known about the Electarian tariffs on Vitrian products— they raised prices for all the ingredients that the bakery needed to operate. While she wasn't sure if she agreed with Leo's decision to keep them in place, she was interested in the turn of the conversation to the ports.

Leo stroked his beard, his eyebrows furrowed in concentration. Finally, he moved a piece forward and offered, "What if, instead, you increased the cap you have placed on Electarian textiles?"

Studying the board and moving her piece, Renee frowned. "In order to do that, we would have to negotiate down the number of textiles that the Aurjnegh send us. Our factories are at capacity as we speak—our business owners truly don't need that much more raw material."

"If you adjust the quotas between our countries, you can always go back and offer lower prices on the finished goods to Aurjnegh when you export back into their country."

"I don't have the power to determine pricing, Leo. I'm not like the damned Aurjnegh who think they can control their markets like a chained dog." Renee scowled, moving three pieces in a complex execution that Elle wasn't sure was legal.

Renee paused, her face smoothing out with thoughtful consideration. "Though, I suppose we could offer a higher level of exports within our own agricultural sector to Aurjnegh. I hear they're struggling with getting essential crops to grow on some of that arid land of theirs."

"In which case, you would be able to increase your agronomical exports to Aurjnegh, and your fishing exports to Electaria, and we are able to increase our textile exports to your kingdom. If you could simply promise one more open port to my traders every other day of the week, I think we'd have ourselves a deal." Leo put his hand over Renee's before she could move her piece, extending his other hand to shake.

Renee regarded his outstretched hand for a second. "You drive a hard bargain, Leo. Much harder than you used to, anyhow." She laughed before grinning and shaking his arm so hard Elle thought she would tear the limb right off.

They continued playing the game in silence, allowing the dust of the agreement to settle. Elle paid no attention to the game anymore, mulling over the outcome of the deal. There were so many different levers at play during the conversation. Leo and Renee ran around, pulling them down, shoving them back up, until they found a combination that made the political machine run smoothly. Elle chewed the inside of her lip. These were the kind of talks that affected people of the kingdom the most. Behind the doors of a bedroom, casually over a board game, without any oversight or anyone to speak up in objection. Elle chewed the inside of her cheek, trying to hide her annoyance. This was the kind of thing she wanted abolished as queen.

As Elle contemplated this, Renee moved another one of her pieces, surrounding one of Leo's dragons and plucking it over to her side. Elle faintly remembered Nic saying anybody who chose the extra turns was a fool.

"Son of a *malum*." Renee swore to herself, responding with a sigh of her own as she leaned back, hands behind her head.

Leo chuckled to himself, leaning backward. "I swear, a royal as highly ranked as you are with that mouth of yours comes, perhaps, once in every century."

"A shame, I decree," Renee mumbled.

"What ails you, my friend?" Leo inquired, staring at the board.

Elle blinked out of her thoughts and looked at his side of the board; his poor dragons were all about to be surrounded.

"Dammit if I'm not going to miss having a follower of *Menda* on the throne." Renee chuckled to herself, resting her head on her folded hands as she watched Leo. "Trade deals are so much damn easier when you know the other party is going to keep their word. That is why I hope to have a Vitrian, if not a *Menda* follower, assume the throne." She reached over and tapped Elle's head. Elle's mark pounded, reacting to just the idea of Elle on the throne.

"Ah, well, depending on the outcome in the next week, you may have your wish," Leo said vaguely, eyes trained on the board.

"To be honest," Renee's blue eyes darkened and slowly moved up to meet Leo's, "I wish the Electarians weren't so obstinate about the *Imperium* thing."

Leo's shoulders stiffened. Elle's eyebrows pushed together—the relaxed atmosphere of the room from moments before was quickly freezing over.

"You'll have to make do, I'm afraid. Regardless of who assumes my throne, they will bear the mark of *Imperium*. Surely your future successors will see the irrationality in cutting off ties with a kingdom simply for the mark of its king or queen." Leo paused, frowning. "Dare I say, I should hope they would abhor such an idea. Such discrimination is dangerous."

"Some of the contestants have more *Imperium* running through their blood than others." She gave Leo a pointed look.

Elle shifted uncomfortably. This was the territory of a conversation in which she didn't want to venture. Leo had been kind to her, but Elle knew the king would ultimately stick up for his children. What father wouldn't?

"Besides," Renee continued, "do we not discriminate against the markless? The entirety of *Terrabis* practically spits upon the godless Soj for having such abominations. Tell me the difference between that and disavowing an *Imperium* ruler. Anyone who denies the existence of mark-based prejudice is a fool."

"It is not the existence I deny, but the legitimacy of the claim," Leo protested. "The markless are denounced by the Gods themselves. It's a way of signaling a lack of morality—they quite literally have no path to their virtue. The *Imperium* followers, whether you hold their virtue in esteem or not, still have their Walk."

"And what about those who have marks but do not fulfill them? Those who bear black marks their entire lives?" Renee challenged him, her eyebrows rising. "Do they not deserve the same level of condemnation? Do they not *receive* the same level of abhorrence by their neighbors? How can they claim to be any more virtuous than their markless counterparts?"

"But they at least have a path to enlightenment!"

"Have you ever heard of a person over the age of fifty completing their Walk? Theirs is a path to *nowhere*," Renee said, her blue eyes a hurricane.

Leo fell silent. Elle wanted to flee from the room. Her mind lost itself in the storm of Renee's argument, crashing and turning with the waves and unable to find the sanctuary of purchase on a single thought. Renee sighed, moving her piece to capture Leo's final Dragon. Elle blinked, not having even noticed the closing of the game.

Renee regarded the board, her tone calmer, more confused than combative. "It is something I've struggled with for years, Leo, but I keep coming to the same conclusion. Virtuosity does not partition itself into the haves and have-nots. Even those who have completed their Walk remain on its tenuous spectrum."

"Then what is the point of the marks at all if completing your Walk simply lands you on the same damn gamut as before?" Leo looked at her, exasperated.

"I don't know," she answered honestly, shrugging with a helpless flop of her shoulders. "*Menda* has yet to reveal such a truth to me. If even such a truth is worth knowing. Perhaps being virtuous was once that easy when the Gods first created the marks. But we screwed it all up."

The two fell into a painful silence. Did Elle believe in that idea? It seemed like such an uncomplicated way to look at life, where once people completed their Walk, they were done. But Ma and Da had both completed their Walks, and even they had disclosed to Elle times when they struggled to tell the truth. The day they told Elle she couldn't go to trade school, they admitted not wanting to tell her at all. There was no perfection achieved in a completed Walk, just an understanding and a desire to live up to that understanding. Eventually, she began to shake her head.

"If that's true," Elle spoke slowly, collecting her thoughts like shards of a broken vase, "then there would be no point in completing one's Walk. No point in trying to be wise or honest or humble or strong or powerful. And do either of you two believe that's true?"

Neither responded.

Elle continued, conviction growing. "Of course not. Because there is a point—the point is the Gods think they're things worth being. Even if it's a lifetime pursuit, it's still a worthwhile one."

The two stared at Elle without saying anything for a moment. Their internal warring was obvious, but they managed to break from the existential tidal wave and smile.

"Who knew the city kid was such a philosopher?" Renee pointed over at Elle with her thumb.

"Perhaps we should take her from the competition and put her in the House," Leo said with a small smile, shoulders relaxing.

"With all due respect," Elle interrupted the joke before it could snowball any further, "I *pray* you do not."

The pair burst into laughter. The tense atmosphere of the room, now sedated, returned to as it was before.

Renee stood up, stretching out her long form. She leaned down and clasped Elle on the shoulder with a grin. "You keep me young, Ellegance. And you, Leo! With all those gray hairs of yours." She cackled as Leo grumbled. Renee admired the board for a second before looking back at Leo and Elle. "I'm sorry for that ending, both of you. But, Leo, thank you for letting Elle join us. And for being so terrible at this game. I thoroughly enjoyed destroying your sorry ass."

"And thank you for striking up such an amenable trade deal for our two kingdoms." He smiled back.

"Anything for an old friend." She winked at him. Renee swept out the door past Ro. Abrupt, to the point, no space for unnecessary pleasantries. Elle grinned to herself. Renee could give lessons on what it meant to be a true Vitrian.

Elle got up to leave, and Leo slowly started putting the board away. He began talking, causing Elle to stop before exiting through the door. "You know, she says I make her feel young. *Imperium* help me if she doesn't make me feel twenty years older. We went to university at the same time, and somehow, she manages to exceed me with youthfulness by at least a decade.

"Maybe that's why she has the time to think about such things," Leo cogitated, sliding the board back into its place on one of his many shelves. His walls, covered with trinkets, books, and personal items, looked full once more with the silver set back in its place. "What say you, Ellegance? Those types of thoughts that you and she have age me because I simply don't understand them. I think I'm past the point in my life where I can confront such attacks on my belief system." He chuckled, his voice growing sad. "Because if Renee is right, I have spent a very long time believing in the wrong thing."

The room filled with silence as his words settled into the walls, sticking there with the clinging residue of regret. When remorse went unnamed, it fell from the air easily. It simply lingered in the mind, untouched. Once titled, though, a regret existed in a physical way, occupying a space and a time, serving as a constant reminder of all that was and all that was not. Elle shifted, opening and closing her mouth, unsure of what to say to the sorrowful king.

"I think," Ro said slowly, his voice unimaginably deep and heavily accented.

Elle turned to stare at the guard; she had never heard him talk and honestly never thought he had the capacity.

"Virtuosity. It is...personal. Not objective. This is why you see good people do bad things. Bad people do good things."

"I don't think I see things that way," Leo finally said, shaking his head. "If virtuosity is personal, then there is no being a truly good person, no? As there would be no strict definition of what a good person is. There would be nothing to strive for, nothing to achieve. And at that point, what is the point of being at all?"

Elle thought of the Trials, each and every one designed to test her and reveal what would make her thrive or fail as a leader. She doubted Liliana and Teo experienced the Trials the same way as she, nor did she imagine that they learned the same things as Elle from each new test. She doubted a single one of them achieved the same outcome from any singular trial. So the worth had to be beyond the outcome. It had to come from the effort to grow and be better through them.

"The striving, I think," Elle answered softly, head tilted as she looked at the guard.

He nodded slightly to her then stood as still as a statue once more as Leo turned around to look at her curiously. Elle waved goodbye quickly to the king, walking out with a hurricane of thoughts swirling in her mind.

CHAPTER 20
7055.1.27

Aoran whistled his way across the palace grounds, his traditional stroll closer to a skip. Did his ass hurt? Spectacularly. Did he wince every time he moved his arms? Unequivocally. Was his pride a little wounded? Abso-wrecking-lutely.

He couldn't help the smile that threatened to tear apart his cheeks. After yesterday, Aoran could confidently say he had never so thoroughly enjoyed getting his ass kicked in his life.

Last night, after his and Liliana's...encounter, he received a note from the Captain, informing him of a morning patrol shift so one of the newer shreds of military bait could practice guarding a royal. Aoran was forced to wake up at dawn to begin patrolling the palace grounds.

Normally a hellish duty, today it was just as well to Aoran. Gray clouds shrouded the sun, casting the area in a moody light. Impe weather could be fickle in Electaria, and the season certainly delivered some miserable weather that day. The castle's white stones soured under the sky, the pristine color darkened like ash on a wedding gown. A light drizzle adorned the palace in persistent, miserable crystals, its downpour unyielding the entire day. The flower beds drowned in the unsought irrigating, the poor flower petals drooping to skim the water. Even the statues sagged in a particularly morose fashion, their stony faces crying and drenched.

And yet, the palace grounds had never looked so goddamn splendid.

Aoran perused the area, his feet picking up the eight count of an Aurjnegh tango. *Slow, slow, quick, quick, slow.* Every so often he would turn on a count, whipping out one of his sickle blades to slice through a shrub or cut down a branch. The second he sheathed his blades, his fingers itched to draw them out again. His hips fell back into moving through the tango, hapless to the impulse. His body practically buzzed with a giddy electricity, making him entirely unable to keep still. And making him entirely unable to keep the stupid grin off his face.

The vortex of Liliana's kiss continued to drag him back into its sweet abyss. It hurled him around, looping back the memory and replaying it until he hadn't the will to drag himself out of his own mind. Never had the stinging eddy of his thoughts tasted so delicious. It was just what he had expected out of his royal dragoness—not a hint of sweetness caressed his face in that moment, nor a single tender touch. Liliana lacked such subtlety. Instead, she had fought him with her fists, and when she had won, she continued to brawl him with her lips.

Her cheeks had filled with a shade of red so brilliant a thief could have confused them with rubies. Her mouth had pressed against his with the ferocity of a tsunami crashing into the ocean shore. And her eyes—*Imperium,* her eyes—her hazel eyes had practically liquefied into molten gold, melted by the inferno that always lingered behind them. The flame that drove her intensity and passion had blazed in that moment. Nothing could have been spared from its voracious flames.

Aoran unlocked the cage that harbored his heart, allowing it to caper about to its content. It skipped around, composing sonnets dedicated to the princess's fire. He would lock it up again soon, but for the first time in his life, he allowed the thing a bit of freedom. *Imperium* knew, it had cause for celebration.

That was where his mind stayed, locked in the immutable past. It dared not stray into the territory of the future. As far as he was concerned, the future between him and Liliana stayed its traditional course. Musing otherwise would be the same as diving off a cliff, where the bottom could just as easily be gentle waves as it could serrated knives. Such fantasies had no merit.

Besides, Aoran retained no romantic notion that the brief kiss had any long-term obligations. It gave him no possession over her or her affections. Men who tried to imprison women over brief moments of shared physical affection lacked the ability to detect the difference between an instant and a trend. Aoran considered himself above that line of thinking. The kiss offered Aoran no promises of how their relationship might continue. Liliana would laugh at such antiquated, starry-eyed idealisms. Then she would spit at Aoran for contemplating the notion.

But...if Liliana should ever choose to approach him in such a way again, rest assured, Aoran would get knocked back down to the ground faster than she could blink.

Aoran smiled to himself, both dreading and praying for the recurrence of such a day. He sent a quick prayer up to *Viribus*— Gods help him, he would take any bit of strength his patron God could offer when it came to Liliana.

"You know," a voice sang to him from behind, "normally when a soldier walks by a member of the royal family, at least some acknowledgment is in order. Or has Liliana so thoroughly murdered the era of dignity that none of us need bother anymore? If such is the case, I should like to kick off the whole affair by strutting around the throne room naked."

"I'm sure Dayanara wouldn't object to such a proposal," Aoran called out without turning around.

Eliana's lovely voice could hardly be mistaken for any other. Whether spitting insults or stroking egos, the elder princess managed to caress every word in a sugary tone that could drive any sane individual to their knees.

"I dare say she wouldn't." Eliana's heels squished in the wet grass behind him, the tip of a rain parasol jabbing into his right shoulder blade.

Aoran turned around and gave a small bow at the waist, his eyes flicking up to glimpse Eliana's face. Eliana rolled her dark eyes and shook the tip of her umbrella, gesturing him to rise. As Aoran straightened his back out, Eliana unfolded the parasol and took graceful refuge beneath its black shade.

Nobody could ever argue Eliana's exquisiteness. Men and women alike paused in the palace hallways, unable to help their admiration of her easy sashay in the same way flowers curl their buds toward the sunlight. She modeled a dangerous type of femininity, as if the Gods had decided humans hadn't enough temptation on earth. From her searing black eyes to the elegant way her hand curled around the skirt of her scarlet dress to keep the hem clean, she was the literal embodiment of Electarian gorgeousness.

Aoran had watched her blossom himself. As he took lessons with Liliana growing up, he bore witness to Eliana's bloom into womanhood. Liliana rolled her eyes all throughout, declaring the entire thing a downward spiral into self-perpetuating vapidity.

Aoran, though never close with Eliana, had always gotten along amicably with the elder daughter. In his earlier days as a soldier, he managed weeks at a time without so much as setting eyes on her. When he at last stumbled upon her—it was rarely intentional—she never failed to engage and entertain. Age, unlike with many royals, failed to dull her conversations, and Eliana remained a delightful, though sparse, chatting partner. Still, the famous royal beauty failed to arouse his ire and interest as much as her willowy sister.

Her dark red lips pursed as she appraised him with calculated precision as if he were an insect pinned to a scientist's table. "Why are you so happy?"

"I just learned a novel, little dance and am absolutely itching to try it out. Care to see?" Aoran kicked his heels together and splayed his hands out in front of him in a half-hearted attempt at a Vitrian jig.

Eliana pursed her lips, ignoring the dance and zeroing in on the silly smirk that persisted on his face despite his best efforts. "I've seen squirrels lie more convincingly." She raised one manicured eyebrow.

Aoran shrugged, the rain plastering his fair hair against the side of his face. He could have sworn he had given nothing away during the entire exchange. Though he did not court the concept of stoicism as Teo and Ro so monogamously did, he could hold a neutral expression when needed.

And yet, the essence of mystery pulled up the corner of Eliana's mouth with a feather-light touch. The tiny change replaced her smile with a smirk. "Why, does this have something to do with a certain kiss I've been hearing so much about?"

Aoran could say with swaggered confidence that he had never blushed in his life. He communicated through a quick smile and quicker jokes, not by displaying his heart on his sleeve. Such a thing would have gotten him killed, both as a child and in the military.

That was why, when Eliana threw out this tidbit of information, instead of flushing, Aoran practically choked on his own surprise. Aoran leaned over, hitting his chest and coughing. He would have been less surprised if Eliana had simply come up to him, placed his hand over her stomach, and told him the Captain was expecting. He wheezed, looking up at her with weak, green eyes. "Where'd you hear that?"

"Oh dear. Who can even remember these days?" She pressed a hand against her cheek in mock confusion, a sly glint in her eyes. "A squirrel, I suppose. But they are such notorious liars. Fortunately, dear," she took a step toward him, patting his cheek with surprising firmness, "you've all but confirmed his nutty, little tale."

Aoran groaned, dragging his hands down his face. Son of a *malum*. He would never hear the end of this once Je and Dayanara got a hold of him. His eyes widened between his fingers. *Imperium* help him if the Captain ever found out. Being dismembered, disemboweled, and having his separated body parts pickled would be preferable to facing the woman if she caught wind of him kissing his charge. His knees shook.

Eliana breathed out, watching Aoran crumple in front of her. Her expression stilled, caught between disbelief and delight. "So it *is* true."

Aoran made a strangled noise.

"Frankly, it was a matter of time. Nearly every staff member in the palace has bets placed where the two of you are concerned. There will practically be a bloodbath when the news gets out."

Aoran's head jerked up. "You can't! Eliana, please—you can't let this get out in the castle. I'm begging you."

Sympathy flashed across Eliana's face like a flicker of lightning before disappearing behind her characteristic, shadowy half smile.

"Oh, don't be so ridiculous. I'm not as cruel as my great-aunt to spread that kind of information intentionally. Furthermore, I consider myself far above Teo's clunky—albeit well-meaning—social exchanges to let it slip accidentally," she said and regarded him with what could almost be considered fondness, the way a mother cat might look upon her favorite kitten. "You can trust me."

Gratitude flooded into his body, slumping his shoulders over. Aoran stayed there for a second, a scarecrow removed of its stressful stuffing, leaving behind its corpse held together with stitches of relief.

"But," her mouth curled around the word like a succulent cherry, "if I'm to be silent I must know..." Her voice dropped a tick lower, luring him in with the softer tones. "What are your thoughts on the whole affair? I want details, as many as you've got."

Aoran looked up, trying to arrange his features into as pitiful an expression as he could manage. "Do I have to?"

"Of course! Unless...I could also simply tell the Captain that a member of the royal family gallivanted throughout the palace grounds, unsupervised and unsafe. After all, I did let Dayanara know you would protect me in her stead while I went for a walk."

Eliana's innocent expression gave way to a mock gasp as she looked frantically around the rainy gardens. "*Imperium* only knows the type of accidents that may befall somebody of royal descent on such a dreadful day. And, goodness, what a shame—with nobody there to help."

It was easy to see how Eliana and Liliana had come from the same mother. Loathe as they were to compare themselves to one another, it was still obvious they were cut from the same cloth. Aoran moaned to himself. *Imperium* apparently would not be helping him. For as much as Liliana renounced her siblings, they all shared a common ability to throw Aoran's life around with a few words.

"You are evil," Aoran said to the princess, to which she responded with a supple, little curtsy and expectant smile.

He sighed, staring up at the sky and letting the rain slide down his cheeks. Maybe with enough time, it would be able to wash the nauseating feeling of mortification that smothered him.

"I don't know—what do you want me to say? It was a surprise. I certainly didn't see it coming," he finally said, resisting the urge to follow the statement up with a laugh. No need to provide Eliana with more ammunition than necessary. "It was nice. Really nice. But it was most likely a one-time thing. I don't think it meant anything more than what it was, which I accept." Aoran looked back at Eliana, pleading, "Is that sufficient information for you to not go to the Captain and get me castrated?"

Eliana laughed and nodded, her eyes sparkling with the latest information. "I think you've been sufficiently tortured, yes. I'm surprised at your maturity, Aoran, but nevertheless impressed. It is wise to categorize what is and is not, and a kiss certainly is *not*," her voice sliced through the word with finality, "anything special.

"After all, kisses are their own currency." She sighed, her eyes straying to the periphery, though Aoran saw nothing there upon glancing. "And I'm afraid they are being rapidly devalued these days."

About a dozen questions popped into Aoran's head concerning *that* interesting, little statement. He imagined a vault full of Elianas, ready to offer those who entered kisses. He was pretty sure thoughts like those were the foundations of a damn good drinking song about deadly sirens. *Superbia* help him, every conversation with Eliana always managed to feel like a carriage ride led by a drunk coachman. The twists and turns were unexpected, jolting, and had a high chance of plaguing its victim with an acute case of vertigo.

However, before he could respond, the sound of a whispered conversation slipped between the raindrops, reaching Aoran's trained ears. It was a funny thing—people whispered to avoid eavesdroppers, but nothing drew the attention of an eavesdropper more than a particularly hushed whisper. It was one of the first lessons taught in military reconnaissance. Regular conversations rarely warranted prying, but a whisper nearly always had something of note lurking in its hushed depths.

Eliana cocked her head to the side, one dark curl slipping out from where it was tucked behind her ears. Aoran peeked at the princess in disbelief. Had she heard it too? He strained his ears. Even he could barely hear their murmurs. How in the world had Eliana caught on to their approach? Liliana was stubborn down to her senses—a dragon's roar couldn't distract her when focused. Teo showed no such keenness either when taking his occasional combat lessons with the Captain. Aoran was impressed. Eliana had damn good ears for a royal. Her face drifted from contemplation into a mysterious smile that could rally armies to her banner.

Aoran shook his head. It was best Eliana had been born with the mark of *Menda*. The kingdom would never survive her reign.

She took a step closer to Aoran, gently lifting her black parasol above both of their heads. She temporarily shielded Aoran from the rain, her soft body pressed against his. He looked up at the umbrella, mouthing expletives to himself. *What the wreck was happening*? The whispered conversation got closer, two figures approaching from around the corner.

Aoran glimpsed down at the petite woman, his emotions warring between confusion, discomfort, and surprised pleasure. He opened his mouth to speak, but she pressed one lithe finger to his mouth, shaking her head, her black curls bouncing with the motion. Eliana stood on her tiptoes, her face now inches away from Aoran's own. *Imperium, Superbia, Viribus...*wreck, he would take virtually any God's help if they could spare him from the royal's whims.

He inhaled sharply through his nostrils, as if limiting his breathing made up for the situation in which he found himself. The inhale made it worse. He tasted the syrupy sweet scent that followed her everywhere she ventured.

"I'm going to show you just how meaningless a kiss can be," she whispered, her dark eyes glittering. Eliana covered the distance between the two, her free hand coming up to cup Aoran's jaw as she softly pressed her lips to his.

Aoran's hands fell to his side, and he stared at her, dumb. Was this family wrecking with him, or was he truly that irresistible? The thought and its answer fell through his fingers like rain as Eliana opened her mouth ever so slightly, letting her breath wash over him.

That syrupy scent enveloped Aoran, slowly pouring out his thoughts and replacing them with her aroma. Eliana's eyes stayed closed as she swiped her tongue playfully against his top lip. Her lips moved against his, gentle and warm. She treated the kiss like a dance, beckoning Aoran to follow with deft movements. Where Liliana's kiss had been fire, nearly painful in its blaze, this kiss was a mild breeze in comparison, coaxing and deliberate.

Aoran was pretty sure he was having a stroke.

Eliana pulled closer and kissed Aoran harder with a careful pressure. The conversation finally came within hearing distance. Aoran made a futile move to break apart, but Eliana's hand against his jaw squeezed and held him in place, all the while the pair walked by slowly. The two made a few tittering comments and laughed at the two lovers embracing in the rain, otherwise ignoring the man and woman underneath the umbrella.

"... I'm simply saying I understand Nuwei's point of view. What I *don't* get is their fierce support of Teo."

The swaying accent was a clear indication of a Vitrian. Even without the accent, the noise level was a dead giveaway. Even when whispering, Vitrians couldn't manage being totally quiet. Aoran opened his left eye and caught a glimpse of the light blue robes of one of the men, its silky sheen indicating a high-up position in the Vitrian government.

"A point of agreement, I assure you. Though I can say, your empress's interest in the child has universally baffled us all."

Aoran could practically hear the wrinkled nose that often came in conjunction with the lilting Aurjnegh accent.

Was this some type of diplomatic meeting? Aoran wanted to tail the two more closely and see how such an unlikely pair of diplomats came to be talking. Eliana, as if sensing Aoran's growing curiosity, grabbed his hand and placed it against her hip as she tangled her own fingers in his long hair. Aoran huffed into her mouth and felt her vague smile in return. During his time with the Captain, he had been forced into handcuffs and still felt freer than in Eliana's entrapment.

"The empress likes that she is of Vitrian descent. She likes that she is honest in spirit and good in nature. What of pleasant temperament and a considerate disposition warrants confusion?" the Vitrian's voice grew defensive. And louder, as Vitrians were wont to do.

"Peace. I only mean to say she is the least experienced of the hopefuls. Such youth worries us."

"Then, *Imperium* pray tell, who does the nation of Aurjnegh hope to see emerge from this competition?"

"Liliana, of course. Easternalia has doubled down her support. Liliana has flaws, undoubtedly. Who of us does not? But they can be flattened out and refined with the hammer of experience. The girl has revolutionary ideas—her recent thoughts on the Soj have aroused quite the stir in our court. She is sharp and clever. Our country would rather be lifted by her tide than destroyed by the incoming wave."

The Vitrian made a sound of disgust. "Empress says she's not to be trusted."

"Your empress says many things if you bring her enough mead," the Aurjnegh answered in an innocent voice.

The whispers dropped off from that point on, devolving into the arguing typical between an Aujrnegh and a Vitrian. Shouting disguised as debating grew fainter and fainter. When Aoran confirmed that the two had left the area, Eliana finally separated her lips from his own. She watched his face carefully, waiting for his reaction.

His mouth tingled with an unfamiliar numbness. His head swam, his thoughts still blurred with the scent of Eliana. Her perfume seeped out of his mind like a slow antidote on a powerful poison. As Aoran regained his senses, he found himself growing irate.

Even Eliana, whom he generally liked, had the same persistent tenacity to treat those around her as tools. Apparently, Aoran served as the perfect tool for eavesdropping. At least Liliana had the decency to tell him when he would be used. It was like the royals didn't see people at all, just utilities drawn and measured against one another. Mechanisms for achieving greater goals—though what Aoran had just helped achieve, he hadn't the faintest clue. His mark buzzed, telling him to stay angry. Telling him to fight.

Aoran ignored the feeling, sighing. Such anger was useless to hold on to. After all, the royals meant well. *Usually.* The greater goals had greater interests in mind. Aoran could live with being used as a pawn every so often, so long as it would pay itself forward and help another even more. *Imperium* bless small Elle. He wasn't sure the cheerful girl shared the same skill of wielding and sheathing her humanity like a common blade.

When Aoran got his bearings and didn't feel like he had just hopped onto land after an eight-year sea voyage, he finally looked up at Eliana. He took some satisfaction in the nervous creases around her eyes.

"If you were really that jealous, you could have just told me. No need to put on a show," he told her sternly.

A beat passed, and then Eliana laughed, her head thrown back and hand thrown over her mouth to stifle the spillover giggles. Aoran managed a wry grin of his own.

When Eliana's laughter subsided, she looked at Aoran with mirthful eyes, momentarily losing the enigmatic edge. "My apologies. Could you find it in your heart to forgive me?"

Aoran rolled his eyes, offering the princess one more bow, this one a little bit deeper than the first, to show he truly had forgiven her. "It doesn't exactly look great in my line of work to despise a member of the royal family."

"But you're not too angry?" Eliana, sensing she had made it out of the woods, pressed him.

"Nothing that sunweed and a few days locked in the training arena won't fix." His expression grew strained and took on a greenish tint. "And a promise that you won't tell a goddamn person in that castle what just happened."

"I promise," she said, trying to cover up whatever laughter followed the statement. Aoran looked at her doubtfully. Eliana dismissed her humor off stage, replacing it with the velvet curtain of her secretive smile. "Besides, can a follower of *Menda* truly lie?"

Aoran furrowed his eyebrows, looking at the ground to think about the question. When he raised his head to protest that yes, followers of *Menda* knew how to lie better than anyone, Eliana had already turned the corner of the castle, lithe fingers wiggling goodbye.

CHAPTER 21
7055.1.27

"Do you think they'll make us take a written test?" Elle bounced her knee up and down and chewed on her lip. "*Imperium*, help me, I hope not. I'm such a slow writer—I always failed the essay portions in school. It has to be something else..."

Her violet eyes lit up once more. Liliana closed her eyes slowly with one eyebrow twitching, her arms crossed. She tried to control her breathing, slowly inhaling and exhaling, and bring down her heartbeat. Unfortunately, Ellegance's plethora of theories concerning the Trial made it frustratingly difficult to concentrate.

"Maybe they'll have us engage in some kind of debate. That would be interesting enough. What do you think, Liliana?"

"For what I hope—though the past two times indicate that it won't be—is the last time: I don't *know*." Liliana seethed, trying to push the words through her teeth with as much force and venom as possible. She usually didn't have such a challenging time getting people to leave her alone. Even Aoran scared away with enough application of malice. It wasn't that she detested the young woman, Liliana just didn't have the time or mental space to think about her.

"I, for one, think it's going to be a fight to the death," Aoran announced. He winked at Liliana, a flash of emerald.

Her heart stuttered for a moment before resuming its usual pattern. She all but washed her hands of the...incident. No need to prime herself for a relapse.

He smirked and leaned toward Ellegance, saying with a conspiratorial whisper: "But with textbooks."

"That—that is absolutely it," Ellegance declared with a tiny applause. Her voice arched as ideas flew back and forth between her and Aoran with unbridled excitement.

The two struck Liliana like a pair of gossiping children, though Liliana barely remembered what such a thing looked like. Faint memories of Eliana inviting her to the courtyards when Liliana was newly in school skipped through her mind like a pebble over a pond. All those attempts to chat ended in Liliana reading or her mother bringing her to a meeting as her sister peddled conversation like a broken toy. Eliana found no buyer in Liliana. It wasn't that she didn't want to talk to Eliana, but her mother had been so much more radiant that any time with her outshined any moments with her sister.

Eventually, Eliana stopped inviting her. The memory drained into clearer pictures of lessons, books, screeches at Aoran to leave her alone to her lessons and books, and the like. Liliana all but skipped the frivolous part of childhood like a puddle on the street. She exited her toddler years and reemerged as a prepubescent with a chip the size of a small dragon on her shoulder. No need to dirty herself in the musty waters in between. Liliana snorted softly to herself. How far she had come from those days.

She peeked one hazel eye open to glower at the chirping birds in the room. Ellegance and Aoran leaned in eagerly on the mahogany bench, two mountains naturally sloped toward each other. *How annoying.* Liliana wondered how they had even met. Her eyebrow twitched again. Her personal guard was awfully friendly with a woman whose literal existence was an obstacle to Liliana's dream.

Beyond being a fellow challenger for the throne, Ellegance was an enigma with which Liliana would have to deal once she was queen. People with marks of *Imperium* outside of the royal family simply didn't happen. Period. When Liliana won, Ellegance would return to the city and throw all faith in the Electarian monarchy into chaos. After all, if anybody could bear the mark of *Imperium*, why the royal family? Liliana supposed she could have Ellegance sent to the Riphs, faraway in rural Electaria. Liliana still didn't know if that would mitigate the spread of rumors. A headache started to form in the front of Liliana's skull. These were not things she could solve while waiting for the next trial. She needed to be queen before she started stressing over the duties of one.

Liliana wanted to find whatever magister and diplomat oversaw these trials and strangle them with her bare hands. Today for *Caecus*'s Trial, Aoran appeared at her door and presently escorted her to a small, dark room to wait. And wait. She didn't even have the comfort of Imperium's fur to knot her fingers through and pass the time. Apparently the illustrious Teo had the honor of going first. When told this information, Liliana's look of disgust was involuntary. Simply another minor privilege allowed to the kingdom's golden son.

The spartan room lacked any ornamentation beyond two benches on opposite sides for competitors to sit upon and a torch on both walls. And, of course, the distracting dynamic duo of Ellegance and Aoran. Liliana leaned her head against the wall and wished with all her might that she were alone.

Lost in thought, it took Liliana a moment to realize that Aoran's and Elle's eyes focused on Liliana. The violet and jade kaleidoscopes settled upon her with curiosity, mischief coiling behind the latter. Fantastic.

Her lip curled upward unpleasantly, "What do you two want?"

"You have remained uncharacteristically quiet, princess. I normally would have expected at least one scathing retort at this point." Aoran's wolfish grin emerged. "Isn't it damn rude to not even hazard a guess at the Trial?"

"It's damn rude to pester somebody who wants to be left alone," Liliana snapped at him.

Aoran sighed in relief, "Thank *Imperium*, there's the abrasive princess I know. You had me worried."

"I'd be curious to hear your thoughts, princess," Ellegance interjected, looking at her with an expression so honest Liliana was taken aback.

The girl's fingers rested against the bottom of a dragon pendant hanging from her neck. Liliana catalogued the tick. Otherwise, the girl showed no clear sign of nervousness. Just caution, as if Liliana were a sleeping, rabid dog. *Smart girl*, Liliana admitted to herself.

The sentence, too, caught Liliana by surprise. Words so rare, only ever truly uttered by her mother, that they stopped any snarky retort that might have come otherwise. The sincerity combined with the sentiment sent Liliana in a minispiral. In spite of her desire to be alone, she felt obliged to respond.

"Maybe...they have us play a game of Dragons and Wolves," Arms crossed, Liliana replied, betraying herself. "That could be a conduit of wisdom in its own way."

Ellegance tapped the bottom of her chin before smiling at Liliana. "It's better than any of my guesses."

Liliana didn't know how to respond. A part of her felt so manipulated by the conversation, but another part of her knew the girl in front of her lacked the capacity to manipulate. It was the latter half that reminded Liliana why she would be the greater queen, but it was the former part that made Liliana worry that Ellegance was the better woman.

"Ellegance Fournier, it is your turn," the Captain's steely voice interrupted any weak reply Liliana might have attempted.

Ellegance jumped up, nervous energy causing her to rush ahead of the Captain. Luckily, her simple black tunic and pants allowed her the mobility to spring out of the room. Liliana looked down at her tight, lavender dress. She dressed in proper royal attire, but she envied Ellegance's outfit. The Captain growled something under her breath about obedience, stalking out the door after Elle. In the back of her mind, Liliana registered that Ellegance made virtually no sound moving, even when scurrying out the door.

Liliana let Elle's words roll around in her brain. Maybe there was another solution to taking care of the young woman. Instead of banishing her to the countryside, perhaps there was some kind of place here at the castle for her. Liliana disliked her less than most people, and her mark would be best appreciated inside the castle walls. Or that could be a terrible idea, given that they previously competed against one another for power. The knot behind Liliana's forehead grew. She needed to be focusing on the Trial, not on Ellegance.

"Princess, are you okay?" Aoran's eyes were wide open as he approached her as if to grab her face. "I know kindness is not really part of your particular brand—I was almost worried you would go into anaphylactic shock. Maybe we simply call the day a wash and go to bed. Should I grab a pillow?"

"I'm not in the mood for your particular brand of wolfshit right now," Liliana snapped at him. Aoran pressed a hand against his chest, adopting a wounded expression. "Don't make me throw you to the ground again."

His wounded, puppy face melted away into a dangerous grin. The carefree wolf fled the building, leaving a pleased predator in its place.

"I'll be a son of a *malum*—I swear, princess, you've never given me such a grand incentive to bother you. I'll really have to kick it up a notch."

"I will burn you alive."

"Still wouldn't be hotter than a repeat of what you did to me in that gym," Aoran sang quietly. Liliana's eyes flashed, and her hands curled into fists at her sides.

Aoran must have sensed danger because he held his hands up, his light green eyes sparkling. Those same eyes that twinkled at her for years from across the classroom, promises of trouble and delectation nestled in fields of jade. Damn those eyes. It was impossible to stay mad at them.

"Peace. I promised myself I wouldn't torture you too much about that day. It's such low-hanging fruit after all. Frankly, it offends my comedic sensibilities," Aoran said.

Liliana let go of the breath she held, falling back against the wall. Time froze in front of her as her mind whirred through space. What was she doing, mind hovering over a kiss? She needed to focus on the Trial. Liliana tripped into Ellegance's previous game by accident, playing out possibilities in her mind.

She hated to admit it, but a written test was possible. Awfully dull, but not out of the realm of reality. They could present her with a riddle, of course. The notion had its own timeless truism. What score had Teo received? *Most likely high marks*, she thought to herself with sharp bitterness. Teo could stand in front of the administrators and simply take a shit; he would still be praised as the wisest man in the land.

"Thinking about the Trial?" Aoran flopped down on the bench next to her, casting a glance over to Liliana's rigid form.

"No, just about what I'm going to eat tonight," she responded numbly, continuing to stare into space. She sighed, breaking her concentration. She turned to Aoran, eyebrows raised. "Think you could attempt being useful for once and help me figure out what it's going to be?"

Aoran made a face. "Being useful is far beyond my pay grade."

Liliana rolled her eyes. For a moment, she surrendered to her nerves and briefly leaned her head against Aoran's right shoulder, defeated. She imagined his mark shining through his uniform, a strength so bright it radiated through the clothing. He looked down at her, expression unreadable, posture utterly still, as if afraid to scare her away.

The Captain reappeared in the doorway. Liliana jolted back up, her heart kicking up into a steady trot. There was no way. How long had it been since Ellegance left the room? Liliana wasn't ready. Dammit, she had spent her time daydreaming instead of preparing. She had spent it thinking about Elle, Aoran, and Teo. Only one of which, in hindsight, was really worth her attention. She cast a glance at Aoran before taking a deep breath. She wasn't ready.

"You ready?" Aoran nudged her with his shoulder as the Captain crossed her arms. The older woman could serve as a fire safety team, putting out flames with the mere presence of her frigid persona.

Liliana wasn't ready.

"Of course."

Liliana followed the Captain out the room without a glance backward. The Captain navigated the dark hallways of the castle while Liliana stared straight ahead, seeing nothing. Liliana's heels clicked against the stone floor, the faint sound still echoing around the corridor. The Captain's steps, miraculously, made no noise at all. Liliana's nostrils flared, and she steeled herself, drawing her shoulders back. Maybe she felt ill prepared, but dammit if she wouldn't walk into this room with her back straight and her head high.

They finally stopped in front of a door. The Captain bowed, the movement barely perceptible by the eye, before opening the door. Liliana knew it was small of her, but the heat of annoyance flashed through her heart. Teo undoubtedly received a lower bow than that. Liliana pushed the feeling aside, stepping through the door with her chin up, but her confidence dropped quickly: she had no wrecking clue where she was.

Her eyebrows furrowed together. Two sets of wooden bleachers sat on opposite sides of the room, sandwiching podiums that stood on either end. A group of six, cloaked figures sat on both sides of the room, parchment paper splayed before them. The middle of the room sank below both the podiums and the bleachers by about six feet into a sandy arena. Had they arranged the training arena into the trial stage? Torches pocketed the larger room, but dozens of flames lit the inside of the arena. The reflection of the light against the sand almost made the middle of the room painful to observe. With a quick inhale, the scent of wood shavings assaulted her nose. The taste of rust stained her tongue.

Ro's silent and expressionless form waited behind one podium, the other remaining vacant. Liliana performed a double take. *Ro?* Why the hell was one of the Four in the room?

The Captain cleared her throat behind Liliana, who shook her head and forced her feet forward, one after the other. Liliana took her place behind the other podium, placing her unsteady hands on the edge of the wood. She gripped the structure harder than she would like to admit. What in *Imperium*'s name was going on?

"Liliana Storidian." A rasp echoed through the room from no discernable location.

The sound crawled around the edges of the room with the smoothness of sandpaper, creeping over Liliana's arms and leaving goose bumps in its place. It was grotesquely unfamiliar, not like any dignitary with which she had ever spoken. Was it a magister from the House? Liliana's total blindness in her knowledge made her heart frantic. She gripped the table tighter, fingers turning white. Ro, damn him, stayed entirely still.

"You are now faced with the Trial of *Caecus*, our God of wisdom. Before you continue with the Trial, we will emphasize one point: a leader must be more than knowledgeable." The rasp hissed with the pleasantness of two bricks being dragged against one another. "Wisdom is not cleverness. It is not intelligence. *Caecus* advises *Imperium*, herself. She needs neither a cunning fox at her side nor a book capable of regurgitating its contents to her. Nor does Electaria's future leader.

"*Imperium* needs a cut above the rest—one who is able to take his knowledge and experience, turning it into a weapon when necessary. Everything you have ever done, everyone you have ever met is a tool. Wisdom, in turn, is knowing how to wield your tools.

"In honor of *Caecus*, you are tasked with the challenge of proving your wisdom."

Creaking doors opened and closed beneath her. Liliana turned toward the arena, blinking past the glare of the torches. Their initial glow caused her to entirely miss the door located beneath both podiums. Nine soldiers now stood on Ro's side of the arena, masks on and backs straight. Six stood beneath Liliana. They did not look back at Liliana as she leaned over the podium, their eyes obediently trained on that immediately in front of them. The soldiers on either side looked the same, save for the fact that those on Liliana's side boasted scarlet sword hilts. Each one wore a simple chest plate and helmets that opened in the front, exposing their faces. Other than that, they sported the black uniforms traditional to Electarian soldiers in training.

"You have three rounds." The rasp clawed up a notch. It approached her from every side of the room, dominating her mind. "Each round, your goal is to incapacitate the other soldiers. You may use up to one-third of your soldiers in any given round. Any actions are deemed valid for the sake of victory in this competition. You have sixty seconds before the commencement of each round to determine a strategy with your soldiers."

"Wait, but he has one more soldier for each round!" Liliana protested, regarding her six soldiers with a dark feeling of dread.

Liliana scrutinized them harder, squinting her eyes into needle points. Were her soldiers smaller than Ro's? Did their swords seem duller? Had they seriously pitted her against one of the *Four* in war games?

"A round ends when the other soldiers cannot move, yield, or die, or any combination thereof." The rasp ignored her objections, though it gained a leery edge. "Your score is directly tied to the outcome of the Trial. The amount of rounds you win will be tied to your allocated points."

"Just stop!" Liliana slammed her hands down on her podium, looking furiously back and forth between the cloaked groups on either side. "You can't seriously expect me to kill those soldiers. They're Electarian!"

"This is the Trial, Princess Liliana." The rasp paused, dangling the next words like a poisonous lifeline. "You can, of course, forfeit. You would fail, obviously, but you may save yourself any unnecessary," the rasp crooned the next word, "consternation."

The condescension dripped into Liliana's bones with acidity. It burned holes in her system that could only be soothed with the salve of victory. The familiar pounding thumped throughout her body. So what if she faced one of the Four? The shit didn't matter. Liliana spent years reading texts of war to weasel her way onto the war council. Ro, at the end of the day, was a soldier. Liliana had the training of a damn general.

Liliana had made it through three Trials thus far. This would not be the one to fell her. After weeks fighting like a soldier and years learning to think like a commander, Liliana was as prepared as anyone would ever be in her position. She gritted her teeth. Failure was not a possibility. *Imperium* herself could stand on the opposite podium, and Liliana would still beat her. There was no other option.

She would win the stupid wrecking game. But on her own terms. Her teeth ground together, and she smashed her fist against the podium. "Let's get this over with."

"Excellent. Your sixty seconds begin now."

Ro wasted no time. He hopped over the wall of the arena, hitting the ground without a sound, rolling on impact to minimize any damage. He popped back to his feet, giving his uniform a quick brush of its dirt. He gathered three of his soldiers and began pointing, though his mouth never moved. He paused every other second, waiting for nods of confirmation. *Wreck it.*

Liliana followed his lead. She placed her hands on either side of the arena wall, hoisting herself up and barking at her soldiers, "Catch me."

Liliana barely waited for their confirmation. She threw herself over the wall, the ground closing in toward her. The one closest to her had turned immediately in response to her command, his arms already outstretched. He caught her with minimal grace, more slowing her fall than stopping it entirely. She dropped to the ground, her satin dress throwing up a cloud of dust. Liliana stayed on the ground, beckoning the soldiers to her side. No time to waste.

"You two—you're first." She jabbed her finger at the two tallest soldiers. They saluted in confirmation. The other four stood at attention. "You're outnumbered. Obviously. When you go into battle, don't delay. Ro will probably expect us to take a defensive stance and wait, which is why we must be better than that. Be faster.

"Be the first to attack and don't let them corner you. If you can move fast enough, you might be able to create an advantage for yourself. You need to try and incapacitate one of his men as soon as possible so you can create an even playing field. Do not divide and conquer; move together and work as one. Do you understand?"

The eyebrows of one of the soldiers in the group shot up in surprise. She resisted the urge to snap at him, instead staring at the two in front of her as she waited for a response. The soldiers held their salute and said, "Yes, princess."

Liliana's shoulders rose to her ears. If she had quills—which, she supposed her sister might argue she did—they would be bristling. "Princess" was barely tolerable when Aoran used the term. When the soldiers used it, it served as a burning reminder of everything that she was and everything she was not. It was biting, acerbic evidence of how much she had to lose in this trial. She ignored the pair, feeling the claws of ticking time grinding into her back. She occasionally glanced at Ro while her mouth moved with lightning speed.

"I don't care what you two do, but keep in mind this: You are not to kill any of the soldiers on the opposing side. Anything else is permissible except for that—*do not aim to kill*. Do you understand?"

"Time." The rasp echoed throughout the room.

Liliana's words faded on her lips, and she swore to herself. It would have to be enough.

"Soldiers, to the front of the room."

Her soldiers turned from her, hands on the scarlet hilts of their swords. A drop of sweat rolled down the back of Liliana's neck. The four soldiers fell in line around her, forming a protective layer between her and what would be the fighting. Ro stepped to the corner, his watchful eyes following the coordinated march of his three soldiers.

Liliana's two men faced Ro's three soldiers. They stood there, unmoving as if some being encased each one in eternal ice. Anticipation simmered in the room, and Liliana tensed, waiting for the mixture to come to a roaring boil. The taste of rust grew stronger, bloodying Liliana's mouth with its power. The torches swelled.

"Begin."

Liliana's soldiers moved faster than she could have believed. She blinked, and her soldiers had already rushed the soldier on the far-left side of Ro's trio. The poor man didn't even have time to raise his sword. The taller of her soldiers took the hilt of his sword and rammed the butt into the man's face. The opposing soldier shouted an expletive, raising his hands to grasp his face. As he did so, Liliana's other soldier delivered a solid kick to the man's knee. Her stomach turned as she watched the opposing soldier's knee slide out of place. He fell to the ground with a strangled noise. One down.

Her soldiers quickly extracted. Ro's other two soldiers recovered from their brief shock, settling into Electarian battle positions. True to Liliana's instructions, her soldiers moved as one unit. They feigned in the direction of Ro's soldier on the right before both falling on the man to the left. He raised his sword, parrying the first blow. At the end of the day, though, few common soldiers possessed the skill to fend off two trained swords at once. While he blocked one stroke, Liliana's other soldier swiftly drove his sword into the man's thigh. Blood spurted from the wound, and the man dropped, moaning.

Two, Liliana thought to herself with sickness. This type of fighting lacked the fun of Aoran's training sessions.

The last soldier stood there, glancing back and forth between his injured comrades and the two men in front of him. He looked green. Ro's eyes narrowed. He lifted his hand, closing it into a fist. The soldier nodded, his relief obvious. He placed his sword on the ground, then raised his hands by his shoulders. "I yield."

Barely a beat passed before the rasp returned. "First round goes to Liliana. Your next sixty seconds begin now."

"Are you serious?" Liliana exclaimed. Her soldiers marched back toward her. Hearing nothing in return from the son of a *malum*, she cursed. She needed to stop wasting time. Two of Ro's soldiers dragged his injured men to the side of the arena. One left a trail of scarlet blood in his wake, staining the stand.

Liliana's stomach jumped. She and Aoran rarely fought so hard as to incur severe injury. Ro appeared unfazed by the gore. Liliana's eye twitched. How did the soldier stay so calm? Liliana could watch the thick liquid pour over the sands again and again and still find a way to feel sick. She ground her teeth together. Liliana would be damned if squeamishness stood in her way.

Her mark pounded, its fire burning away the nausea. Leaders had no time to feel squeamish. Liliana had been so overwhelmed with the previous fight, she failed to track Ro's own decisions. In the upcoming round, she had to focus. It was more than just her group of fighters—it was Ro, his fighters, and all their decisions with which she had to contend.

With the dragon on her back thundering, she addressed her group of soldiers once more. "You two worked well together. Go back in for the next round." She nodded at the two soldiers. She paused, squeezing her eyes shut and thinking. She opened them and instructed sharply, "They'll be expecting you to work together, so we're going to do the opposite. The name of this round is 'divide and conquer.' Move quickly. Go for swift strikes. Don't stay locked in a battle for too long. And remember: no deaths."

This time they at least managed a nod before before the rasp called out, "Begin."

All the soldiers jogged to the center of the room. Ro's men bounced back and forth. The three soldiers stood a touch farther apart from one another. Liliana's eyes tracked the distance between each man—they all stood a little farther than arm's reach from one another. Liliana eyed Ro. What was his plan? Ro's men stared at Liliana's men with thinly veiled hatred. Injuring their fellow soldiers probably hadn't helped the feeling. Liliana swallowed hard.

After another beat, her soldiers split to opposite sides, each engaging with Ro's soldiers on either end. This time, Ro's men were ready. It was as if Ro predicted her division strategy, Liliana noted with increasing frustration. By creating such distance between his men, her own soldiers struggled to cover ground as quickly. Ro's third soldier was given extra space to evade her own soldier's reach and more time to find chinks in Liliana's armor.

Her soldier on the left hit his sword against his opponent's. They locked for a moment before Ro's soldier turned his wrist with a minor flick, somehow sending the other soldier's sword clattering to the ground. Before he could turn to pick it back up, Ro's soldier lodged his sword firmly in her soldier's shoulder. He choked and dropped to the ground, his fingers trembling as they found the stream of blood slowly flowing down his arm.

Her other soldier fared marginally better, though he somehow lost his helmet in the confrontation. Ro's soldier lay shuddering on the ground with a vicious cut down his right bicep that exposed the tendons beneath. Not even Ro's unprecedented cunning could account for superior skill one-on-one.

Liliana's soldier turned with raised fists, dropping into a stance more typical for hand-to-hand. Ro's other two soldiers circled him. Despite his best efforts, Ro's soldiers quickly entrapped her lone man. Ro watched with no expression on his face. Her heart dropped. He had known the entire time what her game was. By dividing her soldiers, she all but leaned into his trap of outnumbering her final man standing. Liliana wanted to kick a wall. Or herself.

The entire fall happened in seconds. Before she processed what happened, Liliana's soldier kneeled on the ground with one of Ro's soldiers holding his right arm and the another one grabbing his hair. The one holding his hair yanked his head back, staring over him.

"Do you yield?" Ro's soldier said.

Her soldier glanced over at Liliana. Yield? He couldn't. If he yielded, she would be forced to go another round against Ro, and she wasn't sure if her cleverness could match his experience. For a man who looked as blank as a chalkboard, he did a remarkable job of making Liliana fear for herself and her shot at the crown.

Her answer must have shown on her face because he spit to the side in response. Ro shrugged his shoulder. The soldier released the man's hair while the other one swiftly dragged her soldier's arm over his knee, snapping the limb in half. Liliana's stomach dropped, and she swallowed down the vomit threatening to emerge. Her soldier's face went white and contorted. No scream erupted from his chest, but a tiny whimper trickled out of his mouth. Somehow, that was worse.

Liliana raised her hand, reigning in her nausea as she croaked, "He yields."

"Second round goes to Ro. Your next sixty seconds begins now."

Liliana's voice caught in her throat. All thoughts were dissolved by the bile churning in her system, leaving her mind blank. Her remaining soldiers didn't wait for an order—they hustled forward, dragging the bodies of their injured brethren to the side. Liliana's breath sped up as she shakily shuffled her way through her war memories. Ro had predicted she would divide and conquer and planned appropriately. How did Liliana know he wouldn't simply guess her tactics once more? For as long as Ro could predict Liliana's moves, she would never have another shot of winning. She would never have a shot at being queen.

How much time had passed? Her back burned. The clocked ticked down, taunting her.

"Yes, um, next round we'll o-obviously need to try something different." She swallowed, avoiding eye contact with her injured soldiers. *Get your shit together, Liliana*, she thought to herself. She hid her hands behind her back, squeezing the fabric of her dress and steadying her voice. "I think we should attempt a feigning maneuver that might trick them and give us the element of surprise once more—"

"Princess, with all due respect," a soldier on the ground spoke, holding his broken arm with a pinched face, "we are outnumbered. We won the first round using surprise. We won't have surprise again. You need to give us free reign to fight as we would in battle. They do not train us to incapacitate. We are trained to kill."

"Begin."

It was a sick joke. Last trial they told her to be strong. In this moment, strength meant winning in the face of adversity. Strength meant standing her ground and protecting these soldiers' lives, regardless for whom they fought. But when focusing on wisdom, apparently strength didn't wrecking matter. Wisdom meant throwing her resolve to the side to achieve her goal. She should have listened to the stupid, wrecking voice. Wisdom meant seeing your tools and knowing how to use them.

Liliana pointed at two soldiers, her voice shaking with barely contained wrath. "You two, go. You have permission to use whatever tactics necessary."

A white, burning fury blasted through her body as her soldiers approached the center for the last time. These people didn't want a leader for Electaria. They wanted a puppet. They wanted someone who would be honest when desired but able to conjure humility when asked. They wanted a strong ruler, up until the point that it might be wiser to throw somebody's life away. Each virtue existed in its own vacuum, separate from the others, leaving jagged rulers in their place who couldn't blend the traits into something more harmonious. These people plucked the strings of virtues, refusing to play the full chord.

And who were these trials designed to honor? The Gods. This dangerous bifurcation of virtues was for *them*. Far from her previous annoyance with her Walk, Liliana began to detest the dragon on her back. What was the point in power if she felt so wrecking weak? She could barely blame the people running the Trials. Their fallacy lay in being human and foolish. The Gods had a responsibility to correct such mutations of their vision. If they truly cared about the kingdom, wouldn't they have sent a sign by now, raining down their disapproval for this aberration?

Liliana struggled to identify who she hated more in the moment—the people running these Trials or the Gods themselves.

Liliana watched the fight with dull eyes, her mind barely following the events. When she finally blinked, three of Ro's soldiers lay bleeding on the floor. Two had shallow but bloody wounds in various appendages. The third had an angry gash in his side that bled in a way that made his blood look like prisoners fleeing from their captors. Rushing, flooding, angry. His gaze was unfocused, distant. A tool that would no longer be useful, she supposed.

"Third round goes to Liliana. Congratulations, princess. You have completed the trial of *Caecus*."

CHAPTER 22
7055.1.28

Elle squinted her eyes, moving the note closer and farther away from herself. The royal stationary felt legitimate, and the neat handwriting met her expectations of the author's fastidious print. Even the straightforward, no-frills writing matched what she knew of him. Plus, Elle had met many talented liars in the city; only the most cunning con artists had figured out how to replicate the waxen seal of the royal family. For all intents and purposes, the note was probably real.

But it made no sense. She read the contents forward and backward, searching for a hidden message encoded in the invitation. The problem was that there was only so much to be hidden in three, measly sentences. Leaning in, she gave the cream paper a sniff. She pulled back, confused. The note smelled completely normal, not like someone was trying to poison her.

Of course, it could also be a joke. The twins would've dubbed this kind of comedy simplistic. Elle's frown grew; she hadn't been in a joking mood since the Trial of *Caecus*. But the author didn't really seem like the joking type anyway. Elle read the words again, thoroughly confused.

Ellegance Fournier,

You are cordially invited to join me for tea in fifteen minute's time. There is no specified attire for the occasion. Your presence is anxiously awaited.

Cordially,

Prince Teo

"Who's it from?" Seran chimed from Elle's couch.

The young Guide's small form draped over the velvet piece of furniture, their doe eyes blinking up from the book on their lap. Seran spent hours in Elle's room, pouring over every book they could get their hands on. They approached every page with childlike wonder, fawning every so often on "how remarkable!" they found humanity to be.

Their academic curiosity was perfectly at home with their newfound facade. Seran integrated into the palace easily under the guise of Elle's new "tutor." Most accepted the appointment with little questioning. Elle's status as one of the three contestants allowed her at least the semblance of privacy. Besides, whenever somebody—Renee—pressed too hard, Seran's golden eyes glowed a tiny bit brighter. The individual always instantly strode away with a pleasant skip in their step, no further questions to be had about the arrangement.

"Prince Teo." Elle's nose scrunched up, and she turned to pass the note to her Guide.

Seran took the note, examining it with the same intensely inquisitive lens through which they observed everything. Seran took in the world with marvel, touching, smelling, and tasting (Elle pulled many an inedible thing out of the Guide's hand) with true wonderment.

Elle had eventually acclimated to having a Guide. Not to be misunderstood—Elle still partook in her fair share of freaking out over the confirmation of a supposedly mythological individual's existence. Guides existed in stories and the cheap, religious wares that merchants peddled to convince others that somebody cared about their Walk. To convince those who were old and lacking their golden mark that a servant of the Gods still existed, and hope was not yet lost. As everybody knew, there was little worse than being old and still bearing the black of one's mark. Well, other than being born without a mark entirely. Elle's mind flashed back to her conversation with the king and the empress. She shook her head before losing all concentration to existential ponderings.

That day in the forest, Seran patiently waited for Elle to finish hyperventilating. When Elle finally had enough of her mind and oxygen to listen, Seran explained as much as they could. Which, all things considered, was shockingly little. Guides were real. They took on forms in the mortal world with varying success—human was the goal, but that required immense, and sometimes impossible, precision. Some Guides failed entirely in the transformation process, appearing in the mortal world as trees and the like. Apparently, some Guides focused on a gender before entering the world, but Seran hadn't felt so inclined. Now, Seran, one of the success cases, existed to help Elle complete her Walk.

Unfortunately, on some of the more pressing issues, Seran was as much at a loss as Elle. They had no idea what *exactly* Elle had to do to complete her Walk. They had no revelations concerning Elle's mark, and why a child of a couple bearing the marks of honesty produced a follower of *Imperium*. They had no insight into the Gods themselves, other than a general fondness for those in the pantheon. Though they knew they had some degree of magical abilities, Seran understood little more than that. It was like the Gods had sent Elle an eager puppy—enthusiastic and well-meaning but useless when it came to more complicated tasks. Like spiritual enlightenment.

So Elle sighed and suspended her disbelief. It did her no good to fight against something she might never understand. Besides, Seran's bright smile and sincere desire to help was hard to turn away. And the genderless, God-like creature stayed.

Seran closed their eyes and tapped the side of their temple with their index finger, lips pursed. "Teo is the scary one?"

"No, that's Liliana. Or Eliana, depending on the day," Elle replied, to which the Guide responded with a small "ah!"

She took the note back from Seran's small hands, folding it into the pocket of her trousers. "Well? Should I go?"

Before the trial of *Caecus*, Seran grew antsy leading up to the event. By the time Elle readied to leave for the waiting chamber, the Guide appeared to be on the verge of a nervous breakdown. They paced around the room, shelving and reshelving books. Muttering under their breath. Sweat coalescing around their brow.

Elle had stopped before exiting, giving her Guide a strange look. "Want to tell me what that's all about?"

Seran looked at Elle, their buzzing body still for one moment. Their visage appeared aged by a couple of decades, their posture slumped over. Their eyes looked like someone had left honey in the sun to sour and rot, turning a dark mahogany. Those same dark eyes looked at Elle, drilling into her chest. Seran said in a monotone: "This Trial is designed to make someone like you stumble. You will need to think beyond your heart in order to succeed. If you do not, you will lose your chance at queen entirely."

Elle left, an uncomfortable weight settling in her chest. Wanting to win and being told to win by a representative of the Gods were two very different responsibilities. When called to the Trial, Elle's mark had pounded. True to Seran's prediction, the Trial appalled Elle. Throwing the soldiers into the rink at all had nauseated her, and she had yielded in the first two rounds before any weapons even made contact.

Despite this, Seran's words stayed with Elle the entire time. Without winning at least one round, Elle's score for the Trial would have been zero, turning her margins of winning into the slimmest of chances. And Elle needed to win. She needed to be involved in the closed-door trade deals; she needed to oversee loan offerings to people like her ma; she needed to make the government more accessible and transparent. The idea nearly choked her: if being empathetic lost her the chance at dispensing her empathy on a nationwide level, was she still being empathetic?

Elle didn't come up with an answer at the moment. She still wasn't positive she did the right thing. But with her mark burning,

Elle swallowed hard and ordered her soldiers into the fray, commanding them to disarm if possible, but discharge if necessary. Nobody died, but both of her soldiers and one of Teo's walked away with ghastly wounds that made Elle retch. The round ended with one victory to Elle, keeping her in the race with Liliana and Teo. At 3 points, she still had a fair chance to catch up to Liliana's 3.1 and Teo's 3.6 in the final Trial.

By the time Elle returned and demanded Seran tell her what they knew, Seran frowned and shrugged their shoulders. They were unable to explain the precise nature of their reaction, vaguely citing having had "a feeling." Elle got no more from the Guide, other than an ambiguous satisfaction with Elle's performance. The interaction made Elle want to puke again. What was the purpose of that kind of bloodshed if it didn't even mean anything? Elle's stomach roiled at the thought in the present.

Apparently, Seran had no such ominous feelings about meeting with Teo. They stared at Elle, confused. "Why in the world would *Imperium* care about with whom you fetch tea?"

"Good enough for me." Elle grabbed her necklace and clasped it around her neck, marching toward the door. So long as that haunted look stayed off Seran's face, Elle truly didn't care what the outcome of this meeting was. She waved over her shoulder while Seran snuggled back into the comforts of their book. "Be good."

Seran gave a small hum of agreement, their eyes already glued back to the page. Elle rolled her eyes to herself and left the room without another word.

While Elle made her way to the general direction of Teo's room, her eyes scanned the castle with a lost interest. Whenever she set about the castle, she couldn't help but search for anything out of place. Thus far, she only found one other door like the one Eliana led her through. Hidden under a squeaky floorboard by the throne room, the secret passage led to a tiny exit in the palace gardens. Elle had yelled when she tumbled from its exit, her eyes lit with desire. She sighed, tiredness filling her head with cotton. The idea of uncovering new things felt less exciting than it had before the trial of *Caecus.*

Elle's hand brushed against the expensive walls as she walked to Teo's. Lavish. Excessive. Wasteful, honestly. While part of Elle grew to appreciate the castle's charm, part of her felt disgruntled at the gratuitous nature of Electaria's government. Though the Aurjnegh were probably more liberal in their interior decorating budget, Elle's mind was stuck on how much money was diverted to the wallpaper while children fought at the Crank for a living.

***

After a circuitous route from her absentminded thoughts, Elle arrived at Teo's door. The door, much like the man itself, lacked the normal frills. Amid the gold embellishment of the hallway, the simple oak door protested the neighboring opulence. Elle had a feeling if the door could talk, it would be scolding the surrounding vases and lamps to "shape up!"

She managed a small smile to herself, rapping on the door. A vague curiosity pricked through the curtain of her disillusionment. Elle knew close to nothing about Teo beyond the few words he'd uttered in her presence. Of those few, most of them were prepositions. He existed in almost a mythical—no, *legendary*—way. Seran brought a whole new meaning to the word "mythical."

Of what little the people of the castle had to say of the prince, the comments mostly centered around three central themes: solitary, silent, steady. Considering Elle's salacious and dramatic experiences with his sisters—between Eliana's secret affairs and Liliana's arson—the prospect of a reliably boring sibling intrigued her.

One of the Four—Je?—opened with a crossbow aimed at her chest. The arrow ended in a serrated tip, one that would be sure to lacerate a few internal organs of any unfortunate individual caught in its grasp. And this deadly weapon was held in the hands of an even deadlier weapon—one of the Four.

Elle looked back and forth from the crossbow to Je's face before covering her face with her hands, weakly asking, "Please don't?"

Je froze and waved his crossbow around as he explained, "Shit, wait, no—kid, I'm not..." His own gaze caught his waving crossbow, and he cursed and dropped the thing to the floor.

They both jumped backward as the weapon clattered to the ground.

He cursed again—with a vocabulary of swear words so vast Nic would have been impressed—and put his foot on the crossbow, sliding it back into the room. "Teo failed to mention he was having a guest over." Je threw a withering look over his shoulder.

"You are one of the Four. I should not have to inform you of these things—you should know," Teo's deep voice echoed from behind Je's flustered form, his reproach clear. "Ellegance, do not be afraid. He will not kill you."

"Comforting," Elle muttered to herself.

"Je, let Ellegance enter."

Je obeyed, his expression sheepish and annoyed as he backed away from the door. Elle paused a beat before sighing. If these two had wanted to kill her, they'd had a terrific opportunity a few seconds ago. They were either incompetent or not planning on murder. Seeing Je's rippling biceps and the broadsword sheathed at Teo's side, she opted for the latter. Besides, Elle figured she could at least get some tea in exchange for the heart attack.

Compared to the rest of the castle, Teo's room was almost insulting. Draftiness settled into Elle's bones, the disconcerting symptom of the absence of things. One bed set in a stone frame. Two pillows swallowed by an expanse of white. One wooden table, barely a foot from the ground. Legions of empty space.

The barren chambers looked as though somebody had set fire to every bright object of the room, varying shades of ash settling in their place. The only pop of color came from the most practical of torches that guarded his wall. Honestly, the torches probably lived in shame for their relative ostentation. The room had about as much personality as a loaf of bread. *Maybe even less*, Elle thought to herself, eyebrows raised high.

Teo gestured mutely to the table in the center of the room. Elle shrugged and flopped to the floor, crossing her legs and plopping her head on her hands. Teo watched her, his expression unreadable. After a beat, he carefully lowered himself to the ground. Once settled—Elle used the word "settled" loosely, the man would have looked just as at home sitting on a porcupine—Teo gave a small nod to Je in the doorway. Moments later, a serving girl whisked in, set two steaming cups in front of the pair, and whisked away without another word. The chasms of empty space made the silence that much louder. If the girl had even whispered, it would have been a shout.

Teo sat in front of Elle, back uncomfortably straight. They eyed each other unapologetically. Teo appeared to do so without awareness of the action. Elle did so in spite of knowing how rude Electarians found such things to be. From the neat cut of his hair to the perfect crop of his beard, Teo was made of clean lines and hard edges. Even his face was a slab of unblemished stone.

He reminded her of the kind of man who would lie on a bed of nails and honestly declare it the most luxurious piece of furniture yet known to man. Instead of oozing charm like Eliana, he practically sucked charisma out of the room. Even Liliana, cactus that she was, looked cuddly next to his stoic form.

"Ellegance Fournier," his baritone came so suddenly that Elle jumped, arrested in her observations, "it is my honor to finally make your acquaintance. My apologies for the delay in our meeting. I hope you may forgive me."

His eyes tightened so slightly around the edges. Elle noticed the change, logging it in its own building within the kingdom of her memory. A small shift but clearly signaling distress. By all appearances, the man seemed to be honest.

She waved off the apology. "No apologies necessary. To be honest," she said slowly, gauging his reaction, "your note surprised me. It's a little late in the Trials to try and make friends, no?"

"Don't misunderstand, Ellegance—"

"Elle."

Teo stopped his line of thinking entirely, staring at Elle, puzzled. "Is your name not Ellegance?"

"Only when I'm in trouble" Elle sighed, taking a sip of her cup of tea. "Though I suppose it doesn't matter either way. Even when I try to make people call me Elle in this castle, they usually still use Ellegance."

Elle practically smelled smoke as the gears of Teo's brain worked through her quip. Eventually, he shook his head and moved past the interruption. Apparently, unlike his sisters, wit escaped Teo like a fish through oil-slicked hands.

"Then...Elle, my intention is not to cultivate friendship today. At the end of the day, we are competitors and must respect such a divide in our relationship."

Normally, that would be the point that dissuaded further conversation. The statement, spoken without a modicum of delicacy, acted as a conversational bludgeon. No malice laced his words—just facts. And Elle understood where the thought came from. It would be awfully inconvenient to be forced into beating one who she considered a friend. Elle cocked her head to the side. He and Liliana seemed to share that trait.

"I actually wanted to speak with someone from the kingdom, and you are the only one from the city to whom I may speak readily," Teo said, driving steadily forward through his thoughts. "While I travel to the city and work with its citizens, they oftentimes choose to placate me instead of voicing their true thoughts and feelings. They are kind, but they hurt their own cause. I cannot create more dramatic change if the worst of their problems that I know of is leaky roofs and broken door hinges."

He spoke like a seasoned traveler, mentally marking the familiar checkpoints of his thoughts.

"Wait." Elle shook her head. This was an unexpected, though not unwelcome, turn. "Do you really go into the city? I feel like I would've heard about that."

"Of course, I do." Teo's eyebrows furrowed before smoothing out as he explained, "I work closer to the outer boundary of the city, which is relatively far from your home. This is likely why you are less familiar with what I do."

Elle nodded, understanding. She knew the city well, but the people on the outer boundary were far more withholding to newcomers and strangers. On a few rare occasions, she had managed to converse with a couple of younger kids there, but the adults always turned conversation away, wary. She supposed that kind of isolation would be harder to maintain in the face of royalty.

Teo continued, "Now, your parents' profession is baking, yes?"

"*Etiam*," Elle said, a nostalgic smile creeping across her face. The phantom aroma of freshly baked rosemary bread drifted through her mind, accompanied by the sweet burning of copper candy and powdered donuts. The memories eased the cloud that had ensconced her thoughts since the previous Trial. "They make the best bread in the city."

"And you have four siblings?"

"I do." Elle stared at the prince. "Why?"

"Is the income from your parents' bakery sufficient in providing for your family?" Teo's brown eyes probed Elle carefully.

From a thousand other people, the question could have been uncomfortable or even insulting. Somehow, Teo's straightforward tone circumvented any such insinuations, instead presenting the sentence for what it was: a legitimate question. He searched for knowledge but did not demand its gift. The least Elle could do was oblige the man.

"For the most part, yeah. I can't really remember any nights going to bed hungry or anything like that." Elle shrugged.

"And what about where you lived? Did you own the property?"

Elle snorted. "Of course not. We stay in the building with the bakery because my parents have a loan with one of the banks in the city. My sister understands this stuff better than I do, but I do know that they only pay interest every month. We almost never make enough to pay anything more."

"And—and how high is the interest your parents pay?" Teo faltered, clearly entering unfamiliar territory.

Elle empathized with the prince's journey into a world he had never experienced. He had spent his entire life in a castle that cost five times as much as Madame Dragonia's store. He probably took ownership of land as a fact of the kingdom, instead of one of its greatest luxuries.

"I don't know the exact number," Elle said, brushing her choppy bangs out of her face. "My ma goes back to the bank every month or so to try and renegotiate the rates we pay, but it's only worked a handful of times." Elle gave Teo a half grin. "Doesn't stop her from trying anyway. That's the kind of person she is."

Though Elle's heart ached at the thought of her ma's fierce eyes and heart, her mark gave an affirming pound. The power her ma showed on a daily basis impressed Elle before, but having gone so long without it, Elle recognized the feat for what it was. In the castle, where royals faced so few, *real* challenges on any given day, her ma was practically a warrior on caliber with the Four.

"Could you not try and get a loan from a different bank with a more favorable rate?"

"That's not how it works, Your Highness." Elle gave him a rueful smile. "The banks are owned by a small number of people in the city. And most of those people work together, so they'll offer the same rates to avoid people switching from one to another."

Teo nodded, closing his eyes. His eyebrows knitted together, his rumination animating his visage more than anything Elle had seen thus far. Finally, he opened his eyes, his pupils locking onto Elle's. "Do you believe the kingdom would benefit from taking over the banks itself?"

"Possibly," Elle said slowly, allowing the thought to swirl through her head. "But how would that even be possible?"

"Likely a heavy investment to buy out the outstanding debts the banks have. Some Nuwei academics have written interesting papers on the theory." His eyes grew intense, and he leaned forward toward Elle. "Ambiguous responses do not interest me. Do you think such a measure would help the kingdom, yes or no?"

Elle eyed the prince with clear interest. "I do."

"Excellent." Though Teo's face barely changed, his voice sounded a tinge warmer, heated by his pride. He clasped his hands on the edge of the table, declaring, "I have reason to believe such a measure will include economic gains for the kingdom as well. Less money spent on rent means more money spent in markets, which increases our tax revenue, as well as the number of land-holding citizens who pay property taxes."

"I wish you the best of luck, Your Highness," Elle told him, an honest smile on her face. In some ways, she believed the plan to be a broader undertaking than for which the prince was ready, but she admired his determination nonetheless. She raised her cup to tap his, a Vitrian custom she had yet to see in the castle.

Teo furrowed his brows. "Vitrians are a strange people."

"*Etiam.*" Elle laughed softly in agreement.

Teo tentatively clinked his cup with hers, his motions cautious and careful like that of a newborn fawn. Teo ushered her out of the room shortly after, making sure to remind her that the meeting was purely informational, and she should refrain from expecting shows of friendship in the future.

Her heart warmed as she exited the room, waving off Je's profuse apologies. A man waited patiently outside the door, dressed in the geometric robes of a Nuwei ambassador. He offered a respectful nod at her passing before brushing into Teo's room. She vaguely wondered about the ambassador's business. Perhaps the prince had even more tea with which to settle future policy matters.

Elle liked Teo, she decided. He spoke with confidence but not bravado. He talked with intelligence but not cunning. If Teo's eyes were not a direct copy of Juliana's, Elle could have been convinced that the prince was from Vitria. He was the kind of person her ma and da would be proud to have as a king. Straightforward, smart, and most importantly, well-meaning—a man to respect, though perhaps not adore.

Elle came to her second decision. She was okay with Teo winning the crown.

Of course, Elle had no intention of letting that happen. At the end of the day, she decided to win. She wanted to grasp the crown, feeling the cool silver beneath her fingers and on her head. She wanted to push against the tide of the aristocracy's status quo, establishing change for the people who depended on the kingdom more than anyone. Instead of taking over the banks, she could start with just putting in some regulations. Something to rein in the heartless people who told her ma no every month. Elle wanted to take the kingdom she spent so many years loving and turn it into a place where everybody might find it in themselves to love it, just a little.

But if she were to lie broken on the floor after giving her all in that pursuit, and Teo stood on the winner's podium, Elle found herself strangely content with the idea. Much like a loaf of overbaked bread, it was an undesirable outcome but not unsalvageable. Regardless of her callused fingers or Teo's stony grip, the kingdom would find itself in good hands.

Elle took a deep breath, her body buzzing. The *Imperium* trial began tomorrow. For better, or worse, her city would find its future then.

INTERLUDE
SEVEN YEARS AGO

Kisses, Eliana found, were a lot like people. Some were male, some were female. Some existed somewhere between the two or far beyond. Some were far too long, others woefully short. Some were so natural, they burned, while others were tense with painful awkwardness. Some were so dry they could kindle fire, while others were far too...damp. Some could melt the heavens in one achingly brief instant, and some could leave one aching to read a biographical text on agronomy.

Eliana ended the kiss with a gentle nip, the ghost of a smirk dancing across her face at her partner's sigh in response. While the kiss failed to break any boundaries of passion or pleasure, it had been warm. Nice.

The woman was a lucky find. While magisters weren't exactly forbidden from taking up a lover, it was far from encouraged. Such frivolities left very little time to interpret the whims of the Gods. Most played a perpetual, insufferable game of chicken, waiting for one of the other magisters to blink and succumb. The loser briefly gained relief to a seemingly eternal sexual repression, and the winners gained all the pious righteousness for which they so desperately sought.

Eliana lifted one finger gently, trailing it along the woman's chin. The woman shuddered, her onyx eyes finally opening against a landscape of seashell-colored skin. Eliana's mouth sloped into her half smile. The sexually repressed made it far too easy, she was afraid.

"Isn't it time for you to return home?" she asked, taunting and sugary all at once.

"*Superbia* won't be that lonely without me," the woman said with a short laugh, but her dark eyes shone with longing. *Desperation.*

Eliana gave a small sigh. Perhaps she had dragged this one in a little too far. She took the woman's hands in her own, pressing a soft kiss against both sets of knuckles. Eliana's mark grew cold, the icy feeling grasping her forearm. She gazed at the magister over the woman's knuckles, Eliana's lips moving against the magister's pale skin.

"*Superbia* needs none of our presence. But the people lack such self-assurance. The kingdom needs you still."

The frost in Eliana's forearm grew colder. The words settled in the woman's head like a cat curling up for a nice, long nap. Normal words had no such power of occupation, but these were not just words. They were a truth. A powerful truth. The magister nodded, eyes downcast. Her hands dropped to her sides. Reality took root in the woman's head, blooming with its thorny responsibilities.

Eliana leaned forward and gave the woman a chaste, parting kiss on the cheek. The woman stepped away, her spine straightening and shoulders pushing backward as she returned to her calling. After all, the House couldn't afford a magister of *Superbia* looking anything less than absolutely self-confident.

Unfortunately for the both of them, even if Eliana wanted to continue dragging secrets from the woman's hooded eyes and pursed lips, she couldn't. Eliana brushed out any wrinkles in her dress of dark red, Electaria's revered color of mourning. She examined her person with a critical eye, assuring herself a thread nor hair was out of place. Satisfied, Eliana set about her next task with calm briskness. Not hurried. Eliana rarely felt hurried. But she moved with a level of speed that spoke of purpose with a dash of determination.

After all, Eliana could hardly be late for her own mother's funeral.

The palace halls wept red, dripping in Electarian mourning reds from the curtains to the carpets. The custom came from the conviction that those still living might distract *malum* from the soul traveling to the Gods by wearing the evil deity's favorite color. Eliana understood the practice but abhorred its application. It made the castle look like one gargantuan, bloody wound.

Intent on avoiding the haunting color, Eliana carefully moved the painting of one of many deceased royals to the side. Her fingers traced the tiny indentation of the wallpaper, so miniscule a spider could scurry across without feeling the bump. Fortunately, Eliana had a keener eye than even most spiders. Secret passageways behind paintings tended to be abhorred as clichés. Eliana learned years ago that clichés, when turned on their head, could be fabulous allies.

She pressed her hand against the indentation and the opposite side of the door released inward with a *pop*. Eliana stepped inside, letting the painting swing back over the entrance and quietly closing the door behind her.

The hallways, despite being hidden in the recesses of the castle, were not in terrible condition. So long as Eliana remembered to wipe the dust from her heels upon exiting, nobody was ever the wiser. The wooden, plank walls glowed in the warm light of torches, strategically placed every few feet by a person Eliana would likely never know.

Eliana strolled for a minute, headed toward the castle center. She stopped on the way at a two-foot-deep depression in the wall. A small chest sat nestled in the hollow, a modest mirror hanging above. Another mystery of the castle's bowels, of which Eliana had long been the beneficiary. The mirror reflected Eliana's half smile back at her as she shuffled around in the chest. She likely had about five more minutes before people began to pour into the castle's blood-red halls and wallow in their anguish for the poor, dead queen. Eliana's mouth twisted. *Anguish for Juliana—a novel concept, as it were.*

Eliana finally grabbed the thick, round jar in the chest's depths and with it, a small brush. Popping off its lid, she dipped the brush in black ink and carefully traced the lines of the wave mark on her left forearm, burying any showing of gold that had managed to reemerge throughout the day.

Growing up, Eliana played with truth and lies like a set of paints made to be swirled and combined to her liking. As with most children's paintings, these pictures lacked finesse. Consequently, she spent her childhood with a reputation for mischief. Eliana completed her Walk years ago, her mark turning gold and the colors of her paint suddenly swirling together brilliantly. She transformed from a dilettante into an artist. Despite being twelve then, Eliana's mark sang to her. She began to paint over her mark that night, shielding the truth under layers of black ink.

Maintaining the narrative that her Walk remained incomplete was integral to Eliana's fun in the castle. If people knew Eliana had completed her Walk, she would lose her greatest weapon. Secrets and truths only held power when they moved concurrently. Secrets only gained power when there was a truth to be had, and the truth only mattered when secrets lurked in its presence. If everyone knew her affinity for the truth, the worth of her secrets would be naught.

Each truth held its own weight and punched with its own power. Depending on the person, the force behind the punch could grow stronger or weaker with use. If everyone believed she told the truth, the effect was diminished entirely. Its value inflated to the point where each truth she told meant nothing because it was exactly what was expected. Secrets were integral to her magic and the joy she derived from twisting the world around her.

Eliana's practiced hand finished painting her mark with a flourish. She cast a dark smile at herself in the mirror. Mystery lined the curve of her lips like that of a full moon, bright and shadowy all at once, intrigue curling through every crater and hole.

She always wondered why people assumed followers of *Menda* were so damn honest. Yes, she always knew when people told the truth. She understood other people's truths. But because she understood the truth so deeply, she also knew how to lie. She knew how to spin webs to create narratives that fit into others' world perceptions. She created lies that made more sense than their truthful counterparts. As far as she was concerned, the golden mark made her better at lying than anybody else in the world.

Eliana laughed to herself at the thought, the sound tinkling and dangerous, as she listened for footsteps before stepping outside of the hallway. She exited from a similar painting in almost a completely different area of the castle. She now lurked on the farmost end of the floor of the throne room. It was the only room big enough to accommodate a funeral the size her mother had requested. Eliana supposed it was just as well. Holding the woman's funeral in the House just seemed ironic. Eliana readjusted the painting with swift hands.

As Eliana strode into the funeral with an appropriate amount of solemnity, she couldn't help but wonder what it must feel like to mourn the loss of one's mother. Dissolving into the somber crowd of people slowly swaying to the throne room, Eliana arranged her expression into a simulacrum of the sadness she saw around her. Her mark jumped, an icy reminder that as much as she might posture, she couldn't lie about how little she felt for Queen Juliana's passing.

Perhaps it was all a matter of degree. Perhaps the relationship between a mother and daughter could be measured the same way one climbed a mountain. Perhaps with continued nurturing and mutual affection, the pair reached a threshold of love that plateaued at a trust so irrevocable it could never again dip below that point. Eliana imagined such a threshold was normally reached in childhood. There had to be a point where a child looked at their mother and decided that this woman would be a source of comfort for all their days. Likewise, a mother needed to have an epiphany that the child in front of her, an unrefined, untainted reflection of herself, would be her tether to the world, in life and death.

Eliana was utterly confounded where that point precisely occurred, but regardless of where it lay on this mountain of relation, she and her mother certainly missed it. A simple thread of genetic familiarity had tied their existences together, a connection so tenuous it could be mistaken for a trick of the eye. At what point in a relationship did a woman go from procreator to mother? Eliana supposed she would never know, seeing as the former was dead, and the latter never existed.

Entering the throne room, Eliana was immediately suffocated by the dark red that dominated every crevice of the area. Dark red curtains covered the walls, a dark red rug rolled over the traditional purple, and a dark red casket replaced the normal throne. Eliana clucked her tongue softly to herself. Though most Electarian funerals opted for closed caskets, her mother had demanded years ago to have hers open. Despite being as long as two men lying toe to head, the casket was probably not big enough to hold both her mother's corpse and her ego.

Eliana weaved her way through the crowd, offering teary gratitude and lip-biting nods where appropriate. She stepped toward her brother, who stood next to the casket, his face devoid of emotion and color. Shadows weighed down his mahogany eyes, and the faded color of his brown skin whispered of insomnia. He wore dark red from his tunic to his boots, even discarding his beloved sword to maintain the color continuity.

Eliana's heart panged for the first time that day. She rested her right hand lightly upon his upper arm, head tilted to the side. "How are you faring?"

"Terribly." His voice was hoarse, the ragged strain a stark contrast to the steady face he maintained. "The Captain keeps moving me to a new room every night to sleep as a preventative measure, in case mother's death was truly at the hand of an assassin. The constant change makes sleep impossible. I swear I haven't shut my eyes since I heard it happened."

Eliana squeezed her brother's arm, her mark helping her sense the hope hidden beneath his words. She pulled it out, like dragging an anchor back in from the depths of the sea. "Things will settle down soon enough. You know as well as I do: the investigative team is all but convinced an assassin couldn't have caused this type of natural death."

Her mark froze over, and Teo's shoulders relaxed slightly as the truth he had been hoping for wrapped around his shoulders like a blanket on a frigid night. "You're right, of course." His face grew stonier. "But even when things settle down, she will still be dead."

Eliana didn't respond, her forearm covered in the icy feeling of hearing the truth. She could hardly disagree with him on that front.

A muted hush rippled through the crowd as Eliana's father and sister made their way to the dais. Liliana's face was a ravaged thing. Though she walked with her chin held high, her lip trembled, and she glared straight ahead, her eyes filled with unshed tears. It looked like her sister was using every ounce of anger and willpower in her body to keep from disintegrating into her grief. Liliana stood next to Eliana, her shoulders thrown back, her whole body quivering every time she dared look at the casket at the center of the dais. Eliana wanted to say something but found she couldn't think of a single word that would bring her sister any comfort. Instead, she stared in front of her, trying her best to drown out Liliana's harsh breathing. The two had stopped seeking comfort in one another years ago—there was nothing Eliana could do for her now.

Their father, taking his position at Teo's other side, nodded at the magisters from the House who would lead the day's proceedings. They launched into a sermon on the journey of the soul, the comfort of the Gods, and all that their mother would be blessed with now that she was dead. Eliana couldn't help but hear the entire thing as a florid way of saying that Juliana was lucky to be dead. Imperium, *if death is so good, perhaps we should all give it a try,* Eliana scoffed to herself. If that's all that life amounted to—a fortunate death—then what was the point?

Eliana faded out from the magisters' teachings and found herself craning her neck to look into the casket. A shiver ran down Eliana's spine. Everyone had always said Eliana and her mother were practically twins. Eliana supposed now, at least, she had an idea of what her own funeral would look like. She couldn't decide if that notion was overly macabre or simply poetic.

Clawing into the depths of her emotions, Eliana searched for a kernel of remorse she could spare for the corpse beside her. She tried to find a memory strong enough to force her head above the deafening water and into a place where she would be forced to hear and confront pain. Instead, she was only able to pinch together a touch of gratitude.

While some followers of *Menda* finished their Walk as they discovered the truth of love or the importance of honesty, Eliana's epiphany, and thus, the completion of her Walk, came directly from her mother.

Eliana had never received the same type of love with which Juliana lavished Teo and Liliana. She used to chalk it up to sheer favoritism. As Eliana grew older, she also outgrew such a childish notion. It wasn't favoritism; it was prejudice. At the end of the day, Eliana was not the follower of *Imperium* that her mother so coveted. If anything, Eliana's looks that mimicked her mother were added insults to the wound of Juliana's one failed child. Shared blood was simply not enough, and Eliana paid the price for her mark every day she lived with her mother.

Years ago, after breaking into an argument with her mother that seemed to last for eons, Eliana threatened to run away. It was a dull weapon all teenagers believed to be sharper than it was, and Eliana was no different. She declared she would run off to Vitria or Aurjnegh and go be a princess *there*. Her mother listened to Eliana's rant before finally snapping, "You want to leave? Fine. I do not care."

It was such a simple statement. In hindsight, its harshness was mild relative to the vitriol Eliana had heard spewed in the castle since. And yet, its *truth*...its truth gave the words such a severe power that Eliana had felt paralyzed.

Her mother had marched out of the room, her head held to the same imperious height Liliana always had hers. Seconds later, a painful, icy feeling grasped Eliana's arm, refusing to let go. It felt as though somebody had encased her forearm in a block of ice and dunked the whole thing in a freezing river. Eliana gasped, tears popping to her eyes. When her vision cleared, the waves on her forearm swam with gold.

Eliana let out the tiniest sigh as she looked at her mother's lifeless visage. It was a strange thing, to look at a woman whose face mirrored her own and feel only a resigned appreciation. Her mother, in all her wretchedness, had given Eliana the best gift she could have ever received. Eliana's heart gave a dull thud as she beheld her mother's dead body. There was something ironic and beautiful there, if only she cared enough to dig into the thought.

The evening continued on in the ceremoniously dull way most events did. In Electaria, even funerals could be made to feel bureaucratic. The magisters preached, dignitaries postured, old friends and distant family members spoke, people wailed, and eventually, everyone left. Packaging their sorrow into neat boxes to be stored next to other momentarily sad memories, the citizens filed out of the throne room, at last leaving the royal family in peace.

"I'm going to the library," Liliana stated shortly after the kingdom's departure, her voice pinched and eyes swimming. Before anybody could respond, she marched out of the room, her shoulders slumping forward with every step. Which left only Teo, Eliana, and their poor father.

Their father, in Eliana's kindest possible summation, looked atrocious. Eliana imagined someone dipping her father's eyes in red paint and shoving them back into his skull to create the sunken, bloodshot gaze he leveled at her. His sepia skin faded without the normal rouge of his cheeks, exacerbated by the dark red outfit he wore to the funeral. Her mother's ornate crown leaned haphazardly on his head, in constant peril of falling with every tired step he took. Eliana reached forward and adjusted the crown, receiving a grateful look in turn.

"I apologize for my appearance. The past few days have been …straining, to say the least." He offered a small smile, and Eliana prayed a blood vessel wouldn't burst from the effort. He clasped both Teo and Eliana on the shoulders, squeezing with a weak grip. "How are my eldest children in such trying times?"

Teo and Eliana shared a glance, understanding passing between them. For all that others made fun of Teo's lack of social awareness, Eliana always felt a certain level of connection with her quiet brother. Throughout her life, his and her father's honesty had been two of the most grounding experiences for Eliana and her mark. Eliana dared to think she wouldn't even know the meaning of truth had it not been for the pair of them.

"We carry on. We're more worried about you, Father," Eliana said, forcing her voice to be gentler than a feather. "We know your reign was unexpected, and the kingdom is in disarray. Is there anything we can do to help ease the burden?"

Her father's exhausted face twisted into a wry smile, his bloodshot eyes focusing in again on Eliana. She felt her chest squeeze, unready for the sudden scrutiny.

"There is, actually. Teo will one day be the next king of this country, so he needs to know of the decision I plan on making today. I need him as a witness for something of serious consequence in the future. But you, Eliana, I need you *not* to witness but rather to *act*." Her father pushed up Eliana's left sleeve, exposing her mark.

Eliana's stomach churned, and she resisted the urge to cover up her arm in fear of raising suspicion.

"I know you've completed your Walk," her father told her, voice soft.

Eliana froze in place. Teo looked at Eliana, momentarily leaving his grief behind for total shock. Her father rubbed his thumb firmly against the bottom of the wave on her arm, gradually smudging the paint she had applied hours earlier.

"You can't hide these things from a follower of *Menda and* your father." He shook his head, but his voice held a tired amusement instead of the anger or disappointment Eliana expected.

Eliana eyed her father warily, pulling her arm slowly back to her own body. *What was his plan?*

"But you've managed to hide it from everyone else in the castle, even some other followers of *Menda*." He shook his head once more, this time incredulous. "Even your mother had no idea, and she tried to make it her business to know everything that happened under the roof of this castle. And that, my daughter, is a skill that I believe is vastly underutilized on your current hobby of collecting idle prattle."

Eliana's expression shifted from wariness to curiosity. "And what superior utilization did you have in mind?"

Leo, eyes bleary from stress and exhaustion, weakly clasped Eliana on the shoulder. "How would you feel about serving as Electaria's spymaster?"

CHAPTER 23
7055.1.29

Anticipation tasted a lot like blood.

True anticipation was not to be confused with anxiety or excitement. Those served as anticipation's watered-down cousins, cheap imitations of the real thing. True anticipation rushed through the body quicker and more lethal than any top-shelf booze. It slowed down each moment while accelerating time itself. It blurred the periphery but sharpened the center.

True anticipation was equal parts heart leaping and heart crawling, coalescing into a terrifying exhilaration that threatened to consume all sense unless held at bay. Anticipation meant feeling the wind bite and the air grow thin as the potential of the moment grew beneath you into a mountain. It meant standing on the precipice of that moment, teetering on the edge of something far grander and greater than yourself. In so many ways, it meant daring to step off into its void. Let the vortex take control.

All those sensations condensed into something bitter and coppery, a feeling that Liliana wanted to spit out as soon as possible. To rid herself of the emotion, the taste. She didn't let herself. She swirled the bloody feeling around in her mouth, closing her eyes and finding a way to revel in the flavor. This was satisfaction in its embryonic stage. Glory before it fully matured. She would savor every vile moment.

Liliana wore her future in every stitch of her clothing. Her soft boots had been replaced with the hard soles that soldiers used during war, steel underlaying the fabric at the toe. Her straight, dark hair collected in a tight bun at the nape of her neck, not a strand allowed to stray from perfection. Liliana's sword, appropriated from the training arena, rested comfortably at her side, its metal handle glinting in the afternoon sun. From the lavender of her tunic and pristine white of her pants, to the golden cape that glided behind her, she radiated power.

Her competition looked fragile in comparison. Teo wore his traditional purple cloak, a simple, black uniform underneath its plum-colored fabric. Oh, and of course, he hadn't forgotten his arrogant stoicism. Elle had settled for standards even simpler than what Teo set. She wore a plain black tunic over white, cotton pants, cinched at the waist with a golden belt. The chain of her silver necklace flashed occasionally, but she kept the ornament tucked beneath her shirt. A small smile crept across Liliana's face. On the most important day of all their lives, the two looked less like future kings and queens than they did two actors, separated from their troupe.

Liliana stood between Teo and Elle on a small platform. Impe's air, a blissfully cool break from its usual warmth, nipped at their cheeks, turning Liliana's cheeks pink. Behind the coolness, she could practically smell the sneaky introduction of Supe with the dewy scent of grass.

The highest-ranking dignitaries clustered in front of the three, whispering behind their hands and teeming with excited energy like a dumb school of fish. Imperium sat close by. Even if Liliana had not told him to sit there prior to claiming her spot on the stage, she would have known he was there by the thumping of his tail, which sent small tremors through the earth. The wolf whined incessantly, despite her hushes. Every so often, he nipped at her cape, pointing his nose back at the castle. Liliana did her best to soothe him, but his agitation persisted. The Captain and her forces prowled the nearby areas.

Liliana caught the occasional glimpse of Aoran on patrol. He always managed to find her gaze, as if her notice was a bell beckoning his attention. He raised a thumbs-up. Liliana rolled her eyes, a hint of fondness creeping in without permission. She batted the feeling away, staring at the sun until her eyes watered, letting the feeling evaporate. Today, more than ever, she needed to concentrate.

Her father looked up at the three in the front of the crowd, Eliana, a picturesque statue on his right side. Her smooth face was serene, regarding the world with a vague warmth. Liliana bit the inside of her cheek. What a facade. Tangy blood filled her mouth, almost comfortable in its companionship with the taste of anticipation still seething under her tongue. Warmth and her sister fit together as well as volcanic ash and snow. No wonder Eliana hadn't completed her Walk. The fronts she put forth to the rest of the world probably forced *Menda* to tears daily.

King Leo's brown eyes creased at the edges, for once crimped with stress instead of his typical smile. Instead of wearing his silver crown, he fidgeted, passing the thing from one hand to another. A part of her missed his belly laughs and broad smiles. Unfortunately, that part of her was much smaller than the other parts of her dedicated to sparring with Aoran, preparing for Trials, and serving on the Education Council. Leo had been busy ruling, Liliana busy fighting for his rule. There simply wasn't enough time and goodwill to cement the foundation and intent to repair the bridge that once held them together.

And yet, a question pinched at the back of Liliana's mind, painful and demanding attention. Who did her father seek to win the competition? Who did he believe would ultimately be triumphant? Her entire life, Liliana sought to emulate her mother. While that never changed, after her mother's death, Liliana grew to appreciate her father. Despite everything that wore their relationship thin, the tiny, childish part of her—that which grew to admire his leadership and how he assumed power when the nation needed him—wanted the answer to be Liliana.

Eliana smiled at their father with her signature willowy grace, whispering something into his ear. He glanced at Liliana and then at Teo, his eyes skipping over Elle entirely. His face bore shadows of age, distress. He looked as though a hand shoved invisible splinters beneath his fingernails every waking second, bathing him in constant waves of agony. Recently, he wore this consternation more often than his smile. It reminded Liliana of the days when her mother still lived. After a beat, his eyes finally settled on Teo, and he nodded, almost imperceptibly, to Eliana.

Liliana's hazel eyes hardened. She smothered that voice, that pathetic part of her that still sought her father's approval. She was here for herself and live up to everything she had always known she was capable of. She would win the kingdom on the strength of her own shoulders, not lifted by the others. Every step since her mother's death had been Liliana's and Liliana's alone. A rational piece of her tore from the fold, reminding Liliana that her father was the one to declare Monarchic Trials in the first place. Liliana squashed the lone dissenter.

Every success was a direct result of her efforts and work. Those people, connected to her merely by blood, had no part in her outcomes and would have no place in her pride. Besides, it had been a long while since she saw one of her family members and felt comforted by the sight.

King Leo coughed, and all chatter quickly moved to the side with a collective intake of breath. He edged a step closer to the platform, still leaving a respectful distance between himself and the candidates. The future king or queen stood before him, and the proper shows of Electarian respect began. He withdrew a folded piece of parchment tucked within the plum sleeve of his jacket. His hands trembled as he slowly unrolled the paper.

Liliana regarded the man with pity. Even with the crown and all the finery in the world, her father could never fully present himself as a king. Always a touch too jovial, a dash too unsure. Liliana's mark burned, a dull, comforting warmth. After all, even with a crown on his head, a fool was still a fool.

"Thank you for gathering here today," Leo announced, his voice booming through the small clearing. It traveled with the loudness of one used to speaking but not with the power of one who held conviction in his own words. "This is the final trial. That of *Imperium*, she who bravely leads the pantheon. She who served as the uniting factor between each God's strength in their war against *malum*.

"Each candidate before me has shown unprecedented wisdom, strength, humility, and honesty. They have upheld the light of *Menda*, bowed beneath the weight of *Superbia*, stood with the force of *Viribus*, and borne the burden of *Caecus*. Time and time again, these three have proven themselves worthy before the eyes of the Gods.

"And now, the final test," Leo said, softer. He shook his head, clearing his throat. "The Trial that will determine the fate of Electaria, chosen by *Imperium* herself. This test will pick the most powerful candidate, raising them above the others as the ultimate monarch of Electaria."

How Liliana hated the pomp of royal events. She stared at King Leo's shoes, waiting impatiently for him to finish droning. Too many words. Too little done. A disease that ran through to the core of the government. When queen, Liliana's rule would be built upon action. Results.

"The format will be as follows: each candidate will be left in an undisclosed location within the same forest, a short trip from where we stand," Leo continued. "The trial itself is simple. Find the other candidates and overpower them without seriously injuring one another. Only with true control over one's own power can you manage such a task. As you may remember, this final Trial is worth two points. These points will be allocated on a zero-sum basis. The contestant with the highest score at the end of the Trial will, as you all know by now, be crowned as the monarch of Electaria.

"The current scores stand at 3 points for Ellegance Fournier, 3.1 for Liliana Storidian, and 3.6 for Teo Storidian."

Liliana refused to flinch at hearing her score. She needed to dominate Teo in order to score higher than him. If he received anything more than 0.8 points, Liliana was automatically out of the running. She practically hissed at the thought.

Her father continued, "Your score will be based upon your ability to incapacitate the other contestants. Any contestant incapacitated is equal to 0.5 points. Additionally, the first contestant to return to the site at sundown will automatically receive 0.5 of the allotted points. If points remain after these initial allocations, the magisters assembled will assist in fairly distributing them based upon a candidate's holistic performance.

"Your only weapons will be the forest and your own bodies." Her father made grave eye contact with each of the candidates. Liliana could have imagined it, but she could have sworn her father lingered on her for a beat longer than the others. "No maiming, no killing. Other than that, anything goes. You have until sundown."

Liliana miraculously avoided rolling her eyes during what might be considered one of the holiest moments of her life. So, for the God of power, they would literally have to overpower one another. Of course, for the most important challenge, they decided to take things literally. The Gods were apparently not particular in their metaphors.

King Leo paused. There he stood. King for seven years, on the edge of being dethroned by one of his children or an outsider. The audience waited behind him with understanding. Eliana placed a feather hand on King Leo's shoulder. What her sister and the rest couldn't see was the look of utter relief that graced King Leo's face. The follower of *Menda* relinquished the seat not with grace but with the grateful timidity of a man fleeing from battle. Such a man returned to his troops with his life but without honor. Liliana's eyes narrowed at Leo. *Coward.*

He took a deep breath, a smile breaking through the clouds of his face for the first time all day. "May the most powerful win and have a blessed reign over Electaria. Best of luck to each of the candidates."

With his final words, a familiar hand wrapped around Liliana's elbow. Aoran guided Liliana away from the platform, surprisingly professional, as Je and Ro did the same with Teo and Elle respectively. Liliana turned away from the crowds, her mind discarding all thoughts of them. Eliana. Leo. None of them mattered now.

Once away from the dignitaries, Aoran turned back to face Liliana, a silk scarf in hand. He smirked wickedly at her. "Not the way I imagined tying you up for the first time, but it'll have to do."

Liliana bit her tongue. Today, *today* of all days, she refused to indulge him with a response. Unfortunately, her ostensible seething was its own reward, as the mischievous crook of Aoran's grin sharpened.

Aoran moved behind Liliana, tying the black silk over her eyes. He took no care to be gentle. Though Aoran probably never knew so himself, Liliana appreciated the small gesture. Or, rather, lack thereof. In many ways, through every trial, every spar, every classroom lesson, Aoran had taken her seriously. He treated her as an equal. Given that she could count on one hand the amount of people who did the same throughout her life, she appreciated the soldier even more. Liliana's heart and mark stuttered in unison. When she won, he would be rewarded appropriately.

Decision made, Liliana returned to the present as Aoran completed the knot with a firm tug. To her frustration, Liliana couldn't see a damn thing through the material. A pause passed. Liliana heard a faint whooshing sound that quickly faded. After a second, she said, irritated, "What are you waiting for?"

"Just making sure you couldn't see the sword I put to your neck!" Aoran replied cheerfully.

"The *wha*—"

And they were off. Aoran dragged her behind him, knitting this way and that as he guided her to her starting point. Her feet never stumbled, trusting the steady direction of the person in front of her. Her mark ticked up a notch in the frequency of its pounding, thumping with every quick step they took.

Liliana couldn't see her surroundings, but that did not immobilize the rest of her senses. By the way they bobbed and weaved, Liliana pictured a forest with trees closely packed together. The tops of her feet brushed over roots crawling through the ground. Easy to trip on if she got sloppy. They never ducked, indicating any existing branches were positioned too high to be of any use.

She breathed in deeply every other step, her nose twitching as it tried to capture every scent that swam through the air. Grass, of course. Bark. A damp something but no sound of running water. Likely a pond nearby. Dirt, assorted flora. Her lip curled upward. Nothing useful there.

As they trekked, Liliana found herself surprisingly content. Not content in any spiritual calmness, but rather content with her circumstances. The anticipation that roiled through her blood and rose to the surface of her skin sat well with her. The unceasing pound and dull warmth of her mark provided a steady backdrop to her thoughts.

For perhaps the first time in any of the damn trials, Liliana found herself with no desire to pray to the Gods. Their messages mixed in confusing and hypocritical ways. It was a wonder the Pantheon didn't tear itself apart in the lacerations of its contradictions. If anything, she had made it so far *in spite* of the Gods, certainly not because of them. When Liliana won today, they would not share in her laurels.

Finally, the pair stopped. Aoran made quick work of untying the silk from around her eyes. Once free, Liliana greedily drank in her surroundings. To her dismay, she found nothing new with her sight. The forest looked almost exactly as she pictured. Lots of trees, high branches, an abundance of roots with which to break her ankle. The only noticeable difference between her vision and reality were the small rocks scattered about at the base of a handful of trees.

Unlike the forest east of the castle where the trial of *Viribus* took place, afternoon sunlight broke through the canopy of trees. Based upon the predominantly needle-like leaves, Liliana figured they had dragged her to the western forest for the final trial. A sharp improvement—being able to see the ground on which she walked would be essential.

Liliana's neck warmed, sweat slowly accumulating at her hairline. Bugs flew about lazily, the first dredges of colonies that would emerge in full force during Supe.

Aoran continued to stand nearby, staring pointedly at the sword strapped to her side. Liliana huffed, unsheathing the lethal beauty and shoving it in Aoran's waiting hands. His mouth quirked up into a fanged grin. Before turning to leave, he bowed. Instead of stopping at a traditional angle, he continued to bend down, lower than ever before.

Low enough to befit a queen.

He glanced up at her, his jade eyes sparkling from the light that broke through the trees. "Don't disappoint me now. I want somebody on the inside I can threaten Je with when he pisses me off."

"Failure isn't an option," Liliana said simply.

"Of course, it isn't." Aoran chuckled to himself. He straightened and gave her one last, firm clap on the shoulder. "Good luck, Your Majesty."

Aoran retreated into the woods, and Liliana quickly lost sight of him. She took one more breath, steeling herself. That bloody taste returned to her mouth, far more pungent. She relished it. That taste was a harbinger of change. Liliana glared ahead, beginning her quiet dive into the forest. It was far past time to shed the skin of her life as the second-place princess.

Now began her story as the damn queen.

Liliana stalked her way through the forest. She shifted seamlessly through the trees, hiding and moving forward every couple of steps. Her blood rushed in her ears, every sound sharper, every bird call magnified, every leaf shuffle uproarious. Liliana gritted her teeth. She didn't think the heightened awareness would be much help. She remembered the way Elle exited the waiting room long ago—the girl had practically levitated out.

The stones continued to crop up in small piles by the trees. Namans tended to accumulate such piles so they could hide their goods underneath. When they needed to regain access, they used their acidic mucus to melt the exterior away and dig out their treasure. Clever little *malums*. Little nightmares though they were, they knew how to make the most of the tools at their disposal.

The anticipation swelled within Liliana as she shadowed through the forest. A fierce excitement underlaid the feeling. A vicious part of Liliana relished the idea of being able to take the other two down herself. Much like everything else in her life, it would be the manifestation of so many hours of work. All that time spent in that stupid gymnasium with Aoran would show no mercy when she incapacitated those two.

Liliana struggled to draw contempt for Ellegance but knew she would still be able to dispose of the other woman with few qualms. *On the other hand....* The corner of Liliana's mouth lifted into a sardonic smile. She practically salivated at the idea of seeing Teo's proud face swollen, his pride beaten back.

The longer Liliana went without seeing either of the other candidates, the more wired she became. Tense but filled to the brim with a restless energy, Liliana felt like a thousand bees hummed beneath her skin, calling her to action.

A voice low and feminine laughed in her mind. "*It's almost time, Little Dragon.*"

Liliana jumped through her own skin, her shoulders hitching up to meet her ears as she scanned her surroundings for the source. The voice, sometimes so wispy in her mind it seemed like a passing breeze, was far clearer, if still quiet. Her fingers curled into loose fists, her body primed for fighting. The comment came like a distorted whisper, passing over her skin and through her brain as carelessly as the brush of a feather. Though the words registered as human, there was something unnatural about its smooth fineness. Her mark bellowed. Liliana saw nobody in her vicinity. She could not say whether this provided a semblance of comfort.

As much as she wanted to believe it was *Imperium,* the God had done so little for Liliana through the course of her life that she struggled to believe she would intervene now. *Then who?* Liliana dared not speak. Better to continue ignoring the apparition than lavish it in attention that would give away her position. She sealed her mouth shut, thinking intensely to herself, *Who the wreck is that?*

Liliana held the faint impression of a pressure in her head, as if somebody or something dipped its toes into the space of her mind. Not overwhelming in its pressure but wildly disconcerting. Her mark beat harder than Liliana remembered ever feeling, its pulse painful in its burning.

A satisfied sigh swept through her head with the same tendril of tangibility: "*The one that will deliver you your queendom, Little Dragon. Now pay attention. He comes.*"

Liliana certainly had lost her religiosity over the past few Trials, but she still found it difficult to argue with a supernatural voice whispering in her head. When Liliana's ears perked up, she quickly caught on to the snap of twigs, the chattering crumble of leaves beneath a leaden foot.

Teo.

Rapid reflexes from hours spent reacting to Aoran's lightning movements allowed Liliana to take cover behind a tree. She moved soundlessly. She smirked slightly to herself. She would not be as gracious as Teo in alerting him to her presence.

The real question was: How to use her advantage? Judging by the unbroken steadiness of his gait, Teo had no idea she hid nearby. *Viribus* recommended putting Liliana's strength on display, jumping in front of Teo and proving her mettle. *Superbia* cautioned overestimation of one's own skills, opting for a more subtle approach from the back. *Menda* loathed such an underhanded tactic, crying for direct confrontation. *Caecus* sided with *Superbia,* advising a surprise attack from behind. She could aim for Teo's legs, knocking him to the floor before he had a chance to retaliate.

Another option gave a firm tug at her mind. Liliana could walk away. She could walk away and relegate herself to some faraway place, no longer a threat to the monarchy, and instead serve as another cautionary tale for young girls who dared to rise above their station. Teo would take the throne. He would be a dispassionate king but a steady one. Under his rule, the kingdom would not change. It would not grow, but it would continue to eke out a meager existence for itself.

Liliana's eyes tightened in sync with her resolve. Or the kingdom could have something more. It could have a queen who spent her life studying its intricacies. It could have a queen who knew the political landscape and how to manipulate the diplomatic ecosystem to her benefit. It could have prosperity and growth, the likes of which never could have been entertained. It could have a queen who refused to be pushed around and who stood her ground for what she knew to be right. It could have a queen who could make the kingdom so much stronger, so much better than it could have ever dreamed of being.

A mess of contradictions, each path lauding its own morality at the expense of the others. Liliana wanted to scream. The paralysis of what was right, what was good, would lose her everything. What was she to do?

"Take the stone beneath your feet and strike him over the head. Show your power. If done well, you can incapacitate him quickly."

No pride or glory in that. Illegal, technically. Leo specified no tools, no maiming. The action would not only be shameful but also worthy of disqualification, should she be cuaght. Ellegance or Teo would assume the throne by default. Liliana could hardly imagine the ballads the troubadours would sing of the bitter princess, eliminated by her own folly.

Unless, of course, the bitter princess was very careful with the evidence.

Liliana found a small smile creeping across her face. Anticipation lined her muscles with its buzzing electricity. Less of a feeling than it was a description of her momentum. And Liliana had plenty of anticipation and momentum in that instant.

No, there would be no pride or glory in what was to come. But she would enjoy plenty of pride and glory later when they put the damn crown on her head.

Liliana wasted no more time thinking. She smoothly picked up the stone, leaning around the tree to catch the flash of Teo's cape fluttering behind him. His stupid, wrecking cape. A symbol of his power but also a weakness when snagged or grabbed. Her mark thundered, roared, feeling as though somebody melted hot wax over its every line. The dragon she carried with her, the first sign she might be worth a damn, practically screeched. When Liliana tensed to leap, she found no part of her body rebelled. She may have looked like her father, but she was her mother, through and through. She would not hesitate.

Liliana lunged. She moved with inhuman speed, muscles taut. She exploded from behind Teo, stepping on his cape to prevent him from moving. Teo turned to retaliate, but he had as much luck as if he moved to prevent the rain from falling. Liliana was a force. He was better off standing in the storm gracefully instead of uselessly struggling through the downpour.

She brought the stone down on the back of his head. Her arms swelled with power. Her rush forward increased her acceleration, magnifying her force. Liliana saw the angry energy rush from her hands to the stone to Teo. All the anticipation in her body shattered as the stone creased the back of her brother's skull. He crumpled to the ground, unconscious before even hitting the leaves.

He lay on the ground, his fingers twitching. Liliana dropped the stone to the side. She stared at his fallen form, unblinking. She saw no sign of his traditional pride. Passed out and on the ground, Teo lost so many of his statue-like qualities. He nearly looked human.

The weight of an unfamiliar feeling settled in her chest like a body dragged down to the bottom of a lake. Liliana knew exactly what she should be feeling. Regret. Guilt. Shame. She cheated. She hurt her brother. Liliana knew little of moral equivalency, but she felt certain that a history of enmity failed to excuse her actions in that moment. She forsook so many virtues in one leap that it was difficult to identify which ones were left behind.

But guilt wasn't quite it. Guilt traveled through the blood with the caustic sting of vinegar. This was heavier but less ruinous. It provided her no solace but a sense of purpose. Liliana could not excuse her actions. Yet she still might reap their benefits for a higher good. The prospect of her sitting on the throne in place of her unfeeling brother did not *excuse* her strike. But dammit, it made it *worth* it.

The unfamiliar feeling was conviction. Grim, dark, ugly conviction. Never had such a thing felt so substantial or so necessary. Liliana needed to move. She turned to leave. She needed to find Elle, and she needed to win the competition.

A trickle of blood wound its way through his hair. She needed to move *now*. Act. Do *something*. And yet, Liliana found the idea of moving her legs impossible. She couldn't stop staring at her brother's face, the cool brown tones of his skin ashier than she had ever seen. His skull looked dented where the stone struck, as if a carver's hand had slipped, accidentally chipping the marble. The blood flowed faster, thicker.

The faint taste of bile replaced the bloody flavor of anticipation. Liliana put a hand to her mouth and stomach, sure she would be sick. Her mark continued to pound, almost torturous. She needed to move and find Elle.

But...

Liliana's head pounded with a growing pain, the tether on her heart keeping her at the scene. Why had Teo stopped moving? His earlier twitching had ceased, but it looked as though even his chest had stopped moving up and down. Her heartbeat and the pound of her mark slowed as she examined her brother's body, her mind processing the scene ten seconds after her eyes took it in. Liliana's eyes widened, and she struggled to find the air to breathe.

Inching closer to her brother, Liliana found the resolve to kneel next to his body. Breathing heavily, she extended her index and middle finger to the crook of his throat. She searched for a reason to believe her suspicions were wrong and held her hand there for more than a minute, but nothing changed. And yet, she kept her hand there in a stubborn insistence. That perhaps she hadn't committed the atrocity she thought she had. Because—she hadn't meant, in spite of everything she never wanted—it was an *accident*—but then how—

Liliana's eyes burned. She moved her fingers around and kept finding more nothing. No pulse, no breath. Nothing.

Liliana flashed back to her conversation with Teo. "You've always been brash, but all this? I simply don't understand. Why, Liliana?"

Her back burned so furiously she thought her mark might very well melt right off her body. She gritted her teeth against the pain and against her action.

Teo was dead.

"*And now your reign begins,*" the voice said, quiet. Thoughtful.

As Liliana pulled her trembling hand away, her mark burst into flames. Agony like she had never experienced engulfed all her senses. She smelled burning flesh. She tasted charcoal and ash in her teeth. She bit her tongue with all her might, willing no moans to escape. Tears streamed down her face, hot and vicious. White spots burst in her vision. Liliana gasped through the agony, trying to reach for her back and put out the fire.

Liliana had killed her brother. A truth that hammered at her as she grabbed her head and gasped. She had never loved Teo, but she had never wanted *this*. It was too far. It was too much. He was dead. This thought picked her apart like a hawk tearing through the carcass of a dead animal. *Teo was dead.*

Liliana clawed for a way through the blaze. A reason to grit her teeth and muffle her shrieks. She was convinced, in that moment, that she suffered from the retributions of the Gods. Each took their turn, delighting in pressing an invisible, scalding poker to her back. Melting her from the outside in, they would burn through her skin, her muscle, her bones, until nothing was left but the ashy remains of an irredeemable girl. For taking her brother's life, they would take hers.

In that torture, Liliana tried to force herself to find the other end. She tried to force her mind to the center of the fire, where the flames burned so hot that she became numb to the pain. While her physical body moaned and convulsed, her mind found a spot so terrible it was insensate. And in that numbing, all-consuming pain, Liliana forced herself to find her purpose.

Liliana had killed her brother. This was beyond a frayed relationship—this was an eternal mistake Liliana would always carry. But it had to be more than just a mistake. She had to make it mean more than a simple, stupid—*so, wrecking stupid*—mistake. Teo's life was more than human error.

If Liliana stayed on the forest floor and let the inferno consume her, then she would consign herself to the reality that her brother's death meant nothing. *Don't wrecking kid yourself.* That her brother's *murder* meant nothing. She couldn't simply send him to the grave and condemn herself to follow. If she did, what had it been for? He deserved more. Whatever their previous wrecking qualms, Liliana owed him more.

That meant standing up. That meant continuing to fight.

After a millennium of blinding pain, the feelings gradually subsided. Liliana, shaky, grabbed the tree to her right. Teo, unsurprisingly, lay prone in the same position she left him. What had happened? Stumbling to her feet, Liliana squinted her eyes. Hours must have passed; it was practically sunset. She didn't have time to question anything. She needed to move and find Ellegance. If she couldn't find Ellegance, she needed to get back to the clearing to get the extra points and secure her victory.

Liliana shook her head, trying to dismantle the cobwebs of pain that coated her brain. She had to track down the girl and incapacitate her. Carefully, this time. Liliana's clarity through the fire meant seeing the damn Trials through. Liliana put one foot in front of the other, beginning her slow return to the waiting crowd.

As her legs wobbled through the forest, Liliana's clarity slowly returned, a stream of water that cleared out the fuzziness.

Liliana needed every ounce of lucidity she could get. Her mind flashed to Teo's dead body. She had done what she had done. In the meantime, she would lie through her teeth until they came as easily as the red to her cheeks. All she needed to do was bend the truth. Screw *Menda*. A true leader knew when to manipulate reality to her will for the sake of her people. For the sake of the fallen. *For the sake of Teo*. It was time to sell her version of the story and take her crown.

Liliana's stride slowly gained speed and confidence as she scoured the forest for Ellegance, searching for her path to ascension. All the while, the mark on her back glowed with a dull warmth, her black dragon having turned a deep, scarlet red.

CHAPTER 24
7055.1.29

E lle, not prone to fits of anger, wanted to scream in frustration.

She walked through the forest for hours. Held her breath at every shuffle of leaves, froze in place at any brush of wind, and scoured the forest for the other contestants. Elle hunted through the forest for Liliana and Teo, praying the entire time that *Imperium* would give her the power to take one of them down should their paths cross.

"And not a wrecking thing." Elle kicked at a stick in her path. She didn't typically swear, but Trials involving her potential queenhood were a different category.

It didn't even seem possible. The forest was only so big; the likelihood that Elle couldn't find either Storidian was so low, the whole thing was nearly miraculous. Definitively annoying but nearly miraculous.

Dusk stretched lazily into the sky, taking no hurry as it splayed its orange and red fingers across the horizon. It descended with the same languid care of a feather caught on a gust of wind drifting downward. Elle hurried toward the clearing, away from the crisp silence of the forest. If she couldn't find the other contestants, the least she could do was try and get the points automatically allotted to the first who returned. The air swept past Elle's face with its sweet, fresh sigh. It was one of the nicest days Elle had seen in a while.

Elle decided the Gods had quite the sense of humor—why else would they provide such damn pleasant weather on such a momentous day?

Eventually, Elle reached the edge of the forest. Though the hum of conversation slowly seeped through the air, Elle took one more moment to scan the area before exiting the brush.

Still seeing no sign of Liliana and Teo, Elle looked at the sky and shook her head. "I swear, you are conspiring against me. Next time, if you want me to lose, save me the effort of going through all the damn Trials, *etiam?*"

The wind blew a puff so hard against her face, Elle stumbled back a little bit.

Cowed, she slowly emerged from the trees. Taking note of the clearing, Elle decided that little had changed since she and the others had been escorted into the Trial, with the exception of a group of magisters now gathered on site. Most of the other kingdoms milled about, talking in hushed voices as if the significance of the day compressed their voices down with its sheer weight. Renee and Kai laughed with Seran at a distance from the group. Renee, taken with Imperium, occasionally reached out to scratch his floppy ears. Perhaps they found common ground in their overwhelming size. Imperium, for his part, looked pained, his head drooped to the ground.

Easternalia and the Aurjnegh court passed around their own gossip like sunweed, each of its members inhaling deeply and savoring the smoke. The Nuwei Council floated to the side, its members scribbling almost absentmindedly against parchment. While the rest of the kingdoms provided anecdotes and exhibits, Nuwei ultimately wrote history. The Soj, in true fashion, stood away from the group, silent.

Naturally, nothing escaped Eliana's burning gaze. Elle watched Eliana tap Leo with her heel, nearly inconspicuous beneath the draping of her long dress. He squinted in Elle's general direction before his eyebrows flew up, finally taking note of Elle. The sun ducked beneath the stretch of the trees, its golden glow guiding her way back to the group.

Leo searched her for any sign of an altercation, of harm. Elle knew he wouldn't find anything. Her skin was unblemished, her clothes unwrinkled. Instead of emerging tattered and torn, Elle simply looked like she had just completed a very long stroll. Seran rushed over to Elle, breaking her staring contest with the king. Their eyes had the same haunted, darkened look as they'd had before the Trial of *Caecus*.

"You didn't find anybody, did you?"

"No." Elle was about to scowl at the sky before remembering the fierce gust of wind and deciding better. Elle eyed Seran. "Why?"

"I don't know." Seran shook their head, rubbing the spot in between their eyebrows. Finally, they looked back at Elle with a small smile, eyes returned to their normal, honeyed color. "But I think that's what was meant to happen. Now go! The world awaits."

A hush fell over the crowd as Elle uneasily made her way over to Eliana and Leo. With the eyes of *Terrabis* upon her, Elle's chest pushed forward, her shoulders sloping backward. While at the bakery, she always had a natural slump to her posture. She found herself unable to resume that position since everybody watched her with the expectation that she could be queen.

"So...what happens now?" Elle asked, eyes skipping between Eliana and Leo.

"Well..." Leo's brain appeared to be moving as slowly as Elle's. He ran a hand over his beard, face pinched. "At the very least, you were the first to arrive at dusk. That's half a point to you right there."

"Okay. So then I have 3.5 points, Liliana still has 3.1, and Teo has 3.6, and there are 1.5 points still up for grabs." Elle's heart sunk as she walked herself through the math. Unless Liliana and Teo managed to miss one another like Elle missed them both, there was no shot of her winning.

Her mark gave a short pound, less a reflection of Elle's feelings and more a brief supply of comfort. She tried to savor the warmth for as long as she could, closing her eyes. Until Liliana or Teo came back, Elle still had a chance. She could give herself a few more minutes of hope, if nothing else.

Leo didn't respond to her comment, staying quiet with a far-off gaze toward the forest. Elle cocked her head at the king, wondering where his mind had wandered.

"We won't know anything until the other contestants come forth," Eliana supplied after Leo returned with silence. The corner of Eliana's eyebrow twitched. Her half smile barely veiled her pulsing annoyance at Leo's reticence. "Did you, by any chance, happen to see my siblings while you were out there?"

"I didn't see anyone," Elle said, exasperated, throwing her hands in the air. "I wandered around the forest for hours before deciding to head back. I still don't see how any of that is possible."

"Are you upset about that?" Eliana raised an eyebrow.

"Of course," Elle said, running her fingers through her choppy bangs. "I mean, I spent so long worrying about this *Imperium*-forsaken trial, and now I might lose by *default*? What kind of end is that?"

The beginning of a lump grew in Elle's throat, and she tried her best to force it away before losing her grip entirely. She tried to shove away the prospect that all the change she envisioned was disappearing by the second. Elle's voice grew small. "I mean, seriously, what kind of end is that?"

Eliana's expression, ever withholding, appeared to soften just for a moment. She cupped Elle's cheek with her warm, firm hand, forcing Elle to meet her melting, black eyes.

"A perfectly fine ending to a very grand story. In any book, the ending is nothing more than a few pages. A tale needs much more than a few good pages to be one worth remembering."

Though the prospect of everything slipping through Elle's fingers was still devastating, Elle felt the tiniest bit better.

Just then, Liliana walked out of the forest, her chin jutting into the sky, shoulders thrown back, and eyes blazing such that her normal hazel almost looked red. The setting sun glittered against her cape in a way that inflamed the golden material into a fiery amber. For a moment, Liliana appeared lost in the moment, eyes open without seeing anything. After a beat, the expression faded, replaced with an indignant expression. Liliana marched toward Leo, her nostrils flared.

Her eyes widened slightly upon seeing Elle, stuttering for a second before her earlier confidence covered up any doubt. Liliana demanded in a quiet, hard voice, "How did she get here?"

"She came back at sunset, same as you." Eliana narrowed her eyes. "Where is Teo?"

"Passed out somewhere—I don't know. You told me to incapacitate him, not babysit him." Liliana's eyebrow twitched, and she sneered at her sister. "That doesn't answer my question. I overpowered one of the other contestants. She didn't. That's half a point to me. Even if she came back before me, it doesn't matter. She loses. So why in the hell is she still here?"

The singeing virulence with which the sisters addressed one another made Elle frown. She couldn't fathom speaking to any of her siblings like that. When they made jokes with one another, there was an understood foundation of love and support. The sisters in front of Elle looked like they were constantly in free fall.

Eliana raised one eyebrow at her sister. Despite their height differential, Eliana looked like she had the higher ground. "You!" Eliana turned around and effectively gave a nearby soldier a heart attack. Her voice melted into a sweet syrup, drowning the young boy in a saccharine plea. "Please do me the favor of retrieving my brother. Your time and valor will be greatly appreciated." Eliana emphasized "greatly," her thick eyelashes framing imploring eyes.

The young man practically tripped over himself as he left. Elle shook her head, as if coming out of the spell herself. Liliana rolled her eyes.

Eliana turned back to her sister, her expression calm and absolutely lethal. "The audacity that you have to question Ellegance's presence is astounding. Were you that inattentive during our father's opening speech?" Eliana asked.

Her iciness, instead of cooling down Liliana, only served to feed her flames, but she continued.

"There is still an entire point that is yet to be allocated, which will be determined based upon the judgment of the magisters overseeing this Trial. Should they allocate the entire point to Ellegance, she would win." Eliana's lips stretched into a half smile. "Any more foolish questions?"

Liliana's fingers twitched at her side, faintly curling into fists. Her mouth stretched out in a scowl. Elle took a step back, her instincts crawling beneath her skin like insects and telling her to flee. Leo's head whipped around, likely searching for a guard in case his daughter attacked.

"Wreck it! Fine, then who the hell *wins*?" Liliana growled, catching the attention of every prying ear in her vicinity. Which, of course, was *every single ear*.

Nearly everyone gathered turned to look at Leo. Obviously, none of them had an answer. The Trials were an Electarian custom. The Nuwei held qualifying exams for governance, the Vitrian empress birthed her successor, and the Aurjnegh court appointed a leader when they saw fit, ruling by majority vote until they deemed a leader necessary. They held no insight on the proceedings.

Leo hurried away from Liliana's seething and over to the group of magisters. With their heads all bent together, their robes made the group look like a large, brown boulder. Leo's presence broke the formation apart faster than an earthquake, and then he was seamlessly enveloped into the hushed discussions. Leo talked with the magisters, his veins bulging, sweat dripping from his brow, his face a dark red.

While they discussed in heated and hushed tones all at once, Liliana took the time to look over at Elle. Her clear brown eyes, tinged red, scanned Elle up and down. Finally, she shook her head and looked at Elle with an unnameable expression. Her voice was rough and hard, like a serrated blade. "I need this crown, Ellegance. I can't let you get in my way."

Elle simply stared at the princess's brown-red eyes, unsure how to respond.

Before she could come up with an answer to the overt challenge, Leo's voice cut through all conversation like a blade to the throat. "As you all know, the scoring for this, and the preceding Trials, was clear." His voice boomed through the clearing. "The contestant who arrived first would be awarded half a point. Any contestant who incapacitated another would receive half a point. This leaves Ellegance at 3.5, Liliana at 3.6, with Teo, presumably, out of the contest."

Leo's eyes tightened, and he coughed before continuing. "The magisters assembled have born witness to each Trial, in one way or another. They have remained hidden for the vast majority, allowing the contestants to complete each Trial without thinking about the extra presence in the room. That said, having observed each contestant's Trial performance, they have come to a decision on how to allocate the remaining point to the two contestants."

Leo paused, looking on the verge of a stroke. His face was bright red, sweat showing noticeably through the armpits of his plum jacket. He coughed again, much longer this time. "With 0.6 points allocated to Ellegance Fournier and 0.4 points allocated to Liliana Storidian, I am...glad to announce Ellegance Fournier as Electaria's next queen."

Renee practically squealed, pounding Kai furiously on the shoulder and giving Elle an emphatic thumbs-up. The Nuwei delegation wilted. They muttered to one another, their hands scribbling furiously. Rethinking, most likely. The Aurjnegh delegation remained still, unchanged by the news.

Elle's heart and back thundered. Her body practically burned with the announcement, so much so that Elle was worried she would be set on fire. Her ears rang, and her legs wobbled, and her mouth moved, but she was unable to say anything in response. Her mark pounded so hard that for an instant, Elle thought she might have completed her Walk. Through all this, though, her mind felt fine. Such an enormous shift in the course of her life felt impossible to process, so she emotionally felt the exact same.

"Surely you all realize this is a result that we cannot accept," Liliana called, loud enough to be heard by every delegation.

Leo turned to look at his daughter, eyes wide. Elle, still caught in her own elation, slowly looked to Liliana, feeling hazy. Every member of the crowd gaped at the princess, their attention a helpless fly in the web of her speech.

"This is something we cannot accept," Liliana repeated, ignoring the wild looks she received from both Leo and Eliana. The words registered in Elle's brain seconds after Liliana said them, her mind processing the entire situation too slowly.

"I acknowledge that there are two candidates left," Liliana said, her voice clear and steady. "One is from the city, young and arguably impressionable. One has spent her life baking bread and gallivanting through the streets of the kingdom, doing *Imperium* knows what. One is given legitimacy through her mark but little else. And we put *her* on the throne through the arbitrary decree of a group of magisters? No!"

Liliana raised her voice, rough and strong. "Whereas the other is of royal descent. She has spent her life in the palace walls, learning its inner mechanisms. Learning from its people. She has served on its Education Council, trained with some of its finest military, and championed for its interests at every stage of her life. Giving the throne to Ellegance at this point would be sheer folly when *I* stand ready to take the helm."

Liliana turned her intense, burning gaze to Leo, and a shiver ran down the king's spine. "*I* should be Electaria's queen." Liliana spoke with so much conviction that a large number of people nodded their heads.

As Elle's mind caught up with the present, her mark roared in response. Like two wolves squaring off to fight for alpha, her body instinctively growled at her challenger. Part of it was an instinctive response, but the other part was conviction. Watching the princess grapple for power she had just lost, Elle came upon a realization. Instead of losing to the rules they had agreed to play by, Liliana had now invented new rules to accommodate her victory. The Trials were supposed to find the best leader. Through her refusal of the outcome, Liliana denied Electaria the leader the Trials—the Gods—had chosen. She cared more about her own power than having the best person on the throne. It was the confirmation of a suspicion Elle had cultivated but hadn't dared believe.

It was more than the notion that Elle simply understood the city's people better. It extended beyond Elle's insecurities that Teo and Liliana knew about the country's various policies. It was an idea that emerged from their first conversation, but Elle only understood it now.

Elle would be a better ruler than Liliana.

The confidence startled Elle. Though she had desired the crown before, for the first time, she felt like she *deserved* it. The crowd slowly emerged from Liliana's spell. Titters scattered through everyone, reflecting a clear division in reactions. Some nodded their heads slowly, while others looked entirely unconvinced. Leo opened his mouth to speak, but Elle beat him to it.

"Princess Liliana has a point. I didn't have tutors growing up, and I don't know all the etiquette. The court, if I'm being honest, still terrifies me." Elle smiled, small pockets of chuckles joining her from the crowd. "She's spent her entire life in the castle, and I'm just a daughter of two *amazing* bakers in the city." She shrugged, seeming nonchalant. A breeze blew her choppy bangs away from her face, fanning out and framing her violet eyes beneath. They glowed with a thrilled determination.

"But"—she bit off the word, hanging on to it tantalizingly, letting the crowd lean in, the bulk of their curiosity forcing them toward her—"It's because of those two bakers that I was raised in the city. Not behind walls a rock's skip away. *In* the actual city. I know this kingdom in a way that—no offense, princess—she never will. I understand the way deals are struck on these streets, the way merchants barter and change their prices, the education system, even. Liliana knows about these issues from a distance, but I've experienced all these things in my daily life.

"She's done her homework—I'll give her that. And I applaud the princess for her hard work up until this point. But I don't think it's enough to be queen. Liliana may have learned about the people inside the castle, but I know of the people outside these walls. And, trust me—there are far more people out there," Elle pointed in the direction of the city, "than in here. I won the Trials. The Trials ordained by the House and the Gods themselves. At the end of the day, I've earned this throne. And that's all there is to it."

Silence swirled around Elle, allowing everyone a moment to let her words sink in. Leo's eyebrows were still up. Eliana smiled at Elle, a fondness melting the mystery she traditionally wore in public. Renee watched from the crowd, her face threatening to split apart from the proud beam that stretched across her countenance.

The empress leaped forward, her voice so deep it could start avalanches as she said, "The Vitrian kingdom is in support of Ellegance Fournier assuming the monarchy. She is the only option for the throne and will undoubtedly prove to be a phenomenal leader of Electaria and its people."

The words detonated in the clearing, obliterating any previous notions of how the Trial of *Imperium* was supposed to operate. Leo's jaw dropped. Eliana's face froze. Elle's face became puzzled. She figured different countries supported different candidates, but such preferences had no place in the actual Trials. Each nation operated and traded closely together, but they maintained sovereign borders and governments.

"Through this statement, Renee threatens to undermine the very sovereignty on which an Electarian throne rests," Eliana said through her teeth to Elle, eyes narrowed into slits.

Councilor Pen, one of the dignitaries from Nuwei, stepped forward, blue eyes determined. "Seeing as Prince Teo is out of the running entirely, we stand with the Vitrians in our support of Ellegance Fournier as queen of Electaria." The Nuwei council behind him nodded, affirming their support.

"Foolish—all of you!" Easternalia cried, stepping forward. Elle blinked at the explosion of noise and drama. "Any throne would be threatened by having such an inexperienced plebeian on the throne. Princess Liliana is the only viable candidate left to assume the throne. *She* should be queen of Electaria!"

Each kingdom argued with one another, their voices rising as they defended their chosen candidate. Elle, far from her previous confidence, watched the chaos with wide eyes. Liliana observed the scene, her gaze narrowed and moving quickly around, as if solving a complex math equation in her head.

"Everything I feared is coming to fruition," Eliana muttered before hurrying to reason with a Nuwei councilor. As she jogged to control the damage of the outburst, she looked at Leo, flashing him a quick smile. "You need to do something as soon as wrecking possible."

"What do you all think you're doing?" Leo exploded, his yell easily surmounting all squabbling. "You all are to participate in these Trials as a show of good faith! You do not get a say in our future, nor our leadership! In these statements, you all compromise the very idea of Electaria as its own nation!"

"What would you have us do? What do you propose, Leo?" Renee threw her hands in the air. "We instead let Electaria fall in a downward spiral of instability as your daughter tries to stage a coup? That would be ruinous for all of us!"

The soldier from earlier burst into the clearing, panting, sweating, and shaking. His shoulders hunched over, and his lower lip trembled. His voice, though small, reached every ear from the sheer weight of his words.

"I found Prince Teo's body. He's not unconscious." His expression turned empty, haunted. "He's dead."

CHAPTER 25
7055.1.29

Aoran kept trying to clear the lump in his throat to no avail. He tracked his way through the forest, swiping at his eyes every few steps. They stung with an incessant burn, as if somebody poured lemon juice into already sleep-swollen sockets. He cursed, jamming the heel of his hand against his right eye. *How incredibly annoying.*

When the soldier arrived in the clearing, the Captain took control. A dead prince meant a potential assassin, and a potential assassin meant getting everyone important far away from the crime and one another. Both made the soft diplomats easy targets.

The day meant to crown Electaria's next monarch quickly transformed into a disaster drill as the Four wrangled their charges, alert and scanning for potential threats. Well, except, of course, Je. The soldier had stood there, crestfallen and motionless, until the Captain snapped at him to lead the gathered diplomats back to the castle. In its own way, the Captain's sternness was a blessing that gave Je a modicum of direction amid his own rampaging storm.

The Captain had corralled all her soldiers, ordering them to keep watch as the diplomats and royals made their way back to safety. Aoran watched with detached curiosity as Chauron joined the swarm, his face grim. Aoran wondered how the day's events played into Chauron's mission at the palace. Aoran found he didn't give a shit. The Guide could smoke the Gods out of the heavens for all Aoran cared.

The Captain had ordered Aoran to stay behind, charging him with finding Teo's body and anyone or anything lurking nearby. Beneath the numbness of his shock, Aoran's body managed to remember that he was a soldier first. He nodded his head, turning toward the forest despite Liliana's insistence that he remain at her side. She had gripped his arm, demanding he stay. Aoran assured the Captain that Liliana was quite capable of fending for herself—as demonstrated by their last run-in when she landed him on the floor—and set off to find the prince's corpse.

With the slowly dropping sun, the air grew colder and bit at him beneath his uniform. Aoran couldn't help his bitter laugh as he thought of the royals hunched over beneath the security of the Electarian military, plodding back to the palace. The whole thing had a dark kind of irony. What was supposed to have been a joyous march had all but turned into a funeral procession.

A deep ache resonated through Aoran's body, like he had gotten his ass kicked in training the previous day and was still sore from the beating. Other than that, he didn't feel that much. Yes, he struggled to keep his heart locked away in its familiar, little cage. It gnashed at him with more vehemence than usual, misery feeding its strength. But in its cage, it stayed.

Death was the mistress of military service—a woman he knew he shouldn't mess around with, but into whose clutches he would inexorably fall. The men who ruminated on Death the most—spent their time fearing her, evading her—tended to die the fastest. Much like gravity, Death had to be accepted not as a force with which to be reckoned, but an inevitability with which to bear. Death was as much a part of Aoran's job as taking orders.

But Death ceased to exist in those terms outside the confines of the uniform. When Death made her appearance in the palace or in the city, she came as an unwelcome guest instead of a regular at the bar. Aoran knew Teo would die one day. The same way Eliana, Leo, Je, Dayanara, and Liliana would; hell, even the *Captain* would eventually succumb to Death. But those kinds of deaths were fated tragedies, far in the future. Not devastations in the present.

Aoran swiped at his eyes. Damn things needed to stop burning.

A small, stupid part of Aoran wondered if maybe the soldier had simply been wrong. The young ones always wanted to prove their mettle. Maybe he craved so badly to be the bearer of such all-important news that he rewove the threads of the story into material much finer than it was. Plus, the soldier had gotten orders from Eliana. Aoran had seen plenty of other young guys and girls wreck up an assignment from their heads being so filled with thoughts of the princess. His heart relaxed, just a bit, settling back down behind its bars. Maybe the soldier had simply been wrong.

After what seemed like only minutes walking through the forest, Aoran stumbled upon Teo's body.

Teo's dark eyes stared blankly up at Aoran. His body sprawled out across the forest floor, the purple of his cape a stark contrast against the dirt. Teo's body, splayed out, was frozen in a way that made him look like the main dish of an especially decadent feast. A shiver crawled through Aoran. The blood vessels around Teo's eyes popped and dilated in different areas, looking like red spiderwebs reaching out toward the rest of his face. Aoran's stomach heaved. He locked his disgust away with his heart. He needed to see this.

Teo looked like a mosaic. His skin faded from a reddish-brown into a kaleidoscope of purple and blue hues. Aoran carefully lifted the prince's head, ignoring the way it flopped uselessly about in his hands. Blood matted Teo's hair in the back, sticky from a wound on the top of his skull. Aoran gawked at the injury. His head was indented so deeply that the white of his skull showed. Aoran placed the back of the prince's head down, having seen enough of the beastly damage. He focused on the face. Bruises surrounded his mouth and nose, discoloring the skin of his cheeks. Between the popped blood vessels and the contusions, it almost looked like Teo had been doing his makeup for a stage performance. The thought made Aoran nauseous.

He stood up and gripped the bicep of his right arm with his left hand. He laughed out loud, nerves frayed. "Stop shaking, Aoran. Je will never let you live that down."

Aoran's heart banged against its cage, begging to be let out and mourn. At the very least Teo deserved that. The prince, despite everything and everyone he had been raised around, meant well. Such a small thing as intention meant so much when applied to a world where ulterior motives were so pervasive they managed to outnumber the oxygen molecules in the air.

But mourning meant breaking. And Aoran had to be strong because he was a soldier who'd seen death before. And he was Liliana's personal guard who needed to stay focused. And he was a wrecking follower of *Viribus*, dammit. *It shouldn't be this hard.*

And then he thought, *Strength is not the absence of fear, anxiety, and their many, terrible brethren.*

Aoran gave a half growl, half laugh, running his fingers and pulling his long platinum hair. Son of a *malum*.

"I hate it when you're wise," he said aloud to himself. Thankfully, there was no response.

Aoran unlocked the part of his mind that imprisoned his heart. He let the emotions ravage his body. The news of Teo's death rampaged through Aoran's body like acid, searing its way through every crevice and vein it encountered. His mark burned with an electric pulse at the same time, setting every nerve on fire. Strength, contrary to widespread belief, hurt like *hell*. A single tear tracked down Aoran's cheek.

Teo and Aoran had not been close. Aoran held no idyllic notions of what he and the prince meant to one another. But Teo had always been a man to watch, if not admire. Unwavering, he lived with his own ideals, and he cared about the people he was raised to serve. The prince, like anybody at the throne, would have been a flawed monarch. The prince had been utterly devoid of charm and lacked the dexterity to smoothly navigate court politics. His success in government up until that point relied on his reputation of straightforward reliability. But all monarchs bore faults. Ultimately, Teo would have been a *good* king. Selfless, devoted, intentional.

"Wreck that." Aoran laughed sharply through the swelling in his throat. He thought back to the day when he talked to the prince in the city, returning from Teo's time helping the people. Good king be damned—Teo had been a good man.

Aoran gave himself one more heavy sigh, one more choked cough. The electric pulse of his mark subsided, settling into an almost approving thrum. He closed his eyes, whispering a quick thanks to *Viribus*. He sent another prayer up to *Imperium*. He didn't think the leader of Gods would listen to him, but it was worth a shot. Then he took a breath, doing his best to clear his head.

The Captain had sent him here for a reason. He needed to heed *all* his advice. Strength allowed him mourning, but it did not disavow him his duty.

Aoran searched the area. His jade eyes pulsed with the effort of staying as open as possible, bright and wide as he scoured for evidence. He rifled for anything that contextualized the prince's death. If Aoran was lucky, he would catch a glimpse of signs pointing to a specific kingdom or motive.

Unfortunately, Aoran was trained in combat. Not investigation. Frustrated, he saw nothing. The trees in front of him looked like any normal, stupid forest. Aoran unsheathed one of his sickle swords, slashing down one of the branches above with a growl. *Imperium* help him, he refused to wrecking walk away without an answer to the question that would surely haunt King Leo's eyes. He closed his eyes, focusing on the electricity buzzing from his mark. He had to have some faith in his patron God. He had to trust that *Viribus* endowed Aoran with the strength of the truth. He opened his jade eyes, examining his surroundings with renewed determination.

Teo exhibited few marks other than the vicious dent on the back of his head and his grotesque discoloration. That essentially eliminated all traditional means of assassination. Stab wounds would have been easily noticeable, poison too slow acting. So what in the hell had the assassin used to crush the prince's skull? The branches of the trees were far too high to be of use to anyone—likely nothing there. The roots protruding from the ground might have tripped Teo but failed to explain any of the popped blood vessels and bruises. If anything, the annoying things would have sent him limping away, sprained but alive. Aoran scoured the ground, his eyes settling on a pile of stones a few paces away.

His mark buzzed, jolting him to life. Aoran's head compressed in on itself, as if something pushed his brain to the side of his skull to make room. A firm and distinctly *exasperated* something. Aoran grimaced and stumbled back, holding his skull. His head was full, overflowing with a pressure that threatened to send him to his knees.

Suddenly, he yanked his hand away from his aching temples. He stared blankly at his hand. Aoran hadn't done that to himself.

Before he could begin to process this horror, Aoran's body began walking. His legs moved on their own but with none of his easy-going gait. He...lumbered. A phantom pain pricked at his ankle, making normal walking impossible. Aoran hobbled forward.

"Damn things never heal right."

Except Aoran hadn't said those words. His panic grasped at him with oil-covered fingers, unable to find purchase and sliding off his emotions. As the foreign pressure shoved against his brain, he felt insulated from almost all other sensations. He watched the world through a window, banging on the glass and shouting himself hoarse inside his own mind. He wanted to feel terrified. He wanted to feel *something*—but couldn't. Aoran hammered harder.

"Wrecking stop it!" Aoran roared out loud.

But it didn't sound like Aoran. The voice boomed with the familiar sound of ratcheting thunder and barging feet on a battlefield. His body grasped his head and squeezed his eyes shut. He took an unsteady breath in and a shaky step forward, seething.

"It's hard enough to do this without you fighting back."

In a moment of horrifying clarity, Aoran realized why the voice was familiar. Why he seemed to be a stranger inside his own body, watching from the inside out.

Viribus? Aoran asked within the confines of himself, a sense of petrified dread building. He almost hoped the answer was no.

"Shut up. I need to concentrate."

Aoran approached the stones slowly, his hand reaching out to pick up one larger stone in particular. He turned this stone over, immediately zeroing in on the rusted color that stained its side. The protection around his brain melted away, slowly but surely yielding control back to Aoran. The pressure in his brain dissipated, a phantom of its former self. His mark sent one more electric jolt running through his body. Aoran decided this was an experience best mulled over when he wasn't investigating a royal murder. And when he'd had enough alcohol and sunweed to forget it in the first place.

He gripped the stone harder, giving the blemish a small sniff. He revolted, pulling the rock away from his face. No doubt. Blood.

But that didn't make any sense. Why would Teo's blood be on a stone and not a blade or arrow? A stone was too crude a weapon for an assassin. Aoran looked at the stone, turning it over in his hands with a probing stare. Dammit, no assassin would be so dumb as to leave the murder weapon behind. It lacked any of the finesse in which the profession prided itself.

The more Aoran turned the stone over in his hands, the more confused he became. The murder had obviously been effective but sloppy. Nobody struck another man with that kind of force without intent to kill. But the instrument of death lay barely more than a skip away from Teo's corpse. No attempt had been made to conceal his body. The murder must have been a spur-of-the moment decision but one with pure conviction behind the strike.

A sick feeling dawned on Aoran. It descended in his body, sliding down the walls of his stomach like rancid meat, the pungent taste rising in the back of his throat. The stone in his hand looked to be miles away, held by another man entirely. Aoran was many, many things. Lazy, cocky, apathetic to all who existed outside his tiny world. However, in a man of nearly innumerous flaws, the words "blind" and "stupid" would not find themselves. As much as he wanted to believe Elle capable of murder, he knew the notion was ludicrous. The girl claimed not to have seen Liliana or Teo during the Trial. Pinning the action on her was an impossible stretch, even for his imagination.

Aoran debated chucking the stone into the forest. In many ways, it would be more trouble than it was worth. For the kingdom and for Aoran. The stone was small and insignificant. And yet it meant the end of an era Aoran held dear. If nobody found the wrecking rock, then he could stroll back to the castle and report a tragic assassination, likely the work of an anarchist or rebel group. Each kingdom would emerge unscathed, and nobody had to be persecuted for parricide. Liliana would somehow become queen, and everything would be okay.

His mind flashed back to every single time she threatened somebody, every time the fire in her eyes sent chills down his spine. He imagined her bursting from the trees, stone in hand, her eyes alight with the same wrath that haunted her on her worst days. Bile coated the back of his throat. Or, Liliana would somehow become queen, and nothing would be okay.

As the thought swelled in his mind, his mark sent an electric shock through him so strong he gasped, falling to his knees. His body twitched as the electricity swept through his body, lighting up every nerve. He gritted his teeth and squeezed his eyes shut. The pain was overwhelming. It was also familiar. It was the same agony that gripped him the day he completed his Walk.

Surrounded by the corpses of his battalion, Aoran had forced his eyes open. Then he forced himself to his feet. Every movement took what felt like all his strength, weighed down by the souls of all the dead. The dead gave him no hope, no inspiration. Instead, they threatened to drag him back to the ground, lulling him into their ranks with a sweet song that promised an end. Aoran swatted off their voices. He drove past the feeling of their ghostly fingers gripping his uniform, trying to pull him backward. Slowly, Aoran checked the bodies for anyone living. He guided the three remaining soldiers back to the main military encampment. When they finally made it to the border of their camp, Aoran collapsed to the ground and stayed down for three days. Simply standing up amid the carnage had taken all his strength.

Aoran bit the cloth of his tunic, screaming into the fabric. He wished his heart would let him lie here and cover up the whole affair with his own death. Strength, true strength, hurt viciously. Following his patron God thus far had failed to lead Aoran to happily ever after. It just led him to more ever afters.

Eyes swollen, face detached, Aoran stood once more. His mark gave another faint buzz. Aoran pocketed the stone, unflinching, before reaching to hoist the dead prince over his shoulder.

Aoran trekked out of the forest, bogged down by Teo's dead body and his own thoughts.

His mind replayed its own gruesome reenactment of what she might have looked like, how defenseless Teo must have been. He kept zeroing in on her right arm—Liliana always favored her right hand—and the way she had to have driven the rock into her own brother's head. She had an arm whose strength Aoran had spent time building. An arm whose practice with swords and fighting had turned a bureaucrat's writing hand into a lethal weapon.

That replay warred with the image of Liliana's betrayed face.

Aoran laughed again to himself, the bitter sound watery and muffled. "Oh, it is going to be just *delightful* to spend the rest of my life processing this."

***

Aoran arrived back at the clearing at night. The exhaustion his body experienced from hoisting the prince's weight still paled in comparison to the weariness that captured his mind. It was the kind of fatigue that settled in the bones, refusing to be cured by sleep. Didn't mean Aoran wasn't going to try. His hands twitched, aching for his sunweed in a desperate way that almost took him by surprise. The yellow smoke seemed like the only thing that might bring him a semblance of peace in the coming months.

A quiver at the corner of his eye distracted Aoran. Squinting through the darkness, Aoran watched Eliana emerge from an opening in a small hill about the height of Aoran's chest. Once out, she grabbed one of the large rocks at the base of the hill and dragged it to cover the opening. Despite looking like the rock weighed twice as much as she did, it slid easily into place, as if greased on the bottom. As she backed away and dusted off her dress, the rock seamlessly melted into the hillside background.

Aoran put the pieces together. The final picture combined her ambiguous role in the castle as well as her insistence on eavesdropping on the diplomats. Even her smile, wrapped in mystery and dripping with playful secrets, clued him in. Aoran guessed that wherever a secret in the kingdom, Eliana lay next to it, kissing her way up its neck until its contents sat in her palms. Who better to perform espionage than a follower of *Menda*, after all? If the day hadn't been such an emotional riptide, Aoran might have even been shocked. Instead, he trudged forward, his mind focused on the prince draped over his shoulder.

Eliana met him in the clearing, arms wrapped around herself. Though she kept her face down to remain covered in shadows, the moonlight that fell across her like silk made her form look luminous. Even on such a terrible night, the woman had the indecency to look breathtaking.

Seeing another individual, the earlier events came rushing back to Aoran in full focus. The enormity of what had happened gripped Aoran like a toy, squeezing at his heart and forcing his mouth open. *Viribus* possessed him, took control of his body. His feelings were utterly inexplicable, and in some ways, his instincts said the only way to explain them was to simply speak to someone else.

But as he approached, Eliana looked up, revealing her face. Her bottom lip wobbled, barely noticeable. Her eyes were frozen with an off-putting shine, caught between the glimmers of tears and the glint of somebody holding back her fury. *No*, Aoran thought to himself with a small shake of his head. He would save the incident for another date. He wouldn't be putting an additional burden on her.

Aoran pulled Teo's body off his shoulders and placed it onto the ground. The prince flopped onto the grass with an ungraceful thud. Aoran winced. He should have probably taken care to be a little bit more delicate with Teo's sister standing right in front of Aoran.

"So it's true," Eliana said softly, her velvet voice cracking. She gazed down at her brother, her black eyes unreadable. She watched Teo's body for several minutes before finally looking up sharply at Aoran. No smile played on her face, but no tears streaked her cheeks either. "What did you find?"

"I'm surprised the Electarian spymaster couldn't figure that out herself," Aoran muttered, digging the stone out of his pocket and tossing it to the princess.

She caught the stone without flinching, quickly turning it over in her hands. Eliana looked up briefly from the stone, unimpressed. "Don't pat yourself on the back. Fools only see me when I want to be seen."

Aoran frowned.

"And I need evidence," she said, ignoring Aoran. "My job isn't based in crystals balls and suppositions. It's data based. We listen, we collect, we analyze. I can't, in my right mind, accuse my sister of murder if I don't at least have proof." Her honeyed voice hardened into something sharper, more scathing than Aoran had ever heard from her full lips. "But this should be enough. This combined with some other things I've collected paint a pretty damning picture of what happened today."

"So it was Liliana?" He barely recognized the sound of his own voice.

"Nobody else would have acted so thoughtlessly but so effectively," Eliana said and gripped the stone tighter. "She probably saw an opportunity and just took it. That's my sister for you. Passionate and determined to the core."

Aoran remained silent. The words floated in his head like air, real but lacking in substance. They were nothing he hadn't already figured out himself. Hearing it out loud didn't make him feel any worse. It damn well didn't make him feel any better, either.

"For what it's worth, Aoran," Eliana said, her face bitter but her dark eyes sincere. "I'm sorry."

Aoran was glad she said nothing more. The apology could be for anything. For the grief of Teo's death, the antipathy for Liliana's decision, even the devastating loss of Liliana herself. Each held its own in the tragedy arena.

Aoran wished it was easy to condemn Liliana; if he shook his head and cursed her name into the air, he wouldn't feel the impending loss of her so acutely. If he wished her good riddance, just rolled his eyes and tutted, he would circumvent the pain. Maybe if he could muster up a little more disgust in his princess's actions, this body-aching nausea would leave him now.

But love rarely worked so simply. Humans spent centuries compartmentalizing people and actions. One bad action did not a bad person make, the same as one grandiose gesture failed to produce a saint.

Liliana's name would be muttered in secrecy from now on. It would be tainted, disassociated entirely with the kingdom she grew up loving. Every piece of legislation she fought for, every ordinance she helped to enact, would carry the malodor of her brother's death. Aoran almost envied the kingdom. The affair would be nothing more than a cautionary tale for its people, a story of unfettered ambition and the consequences such uninhibited passions carried.

Aoran wished he could do the same. He wanted to put Liliana in a straight, little box entitled Villain and be done with it. But much like the real princess, she could not be categorized so neatly.

Liliana was the closest thing Aoran had to family. One night, even one terrible, horrifying night, couldn't erase the years he had spent teasing her. The sight of Teo's corpse couldn't expunge the mesmerizing sight of Liliana's burning, hazel eyes when she chased something she wanted. Temperamental and scathing, she was so, so imperfect. But that imperfection had been a constant in Aoran's life ever since Juliana plucked him from the streets.

The thoughts of Liliana made him sick right now. They might make him sick for the rest of his life. But that biliousness would never be able to remove those thoughts. Her memory was tainted but irrepressible from his conscious.

"Where is she now?" he finally asked, unable to say her name out loud. It made every fear tangible, every guilt real.

Eliana looked at him with something caught between pity and bitterness. "I'm having the news spread through my network as fast as possible. Liliana's nowhere to be found."

CHAPTER 26
7055.1.29

Elle never minded chaos. In fact, she considered herself an avid fan of its anarchic touch. Adventures sprung from seeds of disorder. Exploits had no place in an ordered world, their existence undermined by intractable structure. Elle frowned at the notion—how incredibly dreary such a world sounded. Uncertainty sparkled with potential, a diamond of possibilities for her to mine from its cavern. The world would be a dull place without its manic luster.

However, when Elle traditionally thought of chaos, she thought of its macro beauty. She thought of storms raging, oceans crashing. She imagined the wild bustle of people flooding Electaria's streets. She saw the ecstatic dancing of festivals, bare feet burning holes in the roads from the force of their steps. She did not think of soldiers swarming an area like their own breed of pestilence. She did not think of diplomats, each highly ranked in their respective kingdom, attempting to order around one another. She did not think of a frenzied fear looming over every person like a deleterious smog, its fumes smothering each red face and waggling finger.

This was not the kind of chaos in which Elle basked.

This pernicious smoke of chaos took hold the moment their procession arrived back at the palace. Upon returning, everybody pulled away from one another. Each one marched around the halls, a hero with their own mission central in their mind. The Nuwei demanded they all flee the castle, lest they befall a similar fate to the poor prince. The Vitrians called for a military search party, demanding blood of the offending party in retribution for Teo's death. The Aurjnegh cried for a monarch—*she* might be able to restore order. Elle gulped at that exclamation. Each believed themselves to be the hero of this particular narrative.

While such individualistic gallantries produced legacies of valor in storybooks, in reality they produced unencumbered bedlam. Soldiers scattered about, attempting with futility to secure a rapidly fluctuating perimeter as diplomats ran amok. Dignitaries bumped into one another and burst into arguments. People eyed each other warily, insisting on all hands being kept out in the open. Everyone was so focused on their own agendas that they failed to see the one overlapping commonality on everyone's minds: safety.

Elle watched, a helpless feeling smothering any earlier burning from her mark. When Elle had spoken against Liliana in the clearing, her back had pounded in a fierce way. In a proud way. Such bravado had turned to smoke and mirrors, had quickly puffed out.

Teo's death filled Elle with an empty sadness, the kind that faded with a few nights' sleep and the continual churn of daily living. She was sorry the prince died, the same way she would be sorry if a teacher she admired passed. She mourned for the world's loss of Teo's mind and spirit but ultimately knew so little of the prince. She mourned him as a candidate and as a good man but not as a friend.

Elle frowned to herself. It sounded so cold when she phrased it like that. It was almost cruel she should feel so little when no doubt the worlds of King Leo and the princesses had ripped apart at the seams. Elle's mind, as it always tended to do, lingered on Eliana. Eliana's face had immediately lost its playful mystery when the soldier came back with his report. No tears had fallen down her cheeks, but her expression had shifted. Hardened. Elle wondered if such a change might be permanent. The princess had disappeared shortly thereafter, her form vanished in the throngs of escaping royals.

"Elle," Seran urged her, yanking her back to the present, "we need to move. We should go find somewhere to hide until all this blows over."

Elle's Guide had stuck to her side with an impressive tenacity. They gripped Elle's arm, their small fingers digging fiercely into Elle's bony arms. Any attempt to separate the two was met with Seran's mesmerizing, golden eyes. The intruding party always walked away, swaying like they just finished a night of drinking. *Forget being a Guide*, Elle thought to herself. Their talents were wasted—Seran would have made a much better watchdog.

But still, when Seran spoke, Elle listened. Elle cocked her head at the Guide, her eyebrows furrowing. "Are you having one of your feelings?"

"No, but I'm not an idiot either." Seran looked at her like she was crazy. They tugged on Elle's arm, their voice urgent. "One dead candidate can quickly turn into two if you're too intent on being foolish."

"Couldn't have said it better myself," a low voice interrupted Seran and her. "Though you two are slower than a merchant paying his taxes. Let's get a wrecking move on, shall we?"

Elle wistfully imagined Penelope crowing from behind the intruder, "*Language!*" In reality, Elle turned around to behold a middle-aged man draped in geometric Nuwei robes. He ran a weathered hand over his bald, umber head, regarding Elle and Seran with annoyance. The expression reminded Elle of the way her ma looked at a loaf of bread when it failed to rise—one of irritation, inconvenience. Thanks to the faint frown lines on his chin, Elle struggled to say if that expression came from the pair or from his natural propensity to look cantankerous. Elle focused so intently on the stranger with the brash interruption that she almost missed the dark look that passed over Seran's face.

"Who are you?" Elle asked, eager. From his crusted scowl to his carefree use of profanity, he was unlike anyone Elle had met at the court thus far.

"He's a Guide," Seran answered sourly before he could speak. They pulled away from Elle to cross their arms, disapproval screaming from their tiny form. "A lousy one, but a Guide nonetheless." Their eyes narrowed. "What do you know, Chauron?"

"A Guide about four decades this wrecking pip-squeak's senior, and that's a question better asked and answered in privacy," he snarled, making no effort to conceal his distaste. "Of course, we can stay out here and shoot the shit if that's your wish. But remember, every second we spend out here is another second *your,*" spittle flew from his mouth, "charge's life is in danger."

Their pixie face flushed. Seran grabbed Elle's arm with forcefulness. "Fine. Let's go, Elle."

The three dipped out of the room, disregarded while everyone else focused on their individual tempest. Seran forged the way, their angry footsteps barely making a dent in the carpet. More soldiers roamed the hallways than usual. This created an odd little dance for the three, composed of ducking behind walls and holding their breath. A faint melody plucked out the tempo in the back of her head. Step, step, step, duck, step, step, hold. *A strange waltz, no doubt, but far more useful than the Vitrian jig*, she thought to herself, a frown crossing her face. It felt like years since her da taught her the lively bursts and leaps of her ancestral dance.

When they finally arrived at the throne room, they slipped in one by one, careful to not open the door so wide it might arouse suspicion.

Nobody else loitered in the room, naturally. With only the thrones for shelter, the room offered no protection from potential threats. While that made it a pretty terrible place to hide from a killer, the lack of defense made it a wonderful place to hide from everybody else.

The throne room lost some of its splendor in the dark, devoid of the light and people that highlighted its opulence. A few, sparse torches provided some light, likely for servants using the room as a shortcut. Otherwise, the room existed in darkness when not in use by the royal family. Elle soaked in the shadows, a laugh bubbling in her chest.

Elle looked at Seran and Chauron, a painful and strange reminiscence gripping her. "The last time I was in here, I was declaring my candidacy for the throne. It feels like an entire lifetime ago. It feels like another Elle ago," she said softly, shaking her head. "It still astounds me how the empress found me that day."

Chauron stared at her like she was stupid. "You surely don't believe that such an event was a wrecking coincidence, do you?"

"I mean..." Elle blinked and scratched the back of her head. "I've never really had any reason to believe otherwise."

"Never had a reason—" Chauron spluttered, throwing his hands into the air and waving them. "The fact that you've made it this far is the clearest goddamn reason I could give you! This shit doesn't happen coincidentally. The Gods, for whatever reason, chose you. And now we need to make sure you don't get killed so you can see through whatever wrecking plans they have in store for you."

"Now, hold on." Seran stopped him, golden eyes smoldering, their voice firm. "The Gods watch over the humans, but they rarely involve themselves directly with human affairs. Elle is a follower of *Imperium*, but she's made it this far on her own. She didn't even have *me* to help her for most of it!"

Chauron blinked at Seran before moaning, dragging his hands down his face. "*Caecus* help me! *Imperium* sent the kid a wrecking moron as a Guide. Why in the wreck do you *think* Lord-y *Imperium* chose this kid? You know as well as I do that nobody but royalty bears *Imperium*'s mark. But *she*," Chauron shoved a finger upward, gesturing to the ceiling before pointing that same finger aggressively at Elle, "chose *her*. Give me your best guess. Why do you think? Her gargantuan muscles? Her unmatched intelligence? Of course not!" He threw his hands in the air.

Elle frowned. Whatever point the Guide planned on making, he sure wanted to do it as cruelly as possible.

Chauron continued his rant, his onyx eyes practically popping out of his skull. "*Imperium* placed this girl in the path of Renee and Kai because she was open. That's it. To beat the Electarian trials, you either need to grow through the process or outsmart the damn thing entirely. Liliana was set to outsmart the things from the beginning. She needed a challenger. Elle was just undeveloped enough to be prime for that kind of growth. It didn't hurt that she was wrecking Vitrian—Renee practically had no choice but to take her along."

"Wait." Elle's head spun. Seran's face shifted back and forth between distress and fury, as if they couldn't quite decide which emotion took precedence. "Why did Liliana need a challenger? She had Teo. Why bring in someone else?"

"They didn't know. *Caecus* just had a feeling."

Elle wanted to hit something—from the Guides to the Gods, part of her felt cheated that nothing she prayed to throughout her life was remotely omniscient.

Chauron's dark eyes gleamed, an obsidian glow in the darkness of the room. "Sometimes they listen when he does. Sometimes they don't. This time they did.

"I don't yet know why you're here." He shook his head, angry. "*Caecus* reached out to me for the first time in decades to keep Liliana off the throne. Now he's just telling me to keep you alive. You have a role in all this shit, whether you like it or not. Probably has something to do with the precious princess killing her brother and completing her Walk."

His face somehow grew darker. "But she did it on the wrong side."

Wait, what?

"You felt it too?" Seran's voice was soft, vulnerable without the strength of the light.

Chauron grunted. "Pretty sure every wrecking Guide on *Terrabis* felt that."

"Felt *what*?" Elle tried not to let her frustration show, but the conversation existed in the planes of Gods, beyond her reach despite being in her destiny. She felt left behind in the decisions over her very own life.

"Liliana completed her Walk as a follower of *malum*. That kind of thing happens, sometimes. Usually *malum* pulls her followers from the other Gods, people of lesser stations. Liliana was a princess. She was a follower of *Imperium*. She had practically as much spiritual energy as *malum* could possibly hope for."

"When Liliana...you know, *killed* him, she finished her Walk like an explosion. The ripples of *malum's* power were so strong it felt like getting the wind knocked out of you." Seran looked at the ground, as if ashamed. "It wasn't supposed to happen like that. Liliana had Imperium. He was a Guide for *Imperium*. He was supposed to...you know, *guide* her. Be her tether to the goodness in her. It just shouldn't have happened."

"But it did. Her guide failed," Chauron said bluntly.

Seran whirled on him.

"Funny words from you, Chauron." Seran's eyebrows drew together, and their fists balled at their sides.

"Oh?" His scowl molded into a sneer, nasty and condescending. "Why's that?"

"*Every* Guide knows what happened to your charge," Seran exclaimed, hotly. They threw their hands in the air. "You're practically a living cautionary tale for all of us. We come down to earth with so little memory, but we remember our purpose. And part of remembering our purpose is remembering how royally one of our own wrecked it all up."

A cold sweat broke out along the base of Elle's neck. She had never heard her Guide swear.

"I'm thrilled they continue to teach you all campfire stories, without ever preparing you for your actual duty." Chauron's rough voice rose, bouncing around the large chambers. "You're like every other *Imperium* magister. Self-righteous and stupidly ignorant. You all are so sure of yourselves in the light of her goddamn mightiness, but trust me—I've been at this for a lot longer than you, kid. You don't know sh—"

"You all might possibly be the easiest little group to find in all of existence," Aoran remarked, leaning lazily against the doorframe of the throne room. Light spilled in behind him, cloaking his countenance in shadows. "I wouldn't even need to be a sufficiently talented assassin to kill Elle with the ruckus you all are making. I could be any idiot with a knife and a sprinkle of motivation and still take all of you out."

Elle practically leaped toward the guard. Her head throbbed from their conversation. Too much information, too much out of her control. Elle didn't feel like herself. She felt like a piece in Dragons and Wolves, something to be thrown around so long as she pleased the player of her piece. Her brain kept coming back to Liliana's fiery eyes, the depth of determination that lay there. If Elle understood correctly, her next moves would surely put her in Liliana's way. And if Liliana had killed her brother, she would have no qualms with disposing of Elle.

Elle's hands grew sweaty, and her heart thumped in her chest. Adrenaline pulsed through her system, lacking its normal concomitant of thrill. For the first time, the prospect of being queen felt less like an incredible chance to change her country and more like a slow, arduous march to her execution. She needed something real, something corporeal, something *human* amid the divine tensions. Seeing Aoran was like a long drink of water after having burning alcohol forced down her throat.

"Thank *Imperium*—everything's fine, *etiam*? Tell me they're lying about Liliana and everything else. What happened? What's going to happen?"

Closer, Elle finally saw Aoran's face. She stopped in her tracks, a foot away from him. Dark circles drowned the jade of his irises in their shadowed depths. His platinum blonde hair fell haphazardly across his face, lacking the careful control of his soldiered hands. Instead of leaning lazily, Aoran leaned against the wall the same way a wounded man leaned on his comrades. If she ripped the wall away, Elle knew Aoran would fall with it. She wondered what kept him upright, despite the grief and exhaustion warring on his face.

Aoran grimaced at her questions. "While I don't know what 'everything else' is, they're right about the first part." Aoran swallowed the words, as if he couldn't bring himself to name the actual deed. His haunted eyes strayed over to Chauron. "I guess I shouldn't be too surprised that you all figured it out so soon with him here."

"You look terrible," Chauron commented, dark eyes watching Aoran carefully.

"Pleasure to see you, as always, Chauron." Aoran refocused his tired gaze on Elle. "And what happens next is an interesting question, largely because as far as I know, the answer is up to you."

"I'm sorry?" Elle blinked. The mark on her back began to throb lightly. She frowned. In the moment, *Imperium*'s touch felt like an unwelcome house guest.

"Liliana's fled. So has the Aurjnegh delegation. According to Eliana, we don't technically know she's with them. But you have it on damn good authority that she's in the embrace of the Aurjnegh court." Aoran pinched the bridge of his nose, his eyes squeezed shut. "*My* best guess? They decided they'd rather have her with them than against them. Eliana doesn't think I'm right, but I swear to you they're going to appoint her as their next leader."

"But what does that have to do with *me?*" Elle stressed the last word, her mark pounding harder. She felt light-headed.

"Liliana's gone," Aoran said slowly but without condescension. It was as if he understood the panicked, overwhelmed look in Elle's violet eyes. "Even if she wasn't, she broke the rules of the Trial by her use of tools and the murder. You also won the Trials before all hell broke loose.

"Teo's dead. Leo's practically catatonic in his room right now and won't say a damn word. That only leaves one person to lead Electaria." Aoran pushed himself off the doorframe, grimacing as he thumped down to the ground on one knee. He cursed before shakily unsheathing his two blades, placing both tips on the ground. He looked up at Elle, pity in his eyes. "You're going to have a hell of a time. But I'll be here. So I guess consider me your first subject, Queen Ellegance."

"*Etiam,*" Elle whispered, eyes wide.

CHAPTER 27
7055.1.29

The carriage beneath Liliana bounced violently, jarring her. She bit her cheek on the jolt, blood filling her mouth. She leaned against her arm, her focus overriding any pain. Imperium hated carriages. It was probably for the best that he stayed at the castle. The thought didn't stop the twinge in her heart. It was the first time since finding him that Imperium hadn't followed his mistress. She prayed to the presence in her head for the wolf's safety.

Her stomach rose into her chest as they descended a steep hill. Electaria probably was just starting to roll awake. She wondered how much sunlight drenched the forest they bumped and rolled through.

All the Aurjnegh royal carriages looked like plain merchant carts. The Aurjnegh always planned five steps ahead, the court carrying with it contingencies for dozens of outcomes. When the procession returned to the castle, Easternalia pulled her aside during the madness that followed the palace's lockdown. Two others from the Aurjnegh court waited for them, their postures hunched over and hidden in the shadows.

Easternalia had been curt and straight to the point. She narrowed her eyes at Liliana, saying loftily that she had "no real love" for her or any of her attitude.

But, she had said, continuing reluctantly at the prompting of her two companions, the Aurjnegh court wanted a leader. Liliana performed well in the Trials, right up until the end, proving her worth as a leader. They told her, conspiratorially, that they had hoped for her victory from the beginning. They called her a champion of her kingdom, an avatar of radical change. They wanted her—and Aurjnegh—to be at the helm of that change. Liliana stayed silent, filling in the rest of the thought. They wanted her at their helm so they might never find her on an enemy ship. She couldn't fault them for their sense.

Liliana had stood there, her mark seething with a burn that seemed to be ever present. She listened to their pitch. They had taken monumental risk approaching her in such a manner. Interfering in another kingdom's ascension was abhorrent. Were Liliana to report the meeting, Electaria would have grounds on which to declare war. They didn't know that reporting to Electaria wasn't an option. They didn't even know that staying in Electaria wasn't an option.

Easternalia had watched Liliana disparagingly, as if sensing her great niece's thoughts. Liliana remembered her words distinctly.

"You know, when Elle came from the forest, her confidence had dipped particularly low. *Superbia*, you know. I have a read on these things. But when you came out, your confidence soared so high it almost hurt us followers to witness. That kind of resolution would have only come if you knew you knocked out the real competition. It was rather obvious after the scout reported Teo's death what you did."

Easternalia continued airily, as if she hadn't just casually dropped Liliana's parricide into the conversation. "Obviously, if that is the case, your options are limited but rather obvious from my view, dear. You either come with us and lead Aurjnegh to a new level of glory and greatness or get locked away by the new queen on Electaria's throne."

Liliana stood corrected. Her eyebrows furrowed. They knew practically everything.

They didn't have the Vitrian desire to be up-front. They didn't have Nuwei sensibilities for cost, which might stop them from such excessive preparations. They *did* have *Superbia*'s skill for manipulation. If Electaria lacked the will to put Liliana on the throne after she emerged from the forest, the Aurjnegh had planned on and were sure to capitalize on the mistake.

"They know a true queen when they see one," the voice hummed approvingly. It practically draped itself over Liliana's shoulders. *"I've been whispering in their ears for quite some time."*

After Teo's death, Liliana had a sense of who, or rather what, the feminine voice was. In a sense, it comforted her. The voice had been with her since the beginning of the Trials. Liliana had mistaken it for *Imperium,* and now she felt foolish for believing the leader of the Gods gave a shit about her. The entire time, the Gods had forced Liliana to choose between their various ideologies, forsaking one in pursuit of another. There was never any balance. In some ways, *malum* was perfect for Liliana. Instead of being the simple antithesis to *Imperium*, the infamous goddess was the antithesis to them all. The Trials hadn't led Liliana to completing her Walk with *Imperium*, but they had led her to completing her Walk with a God who actually accepted the ambiguities of morality. That, Liliana could work with.

So Liliana had offered Easternalia the smallest smile—the best she could manage—and accepted the offer as magnanimously as possible, given that her emotions were torn to shreds.

The carriage jolted again, popping Liliana out of her reverie. She watched the wooden walls, a small part of her wishing for a window. The back portions of the carriage were entirely closed off and sturdy, ideal for protecting goods from the elements that may attend a merchant on his journey. Excellent for transporting goods. Subpar for transporting people. A small part of her wished she could at least see her city go, say goodbye in person.

"Dear, if you don't smooth this ride out in the next ten seconds, you'll be the one pulling the carriage back to the kingdom!" Easternalia yelled through the wooden walls, thumping her hand against the wall.

Liliana watched her great-aunt critically. If these people truly wanted her as their leader, she needed to make sure her aunt ended up in some faraway place. Liliana could always ship her back to Electaria, she supposed.

Liliana's heart panged once more at the thought of her kingdom. Well, not *her* kingdom. *Ellegance's kingdom.* Even the words made Liliana's heart twist in a uniquely painful way. In light of her vow to make meaning out of Teo's death, there was something especially hideous about losing the kingdom that had raised them both to this outsider.

So be it. She would be returning to Electaria soon enough.

She wondered with a small, pinched smile how panicked the girl was right now. Liliana hoped the young queen managed to keep her panic in check, as she wanted the kingdom kept safe while she was away. Her scowl deepened as she thought of the people within its boundaries. The Gods themselves would not be able to save the girl from Liliana's wrath if Liliana returned to find Aoran or Leo harmed. She didn't need their love. But she did need their safety assured. Being their enemy did not consign Liliana as their executioner.

Liliana leaned on her hand once again, her mind losing itself in the labyrinth of possibilities. There were so many things to be done. Platforms to be formed, policies to be passed. Aurjnegh had atrocious labor rights in place—perhaps she would start with the textile workers and field hands. A contentment swaddled Liliana's heart, and she sighed, the sound so soft Easternalia didn't even flinch.

She would lead the Aurjnegh. She would build its infrastructure and make it into a kingdom to behold, to envy. Liliana had not lost her fixation on Electaria. Ellegance was a good enough woman, but she would never be a good enough queen. Letting her sit on the throne was an insult to Teo's death. Someday, she would have that silver crown; someday, she would fix her nation, which had been so broken by years of political ineptitude and laziness.

For her kingdom. For her mother. *For Teo.* Liliana closed her eyes.

A small smile played on Liliana's face. Queen of one nation was too low reaching anyway. After all, why be queen of one kingdom when she could just be queen of them all?

EPILOGUE

"So you're Cae."

What should have been a question sounded like an accusation coming from Chauron. Cae had heard him speak a handful of times during the Guide's tenure at the castle. Cae still had to fight back the impulse to wince. Luckily, Chauron's rough voice sounded a touch softer at night. Like throwing a velvet rug over a pile of rocks. It still ground uncomfortably in Cae's ear, but the experience became slightly more bearable.

It was far past visiting hours at the House. Due to a combination of an insistent God and the stress of a transient regime, Cae found himself wide awake and unable to move from the very spot he had occupied all day. Waiting. Cae spread his arms wide before patting the spot in front of him, the dirt letting out a flat sound in the empty room.

"Chauron! *Vici*, I swear I've been waitin' a century for ya. Sit, sit! New queen, dead prince—we got things to discuss."

Chauron flopped down in front of Cae, hitting the floor with a dull thud.

Cae grimaced, his bones aching at the sound. "Aye, my body hasn't done somethin' like that in decades, *vici*. How in *Imperium* do ya walk, throwin' ya self 'round like that? Ain't ya goin' on close to a century at this point?"

Chauron replied only with a grunt.

"That's a long time to be livin', *vici*. Lot can happen in a hundred years. Lot." Cae repeated the word softly to himself, the sound of Tyn's tearful goodbye playing louder in his ear than normal. He pressed his fingers into the gritty dirt on the floor, focusing on the sensation at the tips of his hands instead of the ache that echoed emptily in his body.

"I wouldn't say that," Chauron said.

Cae looked up from the dirt, surprised that he had pulled an answer from the Guide. A shiver ran down Cae's spine at Chauron's dark laugh.

"Most meaningful events can be captured in a matter of minutes. And beyond those moments, not a thing really happens. People who pretend their lives are full of anything other than those minutes are just participating in the grand wrecking lie of living. The lie that you humans all whisper to yourselves and each other, that each and every day matters, so that you all can justify your waking up the next morning." Chauron spit off to the side, his voice growing quieter. "Mostly shit happens in a matter of minutes, and you spend the rest of your existence thinking about the damn thing."

The sentiment hit Cae immediately, his heart withering. His mark reacted viscerally to the Guide's statement, a gust of wind hitting the golden tree on his right hand. It had been some time since his mark had reacted to the wisdom of others. Cae assumed so much time speaking to *Caecus* himself had desensitized his mark to the words found on *Terrabis*.

The last touch of Tyn's soft hand against Cae's cheek had seared, a brand that had burned deeper and darker every year since the other magister had left. At a loss, Cae muttered under his breath, "A matter of minutes." Eventually, the words faded from hearing, leaving Cae simply mouthing to himself.

Silence crept into the room the way it tended to do at night, like a swarm of spiders slowly crawling into a space until one found himself surrounded. Instead of feeling comforted by the presence of a Guide, Cae felt more disconnected from the House than he had in years. Holiness tended to lose its glimmer in the silence, stripped of the noise, clamor, and validation of throngs of other people who followed the same creeds. In the silent night, holiness felt more like loneliness.

A presence pushed its way into Cae's mind, shoving aside the isolating darkness of Cae's own thoughts. Chauron inhaled sharply, as the same feeling overtook the Guide. Dispassionate calculation coalesced into a feeling, and then into a familiar voice.

"*Good evening, Cae.*"

"*Vici*!" Cae answered with as much enthusiasm as he could force, shoving the corners of his lips into a smile when they wanted nothing more than to droop in a permanent frown. "How's the heavens been? Hopefully not as interestin' as what we got goin' on down here."

Caecus ignored Cae. With a wave of the air, the pressure of the room and the God's focus shifted toward Chauron. "*I'm surprised you came.*"

"You asked," Chauron growled into the air.

"*Chauron, my asking has only ever achieved so much with you. From the moment you were created, your apathy toward duty and obedience have consistently made you one of my worst Guides to ever exist.*"

"And with such kind words, you wonder how the wreck I could ever say no to you."

"*And yet this time you did not.*" A pause. "*I suppose I should say thank you.*"

"Spare me."

Caecus brushed by Chauron's comment with the same indifferent breeze the God ignored everything he considered immaterial. "*I assume you two know why you are here. Liliana's spirit contained more* vis *than any of us have captured in decades. Without having to spread that energy around,* malum *will be able to pour every drop into her bond with Liliana.*"

Another pause, the air almost seeming to tremble.

"*A war is coming. As a result of the bond I've forged with Cae and the energy required to sustain my link with Chauron, I have precious little energy to spare. Marianne's Walk would have helped me immensely, but due to Chauron's failure to guide her properly, we will have to do without her* vis."

Chauron made a strangled sound. Cae reached forward, finding the Guide's shoulder and pressing down firmly. Chauron tensed beneath Cae's hand but did not say anything else.

"*If we are to win against* malum, *the humans will need me. Without my wisdom, they will fall into passion-driven disarray. And as it stands, you both are the only ones who can receive my words. I will be calling upon you until we force my cousin back into her cage. Work with the queen and the other nations. Speak with the leaders and coax them to the path of applied reason.*

"*A war is coming. And, for better or worse, it appears you two are to be my generals.*"

Acknowledgments

I'm curious if all authors' hands shake while they write their acknowledgements.

An end—or let's call it a "pause"—to the most surreal, most fulfilling experience of my life thus far. As such, I will attempt to pay gratitude as best I can to the amazing people who helped me up to this point. Shaky hands and all.

First and foremost, I want to extend my deepest thanks to Karli Jackson and Monika Dziamka. These two immensely intelligent women helped shape this world into a more immersive and more cohesive experience. The former made the book believable; the latter made it readable.

I also want to thank the team at Warren Publishing. Mindy, for encouraging me to take the leap. Melissa and Amy, for ensuring I didn't fall. Lacey, for turning my landing into a launch pad.

Carly and Nate were some of my biggest cheerleaders, and also some of my first readers. Carly, thank you for caring about my characters and who they were. Nate, thank you for caring about my world and what it was. Thank you both for taking the time to push back on my ideas and point out my typos. Who would have thought orientation would provide me with such incredible friends?

And Colin. These words are small, but the feelings behind them are monumental: Thank you. A long-distance friendship for the years, and a creative partnership for the ages. I will never forget the New Year's Eve we spent with beers in hand and thinking out loud on all the many ways this story could go and grow. I will never feel fully deserving of your time and your mind, but thanking you here is a good enough way to start.

Finally, I want to acknowledge and thank every person who reached out to me when I had first announced the release of this book. Your support means the world to me, and I only hope to continue to be worthy of it.